GUARDIAN OF DARKNESS

A Medieval Romance

By Kathryn Le Veque

Copyright 2009, 2014 by Kathryn Le Veque
All rights reserved. No part of this book may be used or reproduced in any manner whatsoever without written permission, except in the case of brief quotations embodied in critical articles or reviews.

Printed by Dragonblade Publishing in the United States of America

Text copyright 2009, 2014 by Kathryn Le Veque
Cover copyright 2009, 2014 by Kathryn Le Veque

Library of Congress Control Number 2014-013
ISBN 1494870371

Other Novels by Kathryn Le Veque

Medieval Romance:

The Wolfe * Serpent
*
The White Lord of Wellesbourne* The Dark One: Dark Knight
*
While Angels Slept* Rise of the Defender* Spectre of the Sword* Unending Love* Archangel* Lord of the Shadows
*
Great Protector* To the Lady Born
*
The Falls of Erith* Lord of War: Black Angel
*
The Darkland* Black Sword
*
Unrelated characters or family groups:
The Whispering Night * The Dark Lord* The Gorgon* The Warrior Poet* Guardian of Darkness (related to The Fallen One)* Tender is the Knight* The Legend* Lespada* Lord of Light

The Dragonblade Trilogy:
Dragonblade* Island of Glass* The Savage Curtain
-also-
The Fallen One (related)* Fragments of Grace (related prequel)
*
Novella, Time Travel Romance:
Echoes of Ancient Dreams
*
Time Travel Romance:
The Crusader*Kingdom Come

Contemporary Romance:

Kathlyn Trent/Marcus Burton Series:
Valley of the Shadow* The Eden Factor* Canyon of the Sphinx

The American Heroes Series:
Resurrection* Fires of Autumn* Evenshade* Sea of Dreams* Purgatory

Other Contemporary Romance:
Lady of Heaven* Darkling, I Listen

Note: All Kathryn's novels are designed to be read as stand-alones, although many have cross-over characters or cross-over family groups. Novels that are grouped together have related characters or family groups. Series are clearly marked. All series contain the same characters or family groups except the American Heroes Series, which is an anthology with unrelated characters. There is NO particular chronological order for any of the novels because they can all be read as stand-alones, even the series.

A good portion of this book is about brothers;
I only have one,
William Ralph Bouse III
(a.k.a., Billy, Bill, Unco Bee or just plain Bee)
His spirit and character are embodied in the de Reyne Brothers.
We should all be so lucky to have such brothers.

CHAPTER ONE

Scottish Borders
May 1200 A.D.

The knight walked into a trap.

Whack!

The blow landed on his forehead, sending him to the ground. The torch butt was tossed aside as the attacker ejected herself from the tent. From the moment she struck the man who was coming to see to her comfort, she knew that there was no turning back. She had decided on this course of action earlier in the evening when panic and despair were bedfellows in her fragile mind. She wanted no part of this insane agreement her father called a peace accord. She would not be a hostage for the sake of harmony. She wanted to go home.

Unfortunately, she had not thought beyond the initial escape attempt. Thoughts of collecting her horse were quickly dashed when she realized that she would not have the chance. It did not occur to her, given that her tent was in the middle of the Sassenach encampment, that anyone would notice she was missing. She rather hoped she would have the same consistency of a ghost. Unfortunately, she was not difficult to miss; a tiny woman with long hair the color of a raven's wing. In a camp full of soldiers, it had been idiotic to imagine that she would not stand out. The moment she fled from the tent, someone saw her and, of course, the game was afoot.

Alarms went out all over the camp. The sentries sounded the cry in the damp, heavy night air; she could hear them. Her heart began to race as she pounded her way across the wet grass that had been mashed by the contingent of soldiers sent from Prudhoe Castle. She would not cooperate with their assignment.

She did not want to live in an English castle as a hostage, insurance that her father would behave himself and enforce the peace from Carter Bar to Yetholm.

She honestly thought she could outrun anyone who might attempt to chase her down, at least until she lost herself in the trees. She had always been a fast runner. But what she did not count on were the destriers in pursuit, massive war horses bred for battle. They were enormous beasts and she could hear their thunder approach. The trees were in the distance, a dark indistinguishable line too far for her to reach before the warhorses were upon her. She knew she was about to be caught. But she would not give up without a fight.

A huge mailed hand reached down and grabbed her by the arm. Swinging her little fists, she fought and kicked as the English knight unceremoniously threw her over his lap. Though she struggled valiantly, she was no match against an armored warrior. But that did not stop her from resisting him all the way back to the camp.

When the knight finally let her go, she tumbled to the ground and ended up on her arse. Furious green eyes, the color of emeralds, glared up at the warrior. She shook a fist at him.

"Ye should have let me go," she bellowed. "I will only run again."

The knight had his helm on, visor lifted so he could get a good look at her. From what she'd been able to gather, he was the captain of the men who held her captive. He was very tall, with dusky blue eyes and a thin blond mustache. And the look upon his face suggested he would not tolerate her rebellion.

"Lady Carington," he braced his gloved hand against his thigh and leaned on it. "I thought we were clear on this matter. Your father has offered you to my liege, Lord Richard d'Umfraville of Prudhoe Castle, in exchange for peace between Prudhoe and Clan Kerr. This has come after several years of bitter conflict to which I have personally witnessed. Even if you should make it home, which would be a miracle in itself, your father would simply turn you back over to us. You do not seem to understand that you have no choice."

The Lady Carington Kerr picked herself off the ground with as much dignity as she could muster. She knew his words were true, but still, she resisted. Yet her actions were borne of fear more than of true rebellion; she was terrified at the prospect of being a hostage. Her father had been unclear with respect to the duration of her captivity. Surrounded by strangers, enemy strangers no less, she was full of the Devil. Perhaps if she seemed nasty enough, unruly enough, they would leave her alone. It was all purely in self-defense.

"Stay away from me, Sassenach," she growled. "Tell your dogs to leave me be."

Sir Ryton de Reyne could see that he had his hands full. His lovely little hostage had been relatively quiet until just a few minutes ago when she smacked one of his knights so hard that the man was still seeing stars. Dismounting his Belgian charger, he handed the steed off to the nearest soldier and took a few steps towards her. But he made sure to stay out of arm's length, just in case.

"I can personally vouch for my men, my lady," he said, his voice low and quiet. "Like you, we are simply doing as ordered. We are taking you back to Prudhoe. You alone have the power to make this a pleasant journey or an unpleasant one. Rest assured that we can play any game you like, and play it far better than you. So I would ask, for your sake, that you accept the situation for what it is. If I have to tie you up for the rest of the journey back to Prudhoe, have no doubt that I will do it."

Carington gazed into his dusky blue eyes, having little reservation that he meant what he said. For the first time since her mad dash to freedom, she seemed to show some uncertainty. When she did not reply right away, Ryton took the opportunity to present her to the knights surrounding them.

"If you please, my lady," he began casually. "I would introduce you to the knights under my command. You will be seeing much of them and proper introductions are in order. Perhaps it will make you feel more comfortable."

Carington took a step back from him; he had come too close and she was still skittish. Ryton indicated the man immediately to his right. "This is Sir Stanton de Witt. If you do not recognize him, you should - he is the one you tried to behead. Next to him are Burle de Tarquinus and Jory d'Eneas."

Carington looked at the knight with the huge red mark on his forehead; he was young, pale featured, with big eyes and an angular face. He nodded politely at her and she suddenly felt guilty for striking him. Next to him, Sir Burle was a very large man, older, with receding blond hair and round cheeks. He was very nearly as wide as he was tall, but she could see that with age he had mostly gone to fat. His mail jiggled when he moved. The final knight indicated was a short man with nondescript brown eyes and a head of wavy brown hair. But there was something about his eyes that unnerved her. It was like gazing into a bottomless pit.

At this point, however, everything unnerved her. As she continued to gaze warily at the collection, the sound of hooves approached from behind and she started. Thundering down upon them was another knight, a figure that cut a massive path through the grass. He was, in fact, a massive man; Carington had seen quite a few large men in her time, being Scots, and was accustomed to big men with loud voices. But this knight was different; he seemed to take up all of the air around him, sucking it dry as he reined his fire-breathing charger to a halt and dismounted. When he flipped up his three-point visor, focusing on the group of knights and one small lady, she swore she saw lightning bolts shooting from his eyes. That was her first impression of the man. She resisted the urge to flinch and step away.

"The perimeter guards have been calmed," the man's voice was so deep that it was like listening to the sound of distant thunder. His gaze barely lingered on the lady before turning back to the knight in charge. "I see you have captured the escapee."

Ryton nodded, still looking at the lady even as he gestured towards the enormous knight. "My lady, this is Sir Creed de

Reyne," he said. "I would suggest you make no move against him. He doesn't like women in general and you would be taking your life in your hands. If he gives you a directive, I would strongly advise that you follow it without hesitation. In fact, that goes for any of my knights. What we do, we do for your safety and not out of some misguided sense of punishment. We are not here to harm you, but to protect you as we have been ordered to. Is that clear?"

Carington gazed at the host of faces surrounding her. It was clear but she did not like it in the least. For the moment, however, she had no choice. She looked pointedly at the knight in command.

"What is yer name Sir Knight?" she asked in her heavy, yet deliciously sweet, Scots burr. It would have been quite delightful had the tone not been so menacing. "Ye've introduced me to everyone but ye."

"I am Sir Ryton de Reyne, commander of Prudhoe's army."

"De Reyne," she rolled her "r" heavily, looking between Ryton and the enormous knight standing next to him. "Ye both have the same name. Are ye brothers, then?"

Ryton nodded. "We are."

Carington's gaze lingered between the men, noting a slight family resemblance. They both had the same square jaw, like a block of stone, set and hard. But the aura that radiated from Sir Ryton's brother was a thousand times more intimidating. Carington did not like the feel, or the look, of him. There was something dark and bitter there.

With nothing more to say and escape plans thwarted for the moment, the lady remained silent as Ryton motioned to Sir Burle to take her back to her tent. Ryton's gaze lingered on her a moment, watching her lowered head as his men took her back to her temporary residence. Next to him, Creed had already mounted and was directing his fussing charger back to camp. Ryton vaulted onto his steed and reined his horse near his brother.

The night was dark and foggy as they crossed the open area towards the cluster of smoking fires. There was heavy dampness in the air, coating their armor with a thin layer of water. It would need to be cleaned and dried before it rusted, keeping the squires up most of the night.

"What do you think of her?" Ryton asked after a few moments of pensive silence.

Creed's dark eyes, a dusky blue color that appeared nearly black with the lack of moonlight, tracked the three knights and the one tiny lady in the distance.

"It does not matter what I think," he said. "We are doing as we are told. We are returning her to Prudhoe."

Ryton's gaze moved from the lady to his brother; younger by thirteen months, the two of them had served most of their lives together with the exception of the past three. Creed had been commandeered by King John, having seen the man in action in d'Umfraville's ranks and demanding his service. Creed had been honored by the king's request and had served flawlessly up until an escort mission to France to accompany the king's future bride, twelve-year-old Isabella of Angoulệme, back to England. That had been over six months ago. And that was when the trouble had started.

Ryton knew his brother did not want anything to do with another escort mission. He'd known it from the start. But his brother was back in the service of d'Umfraville and they had their orders.

"You are not going to like what I have to say," Ryton said quietly.

Creed would not look at his brother. "Then do not say it."

"I must," he said. "You are the only one capable of handling this girl until we reach Prudhoe. You are the calmest of my men and by far the most astute. You are the only one…."

"Do not even think it," Creed rumbled threateningly, his gaze moving over the camp, the distant trees, anywhere but to his brother who was also his commander. "I do not want anything to do with her."

"You are the only one I can trust with this," Ryton spoke louder so his brother would understand that he did not have a choice. "She has already attacked Stanton; he is young and strong, but I fear he may be swayed by her tears. Burle is not fast enough to corral her should she escape him, and I would not trust Jory with the task simply because I would not trust him with an unescorted, or unprotected, female. He has got a foul streak in him, Creed. You know this."

Creed rolled his eyes, fighting off the inevitable. He yanked his destrier to a halt. "This is the last thing I need," he snapped at his brother, hoping the man would be swayed by a vicious tone. "With everything that happened on the trip from France with that... that girl, the last thing I need is to have charge of another. If you are so worried about her, you take the duty."

"I cannot," Ryton said steadily. "I must be available to command. I need you to do this, Creed. This is not a request."

Creed just stared at him. He could not believe what he was hearing. After a moment, he just shook his head. "Why would you ask this of me?"

"Because you are a knight, the best this land has ever seen. What happened with the king's betrothed was not your fault. You need to understand that."

Creed's angry stance faded somewhat. After a small, painful moment of holding his brother's gaze, he looked away. "It does not matter if it was my fault or not. What is done is done."

Ryton knew the story well. He was also well aware that their liege had whisked Creed away from London under the cover of darkness to avoid the king's wrath. Creed was, in essence, a wanted man. Wanted by the king who believed the lies of a spurned young girl, which is why he wanted nothing to do with another female. His reaction was understandable.

"We both know that the truth shall be known someday," Ryton lowered his voice, not wanting to sound too harsh. "You rejected the advances of an indiscreet young girl who, just to spite you, told the king that you had deflowered her. The truth was that she had been bedded, by many, long before you ever met her. Everyone knows that. Isabella of Angoulệme is a foul, deceitful child who will one day sit upon the throne of England. She is as hated as her husband. You must have faith that this, too, shall pass, and your honor and reputation will one day be restored to you. But until then, you are under my command and you will continue to perform as an honorable knight. Is that understood?"

They had hardly discussed the taboo subject of the Isabella occurrence, mostly because Creed refused to. It made it difficult for Ryton to help his brother deal with it, although he had tried. But now he saw the opportunity to tell his younger brother exactly what he thought of the situation, clearly and without Creed attempting to shut him up. He had to know that what happened with Isabella had not been his fault. He could not let the incident ruin his life.

Reluctantly, Creed cast his brother a sidelong glance; he adored his older, wiser brother, a voice of reason when the world was in chaos. His world had been in chaos for six months. Only Ryton had helped him keep his sanity and he did not want to disappoint him. He knew the man spoke the truth, even when he would be happy to pretend otherwise.

He drew in a long, deep breath. "It is," he responded quietly. "What are my orders, then?"

Ryton spurred his charger forward. Creed followed. "You are to keep her with you at all times," Ryton said. "She is to remain safe, whole and unmolested. If tragedy befalls her, it will seriously jeopardize this peace we are trying so hard to achieve with her father. You must see this task through, Creed. It is important."

Creed sighed heavily again, but this time, it was with resignation. "Very well," he said. "I shall endeavor to fulfill my orders."

"I know you will."

Ryton watched his brother canter off towards the camp. He knew how hard this was for him. But he also knew the man had to resume his life as if nothing had haunted him for the past several months. Creed was too good, too skilled and valuable, to lose to something as unfair as vicious rumors and untruths. Now the man had to face his fear, unfortunately, in the form of a very spirited, and potentially naughty, young hostage. Creed was jumping back into the fire.

Truth be told, Ryton felt sorry for him. But he also knew he was the best man for the job. With a pensive sigh, he spurred his horse after his brother, fading off into the soft smoky glow of the distant camp.

***

Wrapped in the heavy Kerr tartan, its colors of brown and yellow and green blending into a web of earthy colors, Carington sat before the small bronze vizier that had been lit to bring her a small measure of heat in this damp and foggy cold. Her knees were hugged up against her chest, huddling for warmth, as she listened to the soft conversation of the knights outside her tent. The camp was quieting for the most part as the men prepared for sleep.

She glanced around her small tent; there was a bedroll her father had sent along and two massive satchels that held all of her worldly possessions. From sitting on the ground, her hands and feet were freezing, even with the heavy fabric wrapped around her and the vizier blazing gently. The defiance she had felt earlier was fading into despair. She struggled not to let it claim her completely but it was a losing battle. When tears of misery threatened, she angrily fought them off. The English hounds were not going to see her weep. She would not let them see just how despondent she was.

Exhaustion was claiming her as well. It was tiring maintaining such a level of resistance. She had yawned several times while lost in her dark reflections and she glanced at the bedroll more than once, thinking on claiming a few hours of sleep before she was forced to travel again. It would be wise to rest; only then would she be able to resume the energy necessary to maintain her defiance.

She scooted across the ground towards the bedroll, her feet touching the wet and freezing grass. It was beginning to seep through her tartan as well. Stiff, cold hands reached out to unfasten the ties on the roll. As she fumbled with the strips of leather, the tent flap suddenly moved aside and an enormous figure entered her tent.

Startled, Carington looked up into the face of the knight who had launched lightning bolts from his eyes. On her knees as he stood before her in all of his domineering glory, she instinctively clutched the tartan more closely against her chest as if the fabric would magically protect her from his particular brand of intimidation. Her emerald eyes gazed warily at him.

"What do ye want, English?" She made a good show of sounding brave.

Creed did not reply at first; he was looking down at her, studying her, wondering how on earth he found himself in nearly the same situation he had faced six months ago. Granted, this charge was far more pleasing to look at, beautiful if he really thought about it, but the fact remained that he was sequestered with another foolish female. He could hardly believe his luck.

"I am to be your shadow, my lady," he said with some disgust in his tone. "I am your protection."

Her emerald eyes widened. "Protection? Do I need protection?"

"A figure of speech. You are to be my charge."

Reaching up, he pulled off his helm and tossed it irritably in the direction of the tent opening. It landed with a thud. Carington continued to stare up at him, now faced with the full view of the colossal knight; not only was he wide, but he was tall as well. He was not particularly young, nor was he particularly old. He had a sort of ageless male quality, an ambience of wisdom and hardness that came with years of service.

She had only been able to see part of his face before. Now she could see that the square jaw housed full, masculine lips and a straight nose. His hair was very dark, with gentle waves through it, and the eyes that shot lightning bolts now appeared a grayish shade of blue. It occurred to her that the man was profoundly handsome but she angrily chased the thought away. She did not want to think such things about a hated Sassenach.

"I can take care of myself," she said with more courage than she felt. "I dunna need ye."

"Perhaps not," he said, raking his fingers wearily through his dark hair. "But I am here nonetheless. And think not to get any brilliant ideas about running off again. You would not like my reaction."

"So ye threaten me, do ye?" Her outrage was tempering her fear of him.

"'Tis not a threat but a promise of things to come should you rebel."

Her rosebud mouth popped open in indignation. Then it shut swiftly, pressed into a thin angry line. "Just like a Sassenach. The only words out of yer mouth are those of threat and pain. Do ye know nothing else, English?"

He did not react to her other than to pop off pieces of armor. His sword, in its sheath, ended up near his helm. "Rules must be established, lady," he said patiently. "You have already proven yourself untrustworthy. I am simply following your lead. If you are going to act like a delinquent, I am going to treat you like one."

She did not want to admit he was right. In fact, she hated him for making her feel like a fool. Turning away from him, she angrily unrolled her bedding and crawled atop it, settling herself with frustrated movements.

Creed finished stripping off his armor, alternately watching her body language and paying attention to his own. Further inspection of her showed that she was indeed a pretty little thing, with long, curling black hair and eyes the color of emeralds. She had a pert little nose and lips shaped like a bow. And she was petite, no bigger than a large child. But he knew she was no child; the Lady Carington Kerr, the only daughter of Laird Etterick, Sian Magnus Kerr of Clan Kerr, was a full nineteen years old. She was a grown woman and more than a little old for a hostage.

His gaze lingered on her as she settled into her bedding. There was something oddly intriguing about her although he could not put his finger on it. In fact, he did not even want to think about it. His squire appeared at the tent opening, distracting him with food and drink, and Creed thankfully motioned the lad in. The boy set the tray to the floor just inside the doorway and fled. With a heavy sigh, Creed sat on the ground beside the meal and downed most of the wine before he even attempted the bread. He found he needed the drink more than he needed the sustenance. Whenever a woman was around, he needed the fortification of alcohol.

He heard a soft sigh, glancing over and realizing that the lady had finally settled down. But he could also see that she was cold, clutching the tartan close about her and not seeing much relief from the damp cold. He turned back to his cup, ignoring her until she sat up swiftly and climbed off her bedroll. As he watched, she pulled the bedding over to the vizier and lay back down again. The red-hot furnace was against her back as she settled back down again.

Creed gazed at her as she struggled once again to be comfortable. He could see highlights of red in her hair that were reflecting off of the light from the vizier. The nearly black color seemed to mask a rainbow of warm hues only revealed by the light. Her hands, little white things, clutched at the tartan. He found himself watching her probably more than he should have. She was cold and he wondered if he should offer to stoke the vizier more; a chivalrous man would have. But his chivalry had left him a few months ago when it had gotten him into trouble. Never again would he make the same mistake of showing kindness to a woman.

Just as the lady's movements lessened and she seemed to still, the tent flap opened and Jory stuck his head in. Short and compact, the young knight sought out Creed.

"Your brother needs a word with you," he said, eyeing the supine figure. "I shall watch the lady while you are gone."

Creed set his cup down and stood without hesitation. But he paused when he reached the opening.

"You will not go near her, is that clear?" he said. "If she has been touched, harmed or harassed in any way, know that my retribution shall be swift and painful."

Jory's dark eyes widened at the man who was literally more than twice his size. "I would never touch her, Creed."

Creed did look at him, then, lifting a knowing eyebrow. "That is not true; otherwise, I would not have felt compelled to make things plain to you."

He was gone, leaving Jory standing just inside the doorway with an insulted and slightly fearful expression on his face. After several moments of silently cursing Creed, he settled into a crouched position next to Creed's half-eaten meal. Out of spite, he knocked over the remainder of the wine and snorted at his handiwork. He lingered by the doorway, watching the lady's head as it lay partially buried beneath the colors of the hunting tartan.

Jory d'Eneas was something of an erratic and, at times, appalling creature. Fathered by a powerful baron from a common servant, he had been sent away to foster at four years of age. Though sequestered at a noble house, he had become the victim of an older knight who had seriously abused him from the time he was very young up until he became a squire and could muster the strength to fight the man off. Though there were some that knew of the despicable abuse, no one cared enough to stop it.

Consequently, Jory grew up with a twisted sense of morals and an even more twisted view of the world. He was a strong fighter and had moments of sanity in which one might think he was a decent human being, but for the most part, Jory was a man that bore watching. He came to serve Richard d'Umfraville because Jory's father, Baron Hawthorn, had begged it of d'Umfraville. Not wanting to upset his old friend, Lord Richard had agreed.

Even now, as Jory watched the lady sleep, Creed's threat had little effect on him. True, he was frightened of the man, but it would not prevent him from ultimately doing as he pleased. As the vizier glowed softly and the night outside quivered with the soft sounds of the evening, Jory took a few slow steps in the lady's direction. To an outside observer, it would have looked like a predator stalking prey. To Jory, it was simply a normal approach. His dark eyes glittered as he closed in on her.

Carington was not asleep; she had heard Jory entered the tent and heard the subsequent conversation between him and Creed. In fact, as she lay buried beneath the tartan, she was wide awake, her senses attuned to any movement in the tent. She could hear footsteps approaching. When the grass near her head softly gave way, she bolted up so fast that she tipped the red-hot vizier onto its side, spilling the coals to the damp earth.

Jory was no more than a foot away from her as she rolled to her feet. She clutched the tartan to her, backing away from the knight still in slow pursuit.

"Stay away from me, Sassenach dog," she hissed. "If you come anywhere near me, ye'll regret the day ye were born."

Jory smiled. Then he came to a halt. After a moment's deliberation, sizing the lady up, he laughed softly and put up his hands.

"You need not worry over me, my lady," he said, turning away and looking for a place to sit in the small, cramped quarters. "I was simply checking to see if you were adequately resting. However, since you are awake, I can see that you are not. You really should be, you know. We are departing in a few hours."

There is something disturbing about him, Carington thought as she watched his mannerisms. She did not reply but continued to stand several feet away, coiled like a spring. Jory glanced at her as he plopped down at the edge of her bedroll to avoid sitting on the smashed grass beneath his feet.

"You may return to sleep, my lady, truly," he said, now toying with a blade of grass by his boot. "I will not threaten you."

Carington did not move. She continued to stand there, eyeing him. His back was to her. Suddenly, a light appeared in the emerald eyes, something of brilliance and bad judgment. She was closer to the tent flap than he was. Moreover, his back was to her. He probably would not even see her leave until it was too late. Very slowly, she took a step in the direction of the tent flap. Then she took another. But Jory suddenly threw himself at her before she could bolt from the tent and the battle was on.

He had a good hold of her, but Carington was a fighter. She hissed and scratched like a cat, battling the knight for all she was worth. In the course of their struggle, she tripped over the long tartan and fell onto her back, taking Jory with her.

He landed on top of her, listening to her grunt, imagining in his sick mind that they were pants of pleasure. It had been a long time since he had heard such things. He trapped her with his legs, holding her arms fast, watching her porcelain-like face contort with struggle.

"My lady," he breathed, his face very close to hers. "Why do you fight so? There is nothing of the English that should frighten you so."

Not only was she angry, but now she was terrified. Her second escape attempt was thwarted before it began, and now apparently with far more ghastly consequences. She was too small to battle with him, too small to give him a good fight. His weight was smashing her.

"Get off me, ye foul beast," she grunted. "Take yer hands from me."

Jory was not even struggling with her anymore; he simply lay on top of her, feeling her squirm beneath him. It was horrendously exciting.

"Nay, lady," his tone contained both menace and seduction. "You have been caught at escape again. You must be punished."

"Ye'll not lay a hand on me," her struggles increased. "Get... off!"

Her last word was punctuated by bringing a knee up, aiming for the male groin. She made weak contact, enough to cause Jory to transform from one twisted emotion to the next with blinding speed.

"Unwise, lady," he squeezed her wrists so tightly that she let out a squeal of pain. "If you are going to play with unfair tactics, then so shall I."

Horrified, swiftly slipping into panic, Carington had no idea what he meant. But she quickly found out.

***

Creed stood in his brother's tent watching Ryton remove a few pieces of armor so he could obtain a moderate amount of comfort when he lay down to rest. Creed was still not pleased with his orders and, consequently, with his brother at the moment. He sighed heavily, standing half-in and half-out of the tent.

"What is it?" he demanded quietly.

Ryton glanced up at him. "What do you mean?"

"Jory said you wanted to speak with me."

Ryton's hand paused on a leather fastener near his arm, his brow furrowed. "Speak with you? I did not." He resumed working on the fastener. "But Jory and I were speaking just a few moments ago. I asked him to remind me to speak to you about the lady's mount. But it could just as well wait until tomorrow. It was not necessary to send for you."

"What about her mount?" Creed asked, weary and the least bit perturbed.

Ryton yanked off the breastplate that had been restricting him for the better part of the day. He handed it off to a hovering squire.

"That big blond horse she brought with her," he said. "I am not entirely sure she should be riding it. 'Tis a big beast with male instincts. It has been biting at everything that moves, including the destriers. It gave Stanton's charger a nice bite on its flank. I would hate to have the spirited thing somehow gnash her before we reached Prudhoe."

Creed blinked slowly, without patience. "What do you want me to do about it?"

Ryton shrugged, sitting heavily on the three legged stool that was shoved into the ground near the portable vizier. A very small amount of warmth radiated from it and the man held up his hands a moment, attempting to warm them.

"Let her ride with you, I suppose," he said, running his fingers over his scalp and focusing on his brother. "But it was something we could have just as easily discussed tomorrow. You are supposed to be watching a hostage."

"I was."

"Who is with her now?"

"Jory."

Ryton lifted an eyebrow. "Get back to her, Creed."

There was something in his tone. It suddenly occurred to Creed that perhaps Jory had given him the message to get him away from their hostage. He could not believe the man was foolish enough to not only make an idiot out of him, but to attempt something against their valuable captive.

With a grunt of frustration, he marched from the tent and back across the camp. His irritation towards Jory was growing every step of the way and he sincerely hoped the man was sitting quite patiently in a corner of the tent awaiting his return. Anything else would surely be met with hostility, especially after the parting words between them.

He was still several yards away from the tent when he heard what he thought was a muffled cry. Creed broke into a dead run.

***

He had licked her face.

He had licked her face and now he was in the process of making an attempt to grab a body part that was not his privilege to do so. He was trying to kiss her, too, with his slobbering mouth and foul breath. Carington tried to scream but he kept putting his mouth over hers. All that was coming out of her throat were muffled grunts. He was not a big man, but he was strong. His dead weight upon her was rendering her helpless.

Carington finally got a hand free and jabbed her finger into his eye. Jory screamed but only partially rolled off of her. She tried to flip over on her stomach, struggling to crawl away from him, but she was tangled in the tartan and could not get free quickly enough. Jory was back on her in a flash, pulling her long dark hair. He yanked her head up, his face shoved into the side of her hair.

"You will not do that again," he grunted into her ear, listening to her cry softly when he ran a tongue along her earlobe. "Relax and stop fighting, my lady. I will not hurt you; I promise."

Carington was struggling not to succumb to hysterics. It would be so easy to burst into terrified sobs. She swung a hand back, smacking him in the forehead but doing little damage. The vizier was almost within arm's length; she thought to grab it and throw it on him, not thinking that she might burn herself in the process. All she knew was that she had to fight. This man had foul intentions towards her and she was terrified.

Her fingers grazed the leg of the vizier but she could not get close enough to grab it. The knight had a hand underneath her, squeezing her breast. Suddenly, the weight on top of her was removed and she heard the knight shout in pain and, perhaps, fear. Full of panic, she scrambled to her feet and grabbed the nearest weapon she could find, which happened to be a small iron bar that was used to stoke the vizier. The tartan fell on the ground as she swung around to Jory, fully prepared to shove the bar right through his head. But what she saw surprised her.

Creed stood just inside the tent opening with Jory in his grasp. But it was not any grasp; he had the younger knight around the neck, lifting him up off of the ground and squeezing the life from him. Jory was trying to dislodge his grip, but it was like trying to move iron. The man's hands weren't budging.

Seeing Jory subdued, Carington raced to the battling men and smacked Jory on the head hard enough to knock him senseless. As Jory went limp in his grasp, Creed's surprised focus diverted to the lady. Before he could stop her, she took another whack at Jory's head and split his scalp.

Creed dropped Jory to the ground and grasped the lady by the hands. He yanked the iron bar from her panicked grip and tossed it aside. Half-carrying, half-dragging, he took her back over to her bedroll. The lady was furious, terrified, struggling not to cry. Her breathing was coming in sharp little pants. Creed could see how frightened she was and a small amount of guilt crept into his veins.

"Did he hurt you?" he asked gruffly.

Carington's gaze was riveted to Jory as if afraid he would rear up and grab her again. But she tore her eyes away from the supine knight long enough to look into deep blue bottomless pools. Oddly, they eased her somewhat. "I… I dunna think so," she sounded hoarse with fright. "But he tried. Sweet Jesus, he tried."

"But you are well? No broken bones or injuries?"

"Nay."

Creed's gaze lingered on her a moment before returning his focus to Jory. As the anxiety of the moment waned, he took a deep breath for calm but continued to hold on to the lady's hands. They were like ice. He turned back to her, noting that her exquisite face, pale with terror, was still focused on Jory. In spite of his resistance, he felt himself softening.

"He will not hurt you again," he assured her with quiet authority. "You have my word."

He stood up and went to Jory, now stirring slightly on the wet ground. Effortlessly, he slung the man over his shoulder and went to the tent flap, snapping orders to the sentries standing outside.

Hovering by the vizier, struggling to calm her shaking body, Carington could hear him severely reprimanding the sentries outside, berating them for not having intervened when they heard the sounds of struggle. She heard a loud thump and a simultaneous grunt as something, or someone, was thrown to the ground. Realizing that she was indeed safe, the tears of relief came. Creed came back into the tent to find her weeping.

"What is amiss, my lady?" he went to her, concerned. "Are you injured?"

She wiped her eyes quickly, embarrassed that he had seen her tears. "Nay," she sniffled, keeping her head lowered so that he could not see her face. "I… I am well enough. I am simply exhausted."

He stood over her, hands on his hips, watching her lowered head. Carington hoped he would move away from her, allowing her to regain some of her composure, but he did no such thing.

Much to her dismay, she heard his joints pop as he crouched beside her. A massive hand shot out and gently grasped her by the chin. Like it or not, Carington was forced to look at him.

He was studying her, curiosity and nothing more. She was such a delicate little thing, like a beautiful little doll, but somewhere deep down a fire of strength burned. He could see it. She was scared to death and still maintaining a semblance of control. A small amount of respect for the woman took hold.

"Your face looks well enough," he had originally intended to look for bruises but found himself staring at her just because he could not help it. "On behalf of my liege, I would offer regrets for his actions. They are not indicative of our usual treatment of honorable hostages."

Carington gazed into his dusky blue eyes, feeling a strange heat radiating from them. Not the lightning bolts she had imagined earlier, but something more intense and discreet. She did not like it and pulled away from his hand. When the hand went to rest casually by his side, she realized the man had the most enormous hands she had ever seen. One of them could swallow up most of her head.

"Ye are English," she said quietly. "I'd expect nothing less."

He almost smiled; it was a fair statement, at least in her eyes. He continued to gaze at her, still crouched, still watching her lowered features. "This day was supposed to bring about a new understanding between your people and mine. So far, all we understand from one another is a lack of trust and complete brutality. Do you suppose that is what your father and my liege wished for when they set about this plan?"

She wiped her nose. "Nay."

"What did your father tell you that he wished for?"

She was reluctant to look at him, reluctant to carry on a conversation with him. But the man had just saved her from a horrible situation; perhaps she owed him a measure of courtesy.

"No more battles," she said quietly, her gaze moving between his face and her fidgeting hands. "He has lost many a man to wars with the English, including his three brothers. He has no family left but me."

"Then he has sacrificed much."

"Aye."

"Then why would you try to escape and run back to him?"

Her head snapped up, the emerald eyes narrowing. "Because... because I dunna want to be here. 'Tis not fair to pledge me to hostage. There are a number of others that could do just as well."

"Like who?"

She was returning to her normal, belligerent demeanor. "I have six girl cousins," she insisted. "He could have sent any one of them."

"But it would not have had as much impact. You are a laird's daughter. The peace contract holds far more weight with you as collateral."

Carington's emerald eyes flamed out and she looked to her hands again. Her expression rippled, changing from one emotion to another. "Maybe so," she said after a moment. "But he has thrown me into a den of lions."

"It may seem that way," he said quietly. "But I assure you that d'Eneas is not representative of us all. There are those of us who wish peace also and would seek to protect you as the emissary of that peace. We have all lost friends and family against the Scots."

She did not reply. She kept her head lowered, fumbling with her hands, and Creed rose from his crouching position and went back over to where his tray of food now lay scattered. As he lowered his big body to the ground, he heard a soft voice.

"Have ye?"

He paused to look at her, almost seated, and lowered himself the rest of the way. "Aye."

"Who?"

"My younger brother."

As she looked at him, her gaze appeared less hostile. The brittle, hard emerald eyes softened into something liquid. "When did he die?"

"Almost five years ago at Kielderhead Moor."

She nodded in recollection. "I remember that battle," she said softly, almost reflectively. "It went on for three days. I lost an uncle in the end."

He righted the tipped cup and pitcher, realizing there was nothing left of the wine. "Then it seems we both have a need for peace. I only have one brother left and I do not wish to see him perish in a foolish border skirmish."

She nodded, somehow feeling not quite so hostile against the knight. But her guard was still up. Her tartan lay a few feet away and she rose on weary legs, claiming it once again. She wrapped it tightly around her, making her way back to the bedroll. She had no idea that Creed was watching every move she made.

"If I ask a question, will you answer me honestly?" he asked.

She paused, her deep green eyes focused on him. "Aye."

"What did Jory do to you?"

She blinked as if she had to think on an answer. But she had promised him an honest one. "Nothing that canna be forgotten," she said faintly. But she knew that was not what he wanted to hear. "He tried to kiss me and he squeezed something that he had no right to squeeze. But other than that, I canna say he did anything that I willna recover from."

Creed simply nodded, his gaze lingering on her as she finally settled down and pulled the tartan tightly around her. After a moment, he rose and went to the vizier, tipped in the battle between the lady and Jory, and righted it. The embers in the ground were burned out but there were still a few inside the bowl that were glowing. He went in search of the bar that he had stripped from the lady after she had hit Jory and, upon finding it, stoked the dying peat of the vizier into a small flame. As he hung the bar on the side of the vizier, Carington rolled onto her back and looked up at him.

"Thanks to ye," she said softly.

Creed's gaze lingered on her but he did nothing more than nod his head. When he woke up a few hours later, she was gone.

CHAPTER TWO

She did not want to be here. So why was not she running?

The Sassenach knight was asleep, sitting up, in her tent. She had just left him there, his eyes closed and sleeping like the dead. Carington did not think she had slept at all, listening to the sounds of the night beyond the tent and seriously wondering why she was not making another attempt to flee her captors. Perhaps it was because Sir Creed had made a good deal of sense to her. Perhaps it was because he had proven that he was not out to kill her. She was not particularly sure; for whatever reason, she was swept with reluctance every time she thought she might try to run again. And the reluctance was making her muddled.

Creed de Reyne. He was not what she had expected from a Sassenach knight. When his eyes weren't verging on a lightning display, they seemed rather calm and wise. His manner had been very soothing when it was warranted and his words held a great deal of perception. Although he still sucked out all of the air around him with his very presence, she found he was not as fearsome as she had originally thought.

The dawn around her was a dark gray, lightening to shades of silver with the rising of the sun. It was incredibly damp and cold as she pulled the tartan more closely around her. She stood just outside of her tent, staring into the bleak moors and dark forests beyond.

She thought back to the size of Creed's hand when he had forced her to look at him; she had never seen hands so enormous. And although he was not as tall as his brother the commander, he was as wide as an old oak tree. Massive width through his shoulders and chest yet narrow in the waist. His arms were as large as tree branches, ending up in those colossal hands. Aye, he was a big man with a striking face. If she was so inclined to think such a thing about Sassenachs, she might even think him handsome. But she was not ready to go that far yet. She was still in the bosom of the enemy, surrounded by hostiles, and she hated all of them just as they hated her.

The camp was stirring as men began to rise and pack up their gear for the trip home. Prudhoe Castle was nearly three days from her home of Wether Fair. This was the dawn of the second day and she was not particularly looking forward to one more, marching to her dismal future in the heart of a rival army.

In the distance she could hear the horses nickering as men moved into their midst to feed them. One of those horses belonged to her, a tall golden warm blood that her father had given her. His name was Bress, which meant "beautiful" in the Gaelic. She had raised the horse from a tiny colt, watching it grow into a magnificent stallion with a thick neck and muscled hind quarters. She loved the horse as if it were her child and the horse responded to her in kind. She was concerned for the animal, listening to the whinnying of horses grow increasingly urgent. She hoped he was being fed and that he was behaving himself. With Bress, it was hard to tell.

Carington wanted to go to where the horses were tethered, but she thought it might look as if she was trying to escape again. So she stood there, gazing off into the fog, hoping her horse was being adequately cared for. She did not know how she could have possibly considered leaving him behind last night when she'd tried to flee. She was far too fond of him.

A body was suddenly standing next to her and she flinched with surprise, looking up to see Creed's sharp eyes gazing off across the fog and moors. He looked sleepy but alert. She stared at him a good long while before he finally looked down at her.

"You are up early," he said. "Is anything amiss?"

She shook her head. "I... I couldna sleep. I came outside to see the morning."

"Did you sleep at all?"

Again, she shook her head. "I dunna think so."

He lifted a dark eyebrow. "Then this will be an exhausting day for you."

She lifted her slender shoulders and looked away. "It is of no matter."

He watched her lowered head a moment before emitting a piercing whistle. Carington jumped at the shrill sound as a lad came running in their direction from a group of smaller tents. The boy was very tall, very skinny and blond, perhaps around fifteen years of age. He went straight to Creed.

"My lord?" the boy asked breathlessly.

Creed jerked his head in the direction of the tent behind them. "Gather my things for travel. Bring the lady a meal and some warm water."

The young man fled. Carington watched him disappear into the tent, recognizing him from the previous evening when he had brought Creed his meal. "Who is that?"

Creed's gaze lingered over the foggy encampment a moment longer. "My squire," he said shortly. Then he looked at her. "If you wish to wash and eat before we leave, now would be the time."

She went silently back to the tent, tartan still wrapped tightly around her. She was freezing. Creed watched her a moment, truthfully very thankful that he had found her standing just outside the tent. He thought she had fled again and his heart was still racing because of it. But she had surprised him by remaining firm.

He followed her only as far as the tent flap. James, his squire, emerged from the tent with his arms full of armor and mail and raced back in the direction he had come from. As Creed stood sentry outside the tent, watching the increased activity of the camp, another boy with short brown hair and enormous brown eyes appeared shortly with an iron pot of steaming water hanging off one arm and a covered tray in both hands. Creed flipped back the tent flap and allowed the lad entrance. When the youth quit the tent less than a minute later, Creed resumed his post, his mind moving to the trip ahead.

Inside the small tent, Carington was also preparing for the trip ahead. The tartan was folded neatly on the ground and she was in the process of washing some of the dust from her curvaceous body. It was cold in the tent, made bearable by the steaming water the boy had brought her. She had a surcoat of gray wool laid out with a soft white-wool sheath that went beneath it. Her family was not one of wealth or glory, so she owned no pretty belts or jewelry. She came from a functional, warring clan and such things were considered unnecessary. .

But she did own soap and oil, which she used in concert with the warm water to bathe her tired body. She scrubbed her face vigorously and ran a comb through her nearly-black hair. To keep it neat, she wove it into a single thick braid, draping it over one shoulder. The oil she had brought with her was extracted from Elder flower and had a sweet, slightly spicy scent. It was perhaps the only luxury her frugal father had allowed because her skin often became so dry in the winter time that it bled. The Elder oil helped tremendously and she rubbed it sparingly into her skin.

The surcoat and sheath were long of sleeve, of good quality and durable. She dressed in the garments, pulling on woolen pantalets and finally heavy hose, which were the only pair she owned. Sturdy leather boots went on her feet; her father did not believe in wasting money on frivolous slippers. Rubbing some oil on her rosebud-shaped lips, she quickly repacked everything and emerged from the tent.

She ran right into Creed.

"I am ready to leave," she had both her satchels in her hand. "May I collect my horse now?"

He gazed down at her, momentarily startled by her appearance; she was scrubbed and groomed, appearing completely different from the disheveled creature he had associated with since yesterday. Somewhere in his mind, his inherent male instincts told him that she was an exquisite beauty; sweet face, striking coloring, and a body that was as round and pleasing as any he had ever seen. Better, in fact. Though short of stature, she had full breasts and a narrow torso that put all other women to shame.

He had to make a conscious effort not to gape at her. But the logical male instincts were stronger that the lustful ones. So was his sense of self protection. He refused to allow himself to entertain a pleasant thought where it pertained to her. She was a hostage; nothing more.

"There is some trepidation about your horse, my lady," he said, his enormous arms folded across his chest. "We have concern that it is a violent horse, something a young lady should not be riding."

She appeared genuinely surprised. "Bress? I have raised him since he foaled. He is not a violent horse."

"He has already caused quite a few problems with the other horses."

Her emerald eyes flashed. "'Tis because they are Sassenach horses," she spat. "He smells the enemy and reacts in kind. He knows they want to kill him."

He lifted an eyebrow. "Horses do not know if they are English or Scots."

"But they know if they are enemies."

"That may well be, but the commander feels that it would be best if you rode with me."

Her reaction was not pleasing; she scowled deeply as if he had just suggested something horribly offensive. "I am not a bairn in need of constant attention. I have been riding longer than I have been walking. I can ride better than ye."

He almost smiled at her indignation. "Perhaps. But with your horse reacting badly to the chargers, his behavior could be out of the ordinary. The last thing we need is for the horse to throw and injure you. It would be in your best interest to ride with me."

Her pretty mouth pressed into a thin, angry line. "Dunna believe for one moment that I dunna know what ye're up to. Ye're trying to keep me caged by denying me the right to travel on my own horse."

Creed was coming to realize that she flared faster than any woman alive. But if he possessed one particular personality trait above all else, it was that he was a calm man. The world could explode around him and murder could be rampant in the streets, but still, he would be calm and collected. He had never been known to lose his temper, even when all of the madness with Isabella was going on. He had simply remained collected and struggled to deal with it. In fact, he blamed that particular trait for getting him into trouble in the first place; he'd been calm when the girl-child who would be queen tried to seduce him. He had been calmer still when he had refused her. Nothing could have upset the girl more.

It would therefore stand to reason that he was wary of flaring women. He did not trust them. But he remained characteristically cool as she grew more agitated.

"We are simply concerned for your safety, my lady," he said evenly. "It would be safer for you to ride with me."

"I willna do it."

"You have no choice."

"If I refuse?"

"Then I shall tie you up and you can ride in the back of the provisions wagon."

She glared at him for several long seconds before throwing her satchels to the ground. They ended up at Creed's feet. Her little fists worked as if she was contemplating going to fisticuffs against him; Creed was so surprised by her body language that he very nearly laughed. In fact, it was a struggle not to grin. He did not think she would take that reaction too well.

But she did not strike him. She did, however, continued to clench and unclench her fists. When she spoke, it was through clenched teeth.

"If ye willna let me ride my horse, then at least ye'll let me see to him to make sure he's all right," she said. "Take me to him."

He was unfazed by her anger, laboring not to crack a smile. "Polite requests will be granted. Demands will be ignored."

His calm statement only made her madder. Her fist-clenching grew more furious and her cheeks flushed a lovely shade of red. Creed had to bite his cheek to keep from erupting in laughter.

"I'll not beg ye," she seethed.

"Since when is a polite request begging?"

Her little jaw ticked furiously, the emerald eyes blazing at him. They just stared at each other. Creed could feel the heat from her gaze, all of the pent up anger and frustration and fear that she was feeling. He could also see that she was not used to being denied her wishes. As a laird's daughter, she most always got her way. It was difficult for her to comprehend that things were going to change.

"I want to see my horse," she said with forced politeness.

"Please?"

Her lips twitched. "Ye arrogant swine, I'll not have ye teaching me how to ask a question. I already asked. I want to see my horse!"

He could not help it; he did smile. And he snorted for good measure. Carington saw the laughter and it lit a fire within her the likes of which she'd rarely experienced. He was laughing at her. Her little hand came up, opened palmed, prepared to slap him across his supercilious cheek. But Creed saw the movement and he blocked her strike before she could make contact. He held her wrist in a vice-like grip, all of the humor gone from his expression.

"That," he said slowly, "would have been a stupid move on your part."

She tried to yank her hand away but he would not let go. "Release me," she grunted, struggling. "Ye're hurting me."

He did not let go. "I will not release you unless you promise me that you will not attempt to strike me again."

She grunted and struggled, trying to peel his fingers away, but they would not budge. Creed tightened his grip, not enough to hurt but enough to get her attention. His dusky blue eyes focused on her.

"Listen to me and listen well, lady," he lowered his voice into something deep and hazardous. "We have been attempting to explain to you for the better part of two days that you are a hostage for a reason. Your father and Lord Richard have made this so. All of the fighting, screaming, slapping and biting in the world will not change this. You cannot resist and you cannot refuse. And your time with us will be what you make of it; if you are disagreeable and violent, you will be met in kind. If you are pleasant and cooperative, it will make your stay far more agreeable. You might even come to enjoy the experience, as it is Lord Richard's and Lady Anne's intention to treat you like an honored guest. Do you comprehend?"

Somewhere towards the end of his speech she stopped struggling, gazing up at him with those liquid emerald eyes. But there was still fire in the depths.

"I willna surrender if that is what ye are asking," she said defiantly.

"That is not what I am asking. Do you not see that I am trying to help you?"

She did. He had been trying to help her since nearly the moment they had met. But she did not want his help. She hated him and everything about him.

"Let me go," she said through gritted teeth.

He did, immediately. Carington rubbed her wrist where he had squeezed, glaring daggers at him. Creed merely gazed back with his customary cool.

"You will answer my question. Do you understand that proper behavior will gain you far more than resistance?"

"I understand that ye are trying to subdue me."

"Are you so dense? No one said anything about subdue."

"Dunna call me dense, Sassenach," she snapped. "Ye are trying to force me into submission by taking my horse and my freedom."

"Your freedom has already been taken. What do you think a hostage is?"

Her ranting came to an abrupt halt. She stared up at him, still rubbing the wrist, but her expression was morphing from one of fury into one of realization. The emerald eyes begin to waver; the lower lip, to tremble. He had her and they both knew it.

But it was not in Carington's nature to so easily yield. There was much Scots in her, much fight. She had inherited the intrinsic sense of loathing for the English and those who would seek to take away the liberty that every Scots believed was their inherent right. No man should rule over another; race should only rule over the same race. The English believed they were more civilized and, therefore, more intelligent to administer over their brothers to the north. Carington, her father, and her father's fathers, believed they were quite capable on their own. They did not need any interference.

"I hate ye, Sassenach," it all came out as a blurted, passionate whisper. "I'll hate ye until I die."

He was unmoved. "That is your choice. But in spite of that, I am still your shadow and will do what is necessary to ensure both your safety and your suitable manners. You will behave, my lady, or my retribution shall be swift. I'll not have you striking out at everyone who upsets you, for clearly, that is a frequent occurrence. Is that clear?"

She looked away, rubbing her wrist and struggling not to weep. She was so mad that she was verging on tears. But she was also feeling an extreme measure of defeat. At the moment, there was nothing left for her to do but relent. She was not so foolish that she did not realize that. But she was not giving up entirely.

"May I please see to my horse?"

She asked so softly that he almost did not hear her. As the squires began to collapse the tent behind them, Creed held out his hand to her and she understood the gesture to walk with him. When he reached to take her elbow, purely as a courtesy, she deliberately pulled away. She did not want the knight touching her. She did not want to show any capitulation to the man whose directives she would be forced to comply with. She hated him. She would hate him forever.

Some of the horses were being tended by the time they reached the make-shift area where the horses were tethered. The sky was lightening to a pale gray, enough so that Carington could see the blond head of her tall horse back in the herd. Without a word to Creed, she ducked under the roped barrier and wove her way among the horses, occasionally slapping a big horse butt that got in her way. When she came to within a few feet of Bress, she clucked to him softly, calling his name. The horse's ears perked in her direction and he nickered softly.

Carington and the monstrous horse came together in an affectionate clash. Creed stood a few feet away, watching her hug and kiss the big golden head. The horse nibbled on her arm and flapped its big lips at her face when she tried to kiss it. It was actually quite touching to watch, if he were to admit it. He could see just by the way she handled the animal that she was very much in love with it. Without all of the resistance and fight, he could sense that she was a sweet and compassionate woman. He began to have some doubt as to whether or not he should forbid her from riding the animal; she had indeed ridden it yesterday with no ill effects. Perhaps his brother's concerns were overrated.

As he mulled over his thoughts, Carington proceeded to inspect every inch of the horse. When she was sure the animal was unharmed, she turned to Creed.

"Has he been fed yet?" she asked. "I would like to feed him myself."

Creed looked around to the few soldiers milling about, men who usually tended the horses on a long march. "I doubt it," he said. "Stay here a moment. I'll see about procuring him some food."

She watched him as he wandered off into the lifting fog, studying his confident gait. To see a rear view only confirmed that he did indeed have the widest shoulders she had ever seen. He also cut a very pleasing shape with a narrow waist, tight buttocks and thick legs. But just as those warm thoughts rolled across her mind, she angrily chased them away. She hated the man. She refused to think him attractive to look at.

Bress' eyes were half-lidded as she stroked the blond face. He had an even white blaze down his face that was distinctive and lovely. As she petted the horse, a thought suddenly occurred to her and she found herself seeking out Creed's location; he was a good distance from her, speaking with a soldier. A quick glance back at Bress showed the horse with a halter and lead rope only;

no saddle or bridle to make for easier riding. But no matter; she had ridden him with just a halter many a time. She was comfortable with it. And Creed was too far away to give immediate chase.

Carefully, and with one eye still on Creed, she looped the lead rope over Bress' neck and secured it to the other side of the halter to create make-shift reins. Bress was the fastest horse she had ever seen. She knew the fat destriers would be unable to keep pace with him. Aye, she had decided not to run, once. But she had changed her mind, now that she saw what the Sassenachs truly had in mind for her: complete submission and utter humiliation. She would not be a hostage; she would be a prisoner. And the big beast Creed de Reyne would take great pleasure in her surrender.

The last Creed saw of Carington, she and her golden horse made a graceful jump over a rope barricade and were disappearing into the awakening dawn.

***

She could not go home. Carington knew that; she knew that her father would only turn her back over to the Sassenachs and they would probably beat her for her insolence, so she knew right away that she could not return to Wether Fair. That meant she had to flee far enough to be able to start a new life for herself, far from peace treaties and English knights and Scots barons. It was a foolish and desperate thought, but she was foolish and desperate at the moment. She did not want to be a token for peace. She did not want to be a prisoner. She wanted; nay, needed to be free.

Bress was swift; he covered several miles within the first hour. The morning fog had lifted slightly, but it was still cold and wet. In little time she had made it to a larger town far to the south, although she was not exactly sure why she was heading south. More than likely because Creed and his brotherhood of devils would expect her to head for home, so they would turn northward to search for her. She would fool them and go south.

A few hours into her flight, Bress was showing signs of exhaustion. She slowed the horse and directed him off the road, into a cluster of trees to shield them from the highway. The animal was sweating and foaming, so she began to walk him through the thick bramble to cool him off. He tried to munch on the clusters of wet grass but she pulled him up, wanting to cool him before he ate.

The fog had almost completely cleared as they emerged from the bramble into a lovely green meadow with rocky crags in the distance. Some of the peaks had a white cap of snow. She had a fairly good sense of direction and knew she was heading to the southeast, but she had no idea if there were any towns nearby or what she would do when night fell.

She would have to feed and shelter herself, which she was confident she could do. Being the only child of a warlord, her father had taught her a few things he had hoped to teach a son. He had taken her hunting on occasion and she knew how to catch small game. She also knew how to identify edible plants for the lean times when meat was unavailable. Thanks to the cook at Wether Fair, she also knew how to prepare items like bread and ale. She was quite good at making ale and, thanks to her father she was quite good at drinking it, too. She wished she had some if only for the warmth it would provide.

Carington glanced up at the sky; it was late morning, possibly mid-day, and she was famished. Bress needed to eat and rest also. Wandering across the green grass of an early spring season, she could hear water in the distance. She followed the trickling sound, across the meadow, through a thicket, and emerged on the other side. A small stream cut right through the pasture and she allowed Bress to drink heavily now that he was sufficiently cooled. When he was finished with his water, he went to work on the thick grass that lined the stream and she tethered him to a bush so that he would not run off. With the horse munching happily, she could focus on herself.

She needed food. The thicket was not too far away and she

retraced her steps, entering the dark, cool trees and hoping to find some edible foliage. Off to her right, on the outskirts of the trees, was a huge cluster of dandelions. She went to the patch, collecting as much as she could and using the length of her surcoat as a basket.

With a large amount of greens in the folds of her garment, she continued to search for edible plants. She found some dill weed growing wild and collected a good measure. She fingered through a section of the foliage, coming across a blackberry bush that was bursting with fruit. Thrilled, she harvested as much as she could carry. What she could not eat, Bress would. The horse had a sweet tooth. Laden with her harvest, she emerged from the thicket and made her way back to her gobbling horse.

Sitting beside the stream, she washed her meal and ate until she was stuffed. Bress ate the dandelion heads; she ate the delicious leaves. The horse did not want the dill weed, but he munched the blackberries that turned his horse-lips purple. She tried to turn her back on him and gobble down her berries so he would not eat them, but he would bang at her with his big horse head and shove her around until she handed over the goods. In the end, he ate more than she did, but both were satisfied.

Sated, Carington's thoughts began to turn towards the coming night. She had to either find shelter or make it, and she was not entirely sure that staying in this spot was a good idea. She had already given Creed and his evil comrades the opportunity to catch up with her, but it could not have been helped. She decided that she needed to continue on and find shelter as it became necessary. If she thought about it, she had some measure of anxiety since fleeing the English; she was fearful of what would happen if they caught her, fearful of what would happen if someone else caught her. Her flight was foolish and she knew it. But she had to keep going.

Bress was rolling around in the grass when she finally stood up. He seemed particularly happy. Grinning at his antics, she collected his lead rope and coaxed him to his feet. He stood up and shook himself like a wet dog. Pulling the horse along with her, she retraced her steps back out to the road.

The wind was picking up slightly, blowing her black hair about. Shielding her eyes from the weak mid-day sun, she gazed to the north and finally to the south, seeing not a soul in either direction. Mounting Bress, which was no easy feat considering how tall the animal was, she gathered her make-shift reins and began to trot southward along the road.

This was lush country with moors and crags about the landscape. After an hour of riding, she crested a small hill and spied a village in the distance. She could see ribbons of gray smoke rising from a few chimneys, signaling the approach of dusk and the coming evening meal. Night still fell early, even in the spring, and she made haste to the town to find someplace to sleep for the night. She hoped to find a stable or something similar for both her and the horse. Without money, she had little choice in lodgings.

Carington was careful to stay out of sight when she entered the small berg. There was a large tavern near the outskirts and she could hear the laughing and shouting coming forth from the mortar and wood structure. She paused in the shadows, watching the activity, wishing she had money to pay for such a place. She was coming to long for warmth and descent food.

For the first time since fleeing, she was beginning to feel some doubt. She was no longer sure her decision had been the wisest, but she supposed it was better than being a slave. Turning away from the laughter and smells of cooking meat, she reined Bress back in the direction she had come. She had seen a couple of outbuildings near the edge of the town that would do quite nicely if no one was using them. They had looked old and unstable, but it did not matter; shelter was shelter and she was in no position to be choosey.

Suddenly, laughter and shouting burst from the inn as several knights spilled into the avenue. They were very drunk and very happy. With minor curiosity, Carington turned to glance at them as Bress plodded back down the avenue. She did not think anything of them until one of the men looked in her direction and shouted.

"Hey!" he bellowed. "You, wench! Where are you going? Come back here!"

Panic flared in her chest. It was the attention she had feared and she cursed herself for being stupid enough to have walked right into it. Digging her booted heels into Bress' golden sides, she roared off into the dusk. Behind her, the knights attempted to drunkenly mount their chargers. But even intoxicated, they were experienced riders and took off after her. Carington could hear the thunder of hooves behind her.

The chase was on.

CHAPTER THREE

Creed knew they would never outrun her.

The best they could hope for was tracking her horse and the animal had left distinct hoof prints in the dirt where the horses had been tethered for the night. Burle was a master tracker and had kept them on a steady path most of the morning. Surprisingly, she had continued south. He had been positive that she would have turned for home. But instead, she continued deep into English territory. It did not make much sense. But, then again, nothing about the woman did.

The entire Prudhoe escort was mounted and following within minutes of the lady's escape. Ryton did not scold him, although Creed could tell by his brother's expression that he was displeased. He had, in fact, put Creed in charge of her to avoid this. But she had escaped him. Stanton, in spite of being smacked in the skull by the lady, had fared better. The more Ryton stewed about it as they rode south, the more irritated he became.

"You had time to talk to her," he said to his brother. "Where do you think she will go?"

Creed shrugged his shoulders. "We spoke of trifling things. One thing I do not profess to do is read women's minds."

"You should have kept a better eye on her."

Creed did not respond; he would not explain himself to his brother when Ryton already knew that Creed's knightly skills were beyond question. What happened was unexpected, yet in hindsight, Creed supposed he should not have left the lady standing alone with her horse. Truth was he had not given it much thought until he caught a glimpse of the big golden horse leaping over a barrier with its dark haired mistress. Then he'd just felt frustration. Frustration, with help from his brother's remark that was now growing into anger.

Stanton cantered beside Creed on his big brown charger. The

young knight had seemed particularly concerned with the matter of the escapee; in fact, he'd seemed concerned for the lady the moment they had collected her from Wether Fair. Were the man not married with a young child, one might have taken his concern for romantic interest. But Ryton knew, as did Creed, that it was just infatuation. She was a pretty girl and he was naturally fascinated. Stanton just did not have it in him to be devious or deceptive.

"Should we check the woods, Creed?" he asked, his visor flipped up and his angular face flushed. "Perhaps she has gone into hiding?"

Burle was up ahead, aboard his fat gray charger, riding on the side of the road and studying the ground. "Burle has her scent," Creed told him. "We will wait for his opinion."

"Perhaps you should have put someone else to guard her, Ryton," Jory's voice floated up from behind them, over the thunder of the hooves. "Your brother does not seem to have much luck with women."

It was a deliberate dig, vengeance for the beating Creed had dealt him the night before. Jory had a loose mouth but was no good at backing up his assertions. Ryton did not bother turning around.

"Another word and I send you on to Prudhoe alone," he said steadily. "After what you did last night to the lady, you are lucky that you are still in my corps. The baron will know about your actions towards the hostage, Jory. I have no use for degenerates such as you."

Had anyone else said it, Jory would have snapped back. But Ryton was his commander and he wisely kept his mouth shut. But it did not prevent him from feeling as if, somehow, he had been the one who had been slighted.

Burle suddenly threw up a hand and everyone came to a halt. Creed, Ryton and the other knights rode up to him, watching the man point off to the east; there was an enormous meadow, as far as the eye could see, with snow-topped peaks in the distance. The land was lush and green from an early spring.

Burle got off his charger and following the hoof prints that veered off the road. "She went off into thc mcadow."

All eyes moved to the landscape beyond. "There is virtually no cover," Ryton said. "If she was still in the meadow, we would see her."

Creed spurred his charcoal charger down the road for several yards, studying the soft brown earth.

"Here," he pointed to the road as the charger did a nervous little dance. "She came back out here."

Burle went over to where he was pointing, kneeling down as much as his armor would allow and studying the ground. "Aye," he nodded. "She did indeed. It looks as if she has continued south."

"Then south we ride," Ryton lifted a fist to the column of men behind him.

Creed had already spurred his animal forward, cantering ahead of the troops, keeping his eyes alert for the big blond horse with the little lady upon it. As time passed, he was coming to wonder if they would ever find her. There was so much danger in the world, especially for a lone female. He may have been foolish enough to have given her the opportunity to escape him, but he doubted she realized what she was getting herself into when she made the foolish decision to flee.

But one thing was for certain; either way, he was the one to blame. Christ, he felt stupid.

***

The knights were closing in. Bress was fast, but he was also weary. Carington ended up heading back onto the road she had traveled, a straight and wide road that gave Bress plenty of room to pick up speed. She thought she could outrun the knights and was frankly surprised they had followed her for as long and far as they had. She had expected the drunken warriors to quickly tire of the chase. But they had not. The panic she had been so adept at keeping at bay returned with a vengeance; Bress was tiring and his gait was slowing. If the knights kept their pace, they would eventually catch her.

The sky was darkening with dusk as they pounded along the road north. The men behind her were slowly closing. In the distance was a heavy patch of forest and in her fright, Carington directed Bress for the trees. Perhaps she could lose her pursuers in the bramble.

She plowed into the foliage, hearing the shouts behind her. The men were gaining ground. Bress was grunting and snorting as he raced through the trees. Branches whipped back on Carington; one caught her across the neck and she put her fingers on the wound, drawing away bright red blood. She was still directing the horse northward, paralleling the road, when suddenly the forest ended and she was in a meadow, disturbing a flock of pheasants that flew up into the air. Bress startled, reared up, took a bad step and ended up falling over on her.

Twelve hundred pounds of horseflesh pushed Carington deep into the soft, moist earth. Had the ground been hard, the fall would have most likely killed her. But the earth was very soft and the horse's weight did nothing more than shove her down into it. By the time Bress rolled off of her, the knights were upon her.

"See here," one of them shouted, practically falling off his charger and making haste towards her. "You should not have run, wench. Now you have hurt yourself."

She was stunned but not hurt. Arms were reaching down to pull her up and she tried to yank away from them even in her shock.

"Let me go," she hissed, struggling. "Take yer hands off me."

Two of the knights had her by the arms. "By God's Bloody Rood," the same man who had yelled at her spoke. "She is Scots. No wonder she ran."

The knight on her other arm shook her roughly. "What are you doing here, girl? Spying?"

The world was weaving and her ears were ringing, but it did not lessen her resolve to fight. "Let me go!" she shrieked.

The first knight yanked her hard enough to snap her head

back. She ended up pressed against his chest, her small, voluptuous body wedged intimately against him.

"You are a spy, lass, admit it," he muttered, spittle on his lips. "We know how to deal with spies."

Her struggles increased to panicked proportions as she struggled to pull herself away from the English dog dripping spit on her shoulder. As she twisted and pulled, she suddenly noticed in her peripheral vision that Bress was still on the ground.

"Sweet Jesus!" she exclaimed softly, her panic for herself turning into panic for her horse. "Bress! He's hurt!"

The knights would not let her go. A third knight stood beside Bress, eyeing the softly groaning horse critically.

"Broke his leg," he said casually, hands on his hips. Then he looked to the fourth knight who had come to stand next to him. "Give me your sword so I can put this beast out of its misery."

Carington began to weep loudly. "Nay," she sobbed. "My sweet Bress. Let me see him. Oh, please, let me see him."

The first knight ignored her plea, bending down to throw her over his shoulder. He was a younger man with blond eyebrows, short of stature but evidently strong. Carington fought and kicked him with every ounce of strength she possessed, trying to aim for his neck. But he wore armor and the helm protected tender spots.

As he carried her back towards his horse, she caught a glimpse of Bress on the ground, lifting his head as if trying to see where his mistress was. Sobs of grief overcame sobs of terror; she reached out as if to touch the horse, now laying crippled on the ground. She could see a bloodied right rear leg, near the ankle, and the stiff appearance of something that did not look natural jutting out of his leg. It was a bone, and she squeezed her eyes shut at the sight.

Weak with sorrow and agony, she still struggled with the knight who carried her back to his horse.

"Please," she begged through her tears. "Please let me go to my horse. Please let me comfort him."

The knight slapped her lightly on the buttocks. "'Tis just a horse, lady. He does not need you."

The ring of a broadsword being unsheathed caught her attention. She could see the two knights over by Bress; one of them held his broadsword by the hilt, pointing downward as if to ram it into the ground. But he was aiming at Bress' heaving chest. Carington screamed at the top of her lungs as the knight plunged the sword into the soft golden flesh of her beloved steed. Bress twitched and then fell still. But Carington kept screaming.

She struggled weakly with the knight, devastated at the death of her adored horse, devastated that she was being abducted. Her decision to flee the English from Prudhoe had cost too much. It had been stupid, foolish, and ill advised. She knew that now. Slave or no, she would have been better off with the men from Prudhoe and Bress would still be alive.

The knight was trying to load her onto his charger but she was not a willing burden. As he gave her a good shove to get her up on the horse, a thin wail pierced the air, rapidly growing louder until ending in a dull thudding noise a few feet from the charger. Startled, Carington looked to see a long Welsh arrow protruding out of the ground. Another wail and another arrow buried itself deep in the earth a few feet to her left.

The knight dropped her from his horse and shouted to his comrades to gather their weapons. As Carington fell to her knees and struggled to crawl away, she caught sight of chargers racing towards them from the road beyond. Great hooves threw up clods of moist earth, the thunder from the destriers filling the air with power.

She recognized Creed's big charcoal steed leading the pack. Finding her feet, she had two thoughts; to reach Bress and to stay alive. She did not even think about the punishment she might be facing at the hands of Creed de Reyne. There was a good deal of shouting going on around her as she finally reached her horse, falling beside him in the soft, wet grass. He was still warm. Throwing her arms around his neck and laying her head on his face, she closed her eyes to the sounds of death all around her. Grief consumed her and tears started anew, almost uncaring that she was surrounded by danger.

It did not take long for the sounds of the battle to wane. Four knights against the force that Creed had brought was hardly much of an opposition. She felt a hand on her arm, a soft male voice in her ear.

"My lady?" Stanton was standing over her, his sword drawn to ward off any fighting that might come into proximity. "Are you all right, my lady?"

She opened her eyes, looking up at him even as she continued to lie on her horse. She could not even speak. But she did nod, once. Stanton had her by the arm, his angular face laced with concern.

"Please, my lady," he pulled gently. "You must get up. We must get you to safety."

She shook her head, holding the horse tighter. "Nay," she wept softly. "I canna leave him."

Stanton's pale eyes moved over the horse, seeing the chest wound, the leg. "Did they do this?"

She continued to sob as if her heart was broken. "They chased me and my horse fell."

"Did they kill your horse?"

"His leg was broken."

Stanton did not ask anything more. His eyes were up, looking for Ryton or Creed. He spied both of them standing several yards away, interrogating the only enemy knight left alive. The other three had been dispatched and were being hauled away by Prudhoe men. He finally saw Creed break away and head towards them, his massive broadsword still in his hand and his visor lowered. Even though the battle was done, he was still in full battle mode. And Stanton knew, from the atmosphere of their trek south, that his mood was as dark as the coming night.

Creed was nearly on top of them when Stanton spoke.

"Those knights chased her and the horse broke his leg in the process," he said, hoping that Creed would take some pity on her before letting loose his punishment. "She is unharmed."

For a man whose entire reputation was based on an

unflappable demeanor, the full-blown fury Creed was feeling in his veins was uncharacteristic. He paused next to the big blond horse, watching the lady weep quietly over the beast. It was difficult to isolate why, exactly, he was angry; at the lady for escaping, at himself for feeling like a fool, or at the knights for making an attempt against her. But he realized, above all else, that he was angry because he felt fear. He was unused to fear in any form.

"Back on your mount," he growled at Stanton. "Go find someplace to set up camp for the night."

The pale young knight was gone, but not without a lingering glance to the crumpled lady. As Creed stood there, struggling to formulate some manner of communication that did not come blasting out at her, Jory rode up astride his bay stallion. He gazed down at the lady, her dead horse, and snorted.

"Serves her right for running off," he said.

Creed's head snapped to him but he was already gone, digging his spurs into the side of his horse and thundering off. At Jory's words, Carington burst into fresh tears and Creed looked down at her. The longer he watched, the more his anger tempered. Above his fury, he could see what had happened. Aye, her foolish decision had caused all of this. But he was not without empathy for the results. With a deep breath for calm, he sheathed his broadsword.

"Are you all right?" he asked with more composure than he felt.

She was sobbing against the horse's golden coat. "Aye," she wept.

"What is that on your neck?"

She had forgotten about the bloody scratch. She sat up, fingering the wound. "A… a tree scratched me," she sniffled, wiping at her cheeks with the backs of her hands.

"Those knights did not do that?"

She shook her head. "Nay." Her gaze fell back on the horse and she stroked the blond neck, the pale hair of his mane. "Oh, Bress. Forgive me. I am so sorry."

He stood there a moment, watching her kiss the horse. Darkness was falling and he wanted to get her to the safety of the encampment. Now that he knew she was safe and uninjured, it was easier to be calm. But he was still rightly furious.

"My lady," he said quietly. "We must retreat to the safety of camp for the night."

She looked up at him, eyes welling. "I canna leave him."

He gazed into the emerald eyes, the deliciously sweet face, and felt himself soften. It was difficult to maintain his harsh stance when she was so grief stricken.

"There is nothing more you can do for him," his voice was considerably gentler. "I will have my men properly dispose of him."

She let his statement settle, looking back down at the dead horse. Her gaze moved to his torso, his legs, coming to rest on the broken one. Her lower lip trembled.

"He was startled by the birds," she said. "We came through the trees and the birds flew out of the grass. He tripped and fell on me, but I dinna know he was hurt until... until...."

She could not finish and a new wave of tears washed down her cheeks. As Creed stood there and debated if he should physically remove her, his brother came upon him.

"Those knights were from Gilderdale," he said in a low voice. "If we let the survivor live, he will return to Black Fell Castle and we will have the whole of Gilderdale down around our ears."

Creed flipped up his visor, scratching his chin where his hauberk was chaffing him. "It was a fair fight, Ryton. We were protecting our hostage."

"Gilderdale will not care. They are a war machine."

Creed just shook his head. "I doubt Gilderdale would attack us for revenge on a justifiable conflict."

"We killed one of Gilderdale's heirs."

Creed's dusky blue eyes focused on his brother; that subtle statement changed everything. "What do you want to do?"

"I'm open to suggestion."

Creed drew in a long, deep breath. There was reservation in

the tone. "Then I would suggest sending him back to Gilderdale. The man is a knight, and a captured one. It is not honorable or ethical to assassinate him once he has been subdued."

Ryton looked over at the knight in the distance. Creed followed his brother's gaze and they both studied the short, older knight as he stood with Jory. As they mulled over the man's future, Carington successfully calmed herself from the last barrage of tears, her gaze moving to the enemy knight several feet away. She wiped at the last of the moisture around her eyes, stood up, and moved towards the man.

Creed and Ryton watched her with some surprise and mostly curiosity. Then they followed. By the time she reached the knight, they could hear her soft, sweet lilt against the cool evening air.

"Ye were the one who killed my horse," she said.

The older knight looked at her. She could see no panic, no fear in his eyes, simply resignation. "He was in pain, my lady," he replied quietly. "I did what was necessary."

"But I asked ye not to."

"You would rather have the beast suffer?"

She sniffled, studying him in the dying light. Then she shook her head, slowly. "Ye were swift with it. I saw ye."

"It was necessary."

"Where were ye going to take me? Ye and those others."

His faded blue eyes were fixed on her. "Most likely back to Gilderdale."

"And then what?"

"You would have to ask Sir Gregory that."

"Who is Sir Gregory?"

"The man who held you. He is one of Gilderdale's sons."

She was almost completely calm by the time the conversation lulled. She looked over at Creed and Ryton, standing side by side. The wind was whipping up, teasing her black hair and plastering her surcoat against her curves. She had an unbelievably divine figure, a body that most men would move heaven and earth to touch. Her full breasts were bold and inviting, her waist slender and long. But she paid no mind to the gusting wind or to Jory's hot gaze upon her silhouette. She was looking at Creed and Ryton, and both of them were looking at her face.

"He was not like the others," she said. "I dunna want ye to hurt him. Send him home. Please."

She added the final word as almost an afterthought, gazing deliberately at Creed as she did so. Ryton also looked to Creed, but Creed was looking at the lady. She was not full of fire and spark like she had been since nearly the moment he had met her. She was calmer, her manner far more pleasing. Standing in the blowing wind with her black hair swirling around her, she looked like a little doll, beautiful and perfect in every way.

Creed broke away from his brother and went to the lady, reaching out to grasp her elbow. "I am taking the lady to camp," he said, gently taking her arm. "Jory, see to the horse. Ryton, do what you will with this knight. But the lady has asked he be spared and I would suggest that you consider that request."

With that, he led Carington away, back to the tide of men in the distance. The Prudhoe escort was disassembling to the south, preparing to camp for the night. Already the smoke from cooking fires was filling the air as fire after fire was lit to ward off the coming night. Carington glanced over her shoulder to where Bress lay still and alone upon the cool grass. She could feel the tears again and she sniffled, trying to keep them at bay.

"Have you eaten?" Creed asked as if he did not hear the sniffling.

She shook her head. Then she nodded. "Bress and I ate earlier today. We found some blackberries and...," she suddenly looked up at him, curiosity and trepidation in her expression. "How did ye find me?"

He scratched the same spot on his chin that was always chaffed by his hauberk. "By tracking you. Your horse has distinct hooves."

She had not thought on that, although she should have. "How did ye know his hooves?"

"From where he was standing with the other horses this morning." He did not look at her. "Do you care to tell me why you ran?"

"Are ye going to beat me?"

"Not if you tell me the truth."

She wiped daintily at her nose; she suspected he would not beat her, anyway. He was, in fact, very calm as he asked her. He should be furious. And she should have stubbornly refused to answer him, but she could not muster the strength. Being stubborn had gotten her horse killed.

"Because," she said softly; he barely heard her. "I dunna want to be a prisoner."

"I told you that you were not going to be a prisoner. But if you continue to behave like this, we will have no other choice but to lock you up."

She did not have an answer to that. She was still thinking on Bress, the results of her actions, and she looked over her shoulder again to see Jory standing over the golden body in the distance. She came to a halt and Creed with her. He noted the concerned expression on her face.

"That knight," she said haltingly. "I dunna... I dunna like him. I dunna want him tending my horse."

Creed eyed Jory in the distance as well. "My lady, he cannot harm your horse. The horse is dead. He is simply going to dispose of the body."

"How?"

"More than likely, he will burn he corpse."

She sighed; he heard the soft, wistful hiss. He expected more protests but she remained silent. Just as they were turning around to resume their walk, something caught her attention and the emerald eyes flew open wide. Creed turned to see what she was looking at and they both watched as Jory relieved himself on the dead horse. He peed all over him. Carington looked accusingly at Creed, fully prepared to berate him, but the words would not come. She burst into tears instead.

"He... he peed on him," she sobbed pitifully. "My sweet Bress. He fouled him."

Creed sighed heavily, turning her for the camp and putting his enormous arm around her shoulder so she would not turn around again.

"I am sorry, my lady, I truly am," he said, his voice a gentle growl. "I will take care of Jory, have no doubt. I shall avenge what he has done to your horse. Do you believe me?"

She was tucked into the curve of his torso, the plate metal of the armor jabbing her in tender places. But it was a strangely comforting position. She gazed up at him, the dusky blue eyes and square jaw. Something passed between them, a jolting flicker of warmth that almost made her forget her tears. Whatever it was came right out of those amazingly moody eyes. *Lightning bolts*! She thought to herself. *I felt the lightning bolts!*

"I-I believe ye," she sniffled and stammered. "But my horse...."

He gave her a gentle squeeze. "I will see to him myself if it will make you feel better. For now, let us get you some food and into bed. You need to rest."

Carington fell silent the rest of the way back to the encampment. In fact, she was singularly focused on the big knight's arm around her shoulders and trying to figure out why she was not demanding he remove it. Prudhoe men had set up a nice little tent city near the outskirts of the small village where the knights from Gilderdale had found her. Creed took her back to the tent she had occupied the night before, a larger shelter with a large flap of an opening. The rising wind was beginning to whip it about.

He took her into the dark innards, made spooky by the strong breeze. The oilcloth fabric was cold and uninviting, but the vizier was sitting in the middle of the tent, lit and weakly sparking. Carington's possessions lay in a neat pile near the door where someone had put them.

"It should warm up in here shortly," he said, letting go of her the instant they entered the tent. He bent over and began to untie her bedroll. "Now would be a good time to rest before sup."

She stood there and watched him; now that he had removed his thick arm from her, she was able to focus on his demeanor somewhat. He was acting as if nothing in the world was wrong, as if she had not run from him. He had, after all, been relatively considerate the entire time she had known him. To have run from him was to have slapped him in the face and, more than likely, destroyed his trust in her in the process. She was coming to feel guilty for a multitude of reasons.

She stood there a moment, pulling at her cold hands, watching him unroll the bedding. Her mind was beginning to work. Emotional, exhausted, the words came spilling out whether or not she wanted them to.

"If... if I insulted ye with my actions, then I am sorry," she spoke haltingly. "Ye've been kind to me, Sir Knight, and I am sorry if I offended ye."

He did not reply right away. Truth was whatever fury had held him captive for the past several hours was gone. The lady was safe and that was all that mattered, though it might have been very gratifying to spank her for her insolence. Still, it was done. And he was not a beating kind of man. Moreover, she had been punished enough for her actions by the event of her dead horse. He could not have made a greater impact on her than that.

When the bedroll was finally laid out, he stood straight and put his hands on his hips. "How I feel is of no matter. What matters is if you plan to do it again."

She fixed him in the eye with her emerald gaze, her eyes glittering in the weak light like rare and precious stones. After a moment, she lowered her gaze, wringing her hands furiously. "Nay," she said softly. "If I knew that my escape attempt would kill my horse, I would never have gone. I swear I wouldna have."

Creed did not say anything; he was not sure if he believed her. Aye, he knew she was sorry how things had turned out. Frankly, he was too. But had things worked in her favor, she would not have regretted anything. At the moment, he did not trust her in the least in spite of her obvious remorse.

"Rest," he told her, moving for the exit. "I shall see to your animal and I'll bring back something to tend that cut."

She had forgotten about the scratch on her neck, touching it absently when he reminded her of it. But it did not deter her from thoughts of her horse. "Bress," she murmured, her eyes glittering with emotion. "He... he was a good horse. I was...I was hoping...."

She trailed off, unable to finish. Creed paused. "What were you hoping, my lady?"

She was back to wringing her hands. She almost did not tell him, waving him off, but she took a deep breath for courage. "I was hoping ye could say a prayer for him," she finally said. "He was my friend."

Praying over a horse. Creed's first reaction was to snort at the foolishness of the request, but he could see by her expression how serious she was. He should not have felt such pity for her, but he did.

"If that will comfort you."

"It would." He turned from her but she called to him again. "Sir Knight?"

He stopped, hand on the tent flap. "My lady?"

She took a timid step towards him, emerald eyes riveted to moody, dusky blue. "Could I come with ye? I would like to be with him while you... when you...."

She trailed off, hoping he could read her mind and know what she meant. She could not even bring herself to say it. Creed wondered if she had the stomach to watch it; for her own sake, he doubted it.

He shook his head. "My lady, you should remember your horse as he was, strong and beautiful and whole. I would not want your last memory of him to be a stiffening carcass going up in flames."

Her face paled, at both the description and the denial, but she remarkably held her tongue.

She watched him walk from the tent, the big man with the enormous hands. She wondered if she could repair whatever trust she had damaged, but in the same thought, she wondered if she might not make another attempt. It simply was not in her nature to surrender, no matter how foolish or tragic the results.

As Creed quit the tent, he spied Burle immediately. The fat knight was several feet away, driving stakes into the ground to secure another tent. Creed called to him and the man made his way over to him, his armor jiggling on his fat rolls. His thinning blond hair was standing up in wispy strands, blowing lightly in the breeze. It looked like a crown of feathers.

"My lord?" he asked politely.

Creed gestured to the tent. "Stay with her. Do not let her out of your sight. I am going to see to her horse."

Burle nodded. "Would you have me inside or outside?"

Creed thought a moment; though he was sure the lady would prefer to rest alone, he would admit he felt better having her escort by her side. Especially Burle; the man was as strong as ten men, but due to his flab he could not outrun an infant. At least if he was next to her, he would have a chance of grabbing her before she got away from him.

"Inside," he threw a thumb back at the tent.

Burle nodded shortly and the bear of a man went to the tent, disappearing inside. Fighting off a smirk at the thought of the lady's reaction when she saw the big knight seated beside her like a watchdog, Creed headed off in the direction of the dead horse.

By the time Creed reached the carcass, Jory had commandeered a few men at arms to haul the animal to an area where they could get a good fire going. Four men had tied ropes to the horse and were dragging it towards the road where there was more dirt and less wet grass. As he approached Jory, he realized that his anger, so recently fled, was returning at the sight of him. On behalf of the lady, he was outraged.

"I would have a word with you, d'Eneas."

The young knight with the brown eyes gazed at him warily. "What would that be?"

"Privately."

"You can say whatever you have to say right here."

Though Creed was beckoning him out of the hearing range of the men, Jory was not obeying. Irritation growing, Creed stood next to him, easily twice his size and several times his strength, and breathed down into his pale, sweaty face.

"I saw you relieve yourself on this animal," he rumbled. "What's more, the lady saw you. Would you care to give me a reason for your display before I take your head off?"

Jory was intimidated by him, that much was clear. Still, he put up a weak front. "Why are you so concerned about a dead animal?" he asked, almost flippantly. "'Tis just a dead beast that belonged to that Scots wench. Why do you care so much about it?"

Creed's jaw ticked, never a good sign. "Perhaps no one ever explained to you the rights and wrongs of proper conduct. It is right to treat a hostage as a guest, no matter what her lineage. It is wrong to show such disregard to her, and the living in general, by befouling an object that meant something to someone. Why is it so difficult for you to conduct yourself with restraint and common sense?"

Jory lifted a black eyebrow. "You should have been the first one to pee on the horse, de Reyne. She shamed you most of all by running from you. Do not take your anger out on me for your lack of control over the lady."

It was the wrong thing to say, but strangely, Creed's anger went no further. He was beginning to feel a good deal of contempt, and contempt ran like ice through is veins.

"Jory," he said, almost thoughtfully. "You and I are going to come to an understanding here and now. On the battlefield, I shall defend your life as necessary because we serve together. But off the battlefield, my loyalty to you ends. I pounded you when you attacked the lady last night but I should have wrung your damnable neck. The next time I see or hear of an offense against Lady Carington, in any shape or form, you will meet with a beating the likes of which you are unlikely to fully recover from. Do I make myself perfectly clear?"

Jory's smug expression was gone. "Are you threatening me? I shall go to Lord Richard if you are. He will send you back to the king so you can face off against those charges that are lodged against you."

Creed had visions of wrapping his hands around Jory's neck

and squeezing him until his head exploded. But he kept his hands at his sides. And he kept his cool.

"One more offense and you will pay."

"You do not frighten me, de Reyne."

"Then that is your most grave mistake."

With that, he turned on his heel and marched up on the men who were hauling Bress' carcass. After a few short orders, he had the men dropping the ropes and running for shovels. They would dig a pit to fire the carcass in and be done with it. As the men began to shovel out a pit, Creed stood over the big blond animal, crossed himself, and muttered a prayer. He had, after all, promised.

Jory watched the big knight move. He was indeed afraid of him and knew that the man would not hesitate to do as he threatened. Creed de Reyne had a long standing reputation throughout England, and a flawless one, until six months ago. Now he was hiding from the crown until the issues involving him and the king's betrothed cooled. Lord Richard and Ryton de Reyne were shielding him, protecting him like a coward.

Jory wiped at his nose, still glaring at Creed, thinking of ways he could get back at the man. He could turn him over to the king's guard, but he would need help with that and no one at Prudhoe would help him. He could go after the Scots bitch again because in doing so, he could show how ineffective Creed was in protecting her. He would show everyone Creed's weakness. He would make him pay.

Jory wiped his nose again, thinking hateful thoughts about Creed and concocting a thousand ways to discredit the man. If one failed, surely another would work. De Reyne would suffer in the end.

CHAPTER FOUR

It was not that she was frightened of them. On the contrary; she felt absolutely no fear. But Burle, later joined by Stanton, stood next to each other on the opposite side of the tent and just stared at her. Carington was beginning to feel as if they expected her to grow horns or burp thunder. The way they were looking at her was most strange and it was turning into a very odd standoff.

She was supposed to be resting. But she could not sleep with Burle and Stanton watching every move she made. So they ended up playing a very odd staring game, with Carington watching them and the knights watching her. Had she not been so exhausted, she might have found it humorous. But her tolerance was fading.

"Sir Knight?" she was looking straight at Burle. "What is yer name? I have forgotten."

The big blond knight perked up from his post by the tent flap. "I am Burle, my lady."

"And yer skinny friend?"

Burle and Stanton looked at each other. "His name is Stanton, my lady. You hit him in the face when you escaped the first time."

Carington's dark green eyes moved over the slender, pale knight. She was not sure if Burle's comment was supposed to make her feel guilty, so she let it go without acknowledgement.

"Yer not very old," she said to Stanton. "How old are ye?"

"I have seen twenty years and four, my lady," he answered.

"Are ye married?"

"Aye, my lady."

"Are ye, now? How grand. Do ye have children?"

"A son, my lady. And my wife is again expecting."

"I see," she looked back at Burle. "And ye, Sir Burle? Are ye married?"

The flabby knight nodded his head. "Aye, my lady."

"And do ye have children also?"

"Aye, my lady. Three daughters."

"Marvelous," Carington stood up from the small three-legged stool she had been seated on. But her warm expression vanished and fire flashed in the green eyes as she planted her hands firmly on her slender hips. "Do ye think yer wife or daughters would appreciate a strange man staring at them as you have been staring at me? What kind of manners do ye have gawking at me as ye do?"

Burle struggled not to appear off-guard by her sharp tone. "If it was for their own protection, I am sure they would understand. And we were not gawking."

"Not gawking?" She threw up her hands. "Then what do ye call it? Ye're staring at me as if ye've never seen a woman before."

She was quite possibly yelling. Burle and Stanton were somewhat surprised, but both maintained their even disposition. Especially Burle; he was used to emotional females. He had married one.

"I apologize if you think we have been rude, my lady," he said quietly. "That was not our intent. We only mean to keep you safe until Sir Creed returns."

"Ye mean that you only mean to keep me in this tent until he returns," she supplied with a hint of nastiness. "Dunna think for one minute that I dunna know what ye're up to. You are here to keep me from running off again."

Stanton just looked at Burle; he would let the older man provide all of the answers. "Possibly, my lady," Burle answered.

She lifted a dark eyebrow and crossed her arms; so bullying them had not gotten her very far. She did not even know why she had done it, only that she was tired and irritated and overwrought from the events of her misguided escape. But it was a foolish reaction, in truth. She had come to discover over the past day that she was a foolish woman beneath all of the stubbornness and pride. She lowered her gaze and returned to her seat. When she spoke, it was in a more civilized tone.

"I am not planning on running again," she said, almost wearily.

"Ye dunna have to worry about that."

"That would be a pleasant change."

Creed spoke as he entered the tent, having heard her last sentences. His dusky blue eyes fixed on her and he realized, to his surprise, that he might actually be glad to see her. The thought was so startling that he angrily chased it away and his demeanor darkened as a result. "I heard the shouting across the field," he said lowly, enormous fists resting on his hips. "What seems to be the problem?"

Carington stared up at him; he was sucking all of the air out of the room again. Her heart seemed to be fluttering strangely at the sight of him but she pushed the awareness aside, refusing to analyze it. Perhaps she was ill. Perhaps she was just tired. The fact that she started experiencing these strange symptoms the moment Creed entered the tent had nothing to do with it.

"No problem, m'lord," she said, lowering her gaze. "I… I was simply coming to know my guard dogs better."

Creed passed a glance at both knights; Stanton's gaze was steady and wide-eyed, while Burle's was a bit more seasoned. He and Burle had served together for years and they knew each other well. He trusted the older knight's sense of things.

"Is all well?" he asked the man.

Burle nodded with the trained patience of one used to dealing with women. "It is, my lord."

"Then you may go and get your supper. Send someone with the lady's, if you will."

Both men acknowledged his request as they left the tent. Creed removed his gloves, scratched the back of his neck, and generally settled himself without so much as a glance to Carington the entire time. She sat on the small stool, shivering in the chill, watching every move he made. She was attempting to ascertain his mood, trying to figure out if he was still angry with her for her earlier escapade. He seemed rather glum. She had no idea why she should be concerned with his mood but she was.

"My horse," she began hesitantly. "Did… did all go well?"

"It did."

She did not say any more, realizing that Bress was in flames somewhere outside and not wanting to think about it. The thought made her sad again, and sadness brought another round of brimming tears. She discreetly chased them away, not wanting him to think she was weak and weepy. Carington had never been the crying sort. But the past two days had seen that particular characteristic change.

Creed was not immune to her tears; he was well aware of them. His gauntlets, breast plate and greaves ended up in a heap on the floor. As Carington sat with her back to him, he whistled low in his teeth and watched her jump at the sound. Immediately, his two squires vaulted into the tent.

"Steven," he said to the shorter, brown-eyed lad. "Remove my armor. Make sure it is thoroughly cleaned of the sweat and grime; I do not want any rust on the plates."

As Steven collected the solid pieces of armor, Creed turned to the tall blond lad beside him and held out his arms. "Pull," he commanded softly.

James took hold of the chain mail hauberk and pulled it over his lord's head with ease. Considering the boy had been doing it for half of his life, he was adept at the chore. By now, Carington had turned to the activity, watching the squires work around Creed. The boys were silent and efficient, skinny Sassenach lads on the brink of manhood. When James accidentally met her eye, he blushed furious and lowered his gaze. He was the first one bolting out of the tent with Steven right behind him.

"Yer squires are young," she commented softly. "How old are they?"

Creed raked his fingers through his wavy dark hair, glancing up at her as he did so. "Steven has seen sixteen years. James has seen fifteen."

"The tall blond lad?" she said, surprised. "He is so big. He looks much older than his age."

Creed nodded, moving towards the vizier to see why it was not warming up as quickly as he would have liked. "He was a tall boy when he came to serve me at seven years of age. His father was Constable of York until his death a few years ago."

"Oh," she thought of the quiet, fatherless boy. "A pity. He seems like a good lad."

"He is." Creed grunted as he broke up a smoldering piece of peat with the iron bar.

Carington watched him closely, hoping a bit of pleasant conversation might lift both his mood and her spirits. She found she needed some lifting. But the way he was breaking up the peat, she wondered if pleasant conversation would do any good with him.

"Ye are a father to him, then," she stated quietly.

Creed shook his head, slamming the door of the bronze vizier shut. "I am his liege."

"Do ye have sons of yer own, Sir Creed?"

He did look at her, then. "Nay," he replied. "And you may call me simply Creed."

Somehow, Carington felt as if she had accomplished something great by just that simple sentence. She did not understand why it meant something to her, but it did. Her heart began doing the strange leaping thing again, pounding against her ribcage.

"As ye say," she said quietly, almost shyly. "Ye... ye may call me Cari if ye wish. No one calls me Carington; 'tis too long. Father says it exhausts him to say my entire name because he runs out of breath before he can get it out of his mouth."

Her soft sentence had an unexpected result; Creed actually smiled. Carington's heart pounded louder at the sight of it; he had a beautiful smile that dramatically changed his face. If she thought he was handsome before, or rather tried not to think it, then the event of an unanticipated smile confirmed her observations. She could no longer deny the obvious; the man was stunning.

"'Tis his fault," he said, rising on his massive legs. "He is the one who named you."

Carington shook her head. "Nay, my mother did. Her family name was Carington."

"I see," his gaze seemed to linger on her overlong. "I like Cari better. It suits you."

"Why would ye say that?"

He lifted those enormous shoulders, shrugging as he looked around to see if the squires had stocked the tent with something for him to sit on. "'Tis a sweet name. Petite, like you are."

A bashful smile crossed her lips and she looked at the ground. "Kind words, Sir Knight," she said so quietly that he almost did not hear her. "After today, I dinna expect any from ye."

Not finding anything to sit on, he just stood there, fists on his hips as he gazed down at her. It seemed to be his favorite way to stand. "You certainly do not deserve any."

Her head shot up, the emerald eyes flashing at him. "Ah, so now it comes. I knew ye were simply biding yer time until ye were ready to let loose on me." She stood up, matching his fist-on-hips stance. "Well, out with it, then. Do yer worst. Ye canna make me feel any worse than I already do."

He just looked at her. A snort suddenly bubbled up as he struggled to fight off a grin. "You are faster to rise to anger than anyone I have ever seen. Does it not exhaust you expending that much effort?"

His smirk had her unbalanced. "Do ye taunt me, then?"

He shook his head, still snorting as he turned away from her. "God, no. You would probably gouge my eyes out or rip off my ears if I did."

Now it was her turn to struggle against a smirk. "Ye'd be lucky if that was all I did to ye."

He turned to look at her, a full-blown grin on his face. "I have no doubt, Lady Cari. No doubt whatsoever."

They just grinned at each other, her with a furrowed brow as if she were trying to be stern about it and him with an open expression. It was the first moment of levity they had experienced between them and it was an agreeable one.

"And it's just Cari, not Lady Cari," she told him for good measure. "Lady Cari sounds like a disease and I dunna like it."

He burst out in laughter, his big body shaking with mirth.

Carington watched him laugh, enchanted by the straight white teeth and deep dimples that carved big ruts down each cheek. "Christ, you are a spitfire." He was at the tent flap with the intention on searching for the person or persons bringing their meal, but his gaze lingered on her instead of the encampment beyond. "Very well, my lady. Just Cari."

She nodded shortly at him as if she had just won a great argument. The smile was still on her lips as she resumed her stool and he tore his gaze away from her long enough to search for their errant meal. He spied his squires across the camp, hands laden as they headed in his direction. He lowered the tent flap and turned back to her.

"I hope you are hungry," he said. "It looks as if my squires are bringing quite a feast."

"I am," she said, suddenly quite famished. "I could eat a horse."

James and Steven entered the tent carrying trays of steaming food; hunks of meat, bread, and a large slab of white cheese. Creed had the boys set the trays on the bedroll, next to Carington, and they did so with quiet efficiency. As they quit the tent, Carington took a large piece of meat for herself and bit into it with gusto.

Creed lowered his big body down on the bedroll, reaching for another large slab of meat. It was steamy, almost undercooked, but he did not care. He was starving. But the moment he took a bite and sampled the tough, gamey flavor, his chewing came to a halt. He stared at the meat. Carington noticed his puzzled expression.

"What's wrong?" she asked. "Is it not to yer liking?"

He did not say a word, but a flicker of something very disturbing ignited deep in his mind. He put his hand on her wrist, lowering the meat from her mouth.

"Do not eat that," he said quietly. "Eat the bread and cheese. I shall return."

Confusion swept her as she looked down at the meat. "It seems all right," she suddenly looked stricken. "Do ye think someone has poisoned it?"

He shook his head, rising on his big legs and making his way to the tent flap. "Eat the bread," he repeated.

"What on earth is the matter?" she licked her fingers of the meat's grease. "The meat tastes fine. 'Tis venison, is it not?" She licked her fingers again, a puzzled look crossing her fine features. "But it does not have such a strong flavor. And it 'tis a bit tough. What kind of meat is it?"

He paused at the tent flap, unable to say what he was thinking. *I could eat a horse.* Her words echoed horribly in his head. Across the compound, the distant pyre of Bress was burning and he could see, even at a distance, what had happened. His stomach rolled.

Fresh meat was cooking. The soldiers saw no reason to hunt or cook anything else. Horsemeat was tough, but it was not inedible. They would not let Bress go to waste. They were soldiers, hard and bred, and knew when to take advantage of a feast. Then his eyes narrowed, for walking across the encampment was Jory with a massive wooden trencher of meat in his hand. He saw Creed, several yards away, and his brown eyes lit up. He grinned, popped a piece of meat in his mouth, and continued along his way.

Creed's jaw began to tick; had he possessed any less control, he would have throttled the man there and now. But to do so would more than likely let the lady in on the dark secret. For now, he had to let it go, but the veins in his temples throbbed something fierce. It suddenly occurred to him that he knew who butchered the burning horse and it further occurred to him that his brother probably had not known. Ryton would have never allowed it. But now it was too late to do anything about it.

Though he could not bring himself to tell her, by his expression, she knew something was wrong. Creed went to collect the plates with the meat on them, taking them outside the tent. Carington could hear soft conversation as he spoke to his men outside, perhaps his squires. She did not know. All she knew was that he had looked rather disgusted about something.

They finished their bread and cheese in silence.

***

Later that night, Carington lay on her bedroll staring at the tent wall. She knew that Creed was behind her, sitting propped against a post, his moody gaze fixated on the glowing vizier just as it had been for the past hour. He just sat and stared as if deep in thought. She was convinced she had said something to upset him.

It was too bad. The situation had been so pleasant until their meal had been served. Then he became sullen and quiet. She wanted to ask him what the matter was but she did not have the nerve. She did not know the man; it was frankly none of her business.

The vizier was not doing a very good job of warding off the chill and she only had her tartan for warmth. A chill ran through her as she lay there, staring at the faint light flicker off the tent wall.

"Sir Creed?" she rolled over onto her back, looking at him across the vizier. "Do ye suppose there are any blankets or furs about? I'm a wee bit cold."

His moody gaze turned to her. "It is just Creed."

He was on his feet and moving for the tent opening. Outside, there were four sentries and he sent one of them scrounging for covers. He stood there, waiting for the man to return, as Carington tried to huddle down for warmth. The night was growing colder and unless she wanted to sit on the vizier, the little furnace did not have the power to stave off the chill. Just as she actually dozed off, the sentry returned with a riding cloak, the only cover he could find.

It was rough and dirty, but there was warmth to it. Creed took it from the man and closed the tent flap, trying to seal up the gap so that he could keep whatever warmth there was inside the tent. When he had fussed with it enough so that there was some barrier, he went over to Carington.

She lay still with her eyes closed. The top of her dark head and her eyes were all he could see above the faded tartan. He stood there a moment, gazing down at her dark head, wondering why he was feeling so much angst and confusion. It seemed to all center around her; fury at Jory for his imagined vendetta against her, puzzlement because in spite of everything, he felt a certain interest in the petite little lady. As calm as he was, she was equally fiery. As big as he was, she was equally small. He told her not to do something, so she would therefore do it anyway. But she had proven herself humorous and, at times, most amiable. Christ, he could not believe he was entertaining such dangerous thoughts.

Kneeling, he placed the cloak over her, tucking it in about her small body and trying not to wake her. His big fingers tucked it under her legs, his gaze moving up her delicious figure. And that was another thing; the woman had a body that men would kill to taste. As beautiful as her face was, it was her figure that set her apart from the rest. He had noticed it today in the gray surcoat that clung to every crevice, every curve. She was almost surreal in her perfection. Unfortunately, others had noticed it, too. He'd seen Jory's face. It was another suspicion to add to his concern and his sense of protectiveness grew.

He moved away from her with the intention of retreating to his spot near the post. Just as he did so, she suddenly sat bolt upright on the bedroll, emitting a low, teeth-chattering groan.

"Is there no warmth to be found this night?"

Her teeth were rattling as she fumbled with the tartan. Her small hands shot out and she put them up against the vizier in desperation. But as quickly as she touched it, she immediately drew away with a yelp. The bronze was sizzling. Creed was moving back in her direction.

"You will burn your hands if you do that," he admonished.

She looked truly miserable; her entire body was shaking. "But I am freezing," she insisted. "If it will only make me warm, I will gladly scorch my hands."

He instinctively reached out to grasp her fingers, feeling that they were indeed icy. "I do not believe you would be happy with the long-term results of that," he said, enfolding both of her hands in great warm palms. "Allowing a Sassenach to warm your hands is probably the lesser of the evils."

The moment he grasped her fingers, she tried to snatch them away. That lasted about a half a second. When she realized that his hands were indeed quite warm, she forgot about her hatred, fear, pride, or anything else that might have fed her resistance and gave in to his grasp completely. In fact, she buried both of her hands in his heated palms.

"Ye're like a roaring blaze," she closed her eyes as his heat began to draw the cold from her fingers, causing a prickling feeling. "How is it ye're not freezing like I am?"

He was fully aware that they were much closer, for propriety's sake, than they should be. "A body this size gives off a great deal of heat," he replied evenly. "You do not have much flesh on your bones to warm you as I do."

She lifted a dark eyebrow at him. "I am not scrawny if that's what ye mean."

He pursed his lips at her. "Do you always assume I am inferring something negative about you? I simply meant that I am a good deal bigger than you are and, consequently, I give off more heat than you do."

She eyed him, realizing that he was probably right. She did assume everything he said was an insult to her, yet he had never truly outright insulted her. She backed down. "My apologies, then," she said, feeling her hands spring back to life within his warm grip. "I wouldna want to insult the only Sassenach that has come to my aid."

But the silence that fell after that was uncomfortable, as she could sense his gaze upon her but did not know what to say. Her cheeks were growing warm, though she had no idea why. When her heart started its funny little jig again, she silently pulled her hands from his grasp and reclaimed her tartan about her. The cloak, however, was not as easy to manage and she struggled with it, trying to wrap it around the tartan. It was dusty and dirt flew up in her face, making her sneeze.

Suddenly, the cloak took on a life of its own and wrapped itself tightly around her. More than that, there were arms holding the cloak firm; powerful, enormous arms. It took Carington a moment to realize that Creed had bound her up in the cloak and proceeded to pull her into his massive embrace. She stiffened in shock.

"What are ye doing?" she gasped.

"Being practical," he said, shifting her board-stiff body into a comfortable position so her pointy elbows were not jabbing him in the gut. "You are cold; I am warm. Since the vizier is not doing its job of heating you adequately, I am offering my services. Would you rather freeze to death?"

She was still mortified, stunned, but the moment she felt his heat against her arms and back she could feel herself relenting. She could feel his warmth through the material, and it was evil and comforting at the same time. She should be punching him in the nose for his forwardness. But she could not muster the will.

"Of course I wouldna," she tried to sound outraged but did not do a very good job. "But ye... like this. And *me* like this. It isna proper!"

"Proper or not, it is nonetheless warm. Are you going to argue with me all night or do you intend to accept it, shut up, and go to sleep?"

She twisted her neck back to look at him; his face was hovering over her left shoulder, his dusky blue eyes holding nothing lascivious or indecent. In fact, he looked rather neutral about the whole thing and for some reason, she was disappointed. Nay, not disappointed, but certainly she had thought he would treat her more than just a bit of furniture. He might as well have been holding a chair for all of the warmth she saw in his eyes. What had she expected?

Frustrated at her foolish thoughts, she struggled to remain neutral as well. "I willna refuse ye if ye are so determined to help me," she mumbled, turning around so she would not have to look at him. "I will sleep now."

Creed did not reply. With her gathered in his arms, he lay on his left side and took her with him. She was still stiff as he shifted her around to find a comfortable position, but gradually, she began to relax. The initial awkward moments were fading as comfort set in. She settled back against him, wriggling her bum in an effort to get closer to his heat, and he had to close his eyes against the sweetness of it. He had seen the shape of that particular part of her body and it was round and perfect. Now it was brushing against his groin, although there were several layers of fabric in between them. He had to close his eyes, focus on something else, or all would be lost.

He did not know what possessed him to wrap himself around her in the first place, only that she was so cold that her face was pale and her nose was red. He gave off heat like a bonfire. His instincts took over, whether chivalrous instincts or just plain male instincts, he did not know. But now that he had her in his arms, he was sorely regretting it and sorely pleased with it all at the same time.

She sighed in his embrace, a sound of utter contentment. He could feel her body relax and her breathing grow even. Creed lay there with his eyes wide open, staring into the darkness, totally unable to rest. He was taut with the sensations he was experiencing. He knew she was asleep when she rolled back towards him, wedging herself even more intimately against his body. She was half on her back, half on her left side, the side of her head up against his chin.

The black hair licked at him and he could smell the very faint scent of Elder flower in his nostrils. Christ, if she was not a sweet little thing. Slowly, he rubbed his stubbled cheek against the black head, just once, feeling the silken strands against his skin. It had been so long since he had felt anything even remotely feminine that he was almost giddy with it. But he dare not do more. He should not have even done that.

As the night progressed, he could feel himself gradually relaxing. It was hard not to find comfort with her soft little body against him. He was not aware when he finally drifted off to sleep, but when he awoke a few hours later, his first realization was that Carington was now facing him, pressed up against him as far as she could go, and his arms were wrapped tightly around her. Blinking the sleep from his eyes, he wondered if he had not unknowingly orchestrated the death-embrace they seemed to be positioned in. His logical mind was thinking one thing but his body was apparently thinking another. She was warm, soft and wonderful, and his male impulse, even in sleep, had acted naturally. Her face was in his neck, her hot breath against his skin.

Hating himself, allowing a stolen moment to enjoy the sensation, he tightened his grip and drifted back off to sleep again.

Carington awoke at dawn to find herself quite alone by the cold vizier.

CHAPTER FIVE

Without a horse, she had been given the choice of riding with Creed or in the wagon. Because Creed had disappeared before she had awoken and when he returned seemed distant and cold, she chose the wagon. It was not the most comfortable of rides, but it was better than sitting with someone who clearly disliked her.

The escort moved out at dawn, heading south. Carington overheard Ryton say that they should arrive by the nooning meal. With that awareness, her nervousness began to take root. She had no idea what to expect or what her escorts would tell Lord Richard of her behavior. She was back to feeling alone, frightened and defiant. She did not even have Bress to bring comfort. Without Creed's kind support as the only Sassenach who seemed willing to tolerate her, she was retreating into her shell.

Creed rode slightly behind the wagon, just close enough to keep an eye on her but not close enough so that he had to talk to her. Perched beside the soldier driving the team, Carington ignored him just as he was ignoring her. She was not about to show him just how troubled she really was. Ryton was up at the head of the column, Stanton and Burle in relatively close proximity to the front of the wagon, but Jory was nowhere to be found. As the column rode for one solid hour in silence, then two, the morning around them brightened as the landscape flattened out somewhat. Carington had never been this far south before and turned her attention to the lands beyond.

Clad in a soft linen shift and a scarlet surcoat that was striking against her dark coloring, she was enjoying the weak warmth of the sun. Her dusty tartan was folded neatly beside her on the wagon seat. Her long, curling dark hair was pulled back away from her face, secured at the back of her head with a butterfly-shaped pin her father had given her and her lips were coated with the Elder flower oil, giving the slightly-pink lips a glossy sheen. She was unaware that there was not one man in the escort that did not think she was delightful to look at, including and especially Creed.

Aye, he was riding behind her, but it was mostly for self-protection. He had been both disappointed and glad when she had chosen to ride in the wagon. He had never slept so well as he had with her in his arms and the knowledge confused him greatly. He did not want to be her protector in the first place and was angry at himself for being glad that he was. It was stupid. He was stupid. As he watched the back of her dark head, lost in thought, he was caught off guard when Jory suddenly rode up beside the wagon.

The young knight was in fine form that morning, seemingly happier than he had been in a long time. He flipped up his three-point visor as he focused his unwanted attention on Carington.

"My lady looks well today," his brown eyes glittered as he spoke to her. "Did you sleep well?"

Creed could see Carington stiffen, turning to Jory with great contempt in her manner. "Well enough," she replied in a clipped tone.

Creed spurred his charger forward, closer to the wagon, as Jory continued. "And your sup," Jory went on. "Did you enjoy that as well?"

She looked at him, wondering why he looked so pleased with himself. She had no idea why the man was even talking to her after two hours of total silence.

"It was fine," she said as she turned away from him.

By this time, Creed was on the opposite side of the wagon, turning up his visor and glaring daggers at Jory.

"Leave the lady alone, d'Eneas," he growled threateningly.

The brown-eyed knight lifted an eyebrow. "Why? I am doing nothing harmful. I merely asked how her supper was."

"You will keep silent and move back to your post."

Jory's smug expression faded. "You are not my commander, de

Reyne." He refocused on the lady. "You have Creed to thank for the evening's meal, you know. Without him, we would not have had such a feast."

Stanton and Burle turned around to see what was transpiring; they both knew what had happened, well after the fact, and were disgusted with Jory's underhanded actions. Creed had sought them out that morning just after dawn to find out what they had known about it. Neither man had been aware that the lady's dead horse had been on the menu; their squires had brought them supper and they had not questioned the lads as to what it was. Upon questioning the boys, the squires proceeded to inform the knights that Sir Jory had instructed them to feed the army from the smoldering horse. He had, in fact, cut the meat himself.

The normally very calm and very cool Creed had been mad enough to kill after that. Only his brother's intervention and promise of punishment from Lord Richard had kept him from snapping Jory's neck. The knights had vowed not to say anything to the lady, for obvious reasons. But Jory had not been a part of that vow.

Much to Creed's horror, Jory was apparently intent on letting the lady in on his sick little joke. Not a word all morning and suddenly the man was running amuck at the mouth. Before Creed could issue another threat to him, Carington replied to Jory's statement.

"What feast?" she inquired, looking first to Jory and then to Creed. "What feast does he mean?"

Creed met her inquisitive gaze. "The bread and cheese, I am sure," he said quietly, mostly because he did not want Jory to hear him and contradict him. "I did nothing more than bring it to you. I would hardly call that a feast."

"He is much too modest," Jory had indeed heard him, now gleefully shouting it out for all to hear. "He cooked your horse for all of us. We feasted on your tough Scottish steed last night. Did you not recognize the flavor?"

Carington looked to the foolish young knight as he spoke the words, not truly understanding him for a few moments. But as the words settled and became understood, Carington's emerald eyes flew open so wide that they nearly popped from their sockets. Horrified, her hands flew to her mouth and she looked to Creed with an expression of panicked accusation. His dusky blue eyes were steady and intense.

"My lady," he began, feeling as if he was about to stem a mighty flood with a toy shovel. He could see the chaos in her eyes. "'Tis not as he makes it sound. It was...."

She screamed with horror. Before Creed could grab her, she was bolting off of the wagon, landing on her bum just behind his charger, and scrambling to her feet. As she screamed again and ran off, he reined his charger around and tore off after her. Together they plunged into the bramble, one after the other. What Creed did not see was Burle rein his horse in Jory's direction and slug the knight so hard in the face that he toppled off and cracked his head on the side of the wagon. At the moment, Creed was only concerned with a hysterical young lady.

Carington was crying uncontrollably, running full bore like a crazy woman. Creed leapt off his charger, caught her around the torso, and they both tumbled into the tall grass. Once he had her on the ground, he could feel her supple body start to heave. With his arms around her, she proceeded to vomit up everything she had eaten over the past day and then some. Even when there was nothing left, she still continued to retch. Creed just held her.

"'Tis all right, Cari," he murmured. His helm was bumping against her heaving head and he tossed it off, hearing it land several feet away. "'Tis all right, honey. Just relax. Relax and breathe."

She heard his words, soft and soothing, but she could not do as he asked. She was ill, verging on a faint. Horrified beyond description, she went limp against him. The heaving had stopped for the moment but still the tears came. Creed sighed heavily with great regret, and held her tightly against him.

"I am so sorry," he breathed against her dark hair. "I did not know what had happened until it was too late. None of us did."

Carington's hand was at her mouth, covering it, as she

struggled to breathe. "I… I ate him!"

It all came out as a strangled cry that cut him to the bone. "I know, honey, I know," Creed's gloved hand was on her forehead, holding her head against his shoulder in an effort to both support and comfort her. "But I stopped you before you went too far. I am only sorry that I did not prevent the entire circumstance."

"You cooked him!"

"Nay, lass, I did not cook him. I was burning the carcass and the men smelled the meat cooking and thought it was for eating. It was all a horrible mistake."

She wept as if her heart was broken. Creed heard footfalls crunching in the grass behind him and looked over his shoulder to see Ryton and Burle standing several feet away. His brother looked sickened while Burle just looked angry.

"Get her up, Creed," Ryton said quietly. "Do not let her wallow in this. We must be on our way."

"Give her a minute, for Christ's sake," Creed snapped softly. "Keep moving. I will catch up to you when she has calmed sufficiently."

Ryton's gaze was fixed on his brother, apparently trying to keep the hysterical hostage from running any further by the grip he had on her. As he watched, the lady heaved again and more stomach contents ended up on the mashed grass. With a heavy sigh, he motioned Burle back to his charger.

"Do not be too long, then," he said to his brother. "Lord Richard is expecting us around noon. We cannot delay."

Creed gave him a brief nod, feeling the lady's body convulse under him once again as her stomach struggled to bring up more bile. "It would be wise if you kept Jory out of my sight," he rumbled. "I cannot guarantee my control if I see him."

"I will take care of d'Eneas, have no doubt," Ryton replied. "You tend the lady. And do not be over long with it."

Ryton's footfalls faded across the grass, leaving Creed and Carington alone in the cluster of trees. Creed returned his focus to the lady, no longer retching but struggling to calm her breathing. The hysteria of tears had faded to a soft weeping and he continued to hold her in silence, feeling tremendously guilty. At some point, he started to rock her gently, as one would an ill child. It was an instinct and nothing more. Carington clung to his big arm with one hand, the other still pressed against her mouth.

"Ye knew," she said it so softly that he hardly heard her. "That is why ye took the meat away from me last night. Ye knew and ye didna tell me. Ye knew and said nothing!"

There was an accusation in the statement. Creed rocked back on his heels, shifting her so that she was sitting on his thighs and off of the cold, dirty grass.

"You still would not know if I had any say in the matter," he said frankly. "I did not expect Jory to announce it to you but I suppose I should have. The man is an idiot."

"I told ye that I dinna like him," her voice was a breathy whisper. "He is evil and malicious. Any man who would… who would…."

She was beginning to sob anew and he shushed her softly. "No more," he said. "You are going to make yourself ill. What is done is done. It is over with. You have expelled your grief and we must move beyond it."

"I canna move beyond it. Could ye?"

"I would have to if there were more important things on the horizon, such as meeting the family I am going to live with for the next few years. You do not want them to meet a red-eyed and pale faced woman, do you?"

"I dunna care what they think!" she spat, regaining some of the fire he was becoming familiar with. "If they think ill of me, I dunna care."

He lifted an eyebrow; she was starting to sound like her old self and he stood up, taking her with him. "Aye, you do," he said evenly. "You are a strong woman. You will show them this."

It was a good thing that Creed had a strong grip on her because her knees were very unsteady. Her hands were still on her mouth, tears still in her eyes. She folded over at the waist.

"Sweet Jesus," she wept softy. "My sweet Bress."

He still held her, one big arm around her torso as she bent

over and retched one last time. He found himself pulling her long hair back, out of the way, so it would not become soiled.

"Cari," he said softly. "I know you are upset. But you must get hold of yourself. Please, honey. It is important."

She remained folded in half, breathing loudly, struggling to catch her wind. But her hands and legs were feeling strangely tingly, strangely light. As Creed continued to hold her, she suddenly went limp and he had to put both arms around her to keep her from tumbling into the grass. Knowing she had passed out from sheer nerves, and rather relieved that she had if only to force calm upon her, he carefully collected her into his arms and went in search of his horse.

The charger was several yards away, munching on plump green grass. Creed shifted Carington in his arms, a mere featherweight to his strength, and gazed into her pale, lovely face. She'd certainly had a rough time of it already and the day was not even over yet.

"'Tis all right, honey," he murmured, though she could not hear him. "You needn't worry over anything any longer. I'm here."

They caught up to the column in little time. Creed saw the bloodied welt on the side of Jory's face but did not ask where he got it. He had an inkling that he already knew.

***

Prudhoe was a truly impressive sight to see. Built on a strategic crossing over the River Tyne, it sat atop a massive motte that was at least one hundred years old. The castle was unique in that there was a good deal of heavy trees around it, almost right up to the massive wall that encircled the castle. When the bastion had suffered through a bad siege from the Scots about thirty years prior, those trees had proven strategically detrimental to the defense of the castle. The Scots climbed them and launched their weapons from their branches. But the great oaks had stood there hundreds of years and they still stood to this day. No one seemed to have the heart to cut down the mighty grove.

Carington sat behind Creed, her arms wrapped around his trim waist, her eyes drinking in the sight of her new home. Until this very moment, the castle had been a theory, a dream, certainly nothing real. Now that she saw it in all its glory, it was a terrifying and awesome sight. Although she had been calm for a few hours, her nerves began to return again. Stomach twitching at the sight of the mighty bastion, she turned her head away so she would not have to look. She laid her cheek miserably on the plate protection covering Creed's back.

The day was going from bad to worse. She did not know what she had expected, but the enormous castle shocked her. It was gloomy and foreboding even in the bright sunlight. She could feel the doom radiating off of the gray stone, a silent testimony to her dismal future. Face still against his back, she watched the giant oak trees pass by as they plodded along the road towards their destination.

"Sir Creed?" she asked quietly.

"Just Creed," he reminded her.

Since the episode a few hours ago, he had been inordinately considerate with her. It was as if that experience had somehow bonded them together, a new element added to their association. It had brought it to another level, a level of comfort and trust. She was not sure if he still entirely trusted her, but she was coming to trust him. It was an important milestone.

"Are ye going to be my shadow even at the castle?" she asked.

He could feel her leaning against him, her slight body weary and drained. "I am my lady's shadow wherever she goes."

"I feel better knowing that," she said softly. "I dunna know anyone but you."

"Untrue," he said. "You know Sir Ryton and Sir Stanton and Sir Burle. They will be your protectors as well."

"I hit Sir Stanton in the face. I dunna believe he has forgiven me for that."

Creed thought about the young knight he knew, the one who

had too much compassion and pity for his own good. "Aye, he has. You needn't worry over Stan. He would protect you with his life."

She digested that a moment. "But the big man… what is his name? I wasna very nice to him; I yelled at him. I dunna believe he likes me, either."

Creed glanced over his left shoulder, seeing Burle and Stanton several yards behind him and Jory almost to the rear of the column as if exiled there. He turned back around. "Did you see the injury to Jory's face?"

When she had awoken from her dead faint, the dark young knight happened to pass into her line of sight. She had seen that the entire right side of his face was bruised. "Aye."

"Burle did that."

"Why?"

"Because Jory made you cry. Burle has three daughters, my lady. He is very protective of womenfolk in general."

Carington lifted her head long enough to look back at the two knights, now through new eyes. Surprised at their chivalry to the point of being speechless, her thoughts were distracted as they came into the shadow cast by the massive keep of Prudhoe. She glanced up, straining to look around Creed so she could gain a better look. All she saw was more stone and more walls. As anxious as she was, she was also curious about the mysteries the great structure contained.

"Will ye tell me something of the people who live here?" she asked.

His dusky blue eyes moved appreciatively up the massive stone walls, lit by the bright spring sun. Rays of light filtered in through the oaks that lined the road and he was glad to be home again.

"There are Lord Richard and his wife, the Lady Anne," he said. "They are kind and decent people. You must remember that. They have two sons, Edward, who is six years, and Gilbert, who is eight. You must mind the boys; they have a fondness for fighting and spitting and are quite spoiled. There are also two foster girls, the Lady Julia and the Lady Kristina. They are approximately sixteen or seventeen years, I think. You might find companionship with them."

She snorted. "I am older than they are."

"Is that so?"

"It 'tis. I have seen nineteen years."

He fought off a smile at the haughtiness of her voice. "Then you can be an older, wiser friend."

She snorted again, this time making a face. "Pasty-faced Sassenach lasses. I dunna know if I want to be a friend."

He cocked an eyebrow, turning his neck slightly to make eye contact with her. "None of that. You will behave yourself."

She matched his cocked eyebrow, ending when she backed down and returned her gaze to the looming castle. "What if they are mean to me?"

"Then you will tell me. I will deal with them."

"So I canna even defend myself?"

He shook his head with faint regret at her combative attitude. "Cari, they're not going to attack you. Show them how kind and intelligent a Scot really is. You are representing your people, honey. You are here as an emissary of peace. That is a very honorable and important task."

She was still torn between reluctance and acceptance. "But what if...?" she suddenly blinked, looking up at the side of his helmed head. "What did ye call me?"

He lifted his eyebrows thoughtfully, wrestling with the horse when it threw its head. "Cari?"

"Nay."

"What?"

"Ye called me... honey. Ye've called me that before."

The horse tossed its head again and he cuffed it on the top of the head. "Have I? Forgive me for my forwardness, then. I did not mean to offend."

She eyed him. "Ye did not," she said. She lowered her head and looked back to the trees. "Ye may call me that if ye wish."

A grin spread across his lips. "I wish."

Her cheeks flushed furiously and she hid her smile by pretending to look down at herself, fussing with the dust on her scarlet surcoat. She was a mess but almost did not care. Creed's pet name had her caring about little else.

The escort passed through an enormous gate built into the perimeter wall, spilling them out into a massive bailey. The equally massive keep was on the motte to her right, soaring a hundred feet into the blue English sky. It was bigger than anything she had ever seen. Carington was staring at it when Creed brought his horse to a halt and dismounted. He held his arms up to her.

"Come along," he said. "They are waiting to meet you."

She looked at him and he saw the fear, but she obediently slipped into his arms. He lowered her to the ground, his hands loitering on her waist perhaps a bit longer than necessary. Their eyes lingered on one another, appraisingly, until she offered a weak smile.

"Better to get this over with," she said with forced bravery.

He smiled in return, collecting some items off his saddle before taking her hand and tucking it into the crook of his elbow.

"If my lady will follow me," he said.

She would indeed follow him. She had already decided that. It no longer made any difference that Creed was a hated Sassenach; he was a kind man and quite handsome. Having experienced all that she had with him over the past two days, there was a definite attachment beginning and she no longer possessed the will to fight it.

They followed Ryton and Burle across the outer bailey with Stanton bringing up the rear. Jory was under orders to disband the escort and they could hear his high-pitched shouts above the roar of the ward. Gripping Creed's elbow with her left hand, she brushed at her surcoat with the right. There was dust everywhere and she noticed grass stains from when she had fallen in the grass. She lamented the stains as they crossed into the inner bailey.

"My coat is so dirty," she brushed at the green streaks. "These

Sassenachs are going to think I am a filthy little pig."

Creed glanced down at her surcoat, his gaze inevitably falling on her delicious figure. The slender torso and full, succulent breasts caught his attention but when she looked up at him, she only noticed that he was looking her in the eye.

"You have been traveling," he said. "They understand that there is some wear that goes along with that."

"Do I have time to change?" she asked. "A few minutes are all it would take. And I would feel so much better."

Creed did not see anything unreasonable with that request. He turned to his brother, up ahead of him. "Ryton," he caught the man's attention. "The lady wishes to change her coat. It will not take long. Would you inform Lord Richard and Lady Anne that the lady will greet them once she has cleaned up from her journey?"

Ryton's gaze moved over the lady's clothes; she was dusty and there were grass stains on her garment, but even so, she was still the loveliest thing he had ever seen. Besides that, they were already late and he hated not being punctual.

"No need," he replied. "She is presentable."

"It would be the polite thing to do."

Ryton eyed his brother, a mixture of impatience and intolerance. "Nay, Creed," he motioned towards the great hall dead ahead. "Get her inside. They have been waiting overlong for her arrival."

Creed did not look at her; he was busy glaring at his brother for denying a polite request. They closed in on the wide open door of Prudhoe's great hall, a massively long structure that was built on the ground floor of the bailey. It was separate from the keep, unusual for an English bastion. Most great halls were part of the keep and well away from the open bailey.

Carington observed the carved doorway as they were swallowed up by the dark innards, descending into a place that smelled of must and rushes and smoke. It was eerie and unfamiliar, and Carington's eyes widened at the sight.

Creed felt her hesitate. He looked down at her frightened

expression, noticing that she had slowed considerably to the point of stopping. He patted the hand on his elbow.

"'Tis all right," he assured her quietly. "These are kind people. You have nothing to fear."

She gazed up at him, the emerald eyes full of anxiety. "Ye willna leave me?"

He shook his head, his gaze serious. "Nay. I will be with you the entire time."

She smiled gratefully and he felt his heart skip a beat. Odd; he'd never experienced anything like that before and had no idea what to make of it. He gave her a wink and gently urged her forward.

The dark and musty foyer abruptly opened into a grand and warmly-lit hall. The ceilings were thirty feet high and a gallery spanned the upper circumference of the room. Tapestries hung on the north and south sides with a massive hearth along the western wall. Fresh rushes littered the floor and, amazingly, there were no dogs about. Carington had never seen anything so enormous and struggled not to gape like an idiot. Her eyes darted about nervously, trying to keep her wits, as several people came into focus at the great long dining table beyond.

The party at the table rose as the knights and one small lady approached. Carington's eyes fell on an older, well-dressed man, a slender well-dressed older woman, and several children. But she was not particularly interested in the children; she was focused on the adults. The man and woman drew closer to her and she could see they held non-hostile expressions. Not knowing what to think, she tried to maintain a neutral facade.

The man extended his hand. "Creed," he did not take his eyes off of Carington as he spoke. "Will you introduce us to your charge?"

Creed took her hand off his elbow and placed it in the man's outstretched palm. "Lord Richard d'Umfraville, meet the Lady Carington Kerr. Lady Carington, this is your liege."

Richard was gallant without being extravagant. He placed his lips gently on her hand in a gesture of respect and, still holding her hand, turned to the lady beside him. "Lady Carington, my wife, the Lady Anne."

Anne d'Umfraville was a dark-haired, dark-eyed lady with a handsome face. She smiled warmly at Carington and took her hand from her husband's grip. "My lady," she had a deep, husky voice. "Welcome to Prudhoe. We are happy to have you as our guest for a time."

Even though Creed had told her they were kind people, still, she did not expect it. Off-guard, she dipped a brief curtsey for the lady. "My lady," she looked at Richard. "My lord, I am pleased to be here. Thank ye for yer kind welcome."

Over by the table, the children suddenly came alive. Carington looked over to see two young ladies and two small boys, all in varied degrees of giggles. The youngest boy crawled onto the bench, leapt up onto the table, and stomped is feet.

"Papa," he pointed at Carington. "She talks funny!"

The children burst out into loud laughter and Carington's cheeks flushed a dull red. Richard did not react, but Anne cast them all a nasty look.

"She is from Scotland, lad," Richard said patiently. "All Scots talk this way."

"But it's funny!"

"It is their way and you will not laugh at her. Do you understand?"

The giggles muted but did not die altogether. Carington cast a sidelong glance at the little boy, who caught her eye and stuck his tongue out at her.

"That must be Edward," she said quietly, though Richard and Anne heard her. When they turned to her curiously, she hastened to explain. "Sir Creed told me that ye had two sons and that the youngest was Edward."

"Indeed," Richard said proudly. "His brother Gilbert is eight."

A glance to the older boy showed him picking his nose. Carington lifted an eyebrow at his bad manners and the child ripped his finger from his nose and pointed at her with it.

"Papa," he marched over to them. "I do not like the way she

looked at me. It was disresponsible."

Richard's proud stance seemed to waver. "You mean disrespectful, Gilbert."

The boy continued to point the boogered finger at her. "I want her whipped."

"Whipped!" Anne grabbed her son by the shoulder and turned him back towards the table. "You and your brother sit down and remain silent. Another word and I will blister your backside."

"But, Mama, she is our enemy," Gilbert tried to point out to her. "She is our prisoner. Is that not what Papa said?"

"Nay," Anne said firmly, shoving her son onto the bench seat. "She is our guest."

"But Papa said...."

"I do not want to hear any more. You will remain quiet or you will go to bed. Is that clear?"

Gilbert was not happy with his mother but he obeyed. Anne practically yanked Edward off the table and planted him next to his brother. The younger boy whined and she slapped a hand over his mouth, turning to Carington and the rest of the knights with a forced smile.

"If everyone will sit, we will commence with the meal."

Carington immediately sought out Creed but Richard was there, taking her hand and leading her towards the table. As he directed her to sit, she was aware of the two young women standing on the other side of the table. When she met the girls' eyes, they gazed back at her with a mixture of distain and curiosity. She did the only thing she could do; she smiled weakly.

"Ladies," she said as she took her seat.

Richard sat down next to her. "Lady Carington, this is the Lady Julia le Tourneau," he indicated the shorter girl with light-brown hair, "and the Lady Kristina Summerlin. Ladies, you will greet our guest with graciousness."

The girls dipped into a practiced curtsey. There was no warmth to the gesture; they were simply doing as they were told. But the taller blond girl at least appeared civil; the brown-haired lass was glaring. Carington's neutral expression faded and she glared back.

Creed was suddenly on her right, sitting beside her and collecting an earthenware pitcher of watered ale. He poured her a measure himself but when she looked at him with a grateful smile, he gazed back at her quite unemotionally. The moody gaze with the lightning bolt eyes had returned. It was like a dagger to her heart and the smile died on her lips. In a room full of strangers, he had been her only hope of familiarity and he had failed her. She looked down at her trencher.

The young ladies and the boys sat across from them. Anne sat on the opposite side of Richard, chatting pleasantly as the meal was served. Ryton, Burle and Stanton were seated at the end of the long table, mostly keeping to themselves. Glancing up from her trencher of roast beef and boiled carrots, Carington noticed the other knights sitting far away. She suspected that Creed was upset with her because he was sitting beside her, as if she had expected him to. Perhaps he would rather sit with his comrades.

"Ye should go sit with your knights," she said to him, very quietly.

He picked up his chalice. "Yet I am not."

She lowered her head to her trencher. "I dunna need ye, Sassenach. Go and sit with yer men."

He was not looking at her, either; his gaze was moving across the table at the two foster girls and the young boys, who were collectively staring at Carington as if beholding a strange and terrible creature. He could sense a storm coming and he wanted to be at her side to fend off the inclement weather. Moreover, he realized that he simply wanted to sit next to her.

"Eat your meal, my lady," he said steadily, taking a long drink.

His tone was cool. Carington felt tears sting her eyes, having no idea why he was being so moody with her. It had been a long and difficult day and he had been her only source of comfort. Now her source was turning on her. She felt disoriented, sad and furious all at the same time. He told her to eat her meal, but she set her knife down and refused to take another bite.

Creed noticed right away when she stopped eating. But he

continued to devour his food, watching the wolf pack across the table for any sign that they were about to strike. Although they were children, they could still cause a good deal of misery for her. She did not need the added emotional stress of unruly and jealous children.

Jory entered the hall when the meal was about half over, taking a seat on the other side of Stanton and harassing a serving wench for his trencher. Richard saw him come in, eyed the man as he crossed the room, and spoke to him just as he collected his food.

"Jory," he said casually. "What has happened to your face?"

Jory's brown eyes came up, looking at Burle, who glowered back at him. He lowered his head back to his trencher. "I fell off my horse, my lord."

Richard had known Jory a long time. He knew it was not the truth but he did not press. He left the discipline of the knights to Ryton and if Ryton had dispensed brutal justice to an offense, so be it. Jory undoubtedly deserved it. He turned his attention back to Carington.

"Did you enjoy your trip, my lady?" he asked pleasantly.

Jolted from her morose thoughts, she sat straight and faced him. "Aye, m'lord," she replied. "I… I have never been this far south before."

Across the table, the children tittered and pink crept into Carington's cheeks. Richard pretended he did not hear anything. "We are quite happy to introduce you to Prudhoe and the surrounding country," he said. "I am sure you will find the English people very warm and friendly."

She smiled weakly. "I am sure, m'lord. The Scots people are also warm and friendly, in spite of what the English may think of them."

Edward suddenly burst out with loud laughter, spraying food all over the table. "Papa, she talks funny again!"

Carington dropped her face straight down, staring into her lap, as Anne leapt into the conversation. "Edward, another word and you shall leave this table," she said sternly.

Little Edward was a genuinely cute child but he was, as most occupants of Prudhoe believed, a monster in disguise. He looked at his mother with wide-eyed innocence. "Mama, can we teach her to talk like us?"

"You cannot teach a Scot anything," Gilbert snapped from his other side. "Besides, she is too old."

"She is *not* too old," Anne stressed to her eldest. "Gilbert, you will be polite to our guest or you will join your brother in his punishment."

"But I was not being rude, Mama. I have heard Papa say many times that Scots are dense." His gaze drifted to Carington. "She is older than Julia and Kristina. And she is shorter. Is she married?"

Carington had about all she could take. They were speaking of her as if she were not sitting right in front of them, hurling insults with no rebuke. Her head snapped up and she focused on the ill-mannered child.

"I am not married, Master Gilbert," she said, tension in her voice evident. "And I am indeed older than yer pasty-faced companions. I am also far better mannered than the lot of you, so shut yer yap before I drive nails through yer lips to close them."

She was practically yelling when she finished and the reaction to her speech took various courses; Richard sprayed his ale all over the table, Anne's jaw dropped, Kristina and Julia yelped as if they had been mortally insulted. Strangely, Gilbert and Edward were actually silenced; their eyes were as wide as the heavens as they stared at the venom-tongued Scot. For a split second, no one moved, including Creed. The shock was too great. Then, the boys suddenly leapt to their feet and began screaming at Carington. She responded by shaking her fist at them and threatening to jump over the table.

Creed's moment of surprise quickly vanished when he realized the situation was plummeting. In truth, he was having a difficult time holding a straight face. Carington had said everything to Edward, Gilbert and the two haughty girls that he had always wanted to say but could not. It would not do to insult his liege's children or wards, and he was especially unwilling to insult the man who risked his neck to remove him from the king's wrath.

But he had to do something; Carington was all but threatening to throttle Richard's boys. In fact, she was already up and putting her feet on the bench. He could easily picture her hurling herself over the table and tackling the children. Bolting to his feet, he grabbed Carington around the waist and hauled her away from the table.

"My lady is exhausted," he said to Anne as he passed her with his snarling bundle. "Forgive her uncontrolled behavior. Please allow her to rest from this day."

Anne was more concerned for Carington than she was for her boys at the moment. "Do not punish her, Creed," she said as he walked towards the yawning exit. "She is simply overwrought. Please take her to the ladies' chamber at the top of the stairs. We have prepared a bed for her." The last words were shouted as he disappeared from sight.

The knights watched Creed carry her out. Ryton rose and followed. He caught his brother as the man crossed the bailey and was preparing to enter the three storied keep to the north of the hall.

"Creed," he put his arm on his brother's shoulder. "I shall take her. Return to the hall and finish your meal. I fear I have burdened you with an unwieldy task and you have more than performed your duties. I shall take the chore now."

Creed knew his brother meant well. He could hear guilt in his voice. But he shook his head. "No need," he replied. "I assumed this responsibility. I shall see it through. The best thing you can do is to go back and calm the throng so they do not form a lynch mob against the lady. I fear what Gilbert and Edward will do in retaliation."

"Anne will control them," he eyed Carington's red face. "Are you sure you do not want me to take her?"

Creed shook his head as they entered the keep. There was a small spiral staircase off to the left and he half-carried her, half shoved her onto the first step. "Nay," he grunted as she resisted his efforts. "I have grown accustomed to these little tantrums. I think I am better adept at handling them than you are."

"Dunna speak of me as if I am not here," Carington was trying to turn around to yell at them both. "And if ye expect me to apologize to those two spoiled bairns, then I can tell ye that I willna. They deserved everything I said!"

Creed cocked an eyebrow, turning her around and swatting her behind firmly when she resisted. "They may have deserved it, but you have a good deal to learn about decorum and tact."

Carington yelped when he spanked her, a sharp sting. But it was enough to make her stop her struggles and glare at him. "Ye'll teach me nothing, Sassenach. I'll die first."

Creed did not reply. The last Ryton saw of his brother and the lady, he had her under the arms and was lifting her up the stairs.

The smaller chamber that had been prepared for Carington was on the third floor of the massive keep. There were three rooms on the floor, two larger ones to the right and then a smaller one to the left. Creed all but dragged her inside one of the chambers and closed the door.

He released her once they were inside and she faced off against him like an angry wet hen. Before he could speak, she jabbed a finger at him.

"Ye'll not throw me around like a roughhouse wench," she scolded. "I dunna appreciate being tossed about for all to see."

He lifted an eyebrow. "Do not act like a roughhouse wench and you shall not be treated like one. Your actions dictate mine, lady."

She put her hands on her hips, her lovely face red with fury. "Those children were horrible. I had to defend myself."

"Defend yourself against what?"

"Their slander."

He opened his mouth to reply but thought better of it. She probably truly believed that they were slandering her for a darker, evil purpose. Her only history with the English was not a trusting and pleasant one. With a heavy sigh, for he was quite weary himself, he hunted down the nearest chair. Carington watched him closely, taking no notice of the decidedly feminine chamber around her. Creed seated himself in a simple oak chair that groaned under his substantial weight.

"Come here." He motioned with a crooked finger.

She was defiant. "Why?"

"Just come here."

"I'm not going to if ye're planning on whacking my behind again."

"If I have to stand up to get you then I will most certainly whack your behind."

She pursed her lips, torn between anger and reluctance. But her resistance lasted only a split second before she wandered in his direction, coming to within arm's length of the chair. She would obey, but certainly not willingly. Her little fists were still on her hips.

"Well?"

Quick as a flash, he reached out and snatched her. Before Carington could protest, she was seated upon his lap, snuggly secured by his enormous arms. His handsome face was a few inches from her and she went from furious to breathless in less than a second. Emerald eyes gazed with surprise at sensual, dusky blue. She struggled, though not with much effort.

"Now," he voice was low and breathy. "There are a few things we are going to establish here and now. You will listen to me, you will comprehend, and you will obey. Is that clear?"

Her heart was doing that odd leaping thing again, only now it was so violent she could hardly take a breath. In fact, her entire body seemed to be quivering, a weird sort of heat flooding her limbs. It was not enough to dissolve her resistance entirely, but her struggles stopped.

"Ye're not my master, Creed de Reyne," she snapped, without force. "Ye canna command me about."

He lifted an eyebrow at her, realizing above all else that she was too close, too tempting. What had started as a disciplinary move had turned into something else, something warm and inviting, and he struggled to stay on task.

"Aye, I can and I will," he replied. "You will obey me or you will meet with many more whackings in addition to the one you just received. Is this in any way unclear?"

Her emerald eyes darkened. He could see that she very much wanted to refute him. But she nodded reluctantly and looked away. "What, then?"

He fought off a grin at her pouting face, which he found himself studying at very close range. She was magnificent.

"I warned you that Edward and Gilbert were a handful," he said quietly. "They are young, spoiled lads and will do anything they can to get a rise out of you. And it is not just you; they do it to everyone. It is a game with them; the more you respond, the more insults they will hurl. They are looking for a physical altercation."

She looked back at him, somewhat surprised. "But they're so young. Why would they do this?"

Creed shook his head. "The baron has raised his sons to be fearless. But it has only bred confrontation. Lady Anne is probably the only one who can control them, but she cannot always. Know that these boys are beyond punishment and reproach, so you would do well to avoid them at all costs. However, if you cannot avoid them, you must at least keep your temper. Exploding at them as you did will only feed their frenzy."

She looked at him as if he were insane. "Those little boys are monsters."

"Aye, they are. Remember that."

"So I will. And what of the girls? I saw no friendliness in them."

He sighed, settling her in his lap and somehow pulling her closer. Carington ended up with one arm around his shoulder to support the angle at which she was sitting. They were, in fact, very close and enjoying the comfort without being wildly aware of it.

"Julia is the problem," he said quietly. "She is spoiled and petty. Kristina can be sweet, but she becomes swept up in Julia's demands. She is the weaker of the two. And you will be sharing this room with them so you must learn to deal politely with them."

For the first time, Carington looked around, seeing the three beds in the chamber; two were tucked over against the western wall while the third, hers she assumed, was situated in an alcove directly below a large lancet window. Though there was an oilcloth covering, she could see that she would be subject to whatever weather blew in from the window. It was not the most desirable place in the room. She suspected her new roommates had put the bed there for a reason.

A great many things were coming clear to her. Monstrous children, conceited wards... and she was thrust into the middle of it. Closing her eyes briefly, all of the fight and resistance abruptly left her.

"Oh... English," she sighed as if everything had just come crashing down on her. "What is it ye've brought me to?"

He could see the defeat in her face and he leaned forward, resting his chin on her shoulder. "You are strong, Cari. I know you can deal with this. It will just take time. But please; as a personal favor to me, keep your tongue and your control. You are made of better things."

She turned her head; he was so close that if she had stuck out her tongue, she would have licked him. Her heart thumped harder and faster, threatening to burst from her chest as she gazed into his dusky blue eyes with their fringe of thick dark lashes. The lightning bolts were still there but, this time, they were far tenderer and far less shocking.

"How would ye know what I am made of?" she asked.

"Because I can tell."

She cocked her head. "Ye believe that I have strength?"

He smiled in reply, gazing into her lovely face, knowing that he was going to kiss her and there was not a damn thing he could do to stop himself. His grip tightened, pulling her cheek very close to his mouth, and his lips went to work. Very gently, his mouth moved across her cheek to her chin. As it did so, he felt her body quiver violently and it fed both his passion and his curiosity; he was wildly curious to taste her lips. He thought she tried to say something but he could not be sure; before she could get the words out, his lips slanted over hers and he fed his curiosity with her delicious flesh.

Clutched tightly against Creed's chest, Carington knew she should, at the very least, be protesting his actions. She had tried, sort of, but his mouth had claimed her own and the protest died on her lips. Now she was experiencing the searing heat of his mouth, scorching her like nothing she had ever known to exist. She'd never been kissed by a man before and hardly knew what to expect, but Creed's gentle lips wordlessly instructed her on how to respond. In a very short amount of time, she was aptly doing so. In fact, it was as if a flood gate suddenly opened and her passionate Scot nature exploded in ways she never knew it could.

Her small fingers found their way into his inky hair, gripping his head as he devoured her. His tongue licked at her lips, tenderly prying them open, and she gasped as he invaded her honeyed mouth. Carington savored the sensations, each one so new and exciting, feeling his flesh against hers, his massive arms around her slender body. There was such excitement and comfort and passion, sensations she had never felt before, and she mimicked his actions, matching him suckle for suckle because it seemed like the most natural thing to do. She could taste him, his distinct musk and saltiness, and it was exhilarating.

Creed was kissing her so lustfully that he nearly swallowed half her face. She was delectably sweet, like nothing he had ever sampled before, and the fact that she was responding eagerly to him only increased his fervor. She was so small that his arms encircled her torso and then some, and he could feel the swell of her left breast against the palm of his left hand. It was firm and warm. With the figure this woman had, curvaceous and slender in all the right places, having her in his arms only served to excite him more.

The kiss was growing more heated. A bevy of unexpected emotions and sensations were beginning to crop up, seeds of obsession and intimate curiosity that he could not seem to control. Creed was suckling gently on her tongue when a soft knock sounded at the chamber door. Startled, his head came up and they both stared at the door a moment as if unsure they had heard anything at all. But a second knock came shortly thereafter, stronger than the first, and Creed lifted her up and set her on her feet as if she weighed no more than a child. Carington wobbled, giggled, and he smiled in response, putting a finger over his lips to indicate silence. He noticed her face was rather red, her lips glossy-wet from his kiss, and he gently wiped his hand over the lower half of her face to remove all traces of his loss of control. Carington wiped her face with her own hands just to make sure. He could see that her hands were shaking.

"Stay here," he commanded softly.

She remained still, her emerald eyes following him as he moved across the floor and opened the door. The Lady Anne entered immediately, her eyes wide between Creed and Carington.

"I came to see how our guest is faring," she said hesitantly to Creed. Then she looked at Carington. "Are you feeling better, my lady?"

Carington nodded slowly. "Aye, m'lady," she could hardly speak, still reeling from Creed's wicked mouth. She glanced at him before continuing. "Forgive me for ruining yer sup. I... I dunno what came over me."

She said the last part purely for Creed's sake. She really was not sorry and she was fully aware of what came over her. Yet she realized that she wanted to please Creed. But his face was emotionless as Anne moved towards her.

"You are simply exhausted," Anne said, studying her closely as if to gain a better, more in-depth view of her new charge. "I will put Julia and Kristina in another chamber for tonight. I am sure you will want to rest alone."

"I dunna wish to displace them, m'lady."

Anne smiled. "You are not. Enjoy your rest, then."

Carington nodded, somewhat humbled and uncertain. "Thank ye, m'lady."

Anne's dark eyes lingered on her a moment before turning for the chamber door. She was almost out of the room when she paused, turning to Creed as he still stood by the chamber door.

"You did not punish her, did you?"

"Nay, my lady."

"Good. Go and get her some food and then leave her to rest."

Creed nodded obediently and watched as Lady Anne swept out into the hall and down the steps. His gaze moved back to Carington, still standing where he had left her. She had not moved.

"What would you like to eat?" he asked quietly.

She shook her head. "Send a servant with it, Creed. Ye need not cater to me."

"I do not intend to. But I will bring you the meal you were denied."

Again, she shook her head, moving towards him. "I am not particularly hungry."

"You have not eaten all day. I would see you eat something before you retire. Please."

His softly uttered plea cut off her refusal. A faint smile creased her lips as she gazed up at him. "Why are ye so kind to me?"

They were standing a few feet apart but he could feel her heat from where he stood. He found himself staring at her mouth, remembering how her lips tasted. It was horribly unhealthy and he knew it, but at the moment, he did not particularly care.

"Because you warrant it."

She laughed softly, her teeth straight and white in her bow-shaped mouth. "I've done nothing but fight ye all the way back from Scotland. How can ye say I deserve anything kind from ye?"

His dusky blue eyes glittered at her. "Because you do."

She regarded him a moment. "May I ask ye something?"

"You may."

"What possessed ye to kiss me?"

He stared at her; he was wondering about that very thing and had no clear cut answer. He honestly did not know what had possessed him other than an overwhelming feeling. After a moment, he lifted his big shoulders.

"I do not know. It seemed like a good idea."

"Was it?"

He grinned, a coy gesture, as if he did not want her to see just how he really felt about it. "Aye," he muttered. "But it is not something that should become public knowledge. I am in a position of trust and what I did could be considered a violation of that trust."

She looked serious. "I would never betray ye, Creed. And if I hadna wanted ye to do it, I would have whacked ye."

A smile flickered across his lips, but he did not know what to say to that. It was obvious she had responded to him as readily as he had to her, an attachment between them that was deepening by the hour. He was terrified, sickened, and thrilled by it all at the same time. He did to Carington exactly what Isabella had accused him of doing to her, only this time, he was truly guilty. He had kissed the little firebrand and was not the least bit sorry about it. So he had to leave the room, if for no other reason than to clear his head. The mission to collect sup was a convenient excuse.

Creed quit the chamber in silence, leaving Carington standing there, heart fluttering against her ribs and the flavor of him still on her lips.

***

True to his word, he brought her back a huge tray of supper and sat with her while she ate. This time, Ryton was with him and the two of them sat her down at the small table in the ladies' chamber. It was the first time she had seen Ryton without his helm and she was not surprised to note that he looked a good deal like his younger brother; with the exception of very short, light-brown hair, they had similar facial features. But Creed's features were more solid and masculine. In her view, Creed was most definitely the beauty of the family.

He was also the more persuasive of the two. The men discovered early on that Carington was a picky eater, and not a particularly big eater, so after the third bite of bread with butter and honey she acted as if they were torturing her. Creed took the bread from her plate and fed her as if she were an infant. As long as he was holding the bread, she would eat it. But if he put it down, she would make no move to feed herself.

Ryton sat in a sturdy oak chair, still looking as if he'd been on the road for three days without reprieve, and watched his brother force feed their hostage. Not strangely, Creed had a manner about him that would soothe a savage beast, which was exactly what he had on his hands. Creed had always been a gentle giant, more apt to use understanding and communication before force. Carington was responding to him, but not happily. Had it been Ryton, he would have given up long ago. He simply did not have the patience that his brother did.

Halfway through the meal, the lady focused her emerald green eyes on Ryton. He was leaning back in the chair, arms crossed and feeling his exhaustion when she focused in on him. He noticed her intense stare and his guard went up.

"Why are ye here, Sir Ryton?" she half-asked, half-demanded. "Did ye come to make sure yer brother feeds me as he's been ordered to?"

Ryton gazed back at her steadily. "I came to see how you were faring. You have been a handful for my brother and although the man has patience, he is not invincible."

Carington seemed to back down, passing a long glance at Creed as he cut away a succulent piece of beef from the bone.

"I am sorry I have been difficult," she said quietly. "It was never my intention to be burdensome."

"You have not been." Creed held the beef up to her on the knife and she shook her head. Patiently, he removed it from the sharp knife and held it out to her with his fingers. She just stared at him until he put the beef almost to her lips; only then did she open her mouth and he popped it in like a mother bird feeding a chick. He turned back to the beef. "You have had a most difficult few days and you would have to be either dead or stupid not to react in kind."

Ryton scratched his head. "Creed, you are a saint," he muttered. Then he looked back to the hostage. "Can I assume you are beyond any more escape attempts, then?"

She swallowed the beef in her mouth. "I have nowhere to go, Sir Ryton."

"That is not an answer. Do you plan to escape again?"

She made a face at him, mockingly. "Nay, I dunna plan to escape again."

Creed hid a smile at the way she snarled at his brother. He found her to be quite funny at times. But Ryton pursed his lips at her insolence.

"Very well," he said. "Then I will place you in the wardship of Lady Anne and her majordomo. You will no longer have Creed to torment."

Creed did not react; he was cutting another piece of beef. But Carington looked startled by the suggestion. "But... but I dunna know them. I dunna want anyone else to watch over me."

"Creed has other duties to perform," Ryton replied. "He has completed his task by bringing you unharmed to Prudhoe. Now he must go about his regular duties, of which you are not a part."

Her reaction was to stare at Ryton a long moment before averting her gaze. She dare not say any more, fearful that whatever she was feeling for Creed might be obvious. Moreover, Creed was not protesting in the least. Perhaps he was glad to be rid of her.

"As ye say," she hung her head, turning away from Creed when he offered her another bite.

"Eat," he said softly. When she shook her head, he gently grasped her by the chin and pushed the beef into her mouth.

She chewed slowly, laboriously. Creed stopped cutting beef, wiping his hands on a square of linen. She had already eaten a goodly amount and he would not push further. Ryton watched her lowered head a moment before rising on his weary legs.

"You must understand what is expected of you now, lady," he said. He was so exhausted that he was weaving unsteadily. "You will obey Lady Anne and her majordomo without question. If you are insolent in any way, punishment will fall to me. Not Creed, but to me. You will also be assigned certain tasks about the household, of which you shall perform without question. Any disobedience in this will be met swiftly. Lastly, you are not to stray beyond the inner bailey. If you are found in the outer bailey or outside the walls, it will be considered a violation of hostage terms and will be dealt with as an escape attempt. Is any of this unclear so far?"

Her head snapped up, the emerald eyes flashing. Creed watched her face, knowing the storm was rising.

"So ye are to treat me like a prisoner," she hissed. "I am to be confined like a criminal."

"For now," Ryton said evenly. "Until you prove yourself trustworthy, we must establish rules. Already you have tried to run, twice I might add, so you have brought this upon yourself."

There was a soft knock on the door, distracting them from the rising tension. Creed went to the door and opened it; a few servants were on the landing with Carington's baggage. He motioned them inside the chamber where they deposited it quickly and fled. When they were gone, Creed closed the door quietly.

The brief interruption had allowed Carington's temper to cool somewhat. Creed continued to stand over by the door, not wanting to be close to Carington and possibly get sucked into her emotional turmoil. He clearly felt for her, and clearly felt something for her, but his brother could not know. For both their sakes, Ryton had to be oblivious to whatever was occurring. Creed did not even understand the all of it and there was no way he could explain it to his brother.

"Do you have any questions, my lady?" Ryton had softened somewhat by the time the servants departed; he was not truly trying to be cruel. "Anything at all?"

Carington shook her head. Ryton watched the dark head, thinking perhaps to say something more, but thought better of it. It had already been a long and trying day. Any words of solace at this point, however minor, would seem trite.

"If you need anything, please do not hesitate to send for either myself or Creed. Even if we are not directly responsible for you, we are nonetheless at your service."

She just nodded her head, once. Ryton's gaze lingered on her a moment longer before departing the chamber. He motioned his brother to join him as he did so. Creed did not dare look at Carington as he followed his brother from the room, but he knew for a fact that he would be back.

CHAPTER SIX

"Sorry to have troubled you with such a burden," Ryton was into his fourth cup of wine and feeling no pain. "She was a tax on even your steady demeanor, Creed. God help you."

Burle and Stanton laughed at Creed's expense. Seated around the well-used table in the common room of the dismal knight's quarters, the four of them were enjoying some time away from their duties. They oft spent their precious off-duty hours drinking and blowing off tension, just the four of them, as they were close friends that had seen a good deal of life and death together.

"She was not entirely awful once she stopped being belligerent," Creed's lips crinkled with a smile. "She was actually quite humorous when all of the fire and fight was out of her."

"Humorous, did you say?" Ryton repeated. "Then it must have been a momentary lapse in sanity. Surely there is nothing humorous about that firebrand."

Burle and Stanton laughed again, the ever-ready audience for the comedy team of the de Reyne brothers. Creed just shook his head and took a long drink of wine; it was his fifth cup that evening. He had hoped it would help settle his confusion over their earlier kiss when, in fact, it had only increased it. More than that, he realized that he actually missed her. That thought made him drink more.

"She is a firebrand, no doubt," he replied evenly, wanting off the subject because he was afraid the wine would loosen his tongue. "Now that our task is over and she is here, what now, O Great Brother of mine? We are to have alleged peace with Clan Kerr and their allies. Dare we believe it?"

Ryton's eyebrows wriggled. "I do not know. I would hope so. After losing Lenox against the Clans, I would hope all of this would be finally ended." His good humor faded as he stared into his cup. "But the cost was too high. I would rather have my youngest brother back than all of the peace in the world."

Creed's thoughts drifted to their baby brother, killed in a vicious battle at Kielderhead Moor five years ago. He had fallen on the battlefield and they had not found him until hours later. By then, he was dead. The best they could deduce was that he had survived the initial injury only to be killed by the Scots after the battle had ended when he had lain crippled, unable to defend himself.

He could still see Lenox de Reyne on the last day of his life, newly-knighted and ready to kill Scots. His light brown hair and dusky blue eyes were ingrained into their memories. Where Ryton could be emotional and Creed was so calm that he was oft accused of being dead, Lenox had been the excitement of the family. He laughed easily, played pranks, and was generally a thorn in their side. Many a time Creed had captured his mischievous brother while Ryton punished him by good-naturedly beating him. But it had all been in fun and they both missed him tremendously; much more than they would admit when they weren't drunk. It seemed that something was missing now, a hole in their lives. Though death was part of their profession, losing a gifted brother that had only seen twenty three years had been a true tragedy.

But Ryton did not want to linger on the past. It always made him feel horrendously guilty; he had been in command that day and it was a guilt he still lived with.

"So you ask what is next," he shifted the subject as he poured himself more wine. "I am told that Lord Richard has plans to meet with his allies regarding the hostage situation. It should comfort everyone to know that the Kerrs, for the moment, have consented to peace. But more than that, I do not know. I would hope we will know some quiet along the borders for some time to come."

"That may be, but I doubt we will have any peace here at Prudhoe."

The blurted statement came from Jory, entering the room from the bailey with his saddlebags slung over his shoulder. He let the heavy bags plummet to the floor just inside the door. Only Ryton was looking at the knight; everyone else was focused on their drink.

"Why do you say that?" Ryton asked, though he did not really care what the man had to say.

Jory snorted, making his way over the table where the alcohol was. He had a smug expression on his face; but, then again, he always seemed to have some manner of exaggerated swagger. It was one of the characteristics that made him truly unlikable. The question hung in the air as Jory reached for a cup.

"If we do not have trouble with the Scots, we could have it with the king," Jory made sure he was standing next to Creed as he poured his wine. "We have some traveling merchants staying here for the night."

Ryton lifted an eyebrow. "So? What does that have to do with the king?"

Jory took a long, satisfying swallow, making sure to draw out the answer. "I heard some gossip from the travelers," he said, taking another drink. "Most interesting news."

Ryton's patience was at an end. "What in the hell did you hear?"

Jory was enjoying the moment. He gazed at the wine in his cup, casually, swirling the dregs. "Rumor has it that Queen Isabella is pregnant," he said, hoping the statement had as much impact as he thought it would. "Six months pregnant, that is. Of course, she and the king were only married a few months ago, so she conceived this child well before they were wed. On the trip from France, in fact, as rumor would have it."

Creed did not react but Burle slammed his cup to the table and bolted to his feet. "Do you want another beating, d'Eneas?" he jabbed a finger at the shorter, smaller knight. "I would be happy to shut your mouth permanently."

Ryton held up a hand to calm the knight, watching as he angrily sank back into his chair. He gazed steadily at Jory.

"Did you really hear that?" he asked slowly. "Or are we again privy to your lies and assumptions?"

Jory grinned, a hatefully confident gesture. "It could be only gossip, but the merchant's guards were quite free with the information. It seems that all of London is in an uproar because if it and I would suspect the king is not entirely happy, either."

Ryton looked at his brother for the first time to see how he was reacting. "Lies, all of it," he looked away from Creed's emotionless face and back to his cup. "Who is to say the king is not the father? There is no proof otherwise."

"No proof except for the gossip that the queen had a knightly lover in France. Rumor has it that the Church is now getting involved. We certainly cannot have a bastard heir to England's throne, can we? I am told the Church is starting an investigation."

"Then that is the king's fault for marrying a whore."

No one had much to say to that. Jory took another long drink of his wine. "No one would know that better than Creed. He was one of her escorts from France, after all. I would imagine he would be one of the first people the Church will interview."

Burle tensed again but a glance from Ryton stopped him. He wondered just how far Jory was going to go before Burle snapped and there would be no stopping him. Or, worse still, if Creed snapped. His brother was so powerful that he could break Jory's neck and not even raise a sweat. He had never seen Creed lose his control, but there was always a first time for everything, especially when dealing with so sensitive an issue.

"I suggest you drop the subject, d'Eneas," Ryton said quietly. "No one cares about your foolish prattle. If you want to gossip, go congregate with the serving women. They are the only ones who would care what you say."

Jory drained his cup and poured another. He made sure to walk away from the table before he spoke again. "I did not mean to imply that Creed would have first-hand knowledge of the queen's activities. Of course he's innocent. Creed is a fine, upstanding and chivalrous knight. But since he was charged with our lovely hostage, the truth will be known about his knightly character if she turns up pregnant, too."

It was the wrong thing to say. Burle and Stanton were up,

charging at Jory. Cups went flying and chairs were toppled. But Creed shot to his feet, grabbing Burle before the man could get past him. Burle, in turn, grabbed Stanton before the man could get too far. Only Ryton was not holding on to someone or, in turn, being held by someone. But he was on his feet and he was focused on Jory. He moved past his brother, his dusky blue eyes riveted on his knight. The mood of the room was no longer relaxed; it was deeply brittle as Ryton faced off against his subordinate.

"I will say this one time, d'Eneas, so make sure you understand me clearly," his voice was low, controlled. "You will not repeat what you heard from the merchant's guards and you will never again say what you did about my brother. Should any rumors or other slander get started around here, you will be the first one I come for and I can promise that you will not like my reaction. Do you comprehend me?"

Some of Jory's smugness faded as he gazed into Ryton's tense face; he could see serious implications in the glare. After a moment, he shrugged weakly. "I do," he said. "I meant nothing by it. I was simply... thinking aloud. Just the thoughts of a tired man."

By this time, Creed had let go of Burle and was heading from the room. Ryton watched his brother quit the common room and disappear into the darkness of the bailey beyond. Had he not been Jory's commander, he would have throttled the man. Instead, he followed his brother out into the black night without another word in Jory's direction. He was more concerned for his brother at the moment than an idiot knight.

Stanton and Burle were slower to disband; Stanton moved back to the table, glaring daggers at Jory, while Burle still stood where Creed had stopped him. Jory gazed into the knight's fat face, his smile fading completely. Of all the knights, he knew that Burle was the one that would mostly likely move against him. His head was still swollen from the beating he had received earlier.

"What?" he said to Burle's menacing stare. "I apologized. What more do you want?"

Burle did not say anything; he started to turn away but thought better of it. Stanton heard a loud smack followed by a heavy grunt. Something hit the floor hard. Burle joined the table and reclaimed his cup as if nothing in the world was amiss and Stanton did not turn around to see the source of the loud grunt; he knew for a fact that Jory was lying on the floor behind him in a muddled state of unconsciousness.

Outside, Ryton caught up to Creed just as the man was mounting the wooden steps that led into the keep. He put his big hand on his brother's arm, stopping the man before he could get away from him.

"Creed," he said quietly. "Do not let d'Eneas' ramblings get to you. He is a bitter little man with a bitter little mind. I would not believe everything he says."

Creed's face was emotionless. The ghostly moon's glow gave him a stark, phantom-like appearance as he loomed on the steps above his brother. "He is still angry with me for preventing him from taking advantage of our hostage," he snorted softly. "I should have strangled him and left his body for the wolves. It would have saved us much grief."

Ryton nodded in agreement; there was no disputing that bit of wisdom. "Nonetheless, I intend to talk to Richard about him now. I will no longer tolerate his disruptive presence in my ranks."

Creed lifted an eyebrow. "He is a baron's son."

"A baron's bastard son."

"Even so, you have been asked to treat him differently from the rest of us because of his father's relationship with Lord Richard."

Ryton cast his brother a resolute look. "That may be, but I will not allow him to continue to antagonize you like this. He seems to have a special interest in goading you and that is not healthy for any of us. He only succeeds in provoking Burle and I fear the day when he actually incites you beyond reason. It would be like trying to stop a mad bull."

Creed simply lifted his massive shoulders, his gaze moving across the quieting bailey. "He will tire of the game eventually as long as I do not react to him."

Ryton just shook his head. "Creed, you're a saint," he slapped his brother across the shoulder affectionately. His gaze, too, moved over the ward, watching the soldiers on patrol as the night deepened. "I suppose I should find out what those merchants really told him. If there really is trouble brewing, we will want to know."

Creed just nodded, faintly, as if he did not particularly care. "I am going to check on the lady before taking my usual night watch," he said quietly, turning up the stairs. "I will see you upon the morrow."

Ryton watched his brother lumber up the stairs, sensing depression in the man's manner even though he professed otherwise. Jory's words had indeed weighed heavily on him.

"Take a weapon with you to protect yourself in case she gets out of hand," he jested, attempting to lighten the mood. "And watch out for flying torch butts. Remember what happened to Stanton."

Creed snorted in the darkness; Ryton could hear him. Without another word, the men parted ways and went about their duties for the night.

***

Carington decided right away that she would not sleep in the bed by the window. It was probably sabotaged so she made a firm decision to sleep in one of the other beds. The night was cool and she changed from her surcoat into a sleeping shift. Alone for the first time since leaving Wether Fair, she felt disoriented and homesick. Wrapping up in her dusty tartan for familiar comfort, she lay on either Julia or Kristina's clean linens.

As tired as she was, sleep would not come. She ended up lying on the strange bed, sobbing into a pillow that was not hers and wishing with all her heart she could go home again. When an owl in one of the massive oak trees near the walls hooted, she started at the sound. Everything was unfamiliar and frightening.

But she was exhausted and her lids eventually grew heavy in spite of her nerves. Just as she was drifting off into a fitful doze, a soft knock sounded at the door. Instantly and nervously awake, she sat upright in bed.

"Who comes?" she demanded with more courage than she felt.

"'Tis me, my lady," came a deep male voice. "Creed."

She jumped off the bed and ran to the door. Throwing open the panel she was faced with the weary man and his shadowed, beautiful face. His dusky blue eyes gazed intently at her although he had yet to change expression. He was, as usual, calm and emotionless.

But Carington did not care if he did not look glad to see her. She was certainly glad to see him. "Creed," she half-gasped, half-exclaimed. "'Tis good to see a friendly face. I was feeling as if the whole world had abandoned me."

"Nay, lady, you are not abandoned."

"Did ye come to watch over me tonight?"

He had yet to make a move to enter the chamber; he continued to stand, quite properly, in the landing. "I will be watching over the entire castle from my post on the wall," he said. "But I wanted to make sure you were settled for the night. Do you require anything?"

She did not know why her heart sank at his words. Her resistance to the emotionless façade, the coolness, lasted only a few seconds. He sounded detached, politely inquisitive without being truly warm. Not at all like the passionate man who had kissed her this afternoon. Rather than become cold with him with the posture of self-preservation, she grew depressed.

"Nay," she shook her head and lowered her gaze. "I dunna require anything. But thanks for asking just the same."

She started to close the door but he put his hand up, blocking it. Curiously, she looked up into his tired face. "Is there something else?" she asked, not particularly caring but hoping that there was.

His dusky blue eyes glimmered in the weak light of the hearth. "Nothing else." He suddenly pushed his way inside, closing the door quietly behind him. Carington just looked at him, trying to gauge his mood. The man was moodier than anyone she had ever known; sweet and warm one moment, quiet and morose the next.

"Then what?" she asked.

He did not say anything as he paced the room, inspecting the beds, the window covering, finally coming to rest on the hearth when he seemed satisfied with his observations. It was a quiet night, a gentle breeze blowing from the north. In the light of the fire, he faced her.

"Aside from the *enfants horribles*, what did you think of your first day at Prudhoe?" he asked quietly.

She blinked, pulling the tartan more closely about her as the breeze picked up through the oilcloth. "I canna say, exactly. 'Twas an interesting day to say the least."

"I would imagine so." He eyed her. "Why are you wearing the tartan? This room has an abundance of warm and soft coverlets."

She looked down at the dirty material wrapped around her body. "None of those things belong to me," she said. "This is mine."

"It is also very dirty."

She shrugged, her gaze coming up to meet his. "Perhaps. But I would rather sleep on dirty Tartan than clean Sassenach finery."

He nodded faintly, studying the way the light flickered off her dark hair. He was not sure what more he had to say to her; in fact, he did not really know why he had come at all. He knew she was safe, so other than giving himself another opportunity to see her, there was no reason for him to be here. He should not have come. It was only indulging the foolish sentiment he was coming to feel for her.

"As long as you do not require anything," he said quietly, turning for the door. "I shall go about my duties."

But she was not going to let him go so easily. He was the one bright spot in an otherwise miserable situation and she was eager to cling to that brightness, even if he was moody and cold at times. "Creed," she said, stopping him in his tracks. When he looked at her inquisitively, she fought off a blush. "I… do ye have to go? Can ye not stay and talk awhile?"

He sighed faintly; she heard him. "I am expected at my post, my lady," he said. "And you should be sleeping."

"Please, Creed?"

He gazed at her, feeling himself relent and knowing that he should not. His control had snapped earlier in the day when he had kissed her. Now, in the quiet of the night with no one to disturb them, a similar loss of control would not be healthy. He could not guarantee that he would not go further than simply kissing her. With her sweet face and marvelously delicious figure, his male drives would overwhelm him. He had to resist. For both their sakes, he had to be strong. He closed his eyes to block out the temptation and turned away from her.

"Go to bed, Cari. I will see you on the morrow." He closed the door in her face before she could say a word.

Carington stood, staring at the door, a hollow feeling filling her. The only person that had shown her any kindness had effectively shut her down. It was like a stab to her heart and tears sprang to her eyes. Before she could stop herself, she was sobbing. Creed had only served to reinforce the fact that she was alone, unwanted, cast aside... a hostage. A stranger in a strange land. The loneliness made her cry harder, the loss of Bress finding its way back into her thoughts as if to drive home the point. There was no one left for her.

Black, desolate feelings filled her exhausted mind. Perhaps she should simply throw herself from the window and be done with the pain. She could think of no other way to ease it. She was still standing at the door, weeping, when it suddenly flew open. She was too close and the heavy oak panel smacked her in the forehead, sending her falling backwards onto her bum. Startled, she looked up to see Creed descending on her.

"Honey, I am so sorry," he pulled her to her feet. "Are you all right? I did not mean to hit you."

Carington threw her arms around his neck, clinging to him. Her forehead was fine, if not slightly stinging, but if it would keep him with her she would give him the opportunity to feel sorry for her.

"It... it hurts," she sobbed.

Feeling like a lout, Creed swept her effortlessly into his arms and carried her over to the bed by the lancet window. Carington held tightly to his neck, her head on his shoulder. She was not about to let him go. When he sat on the mattress, it was with her in his lap. He held her like a baby.

He let her weep a moment. "Let me see what I have done," he said softly, pulling back to look at her. He took her chin between his thumb and forefinger, inspecting the red welt on her forehead. He sighed. "I have done a good job of bruising your head. I am truly sorry, honey. It was an accident."

She gazed up at him, her eyes like liquid emeralds as water filled them. "Why did ye come back?"

The dusky blue gaze was steady, unrevealing. Why *had* he come back? Should he tell her the truth; because he heard her crying and her tears had destroyed his resolve? He was not sure that she should know that. Moreover, he did not want to admit it. After a moment, he simply lifted his big shoulders.

"It is of no matter," he said softly. "What matters now is that you are going to have a lump on her head that I am responsible for. Lady Anne will have my hide."

Carington shook her head, wiping away the last of her sniffles. "I will tell her I smacked it on the wardrobe. Ye neednа' worry."

"That is noble but unnecessary. I will take responsibility for my actions."

She was still looking at him, studying his masculine features. He was so cool, so professional, his calm demeanor interspersed with moments of genuine warmth. It was beginning to wear on her. She was not very good at controlling her mouth or her emotions, especially given the fact that she had just come off of a crying jag.

"May I ask ye a question?"

"Aye."

"Why are ye so cold to me one moment and so warm the next?"

His brow furrowed slightly. "What do you mean?"

"What do I mean?" she repeated, outraged. "I mean that ye were so kind to me during our trip to Prudhoe and I surely did not imagine yer kiss this afternoon. Yet ye walked from this chamber not a minute ago as if ye wanted nothing to do with me. 'Tis not the first time ye've turned cold and hard on me, Creed de Reyne, and it's making my head spin. Yer the moodiest man I've ever met and I want to know why."

He just stared at her. After an eternal moment of holding her intense emerald gaze, he looked away.

"All you need know is that I am a knight sworn to protect you for your duration at Prudhoe," he mumbled. "Nothing else matters."

Now it was her turn to stare at him. She felt the wind go out of her, as if he had struck her with one of those powerful fists. After a moment, she climbed off his lap and moved a proper distance away from him, her heart hurting in a way that she could not begin to describe. It hurt so badly that her entire body ached.

"Then get out," she said quietly, struggling to keep her voice from breaking. "If ye are simply a knight and I am simply a hostage, then it is not proper for ye to be here alone with me."

He rose wearily, his gaze still averted, moving for the door. He looked as if he had just seen defeat at the hands of his mightiest enemy from the way his broad shoulders sagged. Carington stopped watching him, hearing his footfalls across the floor.

The heavy door opened and softly closed. Her heart shattered. A whimper escaped her lips and she broke for the door, throwing it open.

"Creed!" she cried.

She raced to the top of the stairs, only to run headlong into him; he could not have been more than a few steps down the flight. She did not even think; her arms went around his neck of their own accord and she pressed her lips against his with all of the passion and awakening emotion she was feeling. She knew he would shove her away, but she did not care; at the moment, her mind was only thinking of one thing; to hold the man, to feel him, before he was forever taken away from her.

But a strange thing happened; Creed did not pull back, nor did he shove her away. In fact, he seemed to be much more aggressive with their stolen kiss than she was. More than that, he was completely taking over, kissing her so hard that he drove her teeth into her soft upper lip. Carington gasped softly as he suckled away the pinpoint of blood as his tongue demanded entry into her honeyed mouth. Before she realized it, she was aloft in his arms and they were back in her borrowed chamber. The door was closing behind them and she heard the bolt lock.

She was still in his arms, held off the floor by his amazing strength as his mouth suckled her mindless. She could not form a coherent thought as he blazed a scorching trail across her cheek, down her neck and to the base of her throat. Carington held his head so tightly against her flesh that she was sure she was suffocating him.

"Creed," she murmured into his forehead. "I'm more than a hostage to ye, am I not? Tell me that I am."

He nodded, his lips working their way up her neck. "God help me, you are," he muttered. "But I cannot…."

He trailed off, his lips claiming hers once again. They were in a frenzy of passionate discovery, gently biting, suckling, acquainting themselves with the taste of one another. Whatever attraction had been present from the moment of their introduction was now raging like a fever, out of control. Creed knew, from the moment he put his lips on her, that he was lost. All of the rationalization in the world was not going to help him out of this because it was more than simple lust; there was feeling involved. Once feeling was part of the formula, there was very little he could do against it.

Somewhere in the tumult, he had bumped into a bed and stumbled back on it. Falling with Carington in his arms, she lay atop him as his mouth did wicked things to her. His enormous hands were on her head, wrapped up in her hair, holding her tightly against him and she could hardly breathe through his tender force. He stopped at one point, holding her head in his hands, staring at her perfect face with smoldering eyes. She had gazed back, wide-eyed and flushed, wondering what he was thinking. But before she could ask, he rolled over and laid her upon the bed, his mouth descending on hers with far less frenzy and far more passion.

He was sucking the life right out of her. Carington held him fast against her, feeling his massive arms wrap themselves around her small body and knowing there was nothing sweeter in this world than being enfolded in his enormous embrace. The kiss that afternoon had only been a foretaste of the joy to come. What Creed was doing now went beyond anything she could have possibly imagined.

Her surcoat was a very proper garment, high of neck and long of sleeve. Creed wanted to taste more of her flesh in the worst possible way but the garment was restricting. It was, however, quite clingy; her round, full breasts were outlined and enhanced by the cut of the coat. He unwound one arm from her body, his big hand moving to her shoulder. As he kissed and nuzzled her, the hand moved down her arm, to her hand, and she clutched him fiercely. They held hands a moment, becoming accustomed to the feel of one another, before he let his fingers drift across her flat abdomen. Carington's little hand followed his, fluttering atop his fingers, delighting in her first experience with a man. When his warm palm moved up her torso and closed in around a full breast, she started at the sensation.

He stopped sucking her lower lip long enough to look at her. "Did I hurt you?"

She swallowed, trying to catch her breath. "Nay," she whispered. "'Tis just... it was unexpected...."

He removed his hand immediately. "I did not mean to frighten you," he said, pausing to look at her lovely face, his wits returning now that the frantic kisses had eased. "You make me feel like a weak man, Cari. I am not weak by nature."

She reached up, timidly touching his handsome, weary face. "I wouldna knowingly weaken ye, Creed. Not for anything. Ye're the strongest man I've ever met."

He smiled faintly. "For a Sassenach?"

She grinned, biting her kiss-chaffed lip. "For any man."

They lay there a moment, smiling at each other. He loomed over her, studying the lines of her face, the gentle curve of her neck as it descended to her shoulder. She was so flawless and perfect. And he was terrified.

"I really should get back to my post," he said softly, brushing a stray lock of black hair from her eyes. "Will you be all right tonight?"

"I'd be better if ye stayed with me."

He lifted an eyebrow, thinking of the deeper connotations of that. He knew she had not suggested the more carnal expectations of the statement; still, what she was suggesting was improper. On the road it was one thing to sleep in the same tent with her for protection's sake, but now that they were at Prudhoe, there were no such allowances.

"I cannot, honey," he said quietly. "Already, my presence here is dangerous. Surely you know that."

She averted her gaze, toying with the cleft in his chin. "Creed?"

He was aware she was ignoring his statement. "What?"

"Why are ye so cold to me at times and so… passionate at others?"

He sighed heavily, reaching out to touch her creamy cheek. It was as soft as an infant's. "I am sorry if it seems that way. You must understand that there is a certain demeanor I must present when we are in the presence of others. I cannot act like a besotted fool every time I look at you. But in private moments like this, I am free to show how I feel. Does that make sense?"

She was still playing with his chin; her touch felt just like heaven to him. "Are ye?"

Again, she was evading his question. "Am I what?" he asked.

"Besotted?"

He emitted a long, heavy sigh that sounded suspiciously like a growl. It was evident that he was reluctant to answer her. "What do you think?"

"If I knew, I wouldna have asked."

The fiery little personality in her flared up, like a blaze that suddenly rears and then just as quickly dies. He realized he liked that aspect of her very much. It was entertaining to watch her rise. Kissing her swiftly on the lips, he pushed himself off the bed and discreetly adjusted the bulge in his breeches.

"I think you already do."

She stood up from the bed, a bit unsteadily, still flushed from their whirlwind encounter. He could see the flame in her eye even though she was smiling. "Ye're an evasive man, Creed de Reyne. When I ask a question, I expect the courtesy of an answer."

His reply was to whip her into his arms and kiss her again, so strongly that she was gasping for air when he finally pulled away. He grinned at her as she struggled.

"Was that enough of an answer?"

He was moving to the door, leaving her stunned and breathless. When she did not reply to his question, he paused at the door, his hand on the latch.

"Now go to bed," he ordered softly. "I will see you on the morrow."

She swallowed, her wits making a slow return. It was all she could do to nod her head like an idiot. The man possessed the power to still her tongue as well as flutter her heart. When he winked at her and finally shut the door, she continued to stand there for an unknown amount of time, reliving their kiss over and over in her mind.

When sleep finally claimed her, it was deep and dreamless.

***

"You know that under normal circumstances I would never bring an issue like this to your attention, but I feel that I must in this case. The man is a fool and a danger, and he seriously disrupts the harmony of my knights."

Richard had been listening to Ryton for the better part of the hour. In his private solar in Prudhoe's thick keep, the focus of conversation was Jory d'Eneas, a sore subject for them both. But it was also a very political subject and Richard sighed heavily to Ryton's latest tale of brutality and poor judgment. Though he was not surprised, he was nonetheless disheartened.

"What would you have me do?" Richard finally asked, weary and wanting for the comfort of his bed. "The man is the son of an ally and friend and I cannot cast him aside easily. You know this, Ryton."

"I know it, my lord."

"Then what would you have me do?"

"Send him back to his father. Let the earl deal with his ill-mannered bastard son, for he is only succeeding in upsetting the peace of Prudhoe. I fear that one day he will go too far and have his neck snapped by a fellow knight."

Richard eyed Ryton, hearing the ominous tone. "Is that what is happening within your ranks? Is that why his face is so bruised?"

Ryton nodded slowly. "He attacked the hostage on our trip south. Creed dealt him a harsh blow and so did Burle."

"Then perhaps he has learned his lesson."

Ryton's impatience slipped through. "He has not learned it yet, my lord. In all of the years the man has served me, he has never shown hide nor hair of an ability to take heed of a lesson taught. I am not sure why the latest incident would weigh any differently on him."

Richard's gaze lingered on his captain. "Then I will repeat the question; short of sending him back to his father, what would you have me do?"

Ryton's jaw ticked; he could see that ridding himself of Jory was out of the question. It was not that his liege was weak; it was that he truly worried for the alliance implications of sending the disgraced knight home to his father. Ryton understood very well his fears, but it did not make their issue with Jory any simpler to resolve. Still, he felt some disgust that Richard was unwilling to take the chance of upsetting an ally over the reality of upsetting his entire castle.

"Perhaps you should have a word with him, threaten him with

returning him to his father at the very least," Ryton said, a measure of defeat in his voice. "Even though you have no intention of doing so, perhaps the threat will be enough for him to amend his behavior."

Richard nodded, toying with his chalice that was long since empty of wine. Ryton watched his liege closely, for he could see that the man was thinking.

"The hostage," Richard finally said, somewhat hesitantly. "She is something of a firebrand, is she not?"

Ryton could see their conversation about Jory was over. "She is spirited," he sighed, knowing it would be of no use to try to continue with Jory's punishment.

Richard stood up, stretching his lanky body. "I cannot imagine that Creed took the assignment to protect her willingly."

"He did not. But he is the best one suited for the task. He is the only one of my knights I would trust with her." Ryton cast his liege a sidelong glance. "You should know that Jory seems particularly interested in her. It is my suggestion that we assign Creed to protect the lady even while she is here at Prudhoe. The last thing we need is for Jory to compromise her, or worse, and have the entire Clan Kerr down around our ears."

Richard looked at him, a mixture of disgust and impatience on his face. "She is untouchable, Ryton. Jory must understand that. I will not suffer the wrath of the Kerrs because he cannot keep control of himself."

Ryton merely lifted an eyebrow. "Then that directive should come from you, as his liege. Let him know that if he brings a war down upon us because of his lack of control, we will make sure the Clan Kerr knows him by name. I will not defend a man who would knowingly disrupt a peace accord."

"I will speak to him," Richard said firmly. "God help us all if that man harms one hair on her head."

Ryton was both pleased and surprised that his liege had actually committed to speaking with Jory. He almost always left it up to Ryton unless his captain pushed him into a corner.

"Then I will send him to you immediately," Ryton was moving

for the door, not waiting to be dismissed. "And I will make sure that Creed knows that he is permanently assigned to protect the lady for the duration of her stay."

"Can Jory not wait until tomorrow?"

"Nay, my lord, he cannot."

Richard nodded in resignation. "Very well. Send him to me. But be quick about it. I should like to see my bed before the sun rises."

So would I, Ryton thought dryly. The meeting with his liege had left a foul taste in his mouth; he would have liked to see Richard take a more decisive stand against Jory. The knight was difficult enough to command without strong support from their lord. As Ryton crossed the darkened bailey towards the knight's quarters, he could see the massive outline of his brother on the wall walk.

He was a silent, deadly silhouette against the moonlit sky. Creed had willingly taken the night watch as long as he could remember; even those many years ago when he was newly knighted, Creed would volunteer to take a post deep into the night. Guardian of Darkness, the older knights used to call the powerful young knight with the intense disposition. The man who would guard the night.

Ryton made the decision to deliver Jory his orders before moving on to his brother. He could only imagine what his brother's reaction would be.

He was not looking forward to it.

CHAPTER SEVEN

Carington slept well past dawn. In fact, she would have slept the entire day away had shouts from the bailey not jolted her from a heavy sleep. Yawning, stretching, she rolled over on her borrowed bed, trying to orient herself. It was a bright day beyond the lancet window. It took her a few moments to remember where she was.

She sat up in bed, rubbing the sleep from her eyes. Gazing down at the bed, the room, she suddenly remembered Creed and the passion they had shared in this very room. His warmth filled her veins, the giddy unfamiliar thoughts flooding her. It was enough to prompt her to bolt from the bed, calling to the servants that she knew were lingering within earshot. Two pasty-faced wenches showed themselves at the door and she ordered food and a bath. She was very dirty from her trip and wanted to wash the filth from her body. Moreover, she realized she was starving; she'd hardly eaten the day before and her appetite was back with a vengeance.

In little time, a big copper tub was brought and several servants began filling it with steaming water. Carington was a little stand-offish of the English servants, feeling somewhat intimidated to be alone in a great group of them without her protectors about. She kept herself busy, and away from them, by going through the satchels she had brought with her. She was aware she had only brought four garments with her, plain and serviceable, and she selected the faded yellow wool surcoat that had once belonged to her mother. Due to her father's thrift, she had many recycled garments. In spite of its age, it was the fanciest piece she owned with red and blue flowers embroidered along the scoop neckline. She found herself hoping that Creed would like it.

When the bath was full the two pale serving women remained,

huddled by the hearth and waiting to assist the lady with her bath. But Carington wanted nothing to do with the English servants and sent them away. Removing the Elder flower oil and a precious cake of calendula soap from her bags, she stripped off the dusty and soiled clothing she had both slept and traveled in and plunged into the water.

It was hot and stimulating, and she began to lather away with the calendula soap. From the top of her head to the bottom of her toes, she scrubbed herself furiously. All the while, a sweet little tune came from her lips, an old ballad that was common in her clan. When she was completely soaped, she submerged herself in the water, rinsing the lather off. Her hair was not particularly thick, but she had a lot of it, and it took several rinses to see the water run clear. When the black strands squeaked as she ran her fingers over them, she knew she was finally clean.

Never one to linger in a bath, she leapt out and collected a large square of drying linen that the servants had brought her. Still humming her happy tune, she dried off vigorously and wrapped it around her head to soak the moisture from her hair. After a sparing application of the Elder flower oil to her dry skin, she dressed in soft hose, clean linen pantalets, her spare shift and the pale yellow surcoat.

The peat in the hearth was smoking weakly. Carington stoked it vigorously, added a few more clumps of peat that were in an iron bucket near the hearth, and removed the linen from her head. The warmth of the fire began to dry her black hair into a silken mass and she ran her fish-bone comb through it, letting the heat from the fire envelope every strand.

By this time, an older serving woman with bad skin returned with her meal of bread, cheese and watered ale and she began to wolf it down. The woman watched her eat.

"Ah now, lass," she said timidly. "You'll want to slow down. No sense in everything coming back up again."

Carington eyed the woman. "Get out."

The old woman was not intimidated or offended. "As you wish, m'lady," she turned for the door. "I'll be back in an hour to clean up your mess."

Carington's mouth was full of cheese. She should have just let the woman go but something made her call out. "What mess? There is no mess."

"The mess that you'll make when you vomit everything you just ate," the woman said calmly, almost to the door.

Carington swallowed some of what was in her mouth, now looking uncertain. "I'll not make a mess."

"As you say, m'lady."

The woman opened the door and immediately stepped back; lingering in the doorway were two young women, looking as if they were surprised the door had suddenly opened. Startled, Carington realized that Lady Julia and Lady Kristina had made an appearance and she struggled to swallow the food in her mouth, fumbling with her comb and trying to make sure she was properly dressed to accept visitors all in the same breath. As she hurriedly stood up, the young ladies entered the warm chamber.

For a moment, no one said a word. Everyone seemed to be appraising each other. In their first and only contact, Carington had essentially insulted the girls and she was waiting for a barrage of abuse to come hurling back at her. But the young women made no move against her; they just stared as if expecting her to rise up and breathe fire. Carington could not remember which one was Julia and which one was Kristina.

"It was not my idea to displace ye last night," she was immediately on the defensive, more than likely not a good way to start out a conversation. "If ye're thinking of berating me, I'd hold my tongue. None of it was my doing."

The taller blond girl spoke quickly. "We know," she had a soft, sweet voice. "Lady Anne told us. We came to see if you required any... ummm... assistance this morning."

Carington lifted a dark eyebrow. "Assistance with what?"

The girl shrugged, looking at her companion for support. "Dressing, I suppose. And your bath. But we see that you have already taken care of everything."

Carington studied the tall blond. She was pretty and young.

"Which lady are ye?"

"I am Kristina," the girl replied.

Carington's gaze moved to the second girl; then this one was Julia, the problem that Creed had warned her of. She was short, thin, with not much health about her. She had light brown hair and blue eyes, nothing spectacular about either feature. Carington sensed a great deal of animosity from her.

"Well," Carington averted her gaze and indicated a chair near the hearth. "I suppose we should all become acquainted considering we are to share this chamber. If ye have a mind to sit, I'll not stop ye."

Kristina was definitely the more timid of the two. She looked hesitantly at Julia, who was still fixed on Carington. It was clear that she was sizing her up. But the girls did manage to sit a good distance away from their Scots counterpart after some serious indecision. It seemed that no one wanted to get too close. Carington appreciated the distance, feeling Julia's strong stare as she finished her meal.

"What is it ye wish to know about me?" Carington asked, tearing at her bread. She looked up at the two girls as she popped a piece in her mouth. "Surely there is something ye wish to know."

Julia folded her hands meekly in her lap, her unspectacular face intense with curiosity and hostility. "Aye," she said slowly, her tone low and coarse, surprising for such a small lady. "There is something I have always wished to know about Scots. Is it true that they eat their young?"

The blood rushed to Carington's head but she surprisingly kept her cool. "Nay, lady," she said, putting another piece of bread in her mouth. "Just our enemies. I'd wager to say we've had a few of your kin in our time. I probably cooked them myself."

While Kristina's eyes opened wide with shock, Julia's pale cheeks flushed. "No doubt," she replied smoothly. "There is something quite barbaric about you."

A thin smile came to Carington's lips. "Push me too far, skinny wench, and ye'll find out just how barbaric. I'm a laird's daughter, an instrument for peace. Ye cannot touch me without bringing yer lord's wrath upon ye. But I can do what I please with no punishment. So think twice before tangling with me, lassie. I'll smother ye while ye sleep."

"My lady," Kristina boldly interrupted, seeing that the conversation was plummeting. "Is… is there anything you wish to know about Prudhoe? We have been here for several years and can answer any of your questions."

Carington tore her gaze away from Julia and focused on the young blond. "There is nothing I wish to know about the castle, but thanks to ye for asking."

An unstable pause followed. Kristina piped up again with nervous conversation. "My home is in the south of England. Until I came north, I had no idea there was such snow. And I have never even met a Scots until yesterday. Are there big cities in Scotland, my lady?"

Above her hostile posturing with Julia, Carington could see that Kristina was genuinely attempting to make conversation. Perhaps she was even genuinely trying to welcome her as much as she dared with Julia present. She attempted to soften her manner with the girl.

"Aye," she replied. "There are big cities. My da took me to Edinburgh once and it was the biggest city I have ever seen. There is even an enormous castle in the middle of it."

Kristina smiled timorously. "I went to London with my father when I was a child, although I do not remember much of it. I do, however, remember my mother buying fine jewelry and my father becoming angry with her for spending so much money."

Carington felt comfortable conversing with the girl; her guard was gradually slipping. "My da is frugal also. He doesna believe in spending money on anything foolish."

"Surely he does not mind spending money on his daughter. Would he not buy you whatever you wish?"

Carington laughed, a beautiful gesture that lit up the room. "Hardly; sometimes we have traveling merchants that stop and seek shelter for a night and my da acts as if I am torturing him if I want to buy the smallest trinket. Why, only last month we had a man who had traveled all over France and Italy. He had the most marvelous oils and pastes. I wanted to buy one that smelled of flowers, such a wonderful smell, but my da pretended to take sick and took to his bed until the man left. As soon as the merchant departed, he was miraculously healed. What a deceiver he is!"

Kristina giggled as Carington continued to snort at the memory. Julia, seeing her companion warming to the hostage, suddenly leapt to her feet.

"Since you have no need for us, we will return to Lady Anne and tell her so," she grabbed Kristina by the arm and practically yanked the girl to her feet. "You should be mindful that Chapel is at mid-morning. Lord Richard expects everyone to attend; even you. I would suggest you prepare yourself."

The warmth that Carington had felt for Kristina vanished when addressing Julia. "I will be ready," she said evenly. "I will thank ye both for your offer to assist me this morn."

Julia did nothing more than nod her head and turn away, heading for a large wardrobe that was against the opposite wall. Kristina lingered, still smiling hesitantly at Carington.

"We must get dressed for Mass," she said. "I hope we will not disturb you."

Carington could see that Creed had been right; Kristina was a sweet girl. She was close enough to put a hand on the girl's arm.

"Ye couldna disturb me if ye tried," she assured her.

Removing her hand, she went back to her borrowed bed where the contents of her satchels were spread out. Her leather boots were by the bed, ugly and durable, and she pulled them on over her hose. As she dressed, she could not help but notice that both Julia and Kristina wore fine slippers. She did not own anything so nice.

Sitting on her bed, which seemed the least bit hard now that she was actually resting upon it, she continued to comb her nearly dry hair, all the while watching Julia and Kristina dress. Julia called in a couple of the serving wenches, who were cinching her up in a girdle, while Kristina dressed silently and alone. Kristina's clothes were fashionable while Julia's were quite expensive and lavish.

Carington looked down at herself in her mother's surcoat, thinking she looked sorely out of place among the finely dressed Sassenach ladies. She was coming to feel slightly embarrassed for her appearance but she would not let on. She would act as if she did not care they had fine clothes while she looked like a worn-out peasant.

When her hair was finally dry, Carington pulled the front of it away from her face and secured it on the back of her head with the brass butterfly clasp that had once belonged to her mother. Her dark hair had a natural wave to it and curled down her back, glistening like strands of satin. Some Elder flower oil went on her dry lips. She had no idea that, even for her simplicity, she absolutely outshined every woman in the room.

Julia and Kristina finished dressing while Carington pretended to fuss with her satchels. She probably should have unpacked into one of the wardrobes, but she was not going to lower herself to ask either girl for guidance or assistance. She would just as well keep everything in her bags. When the young women were finished dressing and primping, Julia was the first one out of the door without a word. Kristina, however, paused to speak.

"We should go now," she said to Carington. "Lady Anne will scold us if we are late."

Carington rose and obediently followed Kristina from the chamber. They descended the narrow spiral stairs to the second floor and took a larger spiral staircase to the first floor. The door was open to the bailey and Carington followed her roommates out into the dusty ward. It was only the second time she had been outside any of the Prudhoe structures; she lagged behind as she peered up at the walls, over to the buttery, and back over towards the stables. She found it fascinating and full of activity, much different from her stark and barren home of Wether Fair.

Prudhoe was a massive place, full of soldiers and peasants, and more than once she almost collided with someone when she did not pay attention to where she was going. She did not even know where the chapel was, keeping her eye on Kristina's blue surcoat as they crossed the bustling ward. She trailed the blue garment to the outer bailey in the midst of the organized chaos that seemed to pulse through Prudhoe. Coming around a sharp corner of the great hall, she ran straight into Jory.

From open interest in her surroundings one moment to apprehension the next, Carington's veins ran cold at the sight of his heartless brown eyes. She had hardly seen him since the unfortunate Bress incident and had been thankful to forget about him. But here he was, alive and breathing before her, and she could feel anger and fear stir within her. For Jory, however, his expression was one of naked joy; he peered at her, the sound of intense pleasure in his tone.

"My lady," he said. "How nice to see you this morn. You look ravishing, as usual."

Carington was gearing up for a verbal assault when Kristina suddenly reached an arm around Jory and tugged at her.

"My lady," she said insistently. "We shall be late."

Carington allowed the girl to pull her along and was thankful for the reprieve. All she could feel for the man was hate.

Jory's gaze tracked her as she moved away. "Another time, my lady," he called after her.

She could hear him laugh. Disgusted, Carington was aware that Kristina had not taken her hand away. In fact, her soft warm hand was gripping Carington's fingers. They walked several more feet along a dirt path, into the shadow of the great wall, and ascended a narrow flight of stairs built into a tower. On the second floor of the gatehouse tower was Prudhoe's lovely little chapel.

Burle was standing by the door. Carington looked up into his round face and found comfort with his acknowledging smile. She could not help but smile in return as she allowed Kristina to lead her into the room where the d'Umfraville family was gathered.

It was a small chapel, a tower room that had been converted into a place of worship. The floors were dusty due to its proximity to the main gate, with much dust floating in through the long windows that faced the bailey. Lady Anne and Richard were already kneeling on delicate rugs before a small but elaborate altar while Edward and Gilbert were near the oriel window that faced to the north, thumping each other on the head and generally tussling. But they stopped their battle when they lay eyes upon the latest addition to Prudhoe.

"Do you even know how to pray?" Gilbert walked directly towards Carington with Edward in tow. "My father says that Scots are barbarians. Do you even know who God is?"

Anne looked up from her silent prayers, glaring over her shoulder at the boys. Richard continued praying as if nothing was amiss.

"Gilbert," Anne snapped softly. "Another word and you will go from this room. Be silent."

As his mother returned to her prayers, the little boy dutifully shut up but stuck his tongue out at Carington. She stuck hers out at him in response. He then tried to kick her. She reached out and pinched his arm.

"Ow!" the boy howled.

Jolted from her prayers again, Anne turned sharply to her son. "Gilbert, I said not another word!"

Gilbert was rubbing his arm. "But she pinched me!"

Lady Anne looked to Carington, who merely lifted her shoulders. "An accident, m'lady."

Anne's gaze lingered on her as if surprised she had even admitted such a thing. Truthfully, she was not quite sure what to make of it. Lacking a better response, she did nothing more than return to her prayers.

When the woman's back was turned, Carington glared menacingly at Gilbert and shook her fist at him. He made all manner of fighting gestures in her direction, kicking and throwing his fists to threaten her, but made no actual move to physically touch her. It was apparent he was furious but unwilling to provoke his mother. When his little brother whispered at him, he reluctantly went with his brother back to their seats by the window.

Carington did not take her eyes off the boy. She did not trust him not to slip up behind her and whack her on the head. Julia was already on her knees, head bowed in prayer, as Kristina pulled Carington alongside. When Kristina went down on her knees, so did Carington. The room fell silent as heads were bowed and the boys thankfully shut up.

Carington's father had never been one for the formality of prayer. In fact, her religious education had been very limited. Not wanting to admit such a soul-cursing thing to her new hosts, she simply lowered her head like the other girls and pretended to pray. She honestly was not sure how. Eyes closed, head bowed, her thoughts inevitably drifted to Creed and she wondered where he was on this bright and glorious day. Yesterday morning at this time they had been riding to Prudhoe. She could still feel his arms around her, massive appendages that were safe and comforting. He was such a big man, so powerful, and her heart began to thump strangely as her thoughts of him grew more intense.

She could feel his hands in her hair, his lips on hers. She was becoming warm at the mere memory. And he had a smell about him, something musky and masculine, that stirred her more deeply than she could comprehend. Her breathing began to deepen, to grow heavy, as she remembered the feel of his mouth against hers, his tongue gently yet insistently probing her. It was enough to bring a rush of heat to her cheeks.

Wicked, she thought. I should be praying, yet I am thinking of a man who took liberties with me. She smiled faintly, hoping God would forgive her. God made passion, after all. Perhaps he would not be too upset that she could focus on nothing else.

The prayers seemed to drag on for days when, in fact, it was only a matter of a half hour or so. Carington thought she might have actually dozed off, on her knees to thoughts of Creed's touch, when she was jolted from her kneeling position by Kristina's gentle voice. A bit groggily, she rose, watching Richard and Anne leave arm in arm, followed by Gilbert and Edward. The boys had apparently forgotten about their newest nemesis and paid Carington no mind as they left. They were more interested in tripping each other. Julia was the next one to leave, followed by Kristina. Carington was right behind them, taking a moment to observe the empty chapel with its very precious glass window above the altar. By the time she finished her observation and turned for the door, a very large body was suddenly standing in front of her.

Startled, she gazed up into Creed's dusky blue eyes. His expression was as emotionless as ever, but something in the eyes had warmed up. Until this moment, his eyes always held a cold quality about them when he looked at her. But not today; she could not help the smile that spread across her lips, so very glad to finally see him. It was difficult not to appear giddy.

"Sir Creed," she said, mindful that Burle was still standing near the door a few feet away. "Have ye just arrived? I'm afraid prayers are over."

He looked rested and washed. His skin was smooth, as if he had even shaved. The overall picture was, in fact, striking; she'd only known the man to be dirty and weary from travel for the past few days. But standing in front of her in clean clothing, he looked like an entirely different person. He looked magnificent.

Creed shook his head in response to her question, his dark hair shaking back and forth.

"I have not come for prayers, my lady," he said. "I have come for you."

She lifted her eyebrows. "Me?"

He nodded, sweeping his hand in the direction of the door and indicating for her to quit the chapel. "Indeed. I told you that I would be your shadow."

Clasping her hands primly before her, she obediently left the chamber. "But yer brother said that I was no longer the knights' responsibility. Has something changed?"

A few things, in fact, Creed thought as he followed her down the stairs, but he would not tell her the whole of it. His gaze was predictably drawn to the clinging yellow dress; the soft curve of her backside enough to set his male instincts to raging again. She paused politely at the base of the steps, looking up at him expectantly. He realized she was waiting for an answer. Meeting her emerald gaze, he realized he had never more willingly accepted an assignment.

"It has been decided that, as a special hostage, your position demands more protection," he said, holding his elbow out to her. She took it immediately, her soft fingers clutching his enormous arm. "Since you and I have established a rapport, this duty has been asked of me."

She continued to gaze up at him. "A duty?"

He smiled faintly. "A pleasure."

A broad smile spread across her face. "How kind for ye to say so."

Lord God, he thought as he gazed into her face. Her magnificent smile was enough to cause his knees to go weak, a strange warmth filling him. Never in his life had he felt such giddiness, like a drunken man with too much time and pleasure on his hands. Her smile could make him walk through fire without another thought.

But as foolish and weak as it made him feel, he knew in the same breath that he must conduct himself very carefully. What had happened yesterday would undoubtedly happen again, but he could not, must not, allow it to go further. Creed was not sure what he was feeling for her yet; it had occupied his thoughts all night when he should have damn well been focused on his sentry duties. Even as he tried to catch a few hours' sleep just after dawn, he could not sleep for thoughts of her. When his brother had told him of his assignment regarding the lady, it was all he could do to not shout for joy. Instead, he had showed his brother a clearly bored expression. He was pleased that Ryton had bought into it.

He did not say anything more as they crossed the ward back towards the keep; his wink had said it all. He was aware that he felt oddly puffed up, pleased to have her on his arm, as they made their way across the bailey. He knew every man in the place was watching them and he felt a strange sense of both pride and protectiveness.

Shouts up on the wall distracted him from his thoughts. Glancing up, he could see that the soldiers on the parapet were attempting to gain his attention. He took her hand gently off his elbow, turning in the same motion to Burle several paces behind them.

"Burle," he made sure to put her hand into the big knight's outstretched palm. "Take the lady, if you please. And do not let her out of your sight, for any reason. I shall be right back."

Both Burle and Carington watched him jog across the bailey and mount one of the many wooden ladders up to the wall. Burle watched Creed until he mounted the parapets before turning to the lady.

"Would you like to return to your chamber now, my lady?" he asked politely.

Carington tore her gaze away from Creed's distant form to focus on the big blond man. "Nay," she said after a moment. "I would like to see this place that would be my home for a while. Will ye show me?"

Burle nodded and began walking slowly with her on his arm. "What would you like to see, my lady?"

She shrugged. "Everything. I've never seen a fortress this size before."

He just started walking, pointing out things like the stables, the buttery, the tanner's shack. The outer ward was wide and long and there was much to see. The kitchens were separate from both the hall and the keep, a stone structure that had holes near the roof line to allow the smoke to escape. They must have been baking because she could smell the bread and she was hungry. Burle took her inside the very warm, very smoky structure and procured a newly baked loaf from the red-faced cook. Happy, she pulled the bread apart and tore into it like a common soldier. Crust and crumbs flew all over the place.

Burle watched her with a grin on his face. She stuffed bread in her mouth and asked about the kitchen in general, including the big copper pots used to make ale. The cook was also the ale wife and produced most of Prudhoe's liquor. As she ate, Carington engaged the woman in a conversation about her ale process. Burle stood by the door in silence, listening to Lady Carington discuss the various methods of brewing at her home of Wether Fair. It was apparent that she knew a great deal about it.

Before Burle realized it, Carington and the cook had grasped one of the big copper tubs and were obviously preparing to utilize it. They moved it to the enormous hearth, big enough to cook several people in, and set it upon an extended iron hook that hung from a chain secured into the stone of the chimney.

A conversation with a servant was becoming manual labor. The women could barely move the pot between them but somehow managed as Burle stood there, dumbfounded. He was not sure if he should stop her or not; she seemed very determined and very knowledgeable. He knew it never did him any good to try and stop his own wife from doing something once her mind was set, so he was hesitant to interfere.

"Sir Burle," Carington jolted him from his thoughts, waving him over. "We require yer strength, if ye please."

He moved from his post by the door, eyeing her. "What is your wish, my lady?"

Carington wiped at a stray lock of hair with the back of her hand, gesturing to the pile of massive sacks lined up neatly near the hearth.

"The barley," she said. "Please open a sack."

"And then what, my lady?"

"Dump it into this vat. We are going to cook it."

"Cook it?"

She looked at him then, annoyance on her face. He read her expression and immediately went to the sack without further delay. It was very heavy, but he was very strong; bringing it over to the women, he held it while Carington ripped the stitching in the top. When a small opening was created, he flipped it over and dumped the entire thing into the pot. Dust from the grain billowed up and Carington sneezed several times.

"Do I dare ask what is going on in here?"

The trio of ale cooks looked up at the enormous man standing in the doorway. Creed's shoulders were so wide that they went from one side of the frame to the other, filling the entire opening. More than that, he was sucking all of the air out of the room again. Carington could feel it from where she stood, only it did not intimidate her like it used to. She welcomed it. Creed's expression was curious as he moved into the heated room, his gaze moving between Burle and the little lady.

Carington answered. "I am going to show yer cook how to make a honeyed fruited ale."

Creed's eyebrows slowly lifted, his eyes studying her intently. "You are going to make ale?"

She nodded, completely oblivious to the distain in his tone. "A recipe that has been in my family for generations. It is quite delicious."

He shifted on his thick legs, crossing his arms as he continued to look at her. "You are going to make ale?"

Now she was catching his tone. She cocked her head curiously. "Aye; what is the matter?"

He could not believe she did not see anything wrong with domestic work. But, then again, things were quite different at her home. He knew her father was quite frugal, as she had told him. And he had also seen Wether Fair, a rather desolate keep with a big, dirty army and little else. It began to occur to him that perhaps she was well acquainted with domestic chores. The thought saddened him; such a lovely, intelligent lady was destined for finer things. He never wanted her to lift a finger again.

But he had to be careful with his words. He did not want to insult her when she clearly saw nothing wrong with what she was doing. He took a few steps towards the group until he stood next to Burle, but his eyes never left Carington.

"Nothing is the matter except that I have been asked to take you to town to purchase material for new clothing," he said. "I thought you would want to go now. It is a fine day for travel."

She blinked at him in surprise. "New clothing? Why do I need new clothing?"

"You do not need it, but Lady Anne thought you would like to have some new garments made."

"Why?"

He was on two very touchy subjects and being very careful not to tip the balance against him. First the ale, now the clothing. As he had observed since the day they had taken her from Wether Fair, she obviously did not own any fine clothing. Even the dress she wore now, as much as it clung to her delicious figure, was faded and outdated. Either she did not care how she looked, which he could not imagine was the case, or she did not own anything finer. Lady Anne had noticed it this morning also and had mentioned it to him as he had passed her on his way to the chapel. He was under orders to finely dress her without offending her at the same time. It was a difficult task.

He held out a hand to her. "A word, my lady."

Without hesitation, she placed her hand in his and allowed him to lead her away from Burle and the cook. He took her outside, to a corner of the building where the kitchen met with the outer wall. It was quiet and out of the way, and he faced her in the shadows.

"First, lady, you are a guest of Lord Richard d'Umfraville and to refuse a gift of new clothing would be insulting to your host," he said in a low voice. "Second, finely bred young ladies do not work in the kitchens. Although it is quite generous for you to share your recipe with the cook, I do believe that simply telling her what the recipe is and allowing her to do her job would suffice." He could see the storm brewing in her eyes and he stepped closer to her, his big fingers finding her hand. He brought it to his mouth, his lips against her flesh as he spoke. "You are a beautiful, witty and intelligent woman, Cari. Allow us to treat you as such. Allow *me* to treat you as such. You do not belong in the kitchen. You belong in a fine house with all of the luxury and protection I can provide you."

Her emerald eyes went from flashing to soft in a moment. She watched him nibble on her fingers, her heart doing strange leaps against her ribcage.

"Well," she said slowly, hearing the quiver in her voice. "Since ye put it that way, how can I refuse?"

He grinned, his lips still against her hand. "You cannot. And I thank you for your understanding."

She shook her head at him, a knowing smile on her face as they both knew she had little choice. But she did not particularly care.

"When do we leave for town?" she asked.

"Immediately if you wish."

"Will it just be you and I?"

He shook his head. "Nay. I am taking Burle and Stanton with me and about twenty men at arms."

Her eyebrows rose. "Just for me?"

"Just for you."

Giddy with the thought of spending the day with him, not to mention that her hosts were purchasing finery for her, she was in a splendid mood as he escorted her back to the kitchens. Quite carefully, she explained to the cook what must be done and left the woman to wrangle her magic with the new recipe. With orders to gather an escort, Burle went along his way as Creed took Carington back to the keep to collect her cloak.

As they were preparing to mount the steps to the keep, a few children came running past them, howling in terror. One child, a little girl of no more than four years, fell on the ground and bloodied her knee. Carington naturally felt sorry for the child and was preparing to help her stand when Gilbert and Edward suddenly appeared, small swords in hand. The boys pounced on the little girl before Carington could get to her.

"I have you now, wench!" Gilbert grabbed the child by the hair. "To the vault with you!"

Horrified, Carington made a dash for the child before Creed could stop her. With the little girl in one hand, she shoved Gilbert away.

"Gilbert d'Umfraville, ye're a monster to hurt this child," she scolded severely. "Go away and leave her alone, ye little devil, before I take a stick to ye."

Gilbert's mouth popped open in outrage. Then he thrust his sword at her, barely missing her torso.

"I'll teach you to interfere, you brazen wench," he cried.

Creed was suddenly between them, removing Carington and the weeping child without laying a hand on Gilbert. One had to be very careful with Richard's sons.

"Master Gilbert," his voice was low. "Honorable men do not use weapons against women, and particularly not Lady Carington. She is a guest of your father's and you will not harm or harass her in any way. Another offense and your mother shall be informed."

The threat of Lady Anne's wrath was perhaps the only thing that intimidated Gilbert. But being the spoiled child that he was, he was not easily swayed. He pursed his lips, glaring at Carington and the sobbing girl. He pointed the sword at them.

"Don't you interfere anymore," he threatened Carington. "This is my castle. I will do as I please."

Carington would not let a spoiled boy frighten her. "If I see another wrong doing, ye'll come away with a blistered backside."

"I will kill you first!"

"Make yer move, ye arrogant little fiend. I dare ye!"

It was turning into a shouting match between a grown lady and a horrible little boy. Creed put his hands out, one to turn Carington back towards the keep and the other to gently but firmly turn Gilbert around in the direction he had come. He ended up shoving him into Edward, who was huddled behind his brother in mute support.

"Go, both of you," he ordered quietly. "I will hear no more of this. Master Gilbert, I would suggest you leave those children alone. You have been warned against beating them before."

"But they are my vassals. I may do with them as I please."

"Good lords do not harass their vassals. They protect them."

Gilbert stuck his tongue out at Creed. Carington caught the gesture and she snapped, rushing at him with the intent of whacking him within an inch of his life. Creed was fast and grabbed her before she could fully execute her plan, but she still managed to get a handful of Gilbert's hair and she yanked hard. The boy screamed.

"How do ye like that?" she snarled as Creed hoisted her up and began to carry her away. "That is what ye did to that little girl. It hurts, doesn't it? Ye little beast, I'll...!

Creed slapped a hand over her mouth before she could issue the rest of her threat. He carried her into the keep, only setting her down when they reached the steps. By then, she knew she probably should not have become so angry and she did not fight him as he firmly directed her up the stairs. . He did not scold her; he did not have to. He knew that she was fully aware of the wrongness of her actions, even though the lad had deserved worse. By the time they reached her shared chamber, she was properly, if not reluctantly, contrite.

She would not look him in the eye as he paused at the door. "I shall retrieve my cloak," she said, looking at anything but him. "Please give me a moment."

She started to open the door but he stopped her. Cupping her chin in one enormous hand, he forced her to look at him.

"Cari," his voice was a purr, a rumble that shook her to the core. "No foul moods today. I would see a smile when you return."

She blinked at him with those great emerald eyes. "Are ye going to tell Lord Richard what I did?"

He shook his head, a faint smile on his lips. "Nay."

"But surely that nasty lad will tell him."

"Let him. And then I will tell him of your noble actions in preventing his son from harming a little girl."

She gazed up at him, his words settling. "Ye think I was noble?"

He nodded, the fingers cupping her chin now caressing it. "Indeed I do. But I also think that you need to control your temper where the boys are concerned. It is beneath you to argue with a child."

Her features darkened. "But he was horrible. I wasna going to let him get away with his dastardly behavior."

He was not going to delve into the subject with her. "I will say no more." He let go of her face. "Go and collect your cloak. I shall meet you downstairs."

She nodded obediently, opening the door to the chamber. Creed could see Kristina and Julia beyond and wondered how Carington was getting along with her new roommates. She had not said anything about it and he had not heard anything negative to this point. He eyed the girls in the room beyond as he turned back for the steps.

Carington's gaze lingered on Creed before turning into to the chamber. Kristina was looking at her but Julia had better things to occupy her attention. Julia's eyes were focused on the loom in front of her, an elaborate scene of color blossoming under her skilled needle. Carington smiled at Kristina as she moved to her bed and possessions at the far end of the room. Just as she reached the cloak thrown over the end of the bed, she heard Julia speak.

"Is Sir Creed to be your permanent escort while you are at Prudhoe, my lady?" she asked.

On-guard by the mere sound of the woman's voice, Carington glanced at her. "Why do ye ask?"

"Because he seems to spend a good deal of time around you."

"If he does, it is only his duty. He has been my protector since we left my home."

Julia snorted, a very lady-like sound. "I see," she said. "Have you been warned of Sir Creed yet, my lady?"

Carington's movements paused and her eyes narrowed. "What do ye mean?"

Julia was still focused on her loom; she stabbed at the material. "Then no one has told you."

Carington did not like her tone. She folded the cloak neatly over her arm. "Told me what?"

Julia finally lifted her gaze, noticing that Kristina was shaking her head at her. Julia looked quite innocently at her companion. "Why do you shake your head at me?" she asked. "You know that she must be told. Sir Creed has been with her since her arrival. I was told he was with her the entire trip from Scotland. We would be doing her a disservice if we did not tell her what we know of him."

Carington had had enough of the lady's mystery. She put an irritated hand on her hip. "One of ye had better tell me. What about Sir Creed?"

Julia looked at her with her plain blue eyes. "There is nothing to become upset over, Lady Carington. But you should know the character of the man entrusted with your care, if for no other reason than to be very careful around him."

Carington cocked an impatient eyebrow and her foot began to tap. She had already asked for a reply several times and would not do it again. Julia, sensing she had the Scots attention, put her needle down in a slow, deliberate gesture.

"Have little doubt that Sir Creed is not a great knight," Julia said evenly. "He is the very best in the realm. So great, in fact, that the king requested his service. Creed served the king for nearly three years, until about six months ago."

Carington was torn between impatience and curiosity. "What happened six months ago that he no longer serves the king?"

Julia folded her hands primly; she was enjoying this. "Creed and five other knights were sent to France to escort Isabella of Angoulệme back to England to marry the king. Have you not heard of this, even in your caves in Scotland?"

Carington's cheeks grew hot and she turned away from Julia, moving for the chamber door. "If yer going to insult me, than I have no more time for yer foolishness."

Julia watched her march across the room and proceeded to reclaim her needle. She waited until Carington was at the door before she spoke again, loud enough so that Carington would clearly hear her.

"It is well known that Creed de Reyne and little Isabella had a romance. It is also well known that Creed deflowered her." Julia stabbed the needle into the material again, watching Carington come to a halt in her peripheral vision. "Now news comes to the north that the queen is expecting, but it is not the king's child. It would seem that some believe she is well into a pregnancy brought about by none other than Creed himself."

Carington struggled not to react, but in truth, she felt as if she had been hit squarely in the chest. The lady's words were bitter and nasty; she did not know this young woman and what she knew of her was not pleasant. She was stunned by the words, unsure what to think or believe.

"Why would you tell me this?" she asked in a strange, hoarse voice.

Julia did not look at her. She continued to embroider. "I tell you because you should take great care while in the company of Sir Creed. He has a most unsavory reputation with young women and I would hate to see you fall victim to his lusty nature."

"Ye're lying," she accused quietly.

"Ask anyone. They will tell you the same thing. Sir Creed is not to be trusted."

All Carington could think of at the moment was Creed's passionate kiss, the way his deep blue eyes glimmered so warmly at her. He had made her feel special, safe. Now she was being told that his actions were quite the opposite. But rather than let her emotions flow freely, as was her nature, she steeled herself. She would not let these Sassenach wenches know her thoughts, her turmoil at the shocking words. Woodenly, she swung the cloak over her shoulders, realizing her hands were quaking and hoping neither lady could see it.

Without another word, she quit the chamber and headed down the stairs to the first floor. By the time she hit the entry, she was struggling against tears. But she would not show her feelings. It was a bright morning as she took the stairs faster than she should have, wiping furiously at the moisture around her eyes. It would not do for Creed to see her state and ask her what the matter was. She was not sure she could explain it to him.

But she could not believe what the Sassenach wench said. She would not believe it. Yet she had only known Creed a matter of days. It was not long enough to know his character. Julia had been at Prudhoe a long time; certainly long enough to know. As she drew close to thc cluster of horses and men that were waiting to take her to town, Carington suddenly remember that Kristina had indeed tried to quiet Julia when the woman began to speak of Creed's reputation. If there was no truth to it, why would Kristina have tried to stop her?

The tears of shock were giving way to the posture of confusion. Confusion gave way to belligerence. By the time she reached the group, she in no way wanted anything to do with Creed or their trip to town. She simply wanted to be alone, somewhere, to sort out her thoughts and the horrors that this endeavor to Prudhoe had brought her. But there was no privacy for her, not back in the shared chamber with evil Julia. She was afraid of what she might do to the woman should she say another word to her. Carington was lost in her tumultuous thoughts when Creed approached her.

"Ready, my lady?" he asked pleasantly.

His deep, rich voice broke through her fogged mind. Carington looked up at him, gazing into the dusky blue eyes and realizing that she was fighting off tears. She lowered her gaze; anything so that she would not have to look at him.

"I... I dunna want to go to town," her voice was strangely tight.

His brow rippled. "Why not? I thought...."

She shook her head vigorously. "Nay," she realized that her words were quivering. "I want... I want to go to the chapel. I want to pray."

His face did not change expression, but his piercing eyes were riveted to her. "Now?"

"Aye. Now."

Creed continued to stare at her, wondering why her demeanor had changed so drastically. A few minutes ago she had been warm and agreeable. Now she would not even look at him. He took a step closer.

"Cari," he said quietly. "What is the matter?"

She shook her head and took a step back. She opened her mouth to deny that anything was wrong but a sob bubbled up instead. She slapped a hand over her mouth to keep any more sounds from escaping.

"Nothing," she hissed through her fingers. "Just leave me be. I want to go to the chapel."

He glanced around at the escort he had assembled. Quite a few men wait for them, including Burle and Stanton, mounted on their chargers. Creed held up a discreet hand to the two knights, indicating for them to wait. The men acknowledged his command with a nod. Creed then took Carington gently by the elbow.

"Come along, my lady," he said quietly.

She was not tactful about yanking her elbow from his grasp. Creed let his hand drop as they walked together towards the gatehouse chapel. In silence they mounted the stone steps. At the door, Carington came to an abrupt halt.

"I will go in alone," she said, still not looking at him.

He did nothing more than open the door for her. Carington went inside and he closed the door softly behind her. Now the tears came as she turned to the closed door, knowing Creed was on the other side and feeling such anguish that she could hardly describe it. She could feel the sobs coming and she knew he would hear them. She did not want him charging into the chapel demanding to know what the matter was. Her eyes fell on the old iron bolt and she threw it just as the first sob sprang forth.

On the other side of the door, Creed heard the bolt slide just as sounds of weeping filled his ears. His hand went to the old iron door latch, jigging it and realizing that Carington had locked herself inside.

"Lady Carington?" he did not want to draw attention and rattled the latch quietly. "Unlatch the door. What is wrong?"

Her response was to weep loudly. Puzzled, Creed began to grow concerned. "Cari, what's happened?" he pounded on the door softly. "Open the door and let me in."

Inside the brightly lit chapel with the sun streaming through its many-colored glass panes, Carington wept openly. Her back was to the door; she could feel Creed rattling it. She sank to her buttocks on the cold stone floor, her face in her hands, feeling days of confusion and anxiety gnaw at her. First she was forced to leave her home, then her beloved Bress was killed. Now Creed was apparently not the man of honor and chivalry that she believed him to be; she simply couldn't take anymore.

Creed listened to her weep with deepening concern. She would not answer him and he truly could not fathom what the problem was. But women were confusing creatures he had never been able to decipher. He may have been a stellar knight, but he was not a particularly good mind reader when it came to the opposite sex. Strange thing was that he wanted to read Carington's mind very much. She was upset and he had an overwhelming desire to know why. But his hand remained on the door latch, uncertain what to do.

"Sir Creed?"

A soft female voice met his ears. Creed looked over his shoulder, down the stone steps that led into the bailey, and saw Lady Kristina standing at the base. Her pale face and big blue eyes were laced with apprehension.

"My lady?" he stepped away from the door; he did not want her coming up the stairs and hearing the weeping. "How can I be of service?"

Kristina took the first two steps; Creed descended half the flight before she took another step to prevent her from ascending any further.

"I came to tell you...," Kristina paused when she saw how close he had come; very properly, she traced her steps back down the stairs and stood at the bottom, putting distance between them. "I wanted to tell you that I fear our Lady Carington has heard... well, she has heard gossip and I thought to forewarn you. Since you have been acting as her protector, you have a right to know."

Creed's expression did not change except to cock a dark eyebrow. "Know what?"

Kristina swallowed; Creed intimidated her even though he had never been anything other than kind to her. She began to wring her hands. "She... she has been told of your trip with Queen Isabella. It may have frightened her."

Suddenly, a great deal made sense; Creed glanced over his shoulder at the bolted chapel door before refocusing on Kristina. The girl was uneasy; he could read it in her face. But he had known her for several years and she was not the malicious type. Her companion, however, was.

He sighed heavily. "Lady Julia."

It was a statement, not a question. Kristina nodded reluctantly. "She told her. I tried to stop her, but she would not listen." She took a step towards him, her blue eyes wide and honest. "We all know how Julia feels about you, Sir Creed. She is not threatened by me because she knows I am pledged to another, but Lady Carington is new and exciting and blindingly beautiful, and I can already see that Julia is sharpening her claws."

Creed's gaze was steady on her. "Then Lady Julia is in for a beating. Lady Carington will tear her down to size and never think twice about it. If I were you, I would warn your friend to retract her claws and her tongue before she finds herself in a dire predicament."

Kristina lifted her slender shoulders. "She will not listen to me, my lord."

"Then she will listen to me."

Kristina shook her head vigorously. "Nay, my lord, please do not. If you do, she will know I have told you. And I must live with her."

Creed understood. Though he felt nothing but irritation at the moment for what Lady Julia had done, he nonetheless forced a smile for Kristina's sake. She was a good girl and tried to do the right thing.

"As you say, my lady," he said quietly. "And thank you for telling me the truth."

Kristina bobbed a curtsy and fled, her blond hair wagging in the breeze as she walked briskly in the direction of the keep. Creed's gaze lingered on her a moment before he made his way back up the steps to the chapel. Putting his ear against the door, he could hear sniffling.

He did the only thing he could do. He went for Ryton.

CHAPTER EIGHT

"Damn that girl," Ryton snarled as he pushed past his brother. "If I am not saddled enough with Jory's antics, I have to also deal with a spoiled girl who cannot keep her mouth shut."

Ryton had been seated at the worn table in the knight's quarters, enjoying his first quiet meal in days. With his brother's appearance and subsequent request, he found he'd lost his appetite. In the bright sun of the bailey, he paused long enough for Creed to catch up to him.

"What have you done to Jory and Julia in a past life that they would seek to make you so miserable?" he half-demanded, half-wondered. "Why on earth would she tell Lady Carington about the rumors?"

Creed sighed heavily; he had wished in the past that he'd never accepted the assignment to escort young Isabella to England, but now more than ever, he wished he had run at the first suggestion of such a mission. It was returning to haunt him in more ways than he could comprehend.

"You know why," he said in a low voice. "She is not above such irresponsible behavior."

Ryton nodded his head sharply; aye, he knew why. "That girl has had eyes for you for the past six months. Can she not get it through her thick skull that you are not the least bit interested in her?"

"Apparently not."

"So now I must undo her viciousness." Ryton turned the corner for the stairs that led up to the chapel. "Well? Have you even tried to talk to her?"

Creed cast him a long glance. "Of course I have. She will not talk to me. As I told you, I suspect the only person who has a moderate chance of reasoning with her is you. And I would suspect she wants someone else to be her shadow from now on. I do not think she wants anything more to do with me."

There was something in his tone that made Ryton look at him. His dusky blue eyes studied his brother a moment. "What is her opinion to you?"

Creed met his brother's gaze, suspecting that there must have been too much regret in his tone. He'd tried to keep it from the conversation. "Nothing, except she and I must cohabitate here at Prudhoe together for an unknown duration. I had built a trust with her. I am sorry to lose it, considering I worked hard to achieve it."

Ryton's gaze lingered on him a moment longer. As they mounted the top of the steps near the old oak door, he focused on his brother. "True enough," he replied. "You are the only one who can handle her. If not you, then I must assign Burle and I told you my fears of him before. He will not be firm enough with her, not in the least."

Creed had nothing more to say to that. With an impatient sigh, Ryton moved towards the door as Creed hung back. Ryton knocked softly on the old wood.

"My lady?" he called. "It is Sir Ryton. I would like for you to open this door. I must speak with you."

There was a long pause during which time Ryton knocked again. When they heard her voice, it was muffled and dull.

"What do ye wish, Sir Ryton?"

Ryton was trying to bank his irritation, knowing he must deal with the lady calmly. He rattled the latch; it was still locked. "My lady, Lord Richard and his wife will be in need of their chapel shortly. They pray three times a day and their nooning prayer is fast approaching. You may not commandeer the chapel any longer. You must unlock the door."

There was another long pause. "Sir Ryton, if I unlock this door, I would have yer oath that Sir Creed is not with ye."

Ryton glanced at his brother, who was already descending the stairs. "He is not with me, my lady," he said after a moment, allowing Creed enough time to put distance between them. "Would you open the door now, please?"

The lock slowly unlatched. Ryton stood back as Carington pulled the door open, her red-rimmed eyes peering up at him. He remained impassive as they studied one another.

"Now," he said quietly. "What is the meaning of the locked door? You frightened Sir Creed with this behavior. He thought something was quite wrong."

The door opened wider and she stepped out into the sun. She brushed a stray lock from her face, her eyes never leaving Ryton's face.

"I would ask ye a question, Sir Ryton, and I would have an honest answer," she said.

"You have my vow."

Her lovely face was pale, her eyes still moist from crying. But he saw her take a deep breath and a spark ignited in the emerald eyes. It put him on his guard.

"What kind of man is it that ye've saddled me with?" she demanded quietly.

He lifted an eyebrow at her tone. "What do you mean?"

"Exactly that," she hissed, gaining steam. "Lady Julia told me of Sir Creed and his... his lust for the child queen. She says everyone knows of it. She said that Sir Creed begot Isabella with child and that the whole of England knows it. Is this the kind of man ye would have protect me? A man who would prey upon innocent young maidens?"

It was difficult for Ryton to stay neutral. "Lady," he said slowly. "You seem to be quite willing to throw about accusations without seeking the truth of the matter. Would you truly be so foolish as to believe everything Lady Julia tells you?"

Some of Carington's fire banked, but not entirely. Ryton had a point but she was not yet willing to concede. "Then I would ask ye the truth," she said. "However, being his brother, it is natural that ye would defend him, is it not?"

"Then who would you hear it from that you would believe?"

She was guarded, hesitant. In truth, she was not sure. Everyone at Prudhoe would defend Creed, she suspected, except for Lady Julia and perhaps that lout Jory. Everyone had their opinion and their side to take. She began to cool.

"Who would be honest with me?" she asked.

Ryton was steady. "I would, brother or no. As Captain of the Guard, it is my duty to be fair and honest with all despite family ties."

Carington regarded him a moment. He had always tried to be fair with her, if she thought on it. No matter how she had behaved since they'd met, he had always tried to be even-handed and truthful. He had never been cruel. Sweet Jesus, how she wanted to believe the man if he countered everything Julia had told her about his brother.

"Tell me, then," she whispered. "And tell me the truth."

For a split second, Ryton heard the same tone in her voice that he had heard earlier in Creed's. There was a wistfulness that was difficult to put his finger on. An inkling of an idea formed in his mind but he quickly chased it away. He had not the time to gracefully or rationally deal with it.

"Six months ago, my brother was in the service of the king," he said in a low voice. "The king regarded him very well. So well, in fact, that he sent him as the head of a group of knights to escort the king's bride from France. As always, Creed performed his duties flawlessly. But the child bride of the king took a liking to my brother and sought to make him a conquest. When he refused, she was grievously insulted and sought to destroy him. She accused him of hideous things. But I can assure you, lady, that my brother is completely innocent of all slander charged against him. He is an honorable, trustworthy man and a fine knight. I would not have him in my service if he was otherwise and I certainly would not have assigned him to guard you."

Carington gazed back at Ryton, her expression open with astonishment. "The queen tried to seduce him?"

"Aye."

"But... but why?"

Ryton smiled wryly. "She saw something she wanted. When she could not have him, she made sure to ruin him."

Carington savored the information, digested it, before

allowing herself to form a reply. As she spoke, her head wagged back and forth, slowly. "I've heard tale of Sassenach women of royal blood, how they lack of scruples and morals. I thought it was talk. Most of my countrymen hate the English and the French as well. Can it be that they were right?"

Ryton nodded faintly. "With rare exception."

She was reluctant to give in so easily, still. "Do ye swear what ye have told me is the truth about yer brother?"

"I swear on my mother's grave, my lady. I would not lie to you about something like this, not even to save my brother."

A dark eyebrow lifted. "Then Julia lied to me."

"She was repeating what she had heard. She did not make it up if that is what you mean."

"But why would she do this?"

Ryton looked moderately uneasy; his gaze shifted from Carington to the chapel door behind her to finally his feet.

"Because she is fond of Creed," he said quietly. "She is, in fact, in love with him. He does not return her adoration and for the same reason Isabella slandered him, Julia is also vengeful. Perhaps she is threatened by your beauty and by the fact that Creed has been assigned to act as your protector. In any case, ask me no more."

Carington understood a great deal in that grunted reply, her emerald eyes moving past Ryton and to the ward below. She could see a few servants and soldiers milling about. It suddenly occurred to her that she had believed that slanderous talk before asking Creed his side of the story. He had been honest, protective and forthright since she had met him. She had been difficult, angry and combative. Julia was a snake; she had sensed it from the first. Why she had believed the woman's tale was a mystery. Now she felt like a fool.

With a heavy sigh, she wiped a stray bit of hair from her face and gathered her skirt to take the steps.

"Then it would seem I have some apologies to make to yer brother," she said softly, taking the stairs.

Ryton took her by the elbow, chivalrously, simply to make

sure she kept her footing on the narrow stairs.

"I am sure no apologies are necessary, my lady," he said. "But to ensure your comfort, I shall assign you another escort while you are here at Prudhoe."

She stopped half way down, her emerald eyes snapping to him. "Another es…?" she stopped herself before she sounded too outraged, struggling to remain collected. "That will be unnecessary, Sir Ryton. Sir Creed and I have gotten used to one another. I dunna want to break in another shadow."

He heard that tone again. The same wistfulness he had heard before no matter how hard she tried to conceal it. Now he was sure he was not imagining things but, for lack of a better response at the moment, he simply nodded his head.

"Very well, my lady," he replied.

They reached the bottom of the steps and headed into the bailey. The moment they turned for the keep, they could see Creed in conversation with Stanton over by the gatehouse. Stanton was still mounted on his impatient charger and Creed kept side-stepping the animal. Ryton came to a stop.

"Wait here, my lady," he bade her.

Carington watched him walk towards his brother, watching further as Creed and Stanton turned to him. Ryton spoke a few words to Creed, who nodded his head and headed towards Carington, alone.

As Carington watched him cross the dusty ward in her direction, she was aware of the butterflies in her stomach. Her breathing was coming in strange little gasps the closer he came. All she could focus on was his eyes; he had the most amazing eyes. The lightning bolts were flaring again, shooting giddy warmth deep into her heart. Before she realized it, Creed was standing in front of her.

"Is everything well now, my lady?" he asked softly.

She tried to remain dignified but the moment she heard his voice, she crumbled. "I am so sorry," she whispered miserably. "I shouldna… Julia told me things and I… well, I shouldna have listened to her and I am sorry. Can ye ever forgive me for being so foolish?"

Creed just looked at her. After a moment, he extended his elbow to her. Carington looked at it, then back to him, watching a beautiful smile spread across his lips. It was enough to undo her and she clutched his arm tightly.

"There is nothing to forgive, my lady," he murmured. "Are you ready to go to town now?"

She had almost forgotten about their trip. "Do ye still want to take me?" she asked, surprised.

He slanted her a glance. "Of course. Why not?"

Her lovely brows drew together. "Why not? Because I have been such an imbecile. Why would ye want to have anything to do with me now?"

He paused and turned to her, a smile playing on his lips. "Because I rather like imbeciles; especially beautiful ones." When she blushed madly, his smile broadened and his voice lowered. "Come along, Cari. We have many wonderful things to purchase for you."

She was having a difficult time looking at him; his smile made her go weak in the knees. "Oh, Creed," she sighed. "Ye are too good to me."

"I know."

Stanton, Burle and Ryton could hear her hissing insults at him. They could also hear Creed's low laughter, even when she pinched him.

***

It was a big escort for a little lady; three massive knights and twenty men at arms swooped into the town named after the castle. The berg of Prudhoe was a fairly large metropolis that was populated with almost as many Scots as English. It was a true border town that had persevered through generations of conflict.

Creed knew that there was a seamstress located on the second avenue of merchants, next to the main thoroughfare. It was a woman from the Teutonic region who did a good deal of sewing for Lady Anne. He took the entire party to the woman's shop, clogging up the avenue with men and horses. As the dust kicked up with their cluttered presence, Creed dismounted his charger and moved to the small carriage that contained Carington.

She was practically hanging out of the window, inspecting her surroundings with some fear but mostly awe. Creed opened the cab door and held out a hand to her. He did not have a chance to say a word before she was bubbling over with excitement.

"'Tis such a big town," she exclaimed softly as she put her hand in his. "I dinna know it would be so big. I saw a few Scots when we entered; did ye see them, English? They wore Douglas tartan. My da has been allied with the Douglas clan for many years. They married one of his sisters."

She was prattling. Creed fought off a smile as he tucked her hand into the crook of his elbow and took her to the seamstress' shop. Even then, she continued to chatter like a magpie.

"Do ye suppose they know of my da's alliance with Lord Richard?" she suddenly noticed the shop before he could answer. "Look at all of the fabric; I have never seen fabric like this before."

He directed her into the crowded, dark hut. It was made from stone with only a couple of very small windows for light and ventilation. And it was stuffed to the rafters with fabrics and notions. Carington looked around in awe, tripping on her own feet because she was not paying attention to where she was going. Creed steadied her as a small, round woman approached from the rear of the shop.

The woman snapped herself in half in a brusque bow. Carington instinctively recoiled with equal swiftness because the gesture had been so abrupt. The corner of Creed's mouth twitched as Carington scowled at the woman as if the salute had been something challenging.

"My lord," the woman said in a heavy Teutonic accent. "To what do I owe the honor?"

Creed knew the woman vaguely; they recognized each other from the times he had escorted Anne and Richard into town. The woman was Anne's favorite seamstress. He indicated Carington.

"Lady Anne would like to commission several gowns for her honored guest, the Lady Carington," he replied. "I have been asked to engage your services."

The woman turned her pale blue eyes to Carington appraisingly. Her gaze moved to the old garment she wore, perhaps noting the deteriorated condition. There was distain in her expression, quickly gone. Carington felt self-conscious as the woman mentally dissected her.

"Such a lovely lady," the woman said after a moment. "I could make garments for her that would outshine the sun. She would look magnificent."

"Which is why Lady Anne would entrust this task to you," Creed replied. "Do what you must in order to accomplish it. Meanwhile, Lady Anne was hoping you would have a few garments that were already made that we could take with us until the commissioned garments were completed."

The woman reached out and took Carington gently by the arm. She continued to scrutinize her, turning her around so she could see the width of her buttocks and the breadth of her torso. Carington's emerald eyes fixed on Creed as the woman very nearly manhandled her. Creed gazed back steadily, reassuringly. When the woman put her hands on Carington's waist to measure it, Carington tensed and balled up a fist. She felt the woman was becoming a bit too familiar with her. But Creed shook his head at her and she reluctantly relaxed. She relaxed further when he winked at her.

Finished with her measurements, the woman spoke. "I have three or four garments that I will prepare for you to take with you today," she said. "How many gowns did Lady Anne wish to commission?"

Creed crossed his massive arms and braced his legs apart thoughtfully. "At least five. You will include undergarments and accessories, of course."

"Of course," the woman agreed. "Any preference in color or fabric?"

Creed's eyes found Carington's; he gazed into the emerald depths, feeling an odd liquid warmth spread across his chest. It was a delightful, unfamiliar sensation. The longer he gazed at her, the stronger the feeling became.

"Rich colors," he told the woman, realizing he sounded gentle as he said it. He could not help it. "As you said, she is a beautiful woman. I will trust you to enhance that beauty."

Carington smiled at him, her eyes riveted to his dusky blue orbs. She could feel her cheeks flushing as the intensity of his eyes reached out to grab her. There was an incredibly strong pull between them, something that she had noticed from the beginning of their association but had fought desperately to suppress. Within the past couple of days, her resistance to it had fled entirely. The sweet looks, the stolen kisses, his kindness to her even when she had been horrid had worked their magic. And whatever misunderstanding had occurred back at Prudhoe Castle had somehow strengthened what she was feeling for the man; she knew that she indeed felt something. She just was not sure what it was yet.

As the two of them gazed steadily at each other, the woman ran her hands across Carington's shoulders one last time before finally releasing her.

"Give me an hour and I shall have something prepared for her," she said.

Creed nodded his thanks and took Carington by the arm, gently escorting her to the door. Once outside in the cool sunshine, she turned to him.

"What do we do for an hour?" she asked as she looked at him, shading her eyes from the sun.

His gaze was steady upon her, his handsome face framed by the lifted visor and mail hauberk. He put his hands on his hips.

"I am sure we can find something."

"Like what?"

By this time, Burle and Stanton had come to stand next to them. Burle was smiling at the lady while Stanton looked curiously between the four of them. But Creed only had eyes for

Carington.

"More shopping, perhaps?" he suggested. "There is a merchant on the street behind us that carries all manner of goods from around the world. He has many mysterious things in his shop."

Carington's emerald eyes brightened. "He does? Can we go and see?"

He held out his elbow to her and she took it gladly. As they began to walk down the street, Burle and Stanton followed. The rest of the escort was not far behind. A breeze blew gently, scattering leaves in their path as they proceeded down the wide dirt avenue. It also carried cooking smells and Carington sniffed the air, looking around to see where the delightful smells were coming from. Creed noticed her distraction and realized what she was looking for; he smelled it, too.

They ended up at the food stall of a man selling roast pork and delectable little cakes with a filling of custard. Not usually a hearty eater, Carington gorged herself on the succulent pork and ate at least four of the little cakes with the custard. Creed did not eat anything but Burle and Stanton did; they, too, stuffed themselves on the pork. Creed was more interested in watching Carington eat as he had never seen her eat before; realizing she had eaten very little on their trip to Prudhoe, it was good to see her appetite return. Thoughts of the roasted horse aside, thank goodness, she seemed quite content licking the grease off her fingers and sucking the custard out of the cake.

But there was a negative side to all of the unrestrained eating. She was mid-way through her fifth custard cake when she suddenly stopped chewing, burped most unladylike, and set the cake aside. Creed noticed that she looked a little pale.

"What is wrong?" he cocked his head. "Do not tell me that you have finally eaten your fill?"

He was teasing her gently but she was in no mood for it. She burped again, covering her mouth and looking at him apologetically.

"I dunna feel very well," she said, embarrassed.

He fought off a grin. "I am not surprised with the amount of food you put away."

"But I was hungry," she looked at the cake as if she wished she could finish it. "I have never had treats such as this. They were delicious."

"There will be ample opportunity to have more."

She burped again, only this time she covered her mouth discreetly. Creed grinned at her.

"So," his gaze moved out over the avenue. "Where would you like to go now, my lady? Shall we find an apothecary and purchase something to soothe your over-taxed stomach?"

She scowled at him although it was without force. "Ye're not funny in the least, Creed de Reyne."

"Aye, I am. And there is a name for people like you."

Her scowl grew more forceful. "And what is that?"

"I believe they are called gluttons."

This time, she shook a fist at him. "When I am feeling better, ye're going to regret yer words."

"I apologize, then. I take it all back."

"'Tis too late; ye're a marked man."

He laughed then. "God help me," he sobered, his dusky blue eyes glimmering at her. "I will make it up to you. Shall we proceed to the shop I told you of earlier?"

"Not now," she shook her head, putting her hand on her belly. "I would like to sit down if ye dunna mind."

With a snort, he took her hand and led her back to the carriage. He put his hands on her slender waist to lift her up, but she groaned and batted at his hands. He stood back, smirking, as she climbed in slowly by herself and sat down with a heavy sigh.

"I do hope you feel better," he said quietly.

She rubbed her belly. "Can we bring some of those custard cakes back with us?"

His eyebrows lifted. "Are you serious? You are about to explode as it is."

"But I will be fine by the evening meal. Please?"

He gazed at her a moment before nodding his head in resignation. "As you wish."

"Thanks to ye."

With a wink, he headed back in the direction of the food vendor. Burle and Stanton were still there, shoving down the last of their custard cakes. Creed ordered the cakes from the vendor, adding a measure of pork for himself. All of the eating around him had succeeding in making him hungry. By the time the vendor brought his food, Burle and Stanton had finished and the three of them stood around talking quietly while Creed devoured a massive portion of pork. Just as he neared the end of his meal, Stanton's pale gaze suddenly fixated on something behind Creed and he saw the knight move for his broadsword.

It was an instinctive reaction that they all go for their weapons. Creed had his broadsword unsheathed before he turned around, preparing to defend himself. His gaze fell upon several knights about a dozen yards away. They were mingling with the crowd of shoppers, men dressed in armor and weapons and looking out of place. After a split second of uncertainty, Creed sheathed his sword and turned back to his food.

"Hexham," he said. "Those are de Rochefort's men."

Burle squinted at the bodies in the distance, also putting away his sword. Stanton, however, stood there with his sword in hand as he studied the heavily armed men.

"I have not seen Galen Burleson in months," he finally said, being the last to sheath his sword. "The last time I was in town, I heard that Hexham Castle was going through something of an upheaval. They lost their captain to Newcastle and several men followed him."

The knights from Hexham had spotted the men from Prudhoe; at least four were making their way towards them. Creed picked up what was left of his pork and shoved it into his mouth just as the men from Hexham joined them. Greetings went all around as the men began ordering pork and ale. One man even scavenged Carington's half-eaten custard cake. What had been a quiet meal suddenly turned into a loud party.

Galen Burleson was a knight from Hexham, now captain of their guard. He and Creed had known each other for years and

Creed considered the man a friend. Galen was a big man with black hair and light brown eyes. He was quite handsome and had been known to have his share of women until he married a few years ago. Now he had a lovely wife and three very small boys. Galen greeted Creed with a weary smile.

"De Reyne," he nodded. "It has been a long time."

Creed nodded his head as he downed the last of his ale. "Where have you been hiding yourself?"

Galen shrugged as the vendor brought him a wooden cup of ale. "At Hexham watching my sons grow," he said, taking a healthy swig of ale. "My oldest has seen four years."

"Already? It seems as if he was just born last week."

"Four years ago this past April," Galen nodded and leaned against the table. "He likes to torment his younger brothers. In fact, my boys remind me a good deal of you and your brothers."

That statement brought a smile to Creed's lips. "I am afraid to ask why."

Galen snorted. "Because my oldest is much like Ryton; he is stable and wise. My middle son is much like you; he is the largest and not quite three years old. And my youngest is the wild man in the group. He reminds me a good deal of Lenox. He likes to run around the bailey and scare the horses."

Creed shook his head, smiling as he scratched beneath his hauberk. "Then curb him before he grows too old. Lenox became uncontrollable by the time he was a young man."

"Lenox was hilarious and you know it."

Creed conceded with a smile, reflecting on his younger brother. "I miss him."

"We all do. He was my friend."

Creed lingered on Lenox a moment. Galen and Lenox had, in fact, been the best of friends, so Galen's assertion was an understatement. It was still painful for the man to talk about it. It was painful for all of them.

"What brings you to Prudhoe?" Creed shifted the subject.

Galen scratched his chin. "Summoning a priest."

"What for?"

"Lady de Rochefort's mother. She is dying."

"Lady de Rochefort's mother has been dying for ten years."

Galen wriggled his eyebrows in agreement. "So what brings you into town?"

Creed thought of Carington back in the carriage; instinctively, he glanced over his shoulder at the cab in the distance.

"An errand for Lady Anne," he replied vaguely.

"What kind of errand?" Galen scowled. "Do not tell me that she has you running circles for those two little beasts she harbors in her bosom?"

Creed gave him a lop-sided smile. "Nay."

Galen made a face. "She once asked me to bring my sons to Prudhoe so that Gilbert and Edward would have someone to play with. Do you recall? I had to think of a plausible excuse why they could not come without offending her."

Creed's grin broadened. "I remember. You told her the boys had some kind of pox."

Galen snorted into his cup. "Naturally, she did not want her boys to catch whatever my children had, so I was granted a reprieve." He sobered. "I have no idea how I am going to decline should she ask me again. I will have to tell her that I have sold my boys into slavery and we will never see them again."

"She will not believe you."

"I know." Galen's lips pressed into a flat line of disgust as he thought of Edward and Gilbert d'Umfraville. He noticed that Creed was toying with his empty ale cup as if distracted. It was unlike the man to fidget and his interest grew. "What kind of errand are you on?"

Creed glanced at him, thinking of an evasive answer before deciding to tell him the truth. The man was an ally of Prudhoe, after all, and would find out eventually. "We have a hostage," he said. "I have been instructed to provide gifts for the woman."

Galen's eyebrows lifted. "A hostage?" he repeated. "Who?"

"A daughter of Kerr."

Galen's warm expression faded. "How did this come about?"

"Lord Richard negotiated with the woman's father for peace.

This was the offering."

"Does Lord de Rochefort know that Richard negotiated for a hostage?"

"If he does not now he will shortly," Creed could see that Galen was bordering on hostility. "Galen, he did it for the benefit of all of us. I personally do not want to lose another brother in the battle against the clans. I realize that this woman represents everything we have learned to hate, but if this is the way to achieve peace, then I will take it."

Galen held his gaze a moment longer before reluctantly submitting. He averted his gaze and moved back to his ale. "I am not questioning Richard's motives," he replied. "It… it was simply a surprise, 'tis all. We have heard nothing about a hostage."

"That is because she only came to Prudhoe yesterday."

"A savage Scots in your midst, eh?"

"I think you would be surprised."

Galen thought on that a moment, downed the last of his ale and slammed the cup on the table. "If she can bring peace to our world, then I support her presence. God knows, I want peace for my boys. I do not want them to grow up in a world that is constantly at war. I am weary of it as well."

"You used to be quite eager to kill Scots."

"That was before I was married. I would rather live long enough to see my sons grow up."

Creed did not say anything for a moment. Then he gestured to his friend. "Come with me."

"Where?"

"To meet the savage in our midst."

With a curious expression, Galen followed Creed back to the cab that was parked under a grove of young oaks. He wait several feet away as Creed went to the carriage and peered in through the door window.

Carington was lying across the bench, her eyes closed. Creed hissed at her. "My lady?" he whispered, then more loudly: "Carington? Are you awake?"

Her eyes fluttered open and she sat up too quickly; her dark hair ended up hanging across her face. She blew it away from her lips and wiped it from her wide eyes.

"What is it?" she sounded sleepy. "Is something wrong?"

Creed suppressed a grin; she was half-awake and disoriented. He stuck his head into the cab. "Compose yourself," he whispered. "I would like you to meet someone."

She blinked her eyes, looking at him curiously. Smoothing her hair, she moved to get out of the cab. Creed opened the door and held out a hand, helping her to disembark.

Carington's eyes fixed on the unfamiliar knight with the light brown eyes. He was tall and handsome, looking at her with some suspicion. She could see it in his face. Creed tucked her small hand into the crook of his arm, almost possessively. Carington instinctively moved closer to him, somewhat wary of the enemy knight.

"My lady," Creed said. "This is Sir Galen Burleson, a knight at neighboring Hexham Castle. Galen, this is the Lady Carington Kerr. She is a guest at Prudhoe."

Galen's gaze drifted over her; as most did when beholding Carington for the first time, he could not help but notice her heavenly figure. She was petite, with dark green eyes and black hair. She was, in fact, extremely beautiful. Galen dipped his head in her direction.

"My lady," he greeted evenly. "Welcome to England."

Carington looked at Creed before replying. "'Tis a pleasure to meet ye, Sir Galen."

"I trust you had a pleasant trip?"

She thought a moment about her trip from Wether Fair; the long days, the death of Bress. She could not muster the strength for a fabricated reply.

"It was not worth remembering, m'lord."

Galen glanced at Creed at her strange answer. "I hope you have at least found English hospitality to be warm."

"Warm enough," Carington looked at Creed. "Sir Creed has been very kind."

Galen grinned faintly as he also looked at Creed. "That is

because Creed is a man of astonishing patience and amiability," he replied, his gaze moving back to Carington. "Then I will wish you a good stay at Prudhoe, my lady. Perhaps our paths will cross again someday."

With a lingering glance at the petite Scots, he turned away and went back to his ale and pork. Carington watched him go, turning to Creed only to notice that he was gazing intently at her. She smiled timidly.

"Why do ye look at me so?" she asked.

His gaze lingered on her for a few moments longer before answering. "Because you are the most beautiful woman I have ever seen. Is that not reason enough?"

She flushed furiously and lowered her eyes, too overwhelmed for a snappy reply. In fact, it was the first time he had so openly complimented her. Any other time that he had come close to praising her, she had to practically drag it out of him.

Creed's eyes twinkled at her discomfort. He patted the hand that was still on his elbow. "Let us go and see if your garments are ready," he took pity on her. "I think enough time has passed."

The change of subject was welcome and she nodded, happily accompanying him across the dirt avenue. But they did not quite make it to the seamstress' shop before a knight and ten men at arms suddenly rounded the corner of the avenue and charged straight for them.

It was loud and startling; dust flew into the air and horses snorted. Creed was not particularly worried because Burle, Stanton, Galen and the three other Hexham knights were only a dozen or so feet away. They were close enough and armed enough should any hostilities begin. But it took Creed a moment to realize that the intruding knight was Ryton and oddly enough, only then did his guard go up. There was no reason why his brother should be here unless something unpleasant had occurred. He did not even want to guess.

He left Carington standing a few feet away as he walked up to his brother, who had now come to a halt. The horse danced around and Creed cuffed it in the neck when the beast came too close to him.

"What is wrong?" he asked his brother before the man could speak.

Ryton flipped up his visor, his dusky blue eyes focusing on Creed. "You must return immediately," he lowered his voice before his brother could press him. "A papal representative is at Prudhoe. He wants to speak with you."

Creed just stared at him. "What?" he asked, dumbfounded.

"No questions, Creed. Just come."

Creed, in fact, did not have to ask any more questions; he already knew the answers. God help him, he knew. He met his brother's gaze and silent words of confirmation passed between them; so the rumors Jory told us of were true. Creed's stomach tightened with anxiety but he managed to maintain his composure. He merely nodded his head and turned to Burle.

"Take the lady in hand, de Tarquinus," he told the big blond knight. "I am required back at Prudhoe."

Much to her credit, Carington did not call out to him or demand to know why he was leaving her. She simply stood there and watched as he moved to collect his charger, mounted, and galloped off with his brother. Even when Burle and Stanton joined her and gently took her in the direction of the seamstress, she did not ask questions and she did not utter a sound. Something in the expression on Creed's face told her it was better if she did not.

***

His name was Massimo. He was not English; he was straight from the heart of Rome where the pope had appointed him a special papal legate to London. His superior was the Bishop of London but he answered directly to Rome. He was surprisingly young and well-spoken, but beneath the youth and tact lay the heart of a hunter. Massimo was on a hunt on behalf of the church and he would have his answers.

Creed sensed that from the onset. Father Massimo was in the

small solar of Prudhoe where Lady Anne had settled him. Upon his return to the castle, Creed was directed into the solar by his brother and the door was shut behind him. Alone with the priest, Creed stood by the door with his legs braced apart and his arms folded. All that he had been trying to forget over the past six months was swamping him again like an unwelcome tide and he was growing uncharacteristically furious; furious at the girl-queen, furious at the king and furious that the circumstance had happened in the first place. He was holding a particular hate for the church at the moment for stirring up the bad memories.

Massimo was polite as he introduced himself and asked Creed to sit. The knight did so reluctantly, perching himself on the edge of Richard's great oak chair because it was the only one in the room that could handle his bulk.

The priest watched him sit stiffly, noting the air about the man. He was extremely big and obviously unhappy. Massimo had been involved in the dealings with the queen's pregnancy for almost five weeks now and the name Creed de Reyne had come up again and again. He felt as if he knew the man personally and was not surprised to be met with such resentment. He knew the history of the case. Furthermore, it had taken some wrangling to track the man down because he had been taken from London and hidden by some powerful friends. But Massimo had a job to do and he feared the wrath of God more than the wrath of the knight. He moved straight to the point.

"I have come on the church's business," the priest began. "It would seem that there are matters concerning the queen that must be clarified. I am told you are a man who can give me answers."

Creed looked at him, his jaw ticking furiously. "What answers would those be, my lord?"

Massimo could already tell that this was not going to be a simple thing. The big knight was noticeably hostile. He folded his hands and lowered his voice.

"I am under no false delusions that you do not know why I am here," he said quietly. "Surely you knew this time would come.

Sooner or later, it had to."

"Make yourself clear, my lord."

"Very well," the priest cleared his throat softly. "Six months ago, you led the escort that brought Isabella of Angoulệme to England's shores. She was, at the time, unmarried to the king. That occurred two months later. It is a fact that the queen is now six months pregnant, which means that she conceived before her marriage to the king. Now, you must understand that I am not here on behalf of the king. It is well known that you were rumored to have had an affair with the queen and fled London to escape the king's wrath. I am here on behalf of the church that would ensure the child the queen carries is of royal blood. Only a royal must ascend the throne and I must know the truth, Sir Creed. I must know what happened between you and the queen as it pertains to her pregnancy."

Creed's gaze was steady. "Who told you to seek me out?"

"All of London knows the rumors regarding you and the queen."

"Who told you?"

"It does not matter. Suffice it to say that the rumor was confirmed by several different sources."

"I would know who told you."

Massimo sighed. "Does it matter?"

"It does. It is my right to know."

"Then the queen herself told me."

It was Creed's turn to sigh. But his gaze never left the priest. "What, exactly, did she tell you?"

"That you seduced her and begot her with child."

"So she told you that the child was mine?"

"She did. From her own lips, she did."

Creed was not particularly surprised but he was growing increasingly angry. It was becoming a struggle for him to keep his normally-dormant temper down. He leaned forward in the chair, resting his elbows on his knees as he mulled over the priest's words. After a moment, he simply lifted his massive shoulders.

"It would do no good for me to refute her," he said. "It would be my word against hers and we clearly know who would be believed. Even if she is a lying, petty, spoiled child, by the respect due her royal blood, she will be believed in all things."

The priest shook his head. "Not necessarily."

Creed gave the man a disbelieving look. "Would it do any good for me to tell you that it is a well-known fact that Isabella has not been a virgin since she was a child?" his eyebrows lifted in emphasis. "As you so callously claim that everyone knows of the rumors regarding my association with her, can you also deny the rumors that Isabella has seduced as many men as the king has seduced women? She lists her own uncle as a conquest, for God's sake. Everyone in France is aware of it and her adulterous ways are common knowledge. When I escorted her to London, know that she set her sights on me nearly the moment we were introduced. When I refused her, she flew into a rage and told anyone who would listen that I raped her. She was a little girl spurned, my lord, and nothing more. Now that she is pregnant with what I can only assume is another man's child, she would seek to focus the blame away from her and onto me. She seeks to destroy me for no other reason than that."

By this time, the priest was watching him intently. "Then you deny these allegations."

"With all my heart."

"You will burn in hell for lying to me, Sir Creed. Now tell me again; do you deny these allegations?"

"With my immortal soul at stake, I most certainly do."

The priest gazed steadily at him as if trying to wordlessly persuade him into changing his story. Surely he had enough power behind him to do just that. But Creed held his gaze steady, the dusky blue eyes pure with truth and honor. Massimo eventually lowered his gaze, rising from the small chair he was seated in.

"I do, in fact, know a little about you," he said as he neared the hearth. "It is my duty to educate myself whilst conducting tasks for the church. I know that you served Northumberland flawlessly for many years before going into the service of the king. I did, in fact, speak with most of the knights who accompanied you on your mission to escort Isabella from France."

Creed watched the man pace. "And?"

Massimo paused to look at him. "They have all told me the exact same thing you did," he began to pace again. "Your friends are very loyal. In fact, their criticism of the queen was far stronger than your own. From them I learned that you conducted yourself with dignity and honor, even when she threw temper tantrums and hit you."

Creed just looked at the man. Massimo studied the strong face of the knight before him, pacing thoughtfully around the room as he pondered.

"It would seem, Sir Knight, that the queen has a vendetta against you for spurning her advances," he said as he watched his feet. "But that does not erase the face that she is pregnant with what is presumably not the king's child. The king himself says he did not touch her until their wedding night."

Creed just shook his head and looked at his hands. Massimo paused a few feet away, watching the man's body language.

"You disagree?" he asked quietly.

Creed cast him a long look. "Do you want the truth, my lord?"

"Of course."

Creed sighed heavily and sat back against the chair. "The night we delivered Isabella to the king, he took her into his chamber and we could clearly hear the sounds of lovemaking. It was brutal and loud and she screamed the entire way through it. So, in answer to your question, I strongly disagree with the king's statement. It is simply not true."

Massimo cocked a thoughtful eyebrow. "Your fellow escort party told me the same."

Creed just shook his head and looked to his hands again. "The king's word is law," he muttered. "They can blame this on me all they wish. It simply isn't true."

Massimo watched him a moment before pulling up a chair beside him. He watched Creed's lowered face carefully, feeling some empathy for the man. It was a vicious circumstance he found himself a part of.

"The king has a long and bitter history with the church," Massimo muttered. "One more offense from him will not matter overly. But you, however, are in a bad position."

Creed looked at the man. "Do you believe any of what I have told you?"

Massimo nodded slowly. "I believe all of it."

Creed sighed slowly, wiping a weary hand over his face. It was the first time since entering the room that his guard went down.

"So now what?" he asked a question he had been dreading for six months. "What do I do?"

The priest sat back in his chair, his eyes moving to the fire gently crackling in the hearth. "The king wants you imprisoned."

"I know."

"He does not, as far as I can deduce, know where you are, but that will not hold true forever. He will eventually find out."

"How did you find out where I was?"

"Your loyal friends told me, those who have staunchly defended your honor."

Creed looked at the man, hating that he must face the realities that were intent on following him. He simply could not believe the nightmare was deepening.

"So I will ask you again," he said. "What do I do? More specifically, what do you intend to do with me?"

Massimo scratched his unshaven chin. "I must report back to the papal legate in London," he replied. "I will tell him the truth; that I believe these allegations are untrue. In spite of what you may or may not think of the church, we do hold true to truth and justice. We reject tyranny. And we have indeed heard the rumors of Queen Isabella's infidelity. The rumors have run rampant since the day she arrived in England and we are quite certain she has had more lovers than you can count on your fingers and toes."

Creed could only shake his head in disgust. "Then why me?" he asked. "Why must she seek to destroy me if she has had so many lovers?"

Massimo smiled at him, displaying dingy teeth. "Because you were not a lover. You stood virtuous against her debauchery and she hates you for it. Had you caved into her demands, she probably would have forgotten all about you."

"I was not going to cave into her demands."

Massimo cracked a lop-sided smile. "I understand," he stood up and moved back to the desk where he had laid his things. "And in answer to your question as to what to do, I would say do nothing at the moment. I will return to London to discuss this with the papal legate and we will decide a course of action."

For the first time in almost six months, Creed felt some relief from the situation. He rose on his thick legs, facing the priest. "Is the king actively looking for me? Someone is bound to know where I am."

Massimo shook his head. "He is not as far as I am aware," he replied. "He makes a good game of threatening talk but as far as I know, he has not sent out a search party. You will continue your service here in the wilds until such time as I contact you again."

Creed's jaw ticked faintly. "Understood, my lord."

"Do not lose faith. Good always triumphs over evil."

"Aye, my lord."

The priest picked up his satchel from the desk. "Oh, I nearly forgot," he moved towards Creed with his bag in his hand. "I understand that you have been assigned to protect a hostage of Prudhoe."

Creed nodded. "A daughter of Kerr, our bitter enemy. I am her protection."

The priest shook his head. "No longer," he told him pointedly. "I do not want you involved with any young ladies until this matter is resolved. It would not be viewed, shall we say, favorably."

Creed lifted an eyebrow. "What do you mean?"

Massimo secured the ties on his bag. "You were in charge of a young lady once and the results are coming to haunt you," he lifted an eyebrow at him. "If something happens with this young lady, however innocent you may be, it will only confirm what the queen is telling everyone. It will make you appear guilty as sin. Therefore, until this situation is settled, I would refrain from any association with any woman. You do not want to take any chances."

Creed looked at him, thinking of Carington as he did so. He knew that the priest was right; God help him, he knew. The man made perfect sense. But what he was feeling for Carington was so real, so deep, that the thought of staying away from her tore at him like nothing he had ever known.

"Understood, my lord."

"Good." Massimo faced him, nodding his head to acknowledge that their business was concluded. "Now, I plan to sup here tonight and leave for London on the morrow. Perhaps you and I can come to know one another on more pleasant terms."

"I would be honored, my lord."

"Then take me to the hall and ply me with wine. I find that I am in need of it."

Creed took him into the great hall. But it was Creed who needed a heavy dose of wine, not the priest. The more he drank, the more sullen he became. It was fortunate that Ryton and Lord Richard soon joined them so that Creed did not have to pretend to be pleasant any longer. He kept staring into the fire, seeing Carington's face with every flicker of flame and wondering how she was going to react when he told her he could no longer be her shadow. He wondered how he was going to react, day after day, seeing her but not being able to be near her.

At some point, the priest begged his leave and Richard graciously consented to show him to his chamber. In truth, Lord Richard volunteered so that Ryton and Creed could spend a few moments alone to discuss the results of Creed's meeting with the priest. They were all on edge, knowing why the church had come and wondering how Creed's future was to be impacted. Richard secretly wondered if he was going to have to once again spirit Creed away under the cover of darkness so that the king could not find him.

When Richard and the priest were gone and the fire snapped

softly in the hearth, Ryton changed seats and ended up sitting across from his brother at the long, scrubbed table that had been at Prudhoe for three generations. He gazed steadily at his brother, who seemed more interested in staring into the flames.

"What did he say?" Ryton finally asked the magic question.

Creed continued to gaze into the writhing blaze a moment before speaking. "He said that the church is investigating Isabella's pregnancy. She is telling everyone that the child is mine."

Ryton hissed and poured himself a huge sloppy cup of wine, downing half of it in one swallow. "Christ," he hissed. "That little bitch. Is the king after you?"

"According to the priest, he wants me imprisoned but is apparently not making a concerted effort to find me."

"Because he knows she is lying," Ryton took another swallow. "He knows he has married a whore. That child could be anyone's."

"Anyone but me," Creed looked at him, then. "The priest believes in my innocence. He says that those he could speak to from the escort that accompanied me to France confirmed my story. He says that he is going to go back to London and discuss this with the papal legate. I am to remain here in the service of Lord Richard until such time as the priest contacts me again."

Ryton stared at him, apparently waiting for more information. When none was forthcoming, he lifted his eyebrows expectantly. "That is all?"

Creed's face darkened and he took another cup of wine. "The priest was told that I had been assigned to protect Lady Carington."

Ryton nodded. "He interviewed Lord Richard and me about you. We told him of your performance as a knight, your history and valor. Your assignment to Lady Carington came up during the course of the conversation."

"He says that I am to stay away from her. He says that I am to stay away from all women until this situation has resolved itself."

"Why?"

Creed looked at him; there was tremendous turmoil in the dusky blue eyes. "Because if something were to happen between me and Lady Carington, inappropriate or otherwise, it could be viewed as a confirmation of Isabella's stories. The priest feels that it is best if I stay clear of anything that could become controversial involving women."

Ryton puffed out his cheeks, exhaling heavily. "It makes sense," he conceded. "I will have to turn over the duty to Burle, then. God help him if she tries to run."

"She will not run."

Ryton looked at his brother, then, hearing that wistful tone once more. This time, he had the time and composure to address it. His stomach began to twist, knowing the answer to the question before he even put it forth. He was afraid to ask but knew he must.

"How do you know?" He set his cup down heavily and lowered his voice. "Christ, Creed, is there something going on between you and the lady?"

"Why do you ask?"

"Because I can hear it in your voice."

Creed held his gaze steady a moment. "Something, indeed," he confessed quietly. "Something very unexpected."

Ryton sat back in his seat, not at all sure he wanted to hear the truth. "My God," he breathed. "Please tell me that you have not compromised her."

Creed shook his head. "Nay," he murmured. "But... I would be lying if I said I did not feel something for her. I cannot describe it more than that; all I know is that she fills me as no one else ever has. She is becoming my sun, my moon and my stars. I cannot tell you how this has happened. All I know is that is has."

"I knew it," Ryton hissed, slamming his cup on the table. "When you came to tell me that she had locked herself in the chapel, I knew there was something more to it. I could hear it in your tone. Of all of my knights, you are the last one I would expect this to happen to. How could you do this?"

He was angry, which triggered Creed's well-heeled temper. He slammed his massive fists on the table, shaking the heavy furniture from end to end violently.

"Damnation, Ryton," he fired back. "This is no fickle dalliance. Have you ever known me to show interest in a woman, least of all a charge?"

"Never!" Ryton roared.

"Then trust me when I tell you that this goes much deeper than a trite rendezvous."

"Does it?" Ryton was flaming. "She was your ward. You crossed the line."

"I love her!"

The last two sentences were hotly spoken, overlapping. When Ryton heard his brother's last sentence, his eyes widened and his fury was immediately doused. Staring at his brother, wide-eyed, he plopped back down on the bench as if he suddenly lost all of his strength.

"Oh… Good Lord," he muttered. "Are you serious?"

Creed looked back at him with equal astonishment. He could hardly believe he said it, but on the other hand, he had never said anything more truthful in his life. He could not have denied it in any case.

"Aye," he sighed heavily, regaining his own seat. "I do. She may be aggressive, disobedient and uncontrollable, but she is also the sweetest, most intelligent and compassionate lady I have ever met. She makes me laugh. She makes me feel as if I am important."

"You *are* important," Ryton had no idea why he felt so ill; a mixture of delight and horror swirled in his chest. "You are the most powerful knight the realm has ever seen. The king himself recognized that until all of this madness with Isabella. You can have any woman you want but, instead, you choose a Scots. And not just any Scots; a laird's daughter, a hostage for peace. She is not meant for you, Creed. Do you not understand that?"

"She is meant for me and no other," Creed's dusky blue eyes were intense. "A marriage is a perfect way to cement an alliance with the Scots."

"A marriage?" Ryton blurted. "Do you mean to say that you intend to marry her?"

Creed really had not thought on that until he had said it. Now he could think of nothing else. "I do," he asserted. "I will go to her father and make an offer for her hand."

Ryton could not help it; he put his hands to his face as if trying to hold his brains in. He simply could not believe what he was hearing from his stoic, emotionless brother. His cup was next to him and he realized he needed more wine, but the cup did not hold enough so he drank it straight from the pitcher.

"You certainly do not make things easy for yourself, do you?" he wiped his mouth with the back of his hand. "Just what do you plan to offer?"

"My inheritance."

Ryton's eyes flew open wide. "All of it?"

Creed shrugged. "When father passes on, you and I will split the Hartlepool baronetcy," he said. "I will sell you my half for a trifle of what it is worth. Just enough to purchase a bride."

Ryton stared at him as if he could hardly comprehend was he was hearing. "Nay," he muttered. "I will not let you sell it. We will combine our money if that is what it takes, but I will not let you give up your inheritance. It belongs to you as much as me."

Their conversation fell silent as tempers calmed and they began to weigh the situation. Not only were the circumstances with the queen heating up, but with the added addition of Creed's feelings for their hostage, everything surrounding the man was growing bigger than they could comprehend. . Ryton could not help it; he drained the pitcher until it was empty.

"So now what?" he muttered, glancing to his brother. "You can no longer guard the lady. Now what do we do?"

Creed shrugged faintly. "Give the duty to Burle," he replied quietly. "I will see the lady on my own time."

"Under normal circumstances, I would have a hard enough time with that statement. But given the discussion we have just had, do you think that is entirely wise?"

"Wise or not, those are my intentions."

"Brother or not, I am still your captain."

"Do you intend to keep me from her, then?"

'"I will not let you hang yourself."

Creed cocked an eyebrow but said nothing. His attention turned back to his cup, toying with it as his mind moved over the myriad of thoughts on his mind. Ryton watched him.

"We have one final worry, you know," he said softly.

Creed looked at him. "What is that?"

"Jory," Ryton replied with some disgust in his tone. "He could cause problems. If he catches wind of a romance, he will pounce and you know it."

Creed lifted an eyebrow, tensing. "If he as much as looks in Cari's direction, I will kill him. I could not be in any more trouble than I am now."

Ryton just looked at him; then, he gave him a crooked smile. "Cari, is it?"

Creed met his gaze a moment longer before his façade cracked. He grinned sheepishly, looking back to his cup.

"Aye," he whispered. "Cari."

Further conversation was precluded by voices in the entry. Both men turned to see Stanton enter the keep followed by Burle with Carington on his arm. Ryton could not help it; he looked at his brother when the lady entered the hall and the expression that he witnessed did not surprise him. If there had been any momentary doubt in Creed's statement, it was all dashed at that moment. The man was gazing at her as if the sun, the moon and the stars had just walked into the room.

He was a man in love.

CHAPTER NINE

The surcoat was a lovely shade of gold with a hint of green in it that picked up the color of her eyes. Carington had changed in to the garment in the town so that the seamstress could alter it on her body. A few stitches here and there and it fit like a glove. A link belt of copper with gold leaf hung about her slender hips and the seamstress had taken her lovely hair and caught it up in a golden net at the nape of her neck. She looked elegant and delightful; absolutely stunning.

Carington headed back to Prudhoe with more new clothes and accessories than she had ever owned at any one time in her life. The seamstress included web-fine veils, hair combs, fragranced oils and a cake of hard white soap all the way from Castille. It smelled of flowers after a rain. Carington was delighted with her booty and very eager to show it to Creed.

Burle and Stanton had proven to be pleasant companions on the ride back to Prudhoe. It was only the second time she had been alone with them and this time the situation had been far more pleasant. Burle had quite a sense of humor whereas all Stanton wanted to speak of was his son. He did, in fact, purchase a toy dog for the boy on their way out of town, but no convincing in the world could coerce Burle into purchasing finery for his daughters. According to him, they had already put him into the poorhouse. He was just waiting for the time when husbands would take them off his hands. Then he tried to talk Stanton into a betrothal contract between his young son and Burle's youngest daughter who, at twelve years of age, was seven years older than Stanton's son. Stanton did not believe the marriage to be a good idea.

It was a pleasant trip home, far more pleasant than the trip from Scotland. Carington actually enjoyed herself. But the moment they entered the great outer bailey of Prudhoe, she saw the wagons bearing the seal of the church and was curious. Great yellow crosses decorated the banners. But that curiosity turned to confusion when she saw the expressions on Burle and Stanton's faces. They were apparently not pleased that someone from the church was in residence but she had no idea why. She was, in truth, only thinking of finding Creed and showing him her new gown.

She found him in the great hall with his brother. She pranced into the room, spinning around a few times so both Ryton and Creed could get a good look at her new clothes. With the first spin, the material clung indecently to her divine figure and all they could see was a body that was more feminine, more curvaceous, than anything either one of them had seen. Ryton lowered his gaze uncomfortably, eyeing his brother as he did so and noting that the man was riveted to her. He did not blame him, though; she was spectacular.

"What do ye think?" Carington stopped spinning long enough to propose the question to Creed. "Rita made this for a lady who never paid her for the work. It fits me perfectly. What do ye think?"

Creed tore his eyes off her figure and fixed her in the eye. He realized that he was well on his way to being drunk from all of the wine he had imbibed. Too much drink usually made him emotional and it was a struggle not to give himself away.

"Who is Rita?" he asked.

She cocked her head, looking positively adorable with the gold netting on her hair. "The seamstress; the woman who put her hands all over me."

She was waving her hands around for illustration and he nodded in understanding before the sentence was even out of her mouth.

"Of course," he said quickly. "She is correct; it fits you perfectly. You are a goddess divine."

Carington grinned happily; she had a beautiful smile, something that Ryton was only now noticing. He'd never really paid any attention before but was now seeing the lady through entirely different eyes. He'd only seen her fighting or weeping one way or the other. It was rare when she was calm, even rarer when she smiled. Looking at her at this moment, with her lovely face alight with a smile, he could hardly remember her any other way. And she had his brother positively captivated.

"She gave me three more gowns," Carington went on. "A yellow one, a pink one and a blue one with birds on it. And she gave me soap and oils, too."

Creed was smiling faintly at her. "I am pleased that you are happy."

Carington threw out her arms and twirled around again. "I canna wait to take a bath with my new soap." She suddenly came to a halt. "My da would never buy things that we could just as easily make. I have always had to make my own soap. But Rita gave me soap that has come all the way from Spain."

She made it sound as if the soap had come from the moon. Creed had never seen her so joyful; it made his heart light to watch her, far from the depression of the last several minutes. He was content to forget everything for a few minutes as he watched her dance around.

"We shall buy you soap from all over the world if it pleases you," he said softly.

Carington giggled and plopped next to him on the bench, taking the wine pitcher and realizing it was empty. Burle sat on her other side as Stanton sent a servant for more wine. Carington set the wine pitcher aside and looked around the table.

"My cakes," she looked up at Creed. "Did ye bring them back with ye?"

He realized he had forgotten about her custard cakes and shook his head. "Nay, lady, I did not," he said. "I forgot them. I am sorry."

Her face fell somewhat. "'Tis all right," she said. Then she perked up. "Perhaps we can get more when we go to pick up my other gowns?"

Creed nodded. "We can get as many as you wish."

"And more soap?"

"Do you not think you should use what you have before we purchase more?"

She looked away coyly. "I want new soap for every day of the week."

He cocked an eyebrow at her but he was still grinning. "I see," he murmured. "I suppose I shall have to begin my new career as a highway robber in order to pay for this expensive new habit."

She laughed brightly. Ryton watched the expressions between the two of them, realizing with sickening certainty that the lady felt for her brother the same way he felt for her. It was obvious. But it was further obvious that she needed to be told the change in plans, especially with the papal legate still at Prudhoe. They would need to present the picture that Creed was trying to keep himself out of trouble, at least until the man left. There was no time to waste on that account.

"Well," Ryton stood up, stretching his big body. "I have duties to attend to before the evening meal." He looked at Burle and Stanton, on either side of Creed and Carington. "Good knights, go about your duties."

It took Burle a moment to understand that Ryton was chasing them out of the hall. Stanton, however, did not comprehend the meaning until Burle reached down and grabbed him by the arm. Only then did the pale young knight rise and follow. Carington was left sitting next to Creed, watching the fire pop and smoke and thinking on her new acquisitions. Creed sat next to her, still as stone. When the room was vacated and they were finally alone, a massive hand moved to collect her small one.

She looked up at him, then, smiling into his still-mailed face. She reached up and touched his helm.

"Why are ye still wearing yer armor, English?" she took her hand away from the cold steel. "And why did ye leave me back in the town? Is something wrong?"

He sat there and looked at her, his attitude towards her shifting from that of her assigned protector to that of a man who was clearly in love with her. The line between duty and want began to shape-shift and it was difficult to stay focused. But he knew there was a great deal he needed to say to her. He could only hope that she would be receptive. Gazing into her emerald eyes, he realized that he was actually afraid to tell her, afraid she did not feel the same way. But it was a chance he was willing to take.

"That depends," he said softly, bringing her hand to his lips for a gentle kiss. "It would seem that you and I must have a conversation."

She cocked her head, tendrils of black curls brushing against her cheeks. "What about?"

He sighed, not sure where to begin. He let go of her hand and removed his helm, setting it upon the table. Then he pulled off his gauntlets, peeled back his hauberk and scratched his damp hair. The dusky blue eyes refocused on Carington.

"Earlier today, my brother told you of some trouble I have experienced with the king."

She nodded, looking rather awkward. "He did," she replied timidly. "And I told ye that I was sorry I had reacted so poorly to what Julia had told me. I acted like a...."

He shushed her softly and reclaimed her hand. "Your reaction was natural. I do not blame you for it. But it would seem that the situation my brother has told you of has taken another twist."

Carington stared at him, feeling her stomach lurch. "That canna be a good thing."

He smiled wryly. "It is not," he replied. "You saw the wagons and banners of the church when you rode in, did you not?"

She nodded fearfully. "I did. Did they come to arrest ye?"

He fought off a grin. "Nay," his grin faded as he watched her reaction to what he was about to say. "But they did come to investigate me. It would seem that the queen is pregnant and she is telling the world that the child is mine."

Carington just stared at him. She looked as if she wanted to say something but was not quite sure what to say. Creed continued in a low voice.

"The child is not mine, Cari," he murmured. "I never touched the girl. But that does not prevent her from trying to exact some measure of revenge on me for spurning her attention those months ago."

Carington seemed to snap out of whatever shock held her and she put her fingers against his lips to silence his explanation.

"I know," she assured him. "Sir Ryton told me the entire story. Ye needn't justify yerself to me."

Creed seemed to lose some of his confidence. "In a sense, I do," he ran his free hand through his hair again. "Everything has become far more complicated than it was even a day ago. To begin with, I will no longer be your shadow here at Prudhoe. That duty will be given to Burle."

That bit of information brought a strong reaction; Carington's eyes flew open wide and her mouth popped open in outrage. She shot to her feet and began waving her arms angrily.

"That is ridiculous," she snapped. "Nothing agin' Sir Burle, but I dunna want him to be my escort. Who made this absurd decision? Was it yer brother?"

He looked up at her calmly. "Why do you not want him to be your escort?"

She stopped waving her arms. "What do ye mean?"

"Just that; tell me why you do not want him."

All of the fire seemed to drain out of her as she gazed down at him. Her beautiful emerald eyes were fixed on him and her rosebud mouth worked slightly as she thought of an answer. It seemed like a struggle. Finally, she just shook her head.

"Do ye not know, English?" she whispered.

His voice was hoarse. "Tell me."

Her answer was to reach out and touch his hair, running her small fingers through the inky strands. Creed caught her hand, turning to kiss the palm as she caressed his bristly cheek.

"Because," she whispered. "I dunna want ye away from me, not even for a minute."

His eyes were closed, his mouth against the palm of her hand. "Tell me why."

She sat back down, watching him kiss her palm as if it was the most precious thing in the world. It made her heart flutter wildly, her limbs to go weak. It also loosened her tongue.

"Because I fancy ye, English," she murmured, both hands moving to his cheeks as he reached out and pulled her against his armored chest. Her emerald gaze moved across his handsome face as if memorizing each and every line. "I have never felt this way about anyone. I dunna know exactly what it means but I would suspect that it is something very strong and very wonderful."

"Strong enough to never want to be parted from me?"

"Aye," she insisted. "I will kill anyone who would try it, including yer beloved brother."

His answer was to kiss her, long and hard. But the sane portion of his mind that was not consumed with these wonderful blossoming feelings reminded him that they were in a common room for all to see and he let her go, kissing both hands before putting them back in her lap.

"You cannot know how happy you have made me," he whispered. "To hear that from your lips means more to me than you can know."

Her face was flushed with emotion. "Truly?"

He nodded. "Truly."

It was extremely difficult for him not to reach out and grab her again so he put distance between them, running a nervous hand through his hair once more. When their eyes met again, he chuckled in an edgy burst of energy and she giggled like a child. As he continued to gaze at her, his smile began to fade. There was something in his eyes that should have forewarned her of the words to come but she was too naïve to see it. Therefore, his next question was a shock.

"What would you say if I told you that I wanted to marry you?"

She stopped giggling and her eyes widened to the point of popping from her skull. As he watched, her face screwed into tears.

"Oh, English," she wept. "Why... why...?"

He went to her, concerned. "I am sorry, honey," in spite of his attempt to stay away from her, he took her hands again and kissed them gently. "I did not mean to upset you. I only meant to…."

She responded by throwing her arms around his armored neck, knocking him off balance. "Ye dinna upset me," she sobbed. "I just never thought… I dinna know ye felt that way."

He righted himself and wrapped his arms around her slender body, burying his face in the side of her head. "Of course I do," he murmured. "I cannot explain it better than that, but I do."

She wept. "But I thought… I've been so rotten since the moment we met. I've run from ye, yelled at ye and have made yer duty miserable. How can ye want to marry someone who has been so difficult?"

He laughed softly, kissing the side of her head and pulling back to look at her. "You are not difficult in the least," he winked at her, "once I figured out how to handle you."

She squeaked and wept and he laughed again, kissing her cheeks and gently shushing her. "You must cease your tears, honey," he kissed the end of her nose. "Lady Anne and Lord Richard will be here shortly and they will wonder what horrible things I have said to you to make you cry."

She sniffled and wiped her nose, struggling to stop her tears. "Will ye tell them?"

"Tell them what? You have not yet given me an answer."

She smiled through her tears, a glorious gesture that set his heart to beating wildly. "My answer is that I would be deeply honored to be yer wife," she whispered. "For always, I belong to ye."

He stroked her cheeks with his thumb, never more thrilled about anything in his entire life. "Even to be married to a Sassenach?" he pressed.

He said it with a strong burr, just the way she did, and Carington giggled. "Especially a Sassenach." She touched his face again, her hands trembling with emotion as she did so. "But why? Why me?"

"Because no one else is worthy of you."

"I am not a fine English lady."

The corner of his mouth twitched. "All of the fine English ladies in the world cannot compare with you."

She smiled, her expression hinting that she was reluctant to believe him. He bent over to kiss her again but voices at the hall entry caught their attention. Creed quickly moved a respectable distance away, eyeing the doorway as Burle suddenly bolted through it as fast as his flabby body would carry him. Creed was concerned by the look on the man's face.

"What is it?" he asked.

Burle was focused on Creed as if nothing else in the room existed. "Trouble," he said flatly. "We just received a messenger from Hexham. De Rochefort is calling for aid."

Creed grabbed his helm and gauntlets from the table top. "We just left de Rochefort's men in town."

"I know," Burle replied. "If they are not back at Hexham by now, I am sure they will be shortly."

"What did the messenger say?"

Burle looked at Carington, then, still seated at the table. "A raid," he finally said, refocusing on Creed. "Scots."

Carington bolted to her feet. "It would not be my father," she insisted strongly. "He may be petty and belligerent, but he wouldna break a bargain. He is an honorable man."

Creed plopped his helm on his head, turning to look at her as he pulled on his gauntlets. "No one is saying that it is your father, my lady," he replied evenly. "There are plenty of other clans on the border who like to rattle our cage once in a while."

He turned to follow Burle out the door but Carington ran up behind him just before he quit the hall. She grabbed him by the arm.

"Be careful, English," she dare not say more than that. Already, she felt she was saying too much should someone overhear her. "I dunna want ye returning with holes in ye."

Creed gazed down at her lovely face and felt his heart lurch strangely. He did not like the thought of leaving her and very much wanted take her in his arms. But he dare not make the move. In the bailey, the troops were shouting as they mobilized and he could hear the war horses being brought about. Before he realized it, James was beside him with additional weaponry to prepare him for battle; the lad just popped up out of nowhere. Creed glanced at his tall, blond squire.

"Get my charger," he commanded quietly. "Where is Steven?"

"Already with the horse, my lord," the lad replied. "We are awaiting you."

The young man handed him an assortment of daggers that Creed accepted and began shoving into niches in his armor. As the lad ran back to the swarming bailey, Carington watched Creed as he carefully placed the razor-sharp weapons in strategic positions on his body. Her trepidation for his safety grew. But before she could comment, he turned to her.

"Go to your chamber and bolt the door," he told her softly. "Do not leave that room for any reason. Not until I return. Do you understand?"

She nodded, her emerald eyes full of fear. To her credit, however, she said nothing about it; she simply glanced to the activity outside and forced a smile.

"Ye'd better go," she told him. "They'll not wait for ye."

Creed held her gaze for a moment, feeling as if his heart were breaking just a little. It was an odd experience, something he had never before faced. He had never gone into battle leaving someone he cared very deeply for behind. With a wink, he forced himself out into the dusky bailey.

Carington stood there and watched the troops amass. She saw Ryton astride his big Belgian charger shouting orders to the men. She watched as Creed mounted his enormous charcoal steed and began to carry out his brother's orders. They were efficient and confident, eventually joined by Burle, Stanton and Jory. As she watched the activity, she suddenly realized that someone was standing next to her. Looking over, she noticed that Kristina had joined her. The pale blond realized that she was being watched and smiled timidly at Carington when their eyes met. Carington smiled back.

"It seems we have a bit of excitement," Carington told her.

Kristina nodded. "I have been watching it unfold from our chamber." Her gaze moved from the chaotic bailey to Carington. "How was your shopping trip?"

Carington was distracted from her view of Creed by the question. She stepped back and twirled around for Kristina.

"What do ye think?" she asked.

Kristina smiled as she viewed the surcoat. "It is beautiful."

Carington was interrupted from further conversation by Lord Richard and his boys; the trio descended the stairs and pushed past the women into the bailey. Gilbert and Edward had small wooden swords and they charged out into the ward, swinging their swords and yelling at the men. A couple of times, they nearly got trampled by the warhorses as Richard stood aside, watching his wild sons with pride. Carington found herself wishing that someone would run over the boys and teach them a lesson. But the warhorses always managed to maneuver around them. Eventually, the army began to filter from the bailey into the deepening night.

Carington and Kristina watched the last of the torches fade into the distance as the great gates of Prudhoe were closed and bolted. Night had fallen and suddenly everything was dark and quiet. Richard and the boys were still standing in the bailey, only by this time the boys were thrusting their swords at each other. Richard finally grabbed his sons and shooed them into the hall where the evening meal was about to be served.

The boys ran past Carington without as much as a glance, to which she was grateful. She was hoping they had grown tired of harassing her. When she took her eyes off of the little boys who were now running and shouting all over the great hall, she found Kristina staring at her.

"Well," Carington squared her shoulders, trying not to let her melancholy show. She did not want rumors to get started about her feelings for Creed; from their conversation, she knew it would only bring about great harm to them all. "I have been ordered to retreat to my chamber and stay there. Are ye coming?"

Kristina moved to her side and looped a companionable arm through hers. Carington was a little startled at the familiarity at first but quickly got over it; she was coming to genuinely like Kristina and did not mind after all. In truth, she'd never really had a friend and found the English girl's manner comforting.

"They always order us to our chambers when the army leaves," Kristina told her. "They are always concerned that it is a ruse to draw the army away from Prudhoe so we will be vulnerable to attack."

Carington looked at her with concern. "Is this always true?"

Kristina nodded. "Twice, it has been. We were attacked by a great Scots...," she suddenly trailed off, looking at Carington with horror. "I did not mean to say... that is, they were Scots, but I am sure...."

Carington put her hand up to quiet her. "No harm, m'lady," she said softly. "I know we have been enemies in the past. But I hope no longer."

Kristina sighed, relieved that she had not offended her. "Nay," she nodded. "No longer."

The great hall was warm and fragrant and a grand meal was served in due time. Lady Anne and Julia joined them, Julia seated next to Kristina and clearly attempting to orchestrate her companion's kind attempts towards Carington. But Carington did not particularly give notice to the petty girl; her mind was with Creed, now riding towards Hexham Castle and conflict. She found herself praying twice in one day, this time for his safe return.

So much had changed over the past few days. Her life had become something she did not recognize but was not uncomfortable with. From reluctant hostage to exhilarated bride, she was having a difficult time grasping the turn her future had taken. Not even Gilbert's taunting or Edward's bad manners could dampen her spirits. At the moment, she could think only of Creed and their future together.

When she slept that night, it was with dreams of a Sassenach knight with dusky blue eyes.

CHAPTER TEN

Morning came and Prudhoe's army had not returned from Hexham. Lord Richard seemed unconcerned with his absent army but Carington was so edgy that she could not eat her breakfast. As was customary when the army was not at residence within Prudhoe's walls, the occupants of the castle were allowed to the great hall to break their fast, but afterwards were directed to stay in their bolted chambers and the entire fortress was locked down. Very little activity could be seen, mostly the remaining soldiers on the walls and a few servants dashing from place to place. And because of the lockdown, the papal legate was unable to leave. He was imprisoned in the keep just like everyone else.

Carington remained locked in her chamber with Kristina and Julia. She was dressed in one of her new surcoats, a pale yellow lamb's wool that fit her body like the skin of a grape. It was incredibly flattering, bordering on indecent, but she only knew that it was soft and warm. She never noticed the stares of Richard or a few male servants during the morning meal. She was simply thrilled to be in something other than rags.

Thankfully, Julia had kept silent for the most part during the sequestered existence in their chamber, still working on a great piece of embroidery that was strapped to a large frame. She was very good at sewing and Carington would occasionally glimpse at the ambitious work. But her attention would always return to the window next to her bed, gazing over the lush Northumbrian landscape for any signs of the returning army.

She sat for what seemed like hours. The nooning meal came and went, brought to them by a couple of serving women who provided them with a wide array of fruit, cheese and bread. But Carington hardly touched it, even when Kristina brought her a lovely apple and a great hunk of white cheese. Carington thanked the pale-haired lass kindly but she simply was not hungry. So Kristina returned to her section of the chamber, brought forth a great deck of colorfully painted cards, and came back to sit on the bed next to Carington.

Carington eyed the colorful cards as the girl carefully organized them. "What is it ye have there?" she asked.

Kristina began to carefully lay them out on the coverlet. "These are fortune cards. They can tell your fortune."

Carington smiled faintly at the thought of a piece of wood divining the future. But she was willing to play along. "Did they tell ye that ye would be sealed up with me in a room today?"

Kristina giggled. "They did not," she wagged a card in Carington's direction. "You must be serious or the cards will not tell you anything."

Carington pretended to wipe the smile from her face, finding enough distraction with the game to tear herself away from the window. "Very well," she leaned against the wall and watched her new friend deal out the cards. "What are they telling ye?"

Kristina collected the cards she had just laid out, shuffled them around, and then indicated for Carington to take one. Carington obliged and Kristina took the card out of her hand, laying it on the coverlet. She peered at it closely. Because she was, Carington peered closely at it, too.

"What do ye see?" she asked.

Kristina's brow furrowed in concentration. "It is The Chariot," she said thoughtfully. "It means conquest and pride. It is the card of a warrior."

Carington looked closer. "It does? " She looked up at her friend. "Perhaps it is telling ye something about the battle at Hexham."

Kristina pondered that. "'Tis possible," she said. "It often means strength and battle."

Suddenly, Carington took the cards more seriously. "What else?"

"Take another card."

Carington pulled out another one and handed it to Kristina,

who placed it to the right of The Chariot. She suddenly smiled. "Ah, The Empress," she declared. "It means beauty and desire. Surely that is your card."

Carington blushed furiously. "What else does it mean?"

Kristina was still smiling at Carington's bashful response. "Surely you know how lovely you are," she said. "Why, there is not a man at Prudhoe who has not noticed. You are all anyone can speak of."

Carington looked at her almost fearfully and shook her head. "Ye mustn't say such things."

"Why not? 'Tis the truth."

"Can I pick another card?"

Kristina laughed softly and held out the deck. Carington plucked out another card and Kristina put it to the left of The Chariot. Her smile faded. "The Tower."

"What does that mean?"

"It means Chaos."

The answer came from the other side of the room. Carington and Kristina looked over to see that Julia was addressing them. When she knew she had their attention, she focused her dour predication on Carington.

"The Tower means Chaos," she repeated, more slowly as if to drive home the point. "It also means crisis, disillusionment and ruin. It is horror and destruction."

Carington instinctively stiffened at the woman's hostility. She gazed balefully at Julia for a moment before returning to Kristina. "Can I pick another card?" she asked.

Kristina did not look particularly worried about The Tower and offered Carington the deck. Carington selected a fourth card and handed it back to Kristina, who laid it next to The Empress. Her smile was back.

"Ah," she murmured. "The Lovers. And it is right next to your card, too."

Carington looked more closely at the bright cards. "What does that mean?"

Kristina's eyes twinkled. "It means that you shall find love soon. Is there anyone special you left behind in Scotland, my lady? Someone who has your heart?"

Carington shook her head, unwilling to divulge any information. She prayed her expression would not give her away. "Nay," she replied, still eyeing the card. "No one in Scotland."

"This is a very powerful card. It means eternal love and devotion."

Carington simply shrugged as if she had nothing more to say to that. Kristina, suspecting there was more to what Carington was telling her simply by her evasive stance, held out the deck of cards.

"One last card, my lady," she said. "I need five to tell your fortune."

Carington pulled out the last card and handed it to Kristina. The young lady put it neatly next to The Tower. As she did so, the pleasant expression faded from her face.

"Death," she muttered. "It sits next to The Tower."

Carington already did not like the sound of that. "What does it mean?"

"It means precisely what she said," Julia piped up from across the room. "It means there is Death in your future."

Before Carington could work herself into a snappish reply, Kristina was shuffling them around and putting them back with the deck. She lifted her gaze to Carington's curious face.

"'Tis a silly game," she insisted softly. "Any fortune I have ever told has never come true. Do not take great stock in it."

Carington gazed into her eyes, reading the disquiet, but did not press her. Instead, she forced a smile.

"Of course," she murmured. "Only a game."

Kristina shuffled the cards around furiously, trying to move on from the lingering Death card. "Let us tell someone else's fortune," she said. "Whose should we tell?"

"How about Sir Creed?" Julia stabbed at her embroidery. "Perhaps we can divine his future. Perhaps we can see if a wife is in order."

Carington's head snapped to the girl, attempting to discern if she was mouthing off because she was in possession of secretive knowledge or if she was simply being her usual malicious self. Her statement could have been interpreted both ways. Carington remembered what Ryton had told her of Julia, that she wanted Creed for herself. If Julia had been even the slightest bit kind, Carington might have felt sorry for her. But at the moment, all she felt was venom.

Kristina, thankfully, was oblivious to Carington's mental turmoil. She simply shook her head at Julia.

"We have told his future too many times," she reminded her. "It never comes out the way you wish. I would think that you would give up and look elsewhere for a husband. Marrying Creed simply is not in your cards."

Carington could not even comment on that statement; she turned away, biting off a smile as she returned her attention to the lancet window. It was mid-afternoon now with evening only an hour or so away. She gazed up at the blue sky with its puffy dusting of clouds.

"How far is Hexham Castle?" she asked.

Kristina was shuffling her cards again. "No more than two hours. It is a short and lovely ride."

Carington digested the information, thinking that, in fact, the army had been gone quite some time for so short a distance. But she recollected the days when her father had ridden to battle; he would be gone for weeks at a time. She knew that war was a waiting game for those left behind. Almost as strong as her anxiety for Creed's safety was her desire to know who had instigated the raid. She had told Creed that it could not have been her father; truth be told, she could not be sure. His treaty was with Prudhoe, not Hexham. If allied clans called for Sian Kerr's aide for arms against an English enemy, she knew that her father would not refuse.

So she sat back on the bed and played Kristina's card game. They read fortunes for Burle, Stanton, Lady Anne and Gilbert. By the time they got around to reading a fortune for Edward, an odd sound from the bailey caught their attention. It was a strange grinding noise with echoes of thunder to it. Carington and Kristina looked at each other with some confusion, then apprehension, before they bolted to the window and peered outside.

The great gates of Prudhoe were slowly opening and in the green fields beyond, they could see a smattering of the returning army, hidden in part by the trees. They could hear the rumble of the footfalls and wagon wheels even from this distance. Carington flew off the bed and raced to the door.

"Where are you going?" Kristina demanded.

"To meet the army," she said as if the girl was an idiot. "We must welcome them home."

Kristina shook her head. "We are not allowed to," she insisted. "We must always stay to our chamber until one of the men release us."

Carington's brow furrowed. "Release us?" she repeated. "We are not prisoners. Why must we be released?"

"Because we will only be in the way if we go down stairs," Julia looked at Carington with veiled contempt. "It is the rule of the House; we must stay to our chamber when the army returns until Sir Ryton or Sir Creed or another knight releases us. We are not allowed to be underfoot and must stay to our chamber as good, obedient women."

Carington remembered Creeds words to her; do not leave that room for any reason; not until I return. It never occurred to her that he meant literally. She did not want to disobey him, no matter how excited she was to see him. So she took her hand off the latch and paced back over to the bed, climbing up so she could look through the window again. By this time, the army was pouring in through the gates and a shocking scene was unfolding.

From her vantage point at the window, she could see that two of the wagons they had brought with them were filled with bodies. She could not tell if they were alive or dead, for they were stacked together like cordwood. As she watched in mounting horror, Julia casually rose from her seat and moved to the other lancet window that faced to the north; it did, however, have a narrow view of the front gates. Together, the three of them watched the influx of weary and beaten men and animals.

Carington was not as concerned for the men in the wagons as she was for the knights. So far, she had not seen one of them and her panic was beginning to rise. The army was now filling the bailey in waves; like water crashing upon the shore, wave after wave of men piled into the outer bailey. Eventually, they moved into the inner bailey and that was where she caught her first glimpse of one of the five Prudhoe knights.

It was Jory, waving his arm at the exhausted men, bellowing something she could not hear. Stanton suddenly barreled in to the inner bailey as well, riding without his helm. It was a curious sight. But he turned his head slightly to relay orders and they all noticed a massive bandage that covered one side of his head. Kristina gasped when Stanton turned his head to show them his bloody bindings.

Carington looked at her with concern, keeping her own horror only slightly at bay. She, too, was ready to gasp at the sights she was witnessing. Only by God's good grace was she holding tight as trepidation welled in her chest until she thought she might explode. Eventually, Burle passed into her line of sight as he made his way towards the keep. He was on foot.

"I can see Sir Ryton's charger," Julia suddenly spoke from her vantage point at the other window. "The charger is tethered to a wagon just now entering the main gates."

Carington and Kristina looked over at her. "Do you see Sir Ryton?" Kristina asked; she sounded as if she was about to cry.

Julia shook her head. "The horse is riderless and appears wounded."

Carington was about to jump from her skin. Kristina asked the question that Carington could not bring herself to voice.

"What of Sir Creed?" Kristina went over to Julia's window and tried to gain a better look at the main gates. "Has he returned?"

Julia did not say anything for a moment; both she and Kristina were straining to gain a better look at the incoming army. Suddenly, Kristina gasped.

"I see his charger," she breathed, her hand flying to her mouth. "I see Sir Creed's charger. It is tethered to the last wagon."

That was all Carington could take. She bolted up from the bed and flew to the door before Kristina or Julia could stop her. She threw the door open with the intention of charging down to the bailey but was stopped by Burle's massive form standing in the hall outside. Carington did not see him until it was too late and she plowed right into him.

Burle grunted as she bashed into him, reaching out to steady her as she lost her balance. Carington rubbed her nose where she had smashed it into his mail, gazing up with surprise into his pale, dirty face.

"Sir Burle," she did not realize that she was clutching at him. "What happened? We saw so many wounded and…."

Burle's face was solemn; he could read her panic and he knew why. Since their trip into the town of Prudhoe that day, he had realized what Ryton had; there was something special between Lady Carington and Creed. And, of course, he was informed of the situation when Creed could not keep his excitement to himself as they rode to Hexham.

Burle had never seen the man so happy. It was a trust they had in each other in that the knowledge would go no further; they were old friends that way. That was why Burle had made it his duty upon returning to Prudhoe to seek out Lady Carington; he wanted to get to her before anyone else did. He put his arm around her shoulders and pulled her towards the stairs.

"Come with me, my lady," he said softly.

"Sir Burle?" Kristina's voice called out to him hesitantly. "May we come also?"

Burle paused and turned to see both Kristina and Julia standing in the doorway, apprehensive expressions on their faces. He held out a halting hand.

"Stay there," he told the girls. "Remain until someone returns for you."

Kristina wanted to press him further but refrained. The expression on his face told her not to. Puzzled, she and Julia watched Burle escort Lady Carington down the stairs and out of sight. Only then did Kristina close the door as requested. But she stood against it, tears welling, wondering where Burle was taking Carington and wondered if it was some place horrible as a result of the Scot raid. Perhaps he was taking her to punish her. She was, after all, a hostage. The tears finally fell. Julia watched her friend for a moment before returning, quite unemotionally, back to the window.

But tears were not something that Carington was thinking of at the moment. She was frankly too uneasy at the moment. Burle seemed so grim and that in and of itself scared her to death. She wondered what would make a battle-hardened knight ripe with gloom. When they reached the second floor of the keep and prepared to take the stairs into the inner bailey, Burle finally stopped and turned to her.

"I want to prepare you before we go any further, my lady," he said quietly.

Carington's composure took a direct hit. "Dear God," she grasped at her chest, feeling her knees weaken. "Prepare me for what? What has happened?"

Burle sighed heavily. "We lost Ryton."

She stared at him a moment before his words sank in. Then, the tears welled. "What happened?" she breathed painfully.

It was obvious that Burle was struggling. "Hexham was overrun when we arrived," he explained quietly. "There were Scots everywhere. The bailey had been breached and they were in the process of compromising the keep. Ryton and Creed charged straight into the melee, killing many men. But we only brought three hundred men with us from Prudhoe and the Scots must have had a thousand. It was a brutal battle from the onset."

By this time, Carington was weeping softly, her hands over her mouth and tears coursing down her face. "Is Creed all right?"

"He was not wounded."

That brought more relief than she could comprehend. "Did… did ye recognize the Scots?"

Burle looked at her; it was clear that he did not want to

answer the question. But he had no choice.

"Aye," he muttered. "We did."

"And?"

"Elliot, Graham and Kerr tartans."

Carington's eyes bulged and she pressed her hands against her mouth as if to hold back the scream. But it was not enough and she began sobbing loudly. She tried to turn away from Burle but he grabbed her firmly, forcing her to face him.

"Please, my lady," he begged softly. "I know this is difficult, but you must get hold of yourself. Creed needs your comfort not your tears."

She continued to sob painfully into her hands. "Creed...," she wept. "Where is he?"

Burle's expression took on a distant look as if recalling something of anguish. "He is with his brother. His death has left him devastated."

Carington wept a moment longer before struggling to compose herself, wiping furiously at her eyes and swallowing her sobs. She pulled away from Burle.

"He will not want to see me," she hissed. "He will hate me for this."

Burle shook his head. "You did not lead the attack, my lady. Creed knows this."

"But...," she gasped, struggling to catch her breath. "But my kin did. It may as well have been me."

Burle grabbed her by the arm, again forcing her to look at him. "But it was not you," he insisted quietly. "We will deal with your kin another time. Right now, Creed needs you. You must be strong, if only for him."

Her tears faded as she looked at him, suddenly realizing that he was privy to their secret. His tone, his words, told her so. She wiped at her nose, eyeing him closely.

"He... he told ye?" she asked softly.

Burle shrugged. "I have known Creed for many years, my lady. We are friends. There is not much I do not know about him."

She thought on that a moment, somehow feeling a friendship

with Burle, too. It was as if she were suddenly a part of this very tight, very exclusive brotherhood. Creed had many friends who loved and respected him. She began to understand that by virtue of those relationships, they would love and respect her as well. She had Burle's trust in spite of what happened at Hexham. She could read it in his eyes.

"Where is he?" she asked softly. "Please take me to him."

With a lingering glance, Burle took her by the arm and led her out into the inner bailey. Lord Richard was there, his back to her as he conversed quietly with a man in priestly robes that Carington did not recognize. Burle took her across the ward and into the outer bailey where three wagons loaded with bodies stood parked against the outer wall. There were soldiers and servants everywhere, running about in a frenzy. It was chaos. Burle continued to lead her towards the front gates where a lone wagon sat parked off to the side of the southwest wall. As the wagon came into focus, Carington realized that she was looking at Creed as he crouched in the wagon bed.

Galen Burleson was also standing at the rear of the wagon, his sorrowful gaze fixed on whatever Creed was staring at. He looked weary and beaten, as all of the knights did. Burle stopped several feet away, silently encouraging Carington to continue. She wiped her face one last time to remove all traces of tears as she came upon the wagon. She took a moment to drink in the sight of Creed, relieved beyond words that he was alive yet so incredibly distressed for what had happened.

Creed was still in his armor including his helm. She could only see his profile as he focused emotionlessly on the bed of the wagon. Carington stood against the side of the wagon, gazing into his powerful, handsome face. A soft hand reached up to touch his arm.

"Creed?" she said softly.

He did not acknowledge her for a moment. It was as if he were frozen. Just as Carington opened her mouth to speak again, he suddenly turned his head and looked at her.

The pain in the dusky blue depths reached out to slap her;

Carington literally sucked in her breath at the anguish she was witnessing. Her grip on him tightened.

"I am so sorry," she murmured. "Burle told me what happened."

He just stared at her. Then, both arms shot over the side of the wagon and he lifted her up, pulling her against him. It was a swift, startling movement and Carington grabbed hold of his neck as he settled her into the wagon. His arms, thick and mailed and armored, wrapped around her so tightly that she could barely breathe. Carington did the only thing she could do; she held him tightly.

"'Tis all right, English," she murmured. "I am here now. Everything will be all right."

He still had not said a word; he continued to hold her so tightly that he was squeezing the life from her. Carington struggled to breathe as she unwound one arm from his neck and began to unlatch his helm.

"'Tis all right," she whispered again, releasing the last latch on his helm and pulling it off of his sweaty, mailed head. He had a split scalp somewhere beneath his mail hood and a river of dried blood caked most of the right side of his face. She took the long, trailing sleeve of her new yellow lamb's wool and gently began to wipe the blood away, kissing his cheek tenderly as she did so.

He remained unresponsive as she wiped away most of the blood, speaking softly to him as she gently tended him. She peeled back the mail hauberk, revealing his curly wet hair, whispering gentle words that only he could hear. All the while he simply clutched her and stared at his brother's body, which Carington had yet to see. She caught a glimpse of Ryton's legs when he had lifted her into the wagon bed but she did not want to look further. Right now, her attention was focused on Creed. It seemed to her that he was a hair's breadth away from shattering completely.

"There was nothing I could do," he suddenly said.

Carington stopped wiping at the blood and looked at him. "What do ye mean?"

He blinked as if struggling to process her question. "Precisely that," his voice was a dull echo of his normal deep tone. "A morning star caught him in the head and it was over in an instant. He was beyond help when I came upon him."

Carington tried to keep the horror from her face; she knew now what he was staring at. Swallowing hard, she slowly turned to see what he was seeing. Her gaze fell upon Ryton's torso, his chest, finally his neck. Then she saw his face, which looked normal enough until she noticed that the entire right side of his helm was caved in. Blood and brain matter gathered on his neck and shoulder, pooling in the wagon bed beneath him.

With a groan, she covered her mouth and turned away. "Sweet Jesus," she whispered, putting her other hand down to touch the Ryton's boot at her feet. "God bless the man to not have suffered."

Creed's response was to hold her tighter. "First Lenox, now Ryton," he muttered. "I have lost my brothers in foolish border skirmishes. Now I am alone."

The tears were returning with a vengeance and Carington was struggling not to cry.

"Nay, English, ye are *not* alone," she whispered fiercely. "Ye have me. Ye will always have me."

He was transfixed on his brother's corpse. Carington did not like the edgy blankness in his eyes that seemed to be growing worse by the second. She shifted so that her breasts were at his eye level, blocking his view of his brother. Taking his head in both of her small hands, she forced him to look up at her.

"Listen to me," she whispered fervently. "Ye're brother was a good and noble man. He was fair even during times when he could have easily been harsh, for I experienced his benevolence myself. 'Tis a call for help he answered and paid for that nobility with his life. Ye must not remember him as he is right now; ye must remember him as a powerful knight who followed the path of so many others. He will be remembered well."

He stared up at her, the dusky blue eyes muddled with pain. After a moment, he simply closed his eyes and shoved his face deep into her breasts. Carington held him tightly against the swell of her bosom, her cheek against the top of his head. She did not know what else to say so perhaps it was best if she say nothing. Holding him, at the moment, was enough.

By this time, Burle and Galen were standing at the rear of the wagon, watching the emotional scene. It was heart-wrenching for all of them. Carington was rocking Creed gently, whispering soft words that the knights could not hear. Burle watched them from a distance, surprised at the tenderness the fiery little Scots was exhibiting. He was more than stunned with Creed's reaction to her; he'd never known the man to be anything other than calm, stoic and composed. Moreover, he'd never even seen him truly excited about a woman. But at the moment, he looked like he was clinging to her as if she could save him. The bond of tenderness between Lady Carington and the English knight was truly something powerful to behold.

Burle was abruptly jolted from his thoughts when Stanton suddenly appeared at the side of the wagon.

"Lord Richard is coming along with that priest," the young knight told them, eyeing Carington as she cradled Creed. "We should perhaps... well, you know...."

He gestured at Carington. Understanding the implication, Burle leapt onto the wagon bed and hovered over the pair.

"Creed," he muttered. "Lord Richard approaches. He must not see Lady Carington in your embrace."

Creed's response was to hold on tighter. Carington put her hands on his head; his face was still buried in the valley between her breasts. She was trying to pry his head away from her bosom but was not doing a very good job; he held fast.

"English," she tried to sound firm but gentle. "Let me go. I willna go far, I promise."

After a split second delay, Creed came to his senses and released Carington. Burle lifted her over the side of the wagon and into Stanton's waiting arms. The pale young knight took her by the elbow and led her a respectable distance away from the wagon; it would do no good to remove her completely for Lord Richard caught sight of her as he entered the outer ward. He was marching purposefully with the papal legate by his side. Stanton merely took her off to the side, hoping Lord Richard would not demand to know why she was there.

Unfortunately, Lord Richard moved right for her. He seemed completely oblivious to the sorrow happening in the wagon. His handsome face was lined with grief and anger as he focused on Carington.

"You," he jabbed a finger at her. "Your father was a part of this… this murder raid. What do you know about it?"

He was practically yelling at her. His tone caused Creed's head to snap up, his dusky blue eyes narrowing when he saw his liege moving for Carington in a threatening manner. Suddenly, he was vaulting over the side of the wagon, but Burle and Galen physically restrained him from going any further.

"Nay," Burle hissed in his ear. "Hold fast, Creed. The lady can handle herself."

Creed was an enormous man; they had all been privy to the damage he could do at one time or another when threatened or provoked. He had done a tremendous amount of damage in the battle at Hexham. It took both Galen and Burle to keep him at bay.

Creed's face was tight with emotion. "I will not permit him to blame her for this."

Burle shushed him as the scene before them began to unfold. "Wait," he muttered. "Just wait and see what happens."

As Richard yelled at her, Carington looked over his shoulder to see Creed literally fly out of the wagon. Burle and Galen were there to stop him, but it was clear that he was unsteady. It would not do for Creed to snap and strangle his liege, so she struggled to remain calm so that he, in turn, would stay calm.

"I am sure I know nothing about it, m'lord," she replied evenly. "My father never did divulge his battle plans to me. I am as surprised and horrified as ye are and I would sincerely apologize for this havoc."

Richard was furious; that much was clear. He scowled at her. "Your father pledged you as a hostage against his good behavior," he snarled. "You have only been with us for a few days and already he breaks his word. Do you realize what that means? It means that I can do with you as I wish. I can throw you to the dogs if it pleases me."

In the grip of Burle and Galen, Creed flinched and it took every ounce of strength the two knights possessed to hold him still. It was like trying to pin down a raging bull. But Carington, when faced with a very angry English lord, remained quite calm. Given her fiery nature, her cool demeanor was astonishing.

"Ye may indeed, m'lord," she agreed. "But to do so would not only bring the wrath of my father, but of every other Scotsman from Carter's Bar to Edinburgh. Would ye risk complete destruction to punish me for something ye know I had nothing to do with?"

By the time she was finished, her hands were on her hips and she was scolding him. Richard glared back at her, his mouth working angrily, but knowing in the midst of his fury that she was right. Still, Ryton's death was a blow and he felt the need to blame someone. She happened to be a convenient target who, in fact, was not going to take his abuse.

With a growl, Richard turned away from her and moved to the wagon. He noticed that Burle and Galen were holding on to Creed but assumed it was because of his grief. He went to the knight and put his hands on his enormous shoulders.

"Creed," he sounded strangely calm for a man who had been enraged not moments before. "I am so sorry for your loss. I cannot express what Ryton meant to me, to all of us. My heart aches for him as it would for a brother."

Creed was still unsteady, still in the grip of Burle and Galen. But he forced himself to calm, shrugging off the hands that held him.

"I must take him home," he said quietly. "My father will expect him to be buried at Throston Castle."

"Of course," Richard nodded, peering in the wagon and spying a very unsavory sight. His features twisted with disgust before turning back to Creed. "Go whenever you wish and take whatever resources you need. But hurry back; as callous as this may sound, you are now the commander of my army and I will require your services back at Prudhoe as soon as possible."

Creed just stared at him, a thousand different responses rolling through his head. At the moment, he could not comprehend taking over for his brother although he knew he was the logical choice. Still, it was the furthest thing from his mind. He only had two prevalent thoughts; the death of his brother and Carington. He could not think beyond that.

A small figure in brown robes suddenly passed into his line of sight, moving to the edge of the wagon. Creed recognized Massimo as the priest observed the dead knight and proceeded to make the sign of the cross over Ryton's body. Then he began praying in Latin. Creed suddenly fell to his knees, Burle and Galen with him, as they bowed their heads in prayer. Richard followed shortly, as did Stanton and Carington. They all went to their knees as the papal legate began reciting prayers for the dead.

It was a dismal group that listened to Massimo's prayers. Carington had no idea how long they were on their knees, praying for Ryton's soul, when Creed suddenly stood up and walked in her direction. She barely had time to look up before he was pulling her to her feet and making his way back to Richard.

Carington was actually afraid as Creed practically dragged her across the dirt. She'd never known the man to be anything but gentle with her and his forceful manner was terrifying. But Creed was resolute as he faced his liege with Carington in hand.

"Since Laird Kerr saw fit to attack Hexham and I lost my brother as a result, I am laying claim to Kerr's daughter," he said. "I will not accept anything less."

He said it in a tone that no one had ever heard from him before, especially Richard; the man's eyes widened as he looked between an anxious Carington and a deeply serious Creed.

"What do you mean 'lay claim'?" Richard asked.

Creed lifted a dark eyebrow. "She belongs to me. I intend to marry her."

Richard blanched. "Marry her?" he repeated. "What madness is this, Creed? You cannot...."

Creed cut him off with a finger to the face. "You will not deny me," he countered strongly. "Kerr took my brother and now I am taking his daughter."

Richard stared at Creed, wide-eyed. "If you feel so strongly about it, I will make her your ward. You do not have to marry her."

Creed's stance softened somewhat, averting his gaze from his liege and focusing on Carington. She stared back at him, apprehensively. He realized how antagonistic he sounded and sought to calm himself. This grip on her arm turned gentle and he took her hand in his enormous palm, caressing it.

"Aye, I do," he muttered. "I love her, my lord. I must marry her."

Richard just stared at him. "Are you serious?"

"Never more in my life."

Richard thought on that statement a moment, mulling over the treaty with Kerr, the implication of Creed marrying a Scots hostage. He could tell by the man's expression that there was no dissuading him and he was, frankly, stunned.

"Creed," he said slowly. "I would never deny your heart's desire, but we must look at this logically. Sian Kerr did not have a treaty with Hexham; he is within his rights to support an uprising against an establishment he does not have a treaty with. We hold his daughter as assurance that he will not move against Prudhoe; if you marry her, it could be seen as a breach of our honor."

Creed shook his head. "Untrue. No Scots would dare attack their kin, which is what Prudhoe will become once I marry Carington. It would further cement the alliance."

Richard gazed at him a moment longer before shaking his head. "You would complicate your life more than it already is? Good lord, man, think about what you are saying; you have issue enough with the queen and the church. Now you would complicate your life further by taking a hostage bride?"

Creed looked at Carington, noticing for the first time that she wore one of her new surcoats. It was the most pleasing thing he had ever seen and in spite of his grief, his turmoil, he was able to feel a measure of peace and comfort at the sight of her. She eased his heart in so many ways. It was something he desperately needed.

"I would marry her under any circumstances," he murmured. "I want her, my lord. I need her."

Richard knew a man in love when he saw one. It was more than a surprise; he would have never suspected it, especially from Creed. Richard had been honored enough to have seen service from all three de Reyne brothers. His association with then went back to the time before he was married to Anne when Ryton first came to Prudhoe as a newly ordained knight. Creed had followed shortly thereafter because the brothers had wished to serve together. Lenox had followed five years later and, for a short while, the three de Reyne brothers made the most powerful trio of knights on the border. But then Lenox fell away and now Ryton had followed. Creed was left alone, clearly the most physically powerful of the three but also strangely the most vulnerable.

Richard gazed at the man, knowing he was innocent in all things and glad, when he thought on it, that the man had actually found love. It was a rare thing. Moreover, considering he had just lost his one remaining brother, Richard was not about to deny him an affair of the heart. He could not.

"Very well," Richard finally conceded, his expression one of resignation. "Marry her if you must. But at some point, I am going to have to tell the lady's father."

"You may announce a strong new alliance with Prudhoe," Creed responded.

Richard cocked an eyebrow. "Somehow, I do not think he will see it that way."

CHAPTER ELEVEN

I have a husband.

It was all Carington could think of as she sat in the great hall, watching Creed give several coins to Massimo in payment for having performed the wedding mass. The priest had been initially reluctant to perform the ceremony but had proceeded with a good deal of convincing from both Creed and Lord Richard. Therefore, at dusk before Matins and in front of Lord and Lady d'Umfraville, Kristina and a devastated Julia, Galen, Burle, Stanton and Jory, the Lady Carington Kerr became the Lady Carington Kerr de Reyne in the lovely little chapel at Prudhoe. She still could not believe it.

Creed could hardly believe it, either, but he had never been so certain of anything in his life. In a day that had seen the pinnacle of highs and lows, it gave him comfort to find some joy in it. His grief for his brother was consuming but his delight in his new wife was overwhelming. He was struggling to keep a rein on his emotions, struggling to stay on an even keel. As he finished paying Massimo a goodly sum, he actually began to feel some relief in this most affecting day of days.

As a wedding gift, Lady Anne had given Carington a thin gold band that had belonged to her mother. Creed had placed it on his wife's left hand, a lovely slender band for her lovely slender finger. Carington kept staring at it as she stood with Kristina and Lady Anne while Creed finished with the priest. The women made small talk but Carington's attention was on her husband. He finally turned away from the priest, leaving him standing with Richard as he made his way over to his new wife. She smiled timidly when their eyes met, wondering if he was feeling as disoriented as she was.

"It seems that everything is in order," he told her, then looked to Lady Anne. "I would again thank you for your graciousness in allowing us to be wed in your chapel. And your gift of the ring is priceless. We are deeply touched."

Anne smiled, putting her hand on Creed's enormous arm. "Having no daughters, there was no one to pass the ring on to," she looked fondly at Carington. "I am sure she will take excellent care of it."

Carington looked at her lovely ring again. "It is beautiful, m'lady," she said. "I will always treasure it."

"Of course you will," she reached out and took her hand, giving it a warm squeeze. Then she turned back to Creed. "I am putting you and Carington in the smaller chamber on the fourth floor; you know the one. I will not allow your wife to sleep in the knight's quarters. She belongs in the keep."

Creed scratched his weary head. "Although I appreciate your kindness, my lady, may I point out that Burle and Stanton have their own homes in the outer bailey and that the arrangement has served them quite well. I do not intend that my wife and I should be a burden on your household."

"Nonsense," Anne shushed him. "Lady Carington is an honored guest and you are now commander of my husband's army. 'Tis only right that you should be housed in the keep."

Creed's dusky blue eyes moved to Carington. "Perhaps my wife would like her own home, my lady."

Anne looked stricken as her gaze moved to Carington. "How insensitive of me," she exclaimed softly. Then she lifted her slender shoulders. "We shall discuss it later, then. For now, you will take the chamber on the fourth floor. And no argument."

Before Creed could protest, Carington answered for him. "Ye're most kind, m'lady. We are grateful."

Anne smiled sweetly at Carington, patted her cheek, and went to find her husband. Kristina, seeing that she was now standing alone with a newly married couple, suddenly bolted away. Carington giggled as the girl practically tripped in her haste to give them privacy. Creed merely shook his head and scratched his scalp again. His gaze was warm on Carington.

"Are you hungry?" he asked softly. "Perhaps you would like to eat before retiring."

She gazed up at him with her emerald eyes. "I am a bit hungry," she admitted, yet her expression grew serious. "But what of ye? How are ye feeling?"

His warm expression faded somewhat. "I am weary," he confessed. "And I have no great desire to share you with a room full of people."

She went to him, wrapping her small hands around his great forearm. "That is not what I meant," she said quietly. "I meant to ask how ye are feeling about yer brother. Surely he must be taken care of. I would help ye tend him if ye will allow me."

He patted her hand. "'Tis sweet of you to offer, honey, but there is no need. He has been taken care of for now."

"Are ye sure?"

He nodded. "Galen and Burle saw to it earlier."

She studied his face closely, watching the flicker of grief in his eyes. "They are true friends to do that for ye," she murmured. "They know how sad ye are."

He sighed heavily, thinking back to earlier that afternoon when Carington had returned to the keep to dress for their wedding. He had remained with Burle, Galen and Stanton next to the wagon containing his brother's body, the four of them united in their grief for a fallen comrade and brother. It had been Creed who had lifted his brother's battered body out of the wagon and carried it to Prudhoe's gatehouse, where it had been placed in the lower level of the vault where it was very cold. It was the best place to store the remains until they were able to bury him.

Burle and Galen took over at that point, assuring Creed that they would tend his brother so that he could focus on his pending marriage. More than that, his friends wanted to help him through his grief, and tending his brother's smashed head would not have been the best experience for him. Galen had accompanied them back to Prudhoe for just that reason; he had been there when Lenox fell and felt strongly that he needed to be with Creed for Ryton's death as well. Creed was barely holding himself together as it was. So they put his focus onto Carington and the imminent wedding, and it had been enough to get him out of the gatehouse.

It was a gesture by true friends during a time when he needed it most. Creed was adrift in his reflections when Carington rubbed his arm gently, snapping him out of his thoughts.

"Ye're lost to me," she murmured. "What are ye thinking?"

He gazed down at her, smiling weakly and caressing her soft fingers. "Of my friends," he reached out and touched her cheek. "And I apologize for that. I should be thinking only of you."

Her smiled faded as she gazed into his dusky eyes. "Then let us go to our chamber now," she murmured. "I would rather spend the eve of our wedding alone with ye."

"You are reading my mind," he winked at her, turning to Richard and the priest, a few feet away. "My lord, if you will not be greatly offended, my wife and I will retire."

Richard's gaze passed between Creed and Carington; he still was not over his reserve about the situation but he nodded agreeably. "Understandable," he waved them off. "We will see you in the morning."

Creed started to move for the door but Massimo stepped forward. "I will be leaving in the morning, Sir Creed," he reminded him. "I would speak with you before I go."

Creed nodded to acknowledge him but said nothing more. When he and Carington were descending the chapel steps, she turned to him.

"What does he want to speak with ye about?" she asked softly.

Dusk had fallen and the torches had been lit, giving the outer bailey an unearthly glow. The peace of night seemed far removed from the chaos and horror the past day had seen. Creed's dusky gaze moved across the darkened landscape.

"He simply wants to talk about my issues," he tried to make it sound casual.

"He is concerned with our marriage."

"Aye."

She sighed faintly. "I knew it. I could tell. He is not happy in the least."

His left hand clutched her fingers around his right elbow.

"Nay, he is not, but that did not stop me. He does not control my life."

Carington did not say any more as they crossed the outer ward and into the inner bailey. She knew that now was not the time. The tall cylindrical keep loomed ahead and her gaze trailed upward as if to see their destination at the top. Soft light was filtering from the lancet windows placed strategically around the keep, the gentle illumination beckoning them.

Her hand tightened around Creed's arm as they entered the keep. He squeezed her hand before disengaging it and helping her to mount the narrow stairs. Their eyes met on the way up and she smiled bashfully, full of hope and anticipation and a little apprehension. His response was to wink confidently at her.

They faded up the steps into the darkness.

***

Jory had been watching Julia since he had entered the chapel for Creed's marriage. He knew how the girl felt about Creed; they all did. She had never made it any secret. The event of Creed's wedding had clearly shattered her and Jory watched her for the duration of the ceremony, feeling sparks of wicked thoughts smatter through his brain. Ideas were coming to him fast and furious these days, thoughts that a normal man would have never entertained. But Jory was not normal. In fact, the past few days had seen that trait grow even darker.

When he was not watching Julia, he was watching Carington's backside. She had the most delectable body he had ever seen. Everyone had noticed. And the new gowns she was parading around in did nothing to stifle his twisted imagination. Even now, she stood next to Creed in a surcoat of blue brocade which only emphasized the curves of her figure. Jory began to imagine the wedding bed and how Creed would be touching and tasting her tender flesh. He would be slipping his fingers and tongue into intimate places, finally ramming his great manhood into her virginal sheath. It took Jory a moment to realize that he was engorged and he returned his attention to Julia so that his arousal would go down. Plain, unattractive Julia would serve to calm him. She would also help him.

When the wedding was over and Julia slipped out before congratulating the happy couple, Jory followed. He caught up to her when she was nearly to the inner bailey.

"Lady Julia," he called after her. "Wait a moment."

Julia came to a halt, quickly wiping at her eyes as she turned to him. Jory's dark gaze fell upon her tear stained face and he smiled thinly.

"I am sorry that it was not you standing next to Creed," he made an attempt at sounding sympathetic. "Creed will never know what he has given up."

Julia was struggling to compose herself as she looked up at him. "What is it you want?"

Jory lifted an eyebrow. "Want?" he shrugged, looking about the yard. "I only want to help you."

"Help me with what?"

He looked at her, then. "Punish Creed, of course."

She eyed him suspiciously. Then she began to walk away. Jory caught up to her and took pace beside her.

"He has spurned you, Julia," he said grimly. "And that Scot... what right does she have to marry him? She only met him four days ago. You have known him longer. Certainly you should have been the one to win his heart."

Julia shook her head. "Go away, Jory."

He did not do as she asked. He continued. "By all rights, that woman is a hostage, yet Creed and the others have treated her as if she is royalty," he insisted. "See how they fawn over her? 'Tis not right, I tell you. And what of you? They ignore you. They place this Scots bitch over you. How does that make you feel? How does it make you feel to know that it will not be you that Creed makes love to tonight?"

With a frustrated growl, she came to a halt and faced him. "Enough," she hissed. "I do not need your help or your pity. Go away and leave me alone."

He grabbed her so that she could not walk away. "Listen to me," he said. "I will help you exact vengeance on Creed and his wife."

She looked up at him, struggling to pull away. "What in the world are you talking about?"

His grip tightened. "I speak of a reckoning. Creed has wronged you. His bitch of a wife does not deserve him. Let me help you punish him."

Julia gazed up into his evil, dark eyes and, for a split second, realized she was considering his offer. She was devastated that Creed had married the Scots hostage. But something deep inside her, one last shred of common sense, held her back.

"Why would you offer to do this?" she hissed. "What has Creed done to you that you would be so willing to be the instrument through which my satisfaction is obtained?"

He let go of her, his brown eyes boring holes with their intensity. "My vendetta against Creed has already begun," he said in a low voice. "For every time he has threatened me, for every time his henchman, Burle, has beaten me, and for every vicious word that has ever come out of his mouth directed at me, I can no longer remain still. I will have my vengeance and then some."

Julia did not like the way he was looking at her; it was terrifying. Instinctively, she took a step back. "What do you mean it has already begun?"

A hint of a thin, wicked smile came to his lips. "It started yesterday. He will pay."

"I do not understand."

He just stared at her in a way that made her skin crawl. "The blow that killed his brother did not come from a Scots," he muttered. "It was a Scots morning star, that is true, but I picked it up from the ground where it had fallen. Ryton never saw me come up from behind and smash it into his skull."

Julia's jaw dropped in horror. "You killed Ryton?"

Jory's eyes narrowed. "For every insult, every beating, every offense," he repeated, almost sing-song. "That was just the beginning."

Julia took another step back, thinking quite seriously about running away screaming. "You are mad."

He grabbed her before she could get away. "Tell anyone and I will kill you," he seethed. "Help me to exact my vengeance on Creed and you shall live."

She struggled with him. "So it is your vengeance after all? I thought you said it was mine."

He shook her so hard that her neck snapped. "What I do, I do for us both," he growled, his fingers digging into her soft flesh. "Creed has ever affronted me. He shadows me with his self-righteousness, always ensuring that he has the upper hand. I will not allow him to dominate me any longer. I will not allow him to win."

Julia could see her death in his eyes. She stared at him a very long time before nodding her head, just once. Jory let her go and smiled broadly.

"There, my lady," he said sweetly. "That was not so difficult, was it?"

Julia was trembling and terrified. "What would you have me do?"

He told her.

***

Lady Anne had turned the small chamber on the fourth floor of Prudhoe's keep into a wonderland of warmth and comfort. Slender tapers burned everywhere, filling the room with a gentle glow. Upon the large bed was a fluffy linen coverlet stuffed with feathers, which Lady Anne had covered in the dried petals of wild flowers that grew beyond Prudhoe's walls. Fresh rushes covered the floor and a warm fire blazed in the small hearth.

Carington ran her hand over the coverlet and tossed it back, realizing that the sheets were made of fine cotton and woven until very soft. She fingered the material, never having felt anything so fine. Over her shoulder, she noticed that someone had brought her two satchels and bedroll and had stacked them neatly in the corner. The room was truthfully very tiny and there was hardly enough room to turn around in it, but Carington found it extremely comfortable and inviting. She was much more at home here than in the larger ladies' chamber downstairs. She looked up at her husband as he stood next to her, also inspecting the bed. She smiled when their eyes met.

"I've never seen such a beautiful room," she said. "It looks as if angels sleep here."

His eyes glittered as he touched her cheek. "One does."

She blushed modestly, suddenly feeling very self-conscious. Her nervous eyes darted about the room until her gaze fell upon a small table with a pitcher and two cups. She moved around Creed and went to pour them some wine.

"Libations on yer wedding night, m'lord?" she smiled as she extended him the cup.

He took a step towards her and accepted it, watching her as she collected her own cup. They gazed into each other's eyes as they both drank deeply. He drained his, took her still half-full cup away from her, and set both cups down on the table. Then he took her hand and led her over to the bed. He sat on the mattress as she continued to stand. With his height and her petite size, they were nearly at eye level.

He gazed into her sweet face, studying the woman who had very quickly come to mean the world to him. "Although I had always hoped to marry at some point, I never imagined it would come about like this," he said.

She lifted her eyebrows. "Nor did I."

He laughed softly. "Any regrets, my lady?"

She shook her head and sat down next to him. "Not-a yet."

"Not-a yet?" He repeated in her heavy burr with a snort, watching the firelight play off her nearly black hair. "Hopefully there will never be any. I will do my best to ensure that there are not."

His reached out an enormous hand, gently touching her hair. She instinctively leaned into his hand and he cupped her head gently.

"Tell me something, English?"

He loved hearing her delicate voice, the way her Scots accent enunciated each word. "Anything, honey."

"Are we always to live at Prudhoe?"

His warm expression faded. "Nay."

"Then where will we go?"

His dusky blue eyes took on a distant look. "Throston Castle, eventually. It is where I was born."

"Does yer family live there, then?"

"My father does. My mother passed away some years ago."

She cocked her head, looking at him rather strangely. "Yer father lives there alone? Why do ye not live there with him?"

He took his hand off her head and pulled her into his arms. It was one of the rare times when he did not have any armor on, a harsh barrier between him and her tender flesh. She was soft and warm and he snuggled against her, delighting in the feel of her.

"Because my father has many knights serving him, men whose families have served the Hartlepool Baronetcy for generations," he told her. "I went to foster at a young age, following Ryton. Ryton did not want to serve my father; he wanted to be independent and not under the constant shadow of my father. I wanted the same, as did Lenox, which is how all three of us ended up at Prudhoe. When I return to Throston, it will be as Baron Hartlepool at the death of my father. The title was supposed to go to Ryton, but as of today, it is mine."

His expression dampened at the thought. It had not truly occurred to him until he had said it. Carington could see the mood darkening and she hastened to prevent the fall. She knew the man must grieve for his brother but she did not want him tumbling back in the pit of despair when they had only just risen above it. The days to come would see other opportunities for grieving, but not tonight. Tonight belonged to them.

"Well," she said decisively, toying with the collar of his tunic, "there will be plenty of time before ye assume yer duties as baron. I had no idea I married into such a noble family."

He knew she was attempting to lighten the mood; he could tell by her manner. He gave her a lop-sided smile. "Not only will I hold an English baronetcy but a Scottish one as well, courtesy of my wife. I would assume your father has no male heirs?"

She shook her head. "Just me." Then her eyes widened. "Ye will be commander of my da's men; hundreds of them. Sweet Jesus, they'd just as soon leap over a cliff than take commands from an English knight."

He smirked. "We shall see about that."

Her brow furrowed as her head wagged back and forth. "The Clans are not easily won over, English."

"I won you over, did I not?"

She stopped toying with his tunic and gave him a reluctant smile. "Ye mean ye bullied me into submission. Ye canna do that with every man on the border."

His embrace suddenly turned into a big bear hug and he buried his face in the side of her neck, growling and snorting. She squealed with delight, laughing as he nibbled her ticklish neck.

"Bullied you, did I?" he growled at her again. "You hardly put up a fight."

She giggled again, shrieking one last time when he gave a final nibbling assault and fell still. But she was wrapped up in his embrace, clutched tightly against his chest as they gazed at each other. There was a good deal of warmth and joy in their mutual expressions.

"I did not really bully you, did I?" he asked softly.

She reached up and put a finger to his lips, feeling the smooth warmth beneath her touch. "Nay," she whispered, watching him kiss her finger. "Ye dinna bully me. Ye were a true gentleman always."

His answer was to smile and dip his head low and lower still until he was hovering over her mouth. After a moment's pause to drink in his fill of her lovely face, his mouth slanted hungrily over hers.

Carington submitted to the powerful kiss. He had kissed her before and she was quickly learning to crave the warmth and power that his lips infused upon her. She wound her arms around his neck, holding him fast as the strength of his kiss increased. Soon, he was suckling her lower lip, plunging his tongue gently into her mouth as she responded in kind. She mimicked the movement of his tongue, the gentle licking, the tasting. Her hands moved into his inky hair, holding his head fast against her. The lust, passion, was growing.

Creed could feel her delectable body arching against him, her aggressive little hands pulling his head down to her lips. He laid her back on the bed, one hand behind her head while his free hand went to work removing her new surcoat. He did not want to tear it but he was so eager to remove her from it that he ended up ripping a seam. He came away from her lips, apologizing profusely, but she simply laughed and sat up. Lifting her hair, she directed him to unhook the stays to the rear of the dress and untie the sash. He did so quickly and, in an instant, the blue surcoat with the birds on it ended up on the stool near the door.

Carington sat with her back to him in her shift, unmoving. She could feel his enormous body behind her, the heat radiating from it like a roaring blaze. She turned slightly when she felt him move and realized that he was removing his tunic. Her breathing began to quicken at the sight of his naked skin, tanned and smooth and glistening in the light of the candles. She could see his left arm and part of his torso but not much else. As she gazed at him with her peripheral vision, he came up behind her and wrapped his big arms around her body.

His mouth went to her neck, suckling gently. Carington closed her eyes and collapsed against him as his mouth grew more insistent and his hands began to roam. One arm held her firmly around the waist as the other hand moved up her right arm, into her hair and back down onto her shoulder. He massaged her shoulder for a few moments as his mouth began to work across her jaw. He could feel her breathing growing strong and heavy beneath him and it fed his lust. His hand moved away from her shoulder and came up under her armpit, grasping her right breast from behind.

This time, Carington did not start. She accepted his hand on her breast, feeling the gentle caress and knowing very quickly that she liked it. A sigh of pleasure escaped her lips as his caress grew firmer, kneading her gently, acquainting her with the feel of his hand on intimate parts of her body. His other hand moved from her waist and gently cupped her left breast. With both hands overflowing with her delicious bosom, he pulled her back against him and his lips found hers.

Carington's head was twisted back as his tongue delved deep into her mouth. He was squeezing her breasts gently, his fingers moving to play with her taut nipples. She heard soft gasps filling the air, hardly aware that they were her own. Suddenly, his hands moved to the bottom of her shift and in one clean motion lifted it over her head, leaving her only in her pantalets and hose. Pushing her back gently on the bed, the last two garments on her body came free and ended up on the floor with the shift.

On her back, Carington could only submit as he continued his tender onslaught. She was concentrating on his miraculous hands, unaware when he removed his breeches and boots and kicked them to the floor. There was such passion between them that she was only aware of the heavy breathing as his naked body descended upon her. When she instinctively parted her legs so that his weight would not crush her, Creed's desire moved to a higher level.

His hand was on her breast as he kissed her furiously. But he soon moved away from her mouth, blazing a trail with his mouth that ended up at her breasts. He took a peaked nipple in his mouth, suckling strongly as she writhed and bucked beneath him. Her movements were purely instinctive, a natural reaction to his body and actions, and it only served to fuel his fervor. He was trying to go slowly with her; God knows he was trying. But she was responding to him as if she knew what he wanted and it was driving him over the edge.

As one arm held her close, he continued to nurse at her delightful breasts. Carington's hands were in his hair, harsh little pants coming from her lips. His free hand moved down her flat belly to the fluff of dark curls between her legs. He gently touched her thighs first, very close to the junction where her legs joined, but refrained from touching her most intimate place for the moment. He was attempting to make her comfortable with his touch before forging into virgin territory. But Carington's body was heaving so much that his fingers ended up wedged between her legs when she shifted.

He stroked her wet folds, listening to her pant. It created a wild surge of hunger in him and he inserted his fingers into her before he realized he was doing it. She gasped loudly, instinctively bringing her knees up to accommodated him, and Creed had all he could handle. Returning his lips to her delicious mouth, he placed his enormous manhood at her threshold and carefully pushed his way into her. He felt her stiffen.

"Creed," she breathed fearfully.

He kissed her hard, silencing he words. "Relax, honey," he murmured. "I promise I will be gentle."

She whimpered as he thrust into her, listening to a softly strangled cry when he withdrew and thrust again, pushing deep inside her. He held her tightly, his arms wrapped around her slender body as his hips did the work. She was so slick that in little time, he was seated to the hilt to the sounds of his own gasping.

Carington hands were on his face as he began to move within her, his careful strokes increasing in power and pace. She was so consumed with the feel and smell of him that she could think of little else. There was very little pain from their joining; merely a sense of fullness. But the miraculous feelings he was bringing about as he stroked into her had her head spinning with delight.

His body was creating a raging fire within her loins. She could feel his manroot moving in and out, a primal rhythm that she soon learned to follow. Her hips began to grind against his, lightning bursting every time their bodies would come together. The bursts of lightning grew stronger and brighter. Shebegan to live for that next contact, that next stroke, that finally brought about the roll of thunder and ecstasy such as she had never known rippling through her body. She cried out with the sheer joy of it. Creed thrust into her a few more times, his strokes so hard that her teeth rattled, before spilling himself deep into her beautiful body.

The roll of thunder eventually faded but did not die completely. Carington lay beneath her husband, feeling his massive body atop her with a satisfaction she had never known. But her body was still so highly aroused that when he stroked her gently one last time, out of the sheer pleasure of being inside her, the thunder clapped again and she experienced the thrill of another climax. Creed felt her tremor bursts and he clutched her buttocks against him, thrusting in and out of her sensually and feeling at least four more releases until they faded away completely. As she lay weeping softly beneath him, he realized that he had grown hard again in an extremely short amount of time and he made love to her once more before experiencing a climax so hard that he bit his lip in the heat of passion. He could taste the blood. Carington released again beneath him; he could feel her tight walls throbbing strongly around his deeply embedded member.

When the panting died down and the only sound filling the room was the soft crackle of the fire, Creed just lay there and stared at her. Carington's eyes were closed, her lips softly parted as she dozed exhaustedly. He did not want to sleep, fearful of missing one moment of this glory. He was still entrenched in her delectable body, her legs still parted and wrapped around his hips, and he took a few moments to inspect the perfection of her figure.

As he had noticed from the very beginning of their association, she had a body that put all other women to shame. He found himself gently touching her full, perfect breasts, his enormous hand delicately moving to her flat belly before traveling on to touch a thigh that was wrapped around him. When she suddenly wriggled and thrust her hips up against him, he realized that he was still quite aroused and he leaned forward, gently suckling her lips and feeling her sleepily respond. Extremely gently, he grasped her buttocks and began slow and tender thrusts into her.

Carington responded by winding her arms around his neck, lifting her body against his and imitating his thrusting hips. The more she thrust, the more aroused he became and soon, she was flat on her back while he plunged firmly into her.

Their lovemaking went on well into the night until the soft dawn of a new day found them sleeping soundly in each other's arms.

CHAPTER TWELVE

In spite of a night that had kept him active until an hour or two before dawn, Creed was up at sunrise. He was not accustomed to sleeping during the night at all but last night had been an exception. He was the Guardian of Darkness, after all, and the night was his domain. But in his wildest dreams he could not have imagined the joy and adoration he had experienced and, quite possibly, he thought perhaps that he did not sleep at all. He remembered lying awake for what was surely hours as he watched Carington sleep. He still could not believe he had married her. Leaving his beautiful wife sleeping soundly, he dressed silently and quietly quit the chamber.

He found Richard and Massimo in the solar adjacent to the great hall. Richard was seated behind his heavy oak desk while the priest was perched on a stool near the fire, warming his backside as gentle conversation flowed. Upon Creed entering the chamber, the priest bolted to his feet.

"Ah," he said. "So you did not forget my need to speak with you before I left."

Creed looked relaxed, rested and extraordinarily content. He shook his head at the priest. "I did not forget," he scratched his stubble. "But I would hope that you did not expect me here at daybreak given the fact that I was only married last night. Clearly, I have been quite happily occupied."

Richard cleared his throat at the innuendo, wriggling his eyebrows at Creed when the man turned to give him a lazy smile. Richard, in fact, fought off a smirk at the expression on Creed's face. He was not surprised to see it.

"Be that as it may," he tried to divert the naughty subject matter. "Father Massimo has some concerns before he returns to London. We were just discussing them before you came in."

Creed seemed unconcerned. "Oh?" he began hunting around

for something to eat. "What concerns?"

"He fears that taking a wife might feed the queen's fury."

The relaxed expression left Creed's face. "Then do not tell her," he said, looking between Richard and the priest. "It is a very simple matter; do not tell anyone. There is no reason you need to spread the news of my marriage all over London. It is, frankly, no one's business."

Massimo gaze was intense. "It was not my plan to announce it," he replied. "But I will not lie if I am asked a direct question."

Creed was fast losing his humor. He scratched his head irritably. "I am truly at a loss to understand why my marriage is such a concern."

Massimo pursed his lips as he formulated a reply that would express his reservations adequately. "It would have been better for you to simply keep a low profile while this madness was going on," he explained. "To marry in the midst of it gives you an almost rakish appearance, taking a wife while you are rumored to have gotten another woman pregnant. 'Twould have been preferable for you to have waited. This way, it almost appears as if you are taunting Isabella. I fear that it will cast a shadow on your innocence purely by perception."

Creed's good mood was gone. "I did not get another woman pregnant," he jabbed a finger at the priest. "And I am not going to put my life on hold because a spoiled whore of a girl could not shoulder my rejection."

They were very strong words coming from the usually cool Creed. Richard just looked at the priest, letting the man know with his expression that he supported Creed's assertion. Massimo put up his hands.

"Gentlemen," he said softly. "I am not attempting to be belligerent. I am simply trying to see all angles of this. Sir Creed, I told you before that I believed you. That has not changed. But I want you to understand all sides of the position you find yourself in. I want you to understand this is a very serious matter that is simply not going to vanish no matter how innocent you are."

Creed cooled somewhat. "I do not expect it to vanish. But I do expect to be exonerated."

"I can only promise to try," the priest said. "But you must face the fact that you may have to come to London to be questions before the papal council."

Creed stared at him. "Why?"

"As I said; to answer questions. They will want to hear your side of the tale from your own lips if I cannot convince them that the queen's assertions are baseless."

Creed's jaw was ticking. "Why did you not tell me this before?"

"Because we had your innocence to establish with our first meeting. It was difficult enough given your hostile attitude and I chose not to elaborate on what may, or may not, happen should I not be able to convince the papal legate of your innocence."

Creed gazed at him a moment longer before turning away, emitting a heavy sigh as he did so. "My God," he muttered bitterly. "Does this never end? I have just lost my brother, for Christ's sake; I have just taken a new wife, of which I am extremely happy, but the weight of the entire world is bearing down on my shoulders with the fate of a kingdom hanging in the balance because of something I have been undeservingly drawn in to. How much more sorrow and toil am I expected to bear?"

The priest was not unsympathetic. "God does not give you more of a burden than you can manage, my son," he said quietly. "As with all things, this too shall pass. You must have faith."

Creed fixed on him. "If you believe me as you say you do, then you must help me," he was nearly pleading. "I did nothing wrong."

Massimo nodded, sighing as he did so. "I will do what I can," he muttered. "I can promise you that much."

"Then you have my thanks."

With a lingering glance at the two men, Massimo quit the solar and headed to the outer bailey where his papal escort await. Creed and Richard fell silent a moment, each lost to their thoughts, until Richard finally stood up from his chair and made his way to Creed. He paused, putting a hand on the man's massive shoulder.

"I have holdings in Ireland," he said quietly. "If the king is truly after you, then you can take your wife and go there until this situation blows over. They will never find you in Ireland."

Creed looked at him. "You have always been a good friend to me and my brother, my lord," he replied sincerely. "There is no way I can ever repay you for the risks you have taken on my behalf."

Richard snorted softly. "You and Ryton have repaid me many times over," he said. "You have kept Prudhoe and my family safe. I would take such risks for you time and time again." His expression softened as he looked at Creed. "I cannot tell you how your brother's death has grieved me. I was up most of the night dwelling on it. First Lenox and now Ryton... I can never express my sorrow adequately. When do you plan to take him home?"

Creed had been trying not to think of his brother all morning but now found his attention focused on him. "That depends; when do you intend to tell Cari's father about our marriage?"

Richard gave him a lop-sided smile. "I can wait until you return from burying Ryton if that is what you are concerned with."

"That is exactly what I am concerned with. I do not need an irate Scotsman overrunning Prudhoe while I am gone."

"I thought you said he would not dare attack Prudhoe because he would consider us kin?"

"You are asking me to anticipate a father who had no say in the marriage of his only daughter."

Richard laughed softly. "Having no daughters myself, I can only imagine Laird Kerr's reaction. Put yourself in Sian Kerr's shoes."

"I have," Creed was thinking heavily on going to find something to eat. "If it were me, I would overrun Prudhoe and take great pleasure in it."

"God help us, then. Let us hope you never have any daughters who marry without your permission."

The very idea made Creed grin. "With my luck, I shall have eight of them, all with their mother's disposition."

Richard laughed out loud. "Now there is a happy thought."

Creed was about to reply when an odd sound filtered in through the lancet window. It took them both a moment to realize it was screaming.

***

As she had been instructed, Julia had run to tell Jory when Creed left his marriage chamber. She had been flushed and, Jory thought, weeping as she told him, but he had ignored her distress and ran from the knight's quarters to the keep. It was not particularly busy at this time of the morning and the main entry door had been unmarred by servants or anyone else who might wonder why he was there. It was not normal for the knights to enter the keep. But Jory was on a mission.

It was quiet and dark as he made his way up to the third floor; he could hear Gilbert and Edward fighting in their bower to his right and he quickly slipped up the stairs to the fourth floor before Lady Anne could come out of her chamber and scold the boys. He could already hear her voice as she lifted it, in conversation, behind their closed bedchamber door. Jory's boots were silent upon the stone steps as he spiraled his way to the top of the structure.

His breathing was coming in heavy gasps by the time he came to the landing. Two small chambers were on this level; one to the right and one to the left. Carefully, he put his hand on the latch of the chamber to his right, his heart pounding loudly in his ears as he slowly opened the door. One brown eye peered inside, long enough to note that it was cold and empty. Letting go of the latch, he moved to the chamber on his left.

He half expected to find the door bolted but was both surprised and relieved to find that it was not. He could not keep the smirk from his face as he carefully and silently lifted the latch, opening the door inch by inch, stopping abruptly when it began to squeak. He could see a portion of the chamber now, including the end of the bed. He waited to see if anything stirred. When all remained still, he continued.

The door opened enough for him to slip in without making any further noise. Jory ducked into the room, spying Carington fast asleep upon the bed. He shut the door behind him and bolted it.

He stood there a moment, his gaze lingering on her black head as she lay on her side, snuggled against the linen coverlet. There were flower petals on the floor and burned out tapers everywhere. A small fire burned in the hearth, kicking some smoke into the room. If he inhaled deeply, he could smell the sex that had taken place over the past several hours. He had no doubt that Creed had taken advantage of the lady all night. From the way she was sleeping, heavy and still, he could only imagine the extent of their nocturnal activities. It excited him to think about it.

He thought a moment about his next move. Clearly, nothing gentle or quiet would work. The lady was a fighter and the moment she realized he was upon her, she would resist. It would be loud and violent. He therefore determined the best course of action would be the element of surprise and he intended to take full advantage of it. Ripping the coverlet off, he pounced; a hand went over the lady's mouth and he pinned her small body down with his weight.

Startled out of a deep sleep, Carington's eyes flew open in a panic, her emerald gaze immediately falling on Jory's taut face. Without delay, she began to scream and kick, her cries muffled in his hand.

"If you fight me, I will kill you," he hissed, feeling her naked body struggle beneath him. "Cooperate and you shall live. Those are the terms."

Carington was almost incoherent with terror. She ignored his demands and managed to get a hand free, jabbing him in the eye as hard as she could. Jory howled and fell back, his hand coming free from her mouth. She screamed so loud that it echoed off the thick keep walls.

Jory fell off the bed, his hand on his eye, as Carington leapt up and grabbed the nearest thing she could find. It was a taper sconce, heavy and sharp. Though he was blind in one eye, Jory saw the iron looming over his head and he put an arm up to block what would have surly been a direct strike to his skull. As it was, the sconce hit his head anyway and the sharp edge gashed his forehead.

Naked as the day she was born, Carington wielded the sconce like a club and whacked him several times over the head with it. She was screaming like a banshee, praying she could do enough damage to at least get away. Jory was wallowing on the floor, trying to defend himself, but somewhere in the middle of it he got hold of the sconce and yanked it from her.

Carington almost toppled over as he pulled it out of her grasp. Shrieking, she raced to the door and tried to open it, only to realize that it was bolted. She could hear voices on the other side and she screamed again for help. As she fumbled with the iron bolt, Jory grabbed her from behind and tossed her onto the bed.

She hit her back on the wooden frame, momentarily stunning her. But her fight did not leave her and she put her fists up as Jory came crashing down on top of her. One fist hit his nose but he grabbed her wrists, struggling to pin her arms.

"You little bitch," he growled. "I am going to take my pleasure with you and then I am going to kill you."

Tears were threatening now that he seemed to have the upper hand but Carington refused to give up. She could hear voices on the other side of the chamber door, louder now, and she prayed that someone had run to find Creed. She had no idea where he might be. As she wrestled with Jory in an attempt to prevent him from pinning her arms, he suddenly balled a fist and cuffed her on the side of the head. Dazed, she went limp and bordered on unconsciousness.

When she stopped resisting, Jory went in for the kill. He fumbled with his breeches, groping her tender breasts and slobbering all over her flesh. He could hear the concerned voices on the other side of the door but he ignored them; he knew no one would punish him. No one ever did. It was this false sense of security that helped feed his lust, knowing he would get away with what he was about to do. Lord Richard would surely prevent Creed from exacting any revenge. If the man wanted to keep the alliance with Jory's father, no one would harm him.

He lowered his breeches and roughly pulled her legs apart. Carington suddenly came to life and brought a knee up, catching him in his arousal and Jory fell back with a scream. Moderately lucid, she was preparing to leap over the bed and unbolt the door but Jory grabbed her before she could get close. She still was not recovered from the last blow when Jory began pounding her about the head again, his hands going for her throat. Carington could feel his hands tighten around her neck and she struggled to fight him off as the world began to blacken. She began to think that she was about to die when the door suddenly exploded.

Splinters and debris were still flying through the air as Creed charged into the room like an avenging angel. Burle was right behind him. Creed was not armed but Burle was; it took Creed a half-second to see Jory with his hands wrapped around Carington's neck and he yanked the broadsword from Burle's grasp, driving it deep into Jory's torso. Blood spurted as Jory collapsed with a scream.

Carington fell to the floor, only half-conscious. She was struggling to breathe. Creed left the broadsword in Jory's gut as he scooped his wife into his arms and moved her away from the dying knight. Grabbing the coverlet, he shielded her nakedness from the people now pushing into the tiny chamber. Chaos and the sounds of dying suddenly filled the room.

"Cari," he rubbed her cheeks, her neck where Jory's fingers had left bruises. "Honey, can you hear me? Answer me!"

She coughed as she began to come around. Her emerald eyes fluttered and struggled to open.

"Creed?" her voice was a raspy whisper.

Burst of fury aside, Creed came apart when he realized that he had just saved her from certain death. Had he been a minute later, it might have been another story. Tears welled in his dusky blue eyes as he stroked her face gently, attempting to bring her back to consciousness.

"I am here, honey," he murmured. "Look at me, sweet. Open your eyes and look at me."

Behind him, there was a great deal of commotion going on as Jory went through his death throes. Burle just stood over him grimly, watching the man twitch and foam. Lord Richard was there, watching with horror but making no move to help him. Out in the hall, Kristina and Lady Anne were clutching each other and weeping while Edward and Gilbert just stood in the doorway, jaws agape. Anne finally pushed into the room and made her way to Creed, obviously avoiding Jory. She could not bear to look at him.

"Let me see her, Creed," Anne climbed onto the bed where Creed was holding his wife. "Let me see the damage."

Creed could not even speak; his eyes were swimming with tears as he shifted slightly so that Anne could inspect Carington. The woman ran gentle fingers along Carington's head and neck.

"Look," she stroked a temple. "She has the bruise already. And her neck is quite red but I do not feel anything broken or out of place."

Creed started to say something but emitted an odd noise that sounded more like a strangled sob. Anne looked at him, concerned, only to see that tears were popping out of his eyes and falling onto his wife. She could see, at that moment, that he was far more terrified than he was angry. The man had just lost his brother; now the threat against his wife had put him over the edge. Pity filled her.

"Creed," she murmured, putting her hand on his head. "I do not see any permanent damage. She will be all right."

He emitted a sob and closed his eyes, burying his face in Carington's shoulder. As Anne gently stroked his dark hair, Carington began to grow more lucid.

"Creed?" she blinked her eyes, coming out of a strange fog and realizing that her husband was sobbing against her. She blinked again, seeing his head on her shoulder. "What has happened? Why are ye weeping?"

His head came up, fixed on her. "Because... hell, because I

thought Jory had killed you." He stroked her dark head with a trembling hand. "How do you feel? Are you all right?"

She was feeling much better than she was just a few seconds before. The world was righting itself although her head hurt tremendously. She put a hand to her skull. "I am all right," she said softly, not wanting him to know how weak and achy she felt. He did not look as if he could take any more bad news and she put her hand on his face to wipe away the tears. "I am fine, English. Nothing to worry over."

He emitted a heavy sigh and kissed her gently a couple of times. Then he sat up, taking her with him. "What in the hell happened? How did Jory end up in here?"

She looked over to the corner of the chamber, seeing Burle, Lord Richard and now Stanton and Galen standing over a crumpled form. The latter two knights had heard the commotion way out in the outer bailey and had come armed for battle.

"I dunna know," she said honestly, her head lying against Creed's massive shoulder. "I was asleep when suddenly he was upon me. He told me to cooperate or he would kill me."

Creed's gaze moved to Jory for the first time since he had delivered the death blow. Blood was pooling underneath him and the man was clearly dead. His anger was beginning to return.

"Damn him," he growled. "God damn him to hell."

Richard looked up from Jory's still form, his face pale as he focused on Carington. He took a few halting steps in her direction.

"Did he hurt you, Lady de Reyne?" he asked.

Carington felt a flash of pleasure at hearing her new title but she was too exhausted and hurt to acknowledge it. "He beat me well enough," she replied weakly. "But 'tis nothing I willna recover from."

Richard looked sick. "Perhaps I should call a physic. There is a fine physic in Newcastle; 'tis not too far from here."

Carington tried to shake her head, struggling to sit up in her husband's embrace. "Nay," she said with more strength. "No physic. I will be fine. I just need to rest."

Richard nodded regretfully, passing a lingering glance at Jory's still form. "Get him out of here," he told Burle.

The knights heaved Jory's body off the floor and Burle took him over one of his big shoulders. Creed could not even muster the will to look at the corpse as they removed it from the room. Had he not been more concerned with Carington at the moment, he would have taken much delight in defiling the body. For all of the anger and anguish he was feeling, he would have liked nothing better than to gore the man a thousand times over and call it justice. So it was best that he not look at all.

When the knights had left with a trail of blood behind them, Creed tucked the coverlet in tighter around Carington and continued to rock her gently. Anne remained seated on the bed behind him, her gentle hand on Carington's forehead to give what comfort she could. Kristina stood in the doorway, sobbing.

"Is… is she all right, my lord?" the pale blond asked timidly.

Carington heard her friend and her head came up, her emerald eyes focusing on her. She smiled wearily.

"I am all right," she said. "Dunna stand there; come in here and sit with me a while."

Kristina moved reluctantly into the room, sitting on the edge of the bed and smiling bravely through her tears. Carington moved an arm out from beneath the coverlet and extended her hand to the young girl. Kristina clutched it eagerly.

"I believe ye are more talented than ye know," she said softly.

Kristina sniffled, looking confused. "What do you mean?"

"Yer card game; did it not predict death and chaos?"

She had meant it as a joke but Kristina's eyes opened wide as she remembered her predictions. "I am going to burn all of my cards," she suddenly burst into tears. "I never want to play with them again."

By this time, Creed's head had come up from where it had been resting on top of Carington's dark head.

"What cards?" he asked.

Carington squeezed Kristina's hand. "My friend has magic cards that divine the future. She told my fortune yesterday and, so far, everything has come true."

Creed smiled faintly, noting that Kristina seemed truly despondent. "Cards do not foretell the future, my lady," he assured her. "I would not worry overly."

They continued to sit in silence for a few moments, each to their own thoughts; Kristina of her foreboding cards, Creed of how close he came to losing his wife, Carington of going back to sleep, Anne of how tenderly Creed held his wife, and Richard of how he was going to tell Jory's father that his son had been killed. No matter that it had been in the course of a brutal crime and clearly Jory deserved what he received, the fact remained that Jory's father, Baron Hawthorn, was going to take issue with it. Richard wondered on the repercussions.

Richard finally went to the bed, patting his wife on the shoulder. "Leave them to rest," he instructed quietly. "They have had enough excitement for one day."

With a final stroke to Carington's head, Anne rose from the bed and took Kristina in hand as they quit the chamber. Richard followed, his gaze lingering on the horrific state of the room and wondering if any more horrors await them; in the past two days, Prudhoe had seen its fill.

"I will send Burle back up to you," he told Creed softly. "He will be outside your door should you require anything."

Creed simply nodded, hearing the door shut softly behind him. When they were finally alone, he fixed on her.

"Tell me the truth," he murmured. "How badly did he hurt you?"

She sighed faintly. "He beat me around the head and shoulders, but he dinna do any real damage."

"That is not what I meant."

She gazed at him, realizing what he meant by the expression on his face, and she fought off a blush. "He dinna do what ye are asking," she replied in a whisper. "He tried, but he dinna do it."

"Nothing at all?"

"Nothing, I swear to ye."

He swallowed hard; she saw it. There was an enormous

amount of relief in his manner.

"Will you at least allow me to inspect you for injury?" he asked gently.

She shifted in his arms, moving away from him so that she was in the middle of the bed. She opened up the coverlet, letting it fall. Her soft, thoroughly delicious body was revealed in the weak morning light.

"Look all ye wish," she told him. "I know you dunna believe me when I say that I will be all right. Look and see that I have no broken bones or bloody wounds."

His concerned expression was turning lusty as he gazed upon her perfect breasts and narrow waist. True, she looked well enough except for the red welts around her neck and the lump on her head. She also looked extremely enticing.

"Are you sure?"

She pursed her lips at him irritably and he knew, in that gesture, that she was indeed going to be all right. The sass, the spark, was still there.

"How many times are ye going to ask me the same question?"

He smiled at her, reaching out to collect the coverlet and wrap it back around her body. Like a babe in swaddling, he took her gently in his arms and lay down with her on the bed.

His lips were against her forehead as he held her close. He kept reliving over in his mind how close he came to losing her, thanking God that he had been in time to prevent it.

"I am so sorry this happened," he murmured against her head. "Had I had any idea that Jory would have tried something like this, I would have taken much greater steps to protect you."

She was exhausted, her lids heavy and sleep beckoning. "'Twas not yer fault, English," she replied. "Ye would have had to read his mind in order to know what he was thinking."

"Still," he muttered, "I should have been here."

She sighed contentedly against him, snuggling close. "Yer here now."

"I will always be here, I swear it."

She fell asleep with a smile on her lips.

CHAPTER THIRTEEN

Late November 1200 A.D.

Creed was having a very difficult time that morning. He had been privy to hysterics, weeping, fury and pouting. There was a tempest going on around him and nothing he could say would make a difference. Still, he continued trying. All the while, he could hear Carington in their bower, alternately cursing and crying. She was a mess.

"Honey," he called gently, struggling to be patient. "My dearest, sweetest love, I told you that we would go to town today to visit Rita. Surely she has something lovely and delightful that will fit you."

Two months ago, they had moved into a small cottage that was built into the inner wall of Prudhoe near the great hall. Richard had ordered the cottage constructed when Creed had made the ecstatic announcement that his wife was pregnant. Until that time, they had remained in the tiny room on the fourth floor of Prudhoe's keep but with a baby on the way, they would quickly outgrow the space. Anne had been most insistent that Prudhoe's commander and his wife should have their own home with their growing brood and Richard had agreed.

So the cottage with three rooms was built just for Creed. Carington had been thrilled. But at the moment, in the bedchamber with the big, new bed that had given her so much delight, she was furious because her surcoats had reached the point where they would no longer fit. At nearly seven months pregnant, she was already large with child and growing larger by the day.

But it was the way of things and in spite of Carington's pregnancy-induced mood swings life was very good these days.

Creed had gotten to the point where he simply did not think about the pending trials he was still waiting to face. No information had been exchanged to any regard; of his marriage, Jory's death, or the queen. Prudhoe had kept to itself and hadn't let the rest of the world in. Creed's life was here and now, and he was happy awaiting the birth of his first child. It was all he could focus on. He would deal with everything else when the time came.

As he stood in the main chamber of their cottage, Carington came huffing into the room with her arms full of garments. She dropped them on the table near the hearth.

"I canna fit into any of these," she raged. "Nothing fits anymore. I have grown as fat as a pig."

Creed gazed at his wife who, he thought, had never looked more beautiful. Her lovely face was rosy, her delicious body round and ripe with a gently swollen middle section. He adored making love to her this way.

"You are a goddess divine," he smiled at her.

Her emerald eyes flashed and her lip went into a pout. He could see more tears approaching.

"Will ye take these to Rita and ask her to amend them?" she sniffled.

"I told you I would. Do you want to go?"

She shook her head, wiping at her eyes. "Nay," she squeaked.

He went to her, putting his hands on her shoulders. "Why not?"

She began to weep again, falling forward against him as he swallowed her up in his massive embrace. He rocked her gently, fighting off a smile. She was an emotional wreck these days as the pregnancy wreaked havoc with her thoughts.

"Because I dunna feel well," she wept. "Nothing fits me properly and my belly aches."

"All right, love, do not trouble yourself," he rubbed her back, her arms gently. "I will go into town and deliver these to the seamstress. Shall I get you some custard cakes while I am there?"

She nodded, wiping at her eyes. "I want a dozen of them. And mind ye dunna forget to go to the merchant with the spice cakes. I would have some of them as well."

His grin broke through; she ate nothing but sweets these days and then would cry because she was not fitting into any of her clothes. In truth, he was quite enjoying it because she was animated and humorous when she was not raging with the change of the hour. He kissed the top of her head and let her go.

"Then if I am to go into town, I must get my armor together and collect my horse," he said. "Is there anything else you want?"

"Nay."

"Are you sure you do not want to go?"

"I am sure."

"Do you want to accompany me to the armory?"

She nodded moodily and he took her hand, leading her out into the weak November sunshine. It was cool this day but not tremendously so. Carington was clad in a long sleeved woolen shift and surcoat and was quite warm. But she was pouting and miserable and Creed kept kissing her hand as they crossed into the outer bailey to one of the squatty towers that contained the armory. Somewhere in their walk, Stanton emerged from the stables and ran to catch up to them.

"Good morn to you, Lady de Reyne," he said pleasantly. "It is a fine morning today."

He was making small talk with her but Carington frowned at him. "'Tis a terrible day, Stanton de Witt, and I'll thank ye not to be so sweet and pleasant around me."

Stanton pressed his lips into a flat line, fighting off a grin as Creed cast him a long glance. Now was not the time to laugh at her unless he wanted to end up missing an eye.

Stanton knew that; he'd spent the past nine months with a pregnant woman of his own. "My wife was wondering if you would sit with her today," he asked. "She is bored to tears lying in bed all day awaiting the birth of our child."

Carington nodded. "I know," she lost some of her pout. "Tell her I'll join her for the nooning meal. I'll sit with her a while."

"Thank you," Stanton replied sincerely. "She will look forward to it."

Carington stopped him before he could move away. "What of yer son? Will ye need me to tend him while she sleeps?"

He shook his head. "Your offer is most gracious but Lady Julia is tending him today."

Carington just nodded, watching him stroll off across the compound. She shook her head as they entered the armory tower.

"Stanton's wife is enormous," she remarked. "She looks to be birthing a small city any day now."

Creed did not comment one way or the other; anything he said could be misconstrued as a personal insult or slander, no matter how innocent. As quick to temper as Carington had been before her pregnancy, it was double now and growing worse. So he mounted the spiral stairs in silence, helping her up behind him, until he came to the second floor room that held most of the fine armor. He sat Carington in the corner and began dressing himself. He was about a quarter of the way through when his tall blond squire suddenly joined them.

Carington held her legs up and out of the way as James went to work slapping greaves on his master's shins. The boy moved quickly and efficiently.

"How did ye know he was here?" she teased him gently. "Ye must have eyes and ears everywhere."

The lad blushed furiously; he and the lady had gotten to know each other when Creed had taken Ryton's body back to Throston Castle for burial. Over miles of travel, they had ended up talking to pass the time and genuinely liked one another. While Creed dealt with his aged father's grief, James had kept company with Lady de Reyne in his lord's stead and the two had developed a bond.

"I must have eyes and ears everywhere, my lady, or Sir Creed will have my hide," he replied.

Carington laughed softly, gazing up at her husband. He merely wriggled his eyebrows.

"He'll not touch ye," she told the lad firmly. "I would not allow it."

"Allow it or not, that is my fear nonetheless, Lady de Reyne."

Carington just shook her head sadly. "Dunna be afraid of him, James," she told him. "He wouldna lay a hand on ye. But it is right that ye should respect his strength."

James' head was lowered as he worked on Creed's thigh protection. His fingers moved like lightning. Carington watched the lad a moment before returning her attention to her husband.

"English," she cocked her head as she looked at him. "Do ye not believe it is time for James to become a knight? Young Steven has already been knighted, after all, and he's not much older than James."

Creed held on to the breast plate as James fastened straps. "I believe I know my squire's talents better than you," he scolded gently. "I will determine when the boy is to become a man."

She scowled fiercely. "Dunna take that tone with me. 'Twas merely a question."

He looked at her as James stood up and began fussing with his shoulders. "I am sorry, love," he said sincerely, though he did not mean a word of it. "I simply meant that James will be knighted soon enough and I do not know what I will do without him as my squire. He has spoiled me to anyone else."

James blushed furiously as Carington cooled. She looked thoughtful as she watched the squire finish with her husband's armor.

"I suppose I will go into town with ye," she said, unwinding her legs and standing up. "I want to shop for the bairn."

Creed rolled his eyes and opened his mouth to speak but thought better of it; a strangled grunt came out instead and he quickly pretended to busy himself with his gauntlets as Carington turned a suspicious eye to him.

"Did ye have something to say to that?" she demanded.

He fussed with a glove. "Not really," he said casually. "But do you not believe the baby has enough things right now? He has more possessions than I do and he is not even born yet."

Her lips moved into the familiar pout and Creed put up a

gloved hand in surrender. "As you wish," he said quickly. "Wait a moment and I will escort you home so that you can retrieve your cloak."

She waved him off and began to carefully descend the stairs. "No need. I will meet ye in the bailey."

He watched her dark hair until it disappeared down the stairwell. With an annoyed purse of the lips, he caught his squire looking at him.

"Mind that you remember that women, in general, are mysterious things."

"Aye, my lord."

"Do you plan to marry?"

"Aye, my lord."

"Make sure she is docile."

"You did not, my lord."

Creed eyed him a moment before breaking out into a smirk. "Nay, I did not," he shook his head. "And my life is richer for it. Forget what I said, then. Make sure she is full of spirit and you will never know a dull moment."

"I want a Scots wife just like your lady wife, my lord."

Creed groaned. "God help you, lad."

James finished dressing him with a grin on his face.

Down in the outer bailey, Carington was strolling across the ward towards the inner bailey. She could see Burle across the bailey, running about a dozen new recruit soldiers through a drill, while Steven, Creed's former squire, was on sentry duty up on the wall walk. With Ryton and Jory's deaths, they had quickly promoted the young man and he was proving an excellent asset. All seemed peaceful and bright and Carington was thinking about the fabric she would purchase for the baby when a shout suddenly echoed off the walls.

She looked back to see Steven lifting a hand to Burle, who in turn left his recruits to run to the wall. He disappeared inside the gatehouse only to emerge up on the wall walk. Carington came to a pause, watching curiously.

By this time, Creed and James had emerged from the armory

and Carington watched as her husband and his squire jogged across the bailey towards the gatehouse. Following the same path that Burle had taken, they emerged from the tower onto the wall walk above. After a few minutes of discussion, whereupon Carington grew bored and began to resume her path back to her cottage, Creed suddenly emitted a piercing whistle and the bailey came alive.

Soldiers emerged from the barracks against the north wall and began running. Somewhat startled, Carington scurried out of the way, standing near the gate to the inner bailey as she watched the activity. She was so busy watching the soldiers run back and forth that it took her a moment to realize that Creed had come down from the wall and was heading towards her. She watched him cross the ward, his powerful strides and determined stance. Her heart did a little dance, as it always did when she watched him. There was a time once when she thought he sucked up all of the air surrounding him; it was still true, but now in a good way. The man could positively make her heart sing.

He was upon her in a flash. "Go into the keep, honey."

Fear clutched her at the grim expression on his face. "Why? What is the matter?"

His jaw was ticking as he took her elbow and turned her in the direction of the keep. "Scots," he said softly. "I must assess the threat and until I do, we will assume they are hostile. Get into the keep and bolt the door."

She suddenly dug her heels in. "If they are Scots, then I must be present," she insisted. "They wouldna dare attack Prudhoe with Sian Kerr's daughter within her walls."

The ticking in his jaw worsened. "Cari, I do not have time to argue with you. Please do as you are told. *Please*."

He said the last word as she opened her mouth to protest. With an expression of extreme reluctance, she gathered her skirt and hurried for the keep. Creed stood there and watched her until she entered and the door shut. Only then did he begin shouting at the soldiers to seal up the inner ward.

He joined his men on the wall walk again, trying to spot the colors of the group in the distance. He knew they were Scots simply by the clothing and armor they wore; tartans and leather and very little pieces of metal or mail. They were still too far away to distinguish colors. The next few minutes would tell them who, exactly, approached as their tartans came more clearly into view.

Stanton eventually joined them in their waiting game. Young Steven had grown several inches in the last few months and was now as tall as Burle. He wore Ryton's armor, given to him by Creed because he knew Ryton would not have minded. Moreover, armor was expensive and Steven had not yet amassed any fortune to pay for it. He needed something to wear. The young knight hovered over the edge of the parapet, watching the approaching party with his youthful vision. Finally, the young man straightened.

"Kerr tartan," he said. "That is all I see. And I do not see men riding for battle; it looked like an escort party."

Creed's brow furrowed as his eyes strained to see in the distance. "An escort?" he repeated. "That is odd. Did we receive any missive announcing their arrival?"

The knights shook their heads. "None that we are aware of, my lord," Stanton replied.

Creed did not stand down his troops from alert status but he did go down to the bailey and open the gates. The portcullis remained closed and he stood, watching the Kerr tartans approach, feeling his stomach quiver with apprehension. He was positive they were there with regards to Carington and he wondered if Sian Kerr was, in fact, riding in the party. For months, Richard had refrained from sending any word to Laird Kerr for the sheer fact that he would not take the chance that the man would wage war upon them. He wanted Prudhoe, and Creed, to know some peace after a harrowing summer. Creed did not disagree, especially after finding out that his wife was with child. He wanted her to know peace as well. It was selfish, he knew, and now he worried that his selfishness was about to cost them dearly.

So he waited by the portcullis, peering through the iron grate as the Scots drew closer. Steven had been correct; they did not look like a war party. Still, his heart was thumping with anticipation as the party paused just outside the tree line whereupon several men dismounted. Creed watched as they drew closer, recognizing Sian Kerr right away.

Sian Magnus Kerr was not a large man but he was muscular and very youthful looking. He had Carington's dark hair and the shape of her eyes, but that was where the similarities ended. Sian had vibrant blue eyes, now fixed on Creed as he drew near. He held out his hands as if to show he had no weapons.

"Knight," he called. "I am Laird Kerr. I've come tae see me daughter."

Oh God, Creed thought. He ordered the portcullis raised, standing in the middle of the gatehouse entry with his massive legs braced apart and his arms crossed. It was a defensive stance.

"I am Sir Creed de Reyne, commander of Prudhoe," he responded. "If you truly wish to visit your daughter, then order your men to stand back. You will continue alone."

Sian snapped a hand at the men behind him, burly men with beards and dirty tartans. They came to a halt and Laird Kerr continued. He came to within a few feet of Creed, inspecting him with his vibrant gaze.

Creed examined the man in return; he did not sense hostility but there was something wild and unpredictable in his gaze. When Laird Kerr flashed him a rather big smile, Creed thought he appeared almost mad. It was a peculiar expression. Creed found himself glad he was armed; he anticipated having to defend himself against this erratic bulldog of a man.

"I remember ye," Sian eyed the big English knight. "Ye came tae escort me daughter tae Prudhoe."

"Indeed I did, my lord."

"Where is she? Take me tae her."

Creed did not budge; he remained rooted to the spot. "We did not receive any word of your visit."

"That is because I dinna send any," Sian's smile faded. "Where is me daughter?"

"In the keep," Creed replied, thinking he had better say something before the man saw his daughter and realized she was with child. "Before I take you to her, there is something you and I must discuss."

Sian's smile vanished completely. "What could ye possible want tae discuss wi' me?"

Creed thought it would be best to get him inside the compound where he could not signal his men to charge. With a silent tilt of his head, they began to walk across the outer bailey as Creed ordered the portcullis lowered. He hoped Laird Kerr would not wonder why he was now effectively trapped inside the fortress but Sian was, if nothing else, extremely sharp.

"Ye would treat me as a prisoner, then?" he demanded. "Why do ye close the gate?"

Creed shook his head. "'Tis the way of things at Prudhoe," he explained. "We always keep the fortress locked down. It is Lord d'Umfraville's orders."

Sian cast him a dubious expression but did not argue. "Is my daughter well, then?"

"Very well," Creed replied, "and very happy. But there is something you should be aware of."

"What?"

Creed took a deep breath. "Your daughter has fallen in love," he said softly, coming to a halt just as they reached the inner bailey. "The man she loves is English and of good character and noble birth. He loves your daughter deeply; so much, in fact, that he has married her."

Sian's mouth popped open and the vibrant blue eyes breathed fire; Creed could see it. Before he could work himself up into a substantial rage, however, the door to the keep suddenly opened and a woman screamed at the top of her lungs.

"Da!"

Both Sian and Creed turned to see Carington flying down the stairs from the second floor of the keep as fast as her legs would carry her. When she hit the dusty bailey running, her swollen belly was evident and Sian's astonishment overtook his rage for the moment. As he stood there, dumbfounded, Carington hurled herself into her father's arms.

She was alternately weeping and laughing, squeezing the man to death. Sian embraced her tightly.

"Cari-lass," he murmured into her dark hair. "'Tis heaven tae see ye, child."

Carington pulled back to look at him, her lovely face alight with excitement. "I dinna know ye were coming," she gasped. "I never heard a word from ye."

Sian shook his head. "I dinna send any," he said, his smile fading as his gaze moved to her belly. "I dinna want tae give advanced word because I wanted tae see how they are really takin' care of ye. And now I see."

The thrill on her face dampened, her gaze suddenly moving between her father and Creed. She knew by the look in her father's eye that something very bad was about to happen unless she threw out a block to stop it. She spoke quickly.

"I am very happy here," she said. "I have a wonderful husband and I could never have wished for such happiness as I have found here with my friends. Ye mustna be angry; there is no call. Ye should be happy that yer daughter is expecting a grandson."

Sian's jaw was ticking. "And ye never thought tae get my consent for this marriage?"

She tried to appear firm but her guilt was evident. "It happened rather quickly; there wasna time."

Sian's gaze was on her belly and he could not help the grunt of disgust that escaped his lips. "Good God, lass," he muttered. "Dunna tell me… I raised you better than that, for God's sake. Did ye let him take liberties with ye so that ye had tae marry him?"

Carington shook her head so hard that her black hair snapped in her face. "Ye have no call to accuse me of wrong doing," she glared at him. "Our son was conceived after we married, I'll have ye know. He never touched me before we were properly wed."

It was fairly personal information that she was spouting for all to hear but Creed did not care; he was watching Laird Kerr's body language closely, wondering if he was going to have to protect his wife from the man. But Sian and Carington seemed oblivious to the host of English standing around, listening to them argue.

"Then who is this man who would demand ye marry him without the proper consent of yer father?" Sian demanded.

Carington cooled somewhat. "I love him, Da. He is yer son now and I forbid ye to punish him."

Sian's mouth popped open. "Ye forbid me?"

She was in his face. "Aye, I do. It was my decision to wed just as much as his. We love each other, Dada. Can ye not understand? He is the most compassionate, wise, gracious and powerful man in the world and I'll not have ye scolding him."

It was clear that her father was not pleased. Gritting his teeth, he shook his head. "I can see he's done nothin' tae make ye more obedient. Well? Do ye run all over him as ye run all over me?"

Beside Sian, Creed cleared his throat softly. "Nay, my lord, she does not," he said quietly. "But she is quite demanding, something I personally blame you for."

Sian turned to look at Creed with eyes as wide as the sun. He just stared at him, the enormous English knight that was more than a head taller than he was. He could have taken his statement as a challenge but somehow, he knew it was not. He knew it was the truth. But that did not stop his glare.

"And I will accept the blame, knight," he said with certainty. "But ye still should have asked for my consent."

Creed did not back down. "You are correct, my lord, but we wanted to be married right away. To have sought your consent would have taken time and, quite possibly, you would have denied us. In this case, we chose to marry anyway and beg for forgiveness after the fact."

Sian lifted a disapproving eyebrow at him. "And so ye did. But did ye not stop to think if Cari was already betrothed?"

Creed did not hesitate. "I did not. But it would not have mattered; I love her more than words can express and would have killed anyone who stood in my way."

Sian could see that he was serious. It only made him realize that it was the truth; he could see, plainly, that this was no marriage of opportunity. It was a marriage of love. His harsh stance began to waiver.

"Good God, girl," his eyes moved to Carington. "What is it that ye've done?"

Carington could see her father was surrendering. She wrapped her small hands around his arm and laid her head on his shoulder.

"I've married a very fine man," she murmured, gazing up at him. "And I am giving ye a grandson. Is that not reason enough to be joyful?"

Sian sighed heavily, eventually patting her hand. "Give me time tae settle this in me own mind, lass," he muttered. "Perhaps some ale would help."

For the first time, Creed took his eyes off the man and noticed Richard standing several feet away. He was hovering with Anne, Edward, Gilbert, Julia, Kristina and Stanton's young son, Henry. All of them were gazing at the Scots laird with some measure of curiosity and apprehension. But Richard had heard the man's request; it would not go unsatisfied.

"My lord," Richard stepped forward. "Perhaps you will come with me to the great hall where we may rejoice in our alliance."

Sian recognized Richard; he had seen him those months ago when the terms of the treaty had been agreed upon. He nodded his head resignedly.

"So you would have one of yer knights marry me daughter, eh?" he made one last stand at being indignant. "I wasna aware that hostages were married off to their captors."

Richard eyed Creed, then Carington. "Your daughter is most persuasive. I had no choice."

Sian grunted. "Aye," he shook his head wearily. "I know the feeling."

Richard took them into the great hall, followed by his wife, Carington and the rest of the crowd. Creed kept glancing back to make sure his wife was within sight and she would smile at him on the arm of Lady Anne. Kristina, Gilbert and Edward were somewhere in the middle with Julia bringing up the rear with young Henry. Once inside, the women and children held back while the men seated themselves at the table and servants began to bring out food and drink.

Creed poured ale for his wife's father first before pouring his own draught. Sian watched the man, more than curious about this man his daughter had fallen in love with. He was certainly a big one with enormous hands that gripped the cup.

Richard collected his own cup and held it aloft for a toast. "To our alliance," he said.

Creed lifted his cup and looked Sian in the eye. "To family."

Sian choked but managed to get the liquid down. As Creed sat, he extended his hand to Carington, still standing near the entry with Anne. Carington went to her husband and sat on his enormous knee as he wound his arm around her growing torso.

For a moment, no one said a word. They just stared at each other. Richard eyed Anne for moral support, who promptly joined her husband at the table. Gilbert and Edward followed their mother and climbed on the table, staring boldly at the Scots. Anne eyed her boys grimly but Richard seemed not to notice or care until Gilbert piped up.

"Is he our enemy, Papa?" he demanded.

Richard looked at his son as if fearful of what would come out of his mouth next. "Nay, boy," he told him. "Laird Kerr is our neighbor and ally."

"But he talks funny!" Edward chimed in. "He talks like her!"

He was pointing at Carington, who was gearing up to defend her father until Creed shook her gently. When their eyes met she backed down. Sian's vibrant blue eyes were riveted to the boys.

"Yer sons, Laird Richard?" he asked.

Richard nodded proudly. "They are fine boys, curious and strong. They will make fine allies with the Kerrs someday."

"He does not wear breeches," Gilbert pointed out to his father. "Why do Scots wear skirts?"

"'Tis a kilt, lad," Sian could not decide if he was impressed by their boldness or if they needed a whipping. "We wear it because it is our way."

Gilbert frowned. "Englishmen do not wear kilts."

"Nay, they dunna. That is the difference between us."

Edward suddenly ducked under the table. They could hear the little boy scuttling around underneath until he suddenly crowed.

"He is not wearing anything underneath!" he screeched. "I can see his...!"

"Edward!" Anne cried, reaching under the table and grasping him by the arm. She practically twisted it off in her attempt to flush him out from underneath the table. "Go stand with Julia and Kristina. Go before I take a switch to you."

She had nearly pulled his arm from its socket and he rubbed his shoulder as he did as he was told. Anne yanked Gilbert off the table and shooed him away with his brother. Meanwhile, Richard cleared his throat and prayed for a better subject.

"Did you have a pleasant trip to Prudhoe, my lord?" he asked.

Sian nodded. "Good weather," he returned his attention to Carington, more interested in his daughter's life since her arrival at Prudhoe than in rude English children. "Tell me, lass; when did ye marry Sir Creed?"

Carington's smile faded, remembering that May night when Ryton had been killed. "The night after the Scots attacked Hexham Castle."

Sian's expression did not change; his eyes were riveted to his only child. "When was this?"

"In May."

He scratched his chin and averted his gaze. "I dinna know of this. Attacked Hexham, you say?"

Creed just looked to his cup but he could feel Carington tensing beneath his arm. "How can ye say that?" she hissed at her father. "There were Kerr tartans among those of Eliot and Graham."

Sian lifted an eyebrow. "Kerr, ye say? If that is true, it was not by me own command."

"Do ye not know where yer men are?"

"Of course I do. But we have a large clan, lass. There are those who act on their own with the right persuasion."

Carington knew it was the truth; men from the clan could be bought or coerced by other clans. That was not an unusual happenstance. But this was different; this act of betrayal had resulted in horrific results on someone she had once considered the enemy.

"Creed lost his brother in that raid, Da," she said seriously. "Killed with a morning star to the head; I saw it myself. Do you mean to tell me you have no control over yer men?"

His vibrant blue eyes were piercing on her. "I have no control over me own daughter, 'tis a fact."

She sat back against Creed, as if her father had struck her with his words. He was attempting to unbalance her and had managed to do so. After a moment, she looked at her husband and put an arm around his neck. Her gaze went from hard to soft in an instant as she beheld his face.

"Then what good is a peace treaty if no one but the hostage honors it?" she smiled sadly at her husband as they gazed into each other's eyes. "Although I am deeply sorry for Ryton's death, I am not sorry that I was pledged to Prudhoe for harmony's sake."

Sian watched his daughter's expression as she looked at her husband, the gentleness of it. It was something he had never seen before. Somewhere in the past several months, his daughter had grown up. She had moved from a spirited young girl to a spirited young woman. More than that, there was something in her manner that Creed seemed to bring to it; there was deep compassion and tenderness. She seemed settled and calm. Sian could see it quite clearly. And at that moment, he began to gain some respect for the English warrior. If Carington thought so much of him, then perhaps there was something there.

"Well," Sian turned back to his cup, pouring himself more wine. "I dinna hear anything about the raid on Hexham. If my men were a part of it, they kept it well hidden from me."

"Perhaps because they knew it was in violation of your peace with Prudhoe," Carington tore her eyes away from Creed and looked at her father. "Perhaps they did it behind yer back. That smells of betrayal to me."

Sian lifted an eyebrow at her. "Still yer tongue, girl. I will get tae the bottom of this and find out what my men had tae do wi' it."

"I willna still my tongue," she fired back. "Creed's brother died in that raid and I would know who has betrayed our peace."

"And do what?"

"Punish them!" Carington stood up, agitation in her manner. "I would know who did this to my husband's brother. He was a good man, a fair man, and he dinna deserve for his skull to be smashed by dishonorable savages."

Sian's temper flared and Creed could see, in that brief moment, where his wife got her temper. "I'll not have ye callin' yer kin dishonorable when ye dunna know the entire story," he threw up his hands. "Ye dunna even know who killed the man. It could have been anyone!"

She scowled angrily. "Ye defend men who would go to battle without yer blessing? Since when are ye so ignorant?"

Creed removed her, then. He stood up, pushing her gently away from her father and putting a barrier between them should her father decide to physically demonstrate his fury. Sian leapt to his feet behind Creed.

"Since when do ye speak tae yer father wi' such disrespect?" he bellowed.

Although Creed had her around the shoulders, Carington strained to get a glimpse of her father.

"Since my father is apparently such an idiot," she bellowed in return. "Creed's brother was killed when there was supposed to be peace; killed by Scots, some of whom wore Kerr tartan!"

It was turning into a shouting match. Creed gently but firmly pushed his wife away from the table, attempting to calm her. There was chaos building, so much so that they were all startled when Julia suddenly spoke up from the shadow.

"The Scots did not kill Ryton," she said calmly.

Creed and Carington looked sharply at her; she stood near the hearth, her hands folded primly and appearing calm. She had been, in fact, extraordinarily quiet since the night of Creed's wedding. She had been withdrawn and odd and most attributed it to the fact that the man she had been longing after had taken a wife. Carington, in fact, had barely heard two words from her during all that time and was understandably surprised to hear her voice in the midst of a family argument.

Lady Anne was the first one to speak. "Julia, now is not the time," she said quietly, firmly. "Please take the boys back to the keep. Kristina, go with her."

But Julia would not budge; her gaze was fixed on Creed "I am sorry if I am speaking out of turn, but I meant what I said," she said. "The Scots did not kill Ryton."

Creed's brow furrowed as he gazed at the pale young woman. "How would you know this?"

Julia took a few timid steps toward him. "Jory told me."

Creed's confusion deepened. "What did he tell you?"

Julia seemed quite composed; but suddenly, she erupted into a very odd cry and began to tremble. Her hands flew to her head as if to keep her head on, for she grasped at it and clawed her hair dramatically. By this time, Sian and Richard were on their feet, looking at the young woman as if she were losing her mind. In fact, it very much appeared so; arrogant, surly, proud and plain Julia appeared to be crumbling right before their eyes.

"He made me do it," she suddenly hissed. "He made me do it and I cannot keep silent any longer. Not when... you must not believe that the Scots killed your brother. They did nothing of the kind. Jory killed him."

Creed's expression turned to one of horror. He went to Julia, putting his enormous hands on her arms to trap her. His dusky blue gaze burned into her.

"If you have ever thought to lie to me to get my attention, now would not be the time," he growled. "I will not believe your attempts to gain my trust or my compassion."

She was shaking horribly, her voice littered with spikes and quivers. "The time has long since passed that I would try to gain your attention," she warbled. "Your wife has your attention completely and I am not a fool. But I must ease my conscience on this matter because the knowledge of it is driving me mad."

Creed shook her but Carington was there, her hand on her husband's massive arm. "Nay, Creed," she begged softly. "Dunna be rough with her. Let her speak."

Julia looked at Carington with a wild look to her eye. "You," she murmured. "I hated you. I hated you for what you took from me and Jory offered to help me gain my vengeance. But it was really his own vengeance he was seeking."

"Jory's vengeance?" Creed repeated. "Make sense, woman. What do you know?"

Julia began to cry and laugh at the same time. "The night you were married he came to me and offered to help me exact my revenge upon you for spurning my feelings," she said. "I asked him why he would help me do such a thing and he told me that he was, in fact, determined to get even against you. He said it had already started when he took a fallen morning star and smashed it into your brother's skull. His next step was defiling your wife. He made me help him or he told me he would kill me."

Creed's eyes widened and his grip on her tightened. Carington saw the woman flinch with pain and she put both hands on Creed's arm, trying to pull him away from her.

"English," she said firmly. "Let her go; do ye hear me? Let her go."

But Creed was not listening. He continued to squeeze, unable to voice the sheer horror that was filling his veins. Carington passed a panicked look at Richard, who rushed over to Creed and took hold of the other arm that was preparing to crush Julia. Sian followed on his heels and aided his daughter in removing Creed's hands from the very fragile young woman. When his grip was released, Carington pressed herself against her husband and threw her arms around his tight midsection.

"Creed, calm yerself," she said softly, urgently. "Listen to what she has to say. Ye canna turn yer anger against her for being truthful."

Julia watched, eyes wide with fright and madness, as Creed wrapped his arms around his wife. He seemed to draw a great deal of calm from that gesture. But his dusky blue gaze was still deadly.

"Continue," he said through clenched teeth.

Julia was shaking so badly that it was difficult for her to stand. "He made me tell him when you left the chamber the morning after your wedding," she said hoarsely. "He knew when you had left because I told him. Then he attacked her."

Creed remembered that morning well. He had always wondered how Jory had known Carington was alone. Now he knew.

"It was you," his jaw was flexing dangerously. "You enabled the attack against my wife."

"I had no choice," Julia insisted pathetically. "He told me he would kill me if I did not."

"And so you told him," Creed had no compassion for her. "And my brother? Do you swear he told you that he had killed him?"

She nodded fervently. "With God as my witness, he told me that he had picked up a morning star and came up behind your brother when his attention was elsewhere. Sir Ryton never saw it coming."

Creed could not believe what he was hearing. He stood with Carington in his arms, gazing at the pale young woman with a great degree of shock. He was, literally, speechless. Carington, however, was not; she twisted in her husband's embrace so that she could look at Julia.

"Why did ye not tell us this before?" she asked quietly. "Why wait?"

Julia seemed to falter. "Perhaps there was a part of me that wanted Creed to suffer the death of his brother," she could not look the woman in the eye. "Perhaps there was a part of me that wanted you both to suffer. If I could not have Creed, then I wanted you both to be punished. But the more time passed, the more I realized that you were deeply in love with each other and your marriage had not been one of convenience or lust. And you, my lady… you are kind and vivacious and humorous. I would sit and watch you with Kristina and grow jealous that I was not a part of your games. Creed seemed so happy with you and I began to feel guilty that I hated you. But as the days and weeks went by, the more difficult it became for me to tell you what I knew. I waited for a proper time but none seemed to come and I became terrified of what you would do. But now… with what is being discussed I can no longer hold back. You both must know the truth."

Carington was trying to keep her composure, made worse when she could feel Creed trembling against her. She put a soft hand to his cheek to comfort him, watching him kiss her hand with quivering lips. She turned back to Julia.

"I thank ye for telling us the truth, then," she said. "I understand ye feared for yer life from Jory and I dunna blame ye for what happened. Had you not helped him, he still would have found a way to harm me. 'Twas not yer fault for what he did."

Julia nearly collapsed with relief. "I wanted to tell you, so many times," she murmured. "But I was afraid to."

Carington sighed softly. "You told us now. That is what matters."

Creed was an emotional wreck; he could not be as kind and gracious as his wife was. He turned away from Julia, still clutching Carington, and pulled his wife back to the table with him. Sian and Richard followed. They regained their seats at the table and this time, Sian poured Creed a large cup of wine. Julia simply turned away from the group and left the hall.

Carington watched her go with some sadness. For so long, she had felt no pity for the woman because of her selfish, haughty ways. But that was all changed now; she felt a good deal of sorrow for the lonely, confused young woman. She turned back to her husband.

"Are ye all right?" she asked softly, her hand on his face.

He nodded, staring at his cup of wine. "Aye," he murmured. "But it is as if I am living his death all over again."

She kissed his cheek, leaning her head against his to comfort him. "But ye had yer justice when ye killed Jory whilst defending me. Ye did not know at the time that ye killed the man who murdered yer brother."

He nodded slowly, still staring pensively at his wine. "I did not know it, but God did. Perhaps it was He who orchestrated that event as justice well served for my brother."

She smiled sadly at him, forcing him to look at her. When his dusky blue eyes fell on her sweet face, he suddenly collapsed against her, his face in her tender neck and his arms around her. In the great hall of Prudhoe as life went on around them, Carington could feel his warm tears against her flesh. For Ryton, he would finally weep.

It was only later on that evening that they discovered that Julia had hung herself.

CHAPTER FOURTEEN

December 1200 A.D.

The snows had come early this year. As Carington sat with Lady Vivian de Witt, cooing softly at the newborn girl in her cradle, she kept watching the snow outside as it collected on the windowsill. Lady Vivian was not feeling well after the birth of her daughter and had been growing steadily weaker for days, something that greatly concerned Stanton. Lady Anne had sent to Newcastle for the physic and the man insisted that the lady was greatly taxed from the birth, prescribing such things as boiled beef's blood and other strange things. But still, Lady Vivian was not improving.

Carington and the other ladies would take turns sitting with Lady Vivian to tend both her and the infant who was, in fact, a lusty little girl with her father's blond hair. But Lady Vivian could not feed the child so a wetnurse had been hired from the village. When the woman was not nursing the babe, she was busying herself with little Henry. On this cold and snowy day as Vivian slept, Carington had baby watching duty. She reached into the cradle and scooped up the fussing infant, walking the length of the floor and singing softly to soothe her. She considered it good practice for the day when her own bairn would arrive.

The door to the cottage blew open and two knights entered. Snow blew in after them until the smaller knight shut the door firmly. Carington stood back, shielding the baby from the harsh weather as Creed wiped the snow from his eyes. Stanton went straight into the bedchamber to see his wife.

"The weather is worsening," Creed commented, eyeing the fat-faced baby in his wife's arms. "How is the child?"

"Fine," she said, then lowered her voice. "But Vivian is not well at all. I fear for her, English. She is growing weaker by the minute."

Creed drew in a deep breath, his gaze moving to the open bedchamber door. He could see Stanton seated on the edge of the bed as he spoke softly to his wife. After a moment, he shook his head and looked back to Carington.

"I do not know if I would be half as composed as he is," he murmured, looking into her emerald eyes. "He shows a great deal of strength."

Carington knew he was thinking about her and the perils of childbirth; she had seen this rise in fear in him for weeks. It had worsened since Vivian gave birth to her daughter. She reached up and patted his icy cheek.

"I'm as strong as an ox," she assured. "I'll be on my feet an hour after birthin' this bairn. There is nothing to worry over."

He kissed her palm, watching her put the baby back in the cradle. He was trying not to let the event of the birth frighten him, but in truth, he was terrified and excited at the same time. All he knew was that his wife must survive, no matter what. He did not know what would become of him if she did not; he could not even think about it.

"I came to tell you that we have sighted an incoming party about a half mile out," he changed the subject. "It looks to me as if they are flying papal banners but I cannot be sure. The blowing snow obscures much."

Carington whirled to him, her eyes wide. "The priest returns?"

He lifted his shoulders. "I am not sure," he replied. "But I think you should be with me if it is him."

"Of course I will," she insisted, watching his expression for any signs of apprehension. "The queen's bairn should have been born a couple of months ago. Do ye believe it is news of the birth?"

"It is possible."

She gazed up at him, trepidation in her eyes. "Oh, English," she murmured. "I am frightened. No word for months and then…."

He leaned over to kiss her gently; he did not want to touch her because his armor and mail were like ice. "I know," he murmured, kissing her again. "But we knew this time would come. We expected it. We can do nothing more than face it."

Her eyes began to well. "But what if he wants to take ye to London?"

He pulled off a glove and tenderly grasped her face. "There is no use in worrying about it until the time comes." He let go of her face and hunted around for her cloak. Finding it across a chair, he held it up for her. "Come along, love. Let us to go the great hall and await the visitors."

Sniffling, she allowed him to help her into her heavy woolen cloak with the fur lining. He fastened the ties and pulled her hood on, securing it around her sweet face. Letting Stanton know he was confiscating the baby sitter, he took her out into the snowy ward.

The wind was kicking up something fierce as he took her into the inner bailey and directly to the great hall. Once inside the entry, the heat from the roaring fire was like a slap in the face. It was almost too warm. Creed pulled off his gauntlets and helped Carington remove her cloak.

"Now," he took her gently by the elbow. "Go and sit by the fire and I shall return with our visitor."

She gazed up at him, her lovely little face round and rosy-cheeked. "I'm scared for ye," she clutched at him. "What if... what if we hide and tell Laird Richard to tell the church that we ran off months ago? They'll not know where to find ye."

He put his cold hands on her face, leaning down to kiss both cheeks. "Wife, you worry overly," he said with a twinkle in his eye. "Moreover, it could be good news. If we run, we will never know."

She was not convinced but took a seat at the table with her back facing the fire. It was warm and wonderful and as her belly brushed up against the old oak table, she could feel the babe moving within her. Creed was just putting his gloves back on when she motioned urgently to him.

"English, come here!" she called excitedly. "Hurry if ye want to feel yer son move about."

Creed would take any opportunity for that. He tucked his gloves under one arm and went to her, putting both of his enormous hands on her belly. His hands were so big that they swallowed up the entire bulge. He waited with anticipation for a moment, finally rewarded with strong kicking and a few rolls against her flesh. He grinned as their eyes met.

"He is active today," he said with pride. "He will be a very strong lad."

She smiled in return, putting her small hands over his. There was such intimate joy in their delight, something that meant the world to the two of them. The baby kicked and rolled a few more times, causing Creed to laugh softly.

"I do not believe he is content in there," he told her. "He wants to be born and serve with his father."

She pursed her lips at him. "Ye'll not rush him into battle," she told him. "I would keep him with me for as long as I can."

With a smirk, he cocked an eyebrow at her to let her know how ridiculous he thought her statement was. They had discussed fostering, once, and she had ended up in tears. She did not like the idea of sending her child away. Leaning down to kiss her belly, he stood up and resumed pulling his gloves on.

"I will see to our visitors now," he told her. "I shall return."

Carington's smile faded but she nodded, rubbing her belly as he quit the hall. Trepidation filled her once more as she sat in the quiet room, her imagination running wild with a myriad of horrible scenarios. But Creed had seemed unconcerned. Perhaps she should be as well.

Out in the snow-blown inner bailey, Creed made his way to the outer bailey just as the great gates began to crank open. The wood was frozen and the ropes sodden, making it difficult to move. He could see several soldiers trying to strong arm the gates. As he continued to make his way to the gate, the frozen panels finally jerked open. As they yawned wide, a small party bearing icy banners of the yellow papal cross entered. It took another two dozen men to shut the gates behind them.

The snow was past Creed's ankles and getting deeper as he

made his way to the escort party. There was a small carriage in the center of the group and just as he reached it, the door popped open and a familiar face appeared.

It was Massimo. Creed felt his stomach lurch a little at the sight of the man but he greeted him pleasantly. If the man was traveling in weather such as this, all the way from London no less, then the news must indeed be serious. He was glad that Carington was inside the hall and away from this scene for the moment.

"Your Grace," he said, helping the man from the carriage and into the snow. "You picked fine weather to travel in."

Massimo's young face was bundled up in woolen scarves. His dark eyes fixed on Creed. "It was not by choice, I assure you," he said. "I have come with dreadful news and there is no time to waste."

Creed's stomach lurched a little more. "What news?"

Massimo put his hand on Creed's arm. "Take me into some place warm before I freeze to death and I will tell you."

Creed began to lead the man towards the great hall, wrought with dread as they walked. "Tell me what has happened that would have you traveling in such foul weather?"

Massimo wiped snow from his face. "The queen's child was born three months ago," he told him. "The child was early and did not survive. But it was born with a crown of black hair and, I am told, dark blue eyes. Like yours."

Creed cleared his throat softly. "Be that as it may, it was not mine. And Isabella has black hair."

"I understand," Massimo nodded. "But the fact remains that the king went mad with fury and grief and has been demanding your head ever since. He knew that the church has been in contact with you and he further knew that we advocate your innocence in all things. We have made that clear. When I left London six weeks ago to deliver the news to you, we were followed. A small army of the king's men is not a day's ride behind me."

Creed froze and looked at him. "You led them to Prudhoe?"

Massimo's cold face was lined with guilt and sorrow. "It was a mistake, I assure you," he said quietly. "We had no idea we were being followed until we were almost to Leeds. By then, the best I could do was proceed as quickly as I could to warn you."

Creed just stared at him. "You could have veered away and led them to Manchester or York, for God's sake. As it is, you led them right to me."

Massimo nodded submissively. "A difficult choice to make, Sir Creed. Even if I had diverted them, I could not take the chance that they would somehow wander into Prudhoe or Hexham and catch you unaware. You had to be warned."

Creed sighed heavily, his mind whirling with the news. He resumed his walk towards the great hall. "Then it would seem my choice is to either hunker down at Prudhoe and expect a siege or flee. And I cannot flee."

"Why not?" Massimo demanded. "You must leave right away if you are to have any chance of escaping them."

Creed shook his head. "I cannot leave in any case."

"Why not?" Massimo demanded again.

Creed looked at him, then. "Because my wife is with child. I cannot drag her out in this weather or travel with her in her current condition. Even in fine weather, I would be hesitant to take her into open country."

Massimo stared at him in shock. After a moment, he let out a hissing whistle between his teeth and looked away. "Dear God," he muttered. "I understand your reluctance, Creed, but you have no choice. If you stay, the king's men will lay siege to Prudhoe and you jeopardize everyone here with your presence. Would you really risk so many men, women and children because you do not want to leave?"

They had reached the great hall and Creed turned to look at the priest with a great deal of pain on his face. The dusky blue eyes were full of it. After a moment, he averted his gaze and opened the door.

Hot air hit them in the face as they entered and Creed quickly closed the door behind them. When Creed looked up, he could already see Carington moving across the floor in their direction. Her lovely face was serene yet curious. Massimo unwound the woolen scarf from his head as she drew near.

"Lady de Reyne," he greeted her, eyeing her round belly. "Your husband told me the happy news. Congratulations on your pending child."

She dipped in curtsy. "Yer Grace," she said. "Welcome to Prudhoe. My husband thought it might be ye but he could not be sure."

Massimo forced a smile and took her hand gently. "It was me," he nodded his head in the direction of the table. "May we sit and warm ourselves? I fear that I have barely escaped being turned into a pillar of ice."

Carington smiled at him but her eyes moved to Creed as they made their way back to the well-scrubbed table. Creed simply winked at her, sending a servant for hot mulled wine and food. Then he joined them.

Carington did not mince words; she knew the priest was there for a reason and she would know what it was.

"To what do we owe the honor of your visit?" she asked the priest. "Surely it is not because ye enjoy traveling in the snow."

Massimo smiled weakly. "Nay, my lady, I do not," he cast a glance at Creed. "I have, in fact, come with some news."

Creed made sure to sit beside her as she focused on the priest. "What news?" she asked.

Massimo chose his words carefully; he had caught glimpses of the lady's high strung nature the last time he was at Prudhoe and did not imagine that pregnancy had stilled those tendencies. If anything, they were probably worse. He was very careful how he delivered the news.

"The queen gave birth to a stillborn son three months ago," he said. "It was rumored that the child was the exact image of your husband. The king's grief and fury knew no bounds and he put a price on your husband's head. Even now, the king's men have followed me to Prudhoe and cannot be more than a day's ride behind me. I have been attempting to convince your husband to flee but he will not."

In spite of the devastating news, Carington held her composure admirably. But it was very thinly held. She turned to Creed.

"He is right, English," she said, although he could see her lips trembling. "Ye must flee. Go to Wether Fair and seek sanctuary from my father. Massimo will go with ye and explain the situation."

His heart was breaking as he noted the quiver to her mouth, her pale features. He knew how upset she was. "I will not leave you," he asserted softly, firmly. "I am not afraid to face the king with the church on my side."

"I will go with you," she suddenly bolted up as if she had a million things to do and only five minutes in which to complete them. "I shall pack lightly and we can ride to my father's home. It shouldna take more than a couple of days."

He grabbed her by the hands as she tried to get away. "In this weather?" he was trying to be gentle but he could see that she was beginning to panic. "I will not risk you over miles of open ground. It is foolish."

She had a wild look to her eye as her alarm gained ground. "Then ye must go alone," she insisted, yanking at his hands. "Ye must leave right away. Go to Wether Fair and I will send word to ye when it 'tis safe to return."

He shook his head firmly. "I will not leave you, Cari. There is no telling how long we would be separated and I will not miss the birth of my son."

Her panic broke through and her high-pitched voice began to quake. "Ye'll miss his entire life if the king's men murder ye," she cried. "For the love of God, English, get out of here. Go before it 'tis too late!"

She was yanking fiercely at him and he threw his arms around her to stop the panic. She collapsed against him in terrified tears as he held her tightly.

"I will not run like a coward," he murmured into her dark hair, listening to her weep harder. "I did nothing wrong. God will protect me."

She was weeping pathetically. "Go, English," she sobbed. "I am begging ye; for my sake, please go. I canna stand the strain of knowing ye risked yer life just to stay with me. Oh, please... go...."

She trailed off into heart wrenching sobs. Creed sighed heavily, rocking her gently and trying to soothe her. His dark, anguished gaze found the priest.

"How far behind you would you estimate the king's men are?" he asked quietly.

Massimo wriggled his eyebrows in resignation. "Darlington, perhaps," he lifted his shoulders. "If they are riding harder than I am, then they will be closer."

Carington pulled her face from the crook of his neck, her emerald eyes filled with terror. "Please," she put her small hands on his face urgently. "Please go. The king's men will lay siege to Prudhoe if ye stay and ye will risk much. Yer desire to stay with me is not worth so many lives. And what of Lord Richard? Will ye bring hell upon him because of yer selfishness?"

He gazed deeply into her beautiful eyes. "I do not consider wanting to stay with my wife selfish. Moreover, there will be no siege."

She blinked, looking surprised. "No siege? What do ye mean?"

He leaned down and kissed her wet cheek. "Because I intend to turn myself over to them."

Carington flew into a frenzy. "Nay!" she screamed. "Ye cannot do this, not when...oh!"

She suddenly doubled over and clutched her belly. Creed went from calm to horrified in a split second.

"What is wrong?" he had his arms on her, supporting her. "Cari, what is happening?"

She was panting, holding her rounded belly. "A... pain," she gasped. "'Tis nothing... I will be all right."

Creed was seized with terror. "What is wrong?"

She shook her head; mostly to ease his mind but also because she did not really know. "A pain," she said bravely. "It will pass. I've had a few lately but they go away."

"A few?" he repeated, aghast. "And you did not tell me?"

"There wasna much to tell."

He swept her into his arms, torn between fury and terror. "I am taking you to bed," he told her. "The strain has been too much for you."

Carington was in a good deal of agony as bolts of pain shot through her belly and groin. "Creed," she was struggling to calm herself, realizing that it was now her husband who was on the edge of panic. "I will be all right but I must know that ye are safe. Ye must leave; please. I am begging ye."

He did not reply. A couple of servants were hovering hear the entry door and he sent one of them running for the physic tending Lady Vivian while the other tossed Carington's cloak over her to shield her from the snow outside. Creed was in such a state of horror that he did not realize that it was Massimo who opened the entry door for him and helped them out into the snow. The priest kept Carington's cloak from blowing off as they trudged through the fresh powder snow and into the cottage. Once inside, Massimo removed the cloak as Creed took Carington on into the bedroom.

He laid her gently on their massive bed, gazing into her face with a stricken look. "The physic is coming, honey," he murmured. "What more can I do for you?"

She lay back on the pillows, her hands pressed to her swollen belly. "Ye can go," she whispered. "Please, Creed; I cannot stomach the thought of ye at the mercy of the king. If ye have ever loved me, if ye have ever truly wanted to please me, then ye will flee to Wether Fair and remain there until I send for ye."

He tossed off his frozen helm and removed his gloves, kneeling beside the bed. "I am not leaving you."

She groaned as another pain struck and turned her head away from him so he could not see her fear and anguish. When she spoke again, she was weeping.

"Please," she whispered, extending a hand to him. "Oh, please do as I ask."

Creed realized that tears were very close to the surface for him as well. He took her hand, kissing it reverently, never more terrified in his life. He squeezed his eyes shut, his mouth against her hand.

"My selfishness has brought you to this," he hissed. "I have caused your pain with all of this strife and worry that seems to follow me about like a plague."

"Nay, love, ye have not," she assured him. "But the most important thing right now to me is yer safety. Can ye not understand? Ye are the most important thing in the world to me. I love ye more than my own life. I want ye to save yerself so that ye can see yer son grow up. That is not cowardly."

There were tears on his cheeks as he continued to hold her hand against his face. The dusky blue eyes were in turmoil.

"All right," he murmured. "If that is your wish, then I will do it. But I cannot leave you at this moment."

She nodded firmly. "Aye, ye can and ye will. What becomes of me and the babe will not change if you are here or not and I will feel much more at peace knowing ye are safe."

He gazed at her, his lips trembling. "Please do not make me go."

She reached out and pulled him to her, her arms around his neck as she held him close. "I am not making ye go, English," she murmured against his ear. "I am begging ye to. Please. So ye may live to see yer son grow up."

He sobbed against her neck, a short burst as he struggled to keep his emotions at bay. Suddenly, he was the vulnerable one and she was his strength. The pain of separation was more than he could bear. His massive hands were on her face, her hair, his lips kissing her tenderly as he whispered of his love for her. When she groaned softly with another pain, he gazed at her with sorrow and anxiety.

"My God," he breathed. "I cannot go, not now."

She grabbed hold of his hand and squeezed tightly, her nails digging into him. "Ye promised."

He nodded swiftly, not wanting to upset her further. "All right, all right," he said quickly. "Can I at least wait until the physic has examined you?"

She seemed to calm somewhat. "Aye," she whispered, touching his face to memorize it for the separation ahead. "Everything will be all right, English. Ye must have faith."

He kissed her hand, her cheek, struggling not to fall apart. "I do," he closed his eyes, his forehead against hers. "I love you, Cari. Greater than any man has ever loved a woman, I love you. I will return from this madness and we will know peace and happiness again."

She did not say anything; she continued to clutch him until the physic came and separated them out of necessity. Although it was not the truth, he told Creed that she was simply overwrought. It was a lie that Carington had made him relay because she knew Creed would not have left her otherwise. And it was imperative that he go.

So Creed left into the snowy dusk with Massimo at his side, moving from the outer bailey of Prudhoe and out into the white-encrusted countryside beyond. His destination was Wether Fair in the midst of the Scots border, a place that even the king would not dare breach.

Carington delivered a premature daughter three days later in a complicated birth that nearly claimed her life. The babe did not survive.

CHAPTER FIFTEEN

January 1201 A.D.

"Ye pace enough tae wear holes in me floor," Sian sat in the great hall of Wether Fair, watching his massive son-in-law walk around the room. "Ye're exhausting me, man. Sit down and enjoy yer drink."

Creed lifted an eyebrow at him; they had entertained this conversation many times over the past three weeks, since Creed first arrived at the desolate fortress of Wether Fair.

"I would think you would show more concern than you do," he fired back softly. "It is, after all, your grandson that your daughter is giving birth to."

Sian made a good show at being unconcerned although inside, he was a mess. He lifted his shoulders lazily. "Worrying will not help," he said. "She is in the hands o'God."

Creed stopped his pacing, put his hands on his hips and chewed his lip in a nervous gesture. "Are you really so casual about this?"

Sian's vibrant blue eyes flared at him before turning back to his drink. "Nay," he said. "But I willna worry about something I canna control. I sent one of me men with yer priest tae Prudhoe more than a week ago; they should be returning with some news soon. So sit yerself down and drink before I take a stick tae ye. Ye're makin' me daft!"

The corner of Creed's mouth twitched but he did as he was told. "I should have never left her," he lamented for the thousandth time. "I should not have let her talk me into running."

Sian's expression widened. "And if ye say that again, I am going tae run ye through," he jabbed a finger at Creed. "Ye did what ye had tae. Had ye stayed, the king would have ye now and ye would never see yer son. Is that what ye wanted?"

Creed sighed heavily, gazing into the blazing fire; the hearth was not particularly well made and smoke billowed out to the ceiling. But he drew some comfort being where his wife was born and where she was raised. He could see her traversing the narrow stairs and walking the great hall. He even slept in her old bed just to feel close to her.

"Nay," he muttered. "That is not what I wanted."

"Then stop yer fretting. We will know her fate soon enough."

Creed sighed heavily again, this time with the displeasure of the waiting game, and reclaimed his cup. He and Sian spent nearly every day here, drinking and talking, when they weren't out riding Sian's lands when the weather was better. But this had been a particularly brutal winter and those days were few and far between. Still, it had afforded them much time to get to know one another and Creed was not surprised to realize that he liked his father-in-law. More than that, Sian had formed a strong attachment to Creed. Now, as they sat and entertained one another, it was as friends.

"She is fine," Creed said as if to convince himself. "I am sure that everything is fine."

Sian's vibrant blue gaze lingered on him. "Aye, lad. She is fine."

So it was another day of the waiting game. The New Year came and went two days ago, but to Creed, it felt as if he had been away from his wife more than just a few weeks. It felt like forever. Massimo had stayed with him for a few days until Sian sent the priest, along with a few Scots, back to Prudhoe to see what had transpired. Sian and Creed were still waiting, waiting until Creed thought he would surely go mad. Every day they sat, drank, talked and waited. It was becoming so monotonous that Creed was ready to climb the walls. As the snow blew in through the small, square windows that dotted the keep, all he could think of was Prudhoe and his wife. That made him fairly useless for anything else.

As the afternoon rolled on, Sian tried to interest Creed in a game of dice. Soon they were playing for the assortment of daggers Creed had brought with him against Sian's collection of a fermented barley drink. As they played through the afternoon, Creed ended up with not only all of his weapons, but most of Sian's liquor. The angrier Sian became, the more humored Creed grew. He was, in fact, actually enjoying himself when the door to the great hall suddenly creaked open.

Snow blew in from Wether Fair's bleak bailey as several bodies made their way inside. Creed was not particularly concerned, as there were always Scotsmen walking in and out of Sian's keep, until he recognized one of the men that had escorted Massimo back to Prudhoe. With a start, he rose to his full, considerable height. His jaw began ticking as the men filtered into the hall and began removing their wet winter clothing.

Massimo was the last man in. Creed did not wait; he went right for him.

"Well?" he demanded. "Did you see her? How is she?"

Massimo was fairly close to being frozen. He was having difficulty removing his warm outer clothing and Creed eventually went to his aid. He pulled off the woolen travel cloak, the layers of wraps and scarves, eventually shoving the man close to the fire. The priest just stood there and shivered as Sian stoked the blaze. All of his men were very nearly frozen, indicative of the brutal weather they had endured.

Creed had all he could take of delays regardless of the priest's condition. "Massimo," he demanded again, though in a gentler tone. "Did you see my wife? Is she all right?"

Massimo turned his pale, frozen face to him. His dark eyes were circled and sunken.

"Sir Creed," he said through cold, thick lips. "There is much to tell. Get me a chair before I collapse."

Creed snatched a stool from beside the hearth and practically shoved the priest onto it. The man was so cold that he was having difficulty standing. But he knew that Creed was waiting for an answer; truth was, he was not looking forward to providing him with what he knew. But he had little choice. He fixed Creed in the eye and prayed the man could handle it.

"You are a knight of the realm," the priest began, a chill quiver in his voice. "You have been trained to control your emotions in all things. You must draw upon that strength now to prepare for what I am to tell you."

Creed just stared at him. His face suddenly lost all color; both Massimo and Sian could see it. Next thing they realized, Creed had toppled to his knees before the priest, his expression indicative of his struggle. His eyes were wide with horror.

"She is dead," he breathed.

Massimo shook his head. "Nay, she is not," he told him. "But much tragedy has befallen her since you last saw her."

Creed emitted something of a strangled sob. "What, for God's sake? Why do you not come out and tell me what has happened?"

Massimo reached out and grabbed Creed's massive biceps as if to hold him fast. "Listen to me and listen well," he muttered. "We arrived at Prudhoe nearly eight days ago. We lingered in town for a time and spoke with the seamstress your wife is so fond of. We discovered that King John's men had indeed reached Prudhoe not long after you left. They were still occupying it, interrogating Lord Richard and the knights as to your whereabouts. Somehow, someway, they discovered that you had taken a wife and that she was in residence at Prudhoe."

Creed grew even paler than he already was. "My dear God; what did they do to her?"

Massimo shook his head. "They did nothing to your wife, I assure you. They understood through Lord Richard that the damage, to her, had already been done. There was no more pain or suffering that anyone could inflict upon her."

Creed was so tightly coiled that he was light-headed. "I do not understand."

Massimo's grip softened. He touched Creed on the side of the face comfortingly. "Three days after we left Prudhoe for Wether Fair, your wife delivered a daughter," his voice was soft and soothing. "Creed, there is no way to ease the pain of these facts so I must simply tell you; Carington nearly died in the birth. Your daughter, in fact, did not long survive after she was born and I said Mass for her myself. Her young soul is at rest. But your wife… she lingers still between life and death. I was permitted to see her and to give her last rites and when I left, she had not yet passed. I must be honest when I say that the physic is not hopeful."

Creed shot to his feet before Massimo could finish, pulling the priest off the stool and sending him sprawling. Sian was there, as were some of his burly men, and when they saw their laird grab for Creed they leapt forward to assist. Creed was going mad before their eyes and there was nothing they could do to stop it.

"I must return to Prudhoe," Creed was heading for the door with a half dozen men hanging on him. "I must get to Carington."

Massimo scrambled to his feet and put himself in front of Creed. "Listen to me," he pleaded. "You must control yourself or all will be lost. The king's men are aware that I know of your location; they were there the night I arrived and they knew I gave last rites to your wife. They are further aware that I have been your advocate since the beginning and they have sent me with a message for you."

Creed came to a halt, his dusky blue eyes bordering on insanity. His nostrils were flaring as he spoke. "Who sends this message?"

"A knight named de la Londe."

Creed's brow furrowed and his teeth barred in a frightening gesture. "I know this knight," he hissed. "He was one of the knights who accompanied me on my mission to escort Isabella. What message does he send?"

Massimo hoped that Creed would retain enough sense not to throttle him. "That if you do not return to Prudhoe, they are taking your wife back to London to face justice in your stead."

Those fateful words sealed Creed's fury; the temper he kept so controlled and cool was irrevocably unleashed. With a roar, he yanked away from the hands holding him and proceeded to demolish everything in the hall that was within his reach. The benches at the table were smashed and splintered and when he was finished with those, he proceeded to bash and slam the feasting table until the legs came off and the table itself smashed into a hundred little pieces. The ale cups sailed across the room and smashed into the great stone walls and the stool that the priest had been sitting on ended up in tatters.

Sian and his men stood back and watched Creed demolish the hall. It was a terrifying and awesome sight. Massimo tried to stay clear of the flying debris as he followed the man around the room, trying to talk some sense into him. But it was of no avail; Creed was far gone with lunacy, fury and anguish such as he had never experienced bubbling up from his chest and expending itself in his strength. But it was more than that; months of persecution and hurtful accusations were finding their way free. Finally, he was expending his turmoil. When everything was smashed, still, he smashed it more until he pulverized it.

Eventually, his fury began to wane and he came to an unsteady halt, his hands and arms bloodied, sweat covering his body. It was a rage that none of them had ever seen before, this man who seemed to be followed by such bad fortune and darkness.

Sian waited a reasonable amount of time before approaching him. He understood, more than most, that sometimes a man must physically demonstrate his anger in order to gain control of his demons. Creed seemed to have his share of demons. He came upon Creed as the man stood near the hearth, sweating and bloodied and breathing heavily.

"Creed," he said in a low voice. "She's me daughter. If any man has the right tae feel pain, it is me. I understand your rage, lad, but charging in tae Prudhoe will only get ye killed. Is that what ye want?"

Creed was unfocused and unsteady, staring into the flames and somewhat numb to what was going on around him. But he heard Sian's softly uttered question.

"Nay," he muttered. "'Tis not what I want. But I must go to my wife and I will kill anyone who stands in my way."

Sian scratched his dark head. "I have been fighting the Sassenach for many years and it never ceases to amaze me how the lot of ye will charge in tae a battle and hope that your strength will overcome. Sometimes it is not yer strength that will win but yer mind. Ye must be smarter than yer enemy."

Creed turned to look at him, then. "I have been a knight for fourteen years and in all that time, I have never been accused of being foolish."

Sian shook his head. "Not foolish, lad. Ye simply must think smarter than yer enemy."

Creed gazed at him with his muddled eyes. "The king is my enemy."

"I know."

"You have been fighting the English for many years. What would you suggest?"

Sian cast a long glance at his men, standing around the room, some of them kicking away pieces of the broken table. Now, they were more than allies with Prudhoe; they were family. And family must help family, as Creed had always known. He, in fact, knew the Scots well in that regard.

"This will take more than the support of the Clan," Sian said after a moment. "From what the priest has told me, ye have many friends willing to defend ye, including Laird Richard. He said that Laird Richard has been protecting ye since this madness with the queen started. And Laird Richard has allies that will come to your aid if he calls them."

Creed was not thinking straight but he could grasp the general concept of what Sian was suggesting. "Call upon Prudhoe's allies?"

Sian nodded as he looked at the priest. "How large is the king's force that resides at Prudhoe?" he asked him.

Massimo lifted his slender shoulders. "Fifty men perhaps. They brought more of an escort than an army. They have the backing of the king, after all. They did not expect resistance."

"A king who is hated by his barons," Creed grumbled. "I can take on fifty men by myself."

Sian patted his enormous arm. "Indeed ye can," he humored him. "But yer focus will be on me daughter, not on fighting. Ye must have yer friends hold off the king's men."

"And do what?"

Sian's vibrant blue eyes flashed in that insane expression that Creed was coming to associate with his father-in-law. "Send them back to the king with the message that Creed de Reyne is an innocent man and willna pay for crimes he dinna commit. If the king wants ye then he will have to fight the whole of Northumbria and Scotland to get ye."

Creed was beginning to calm somewhat but he was still on edge. Odd how these men he had been fighting his entire life were suddenly on his side, men his brothers had died against. It was a very strange realization; he remembered telling Carington when Ryton died that he was all alone. Gazing into Sian's face, he realized that he was not alone in the least. In many ways, he was richer than he had ever been.

"Then we ride tonight for Hexham," he said quietly.

"Why Hexham?"

"Because Galen Burleson is there and he is a close friend. Hexham is also Prudhoe's closest ally. If you want large numbers to stand against the king's men, we must have Hexham."

Sian lifted a dark eyebrow. "Ye've not yet seen large numbers until ye've seen the gathering of the Clans," he nodded with confidence. "But ye will, lad. Ye will."

Creed's expression softened. "This is not for me, you understand," he murmured. "It is for Cari."

He heard his father-in-law sigh softly. For the first time since the delivery of the devastating news, his sorrow broke through. "Aye, lad," he replied quietly. "For Cari."

***

Carington was not sure how long she had been awake, but she thought it might have been for quite some time. She could hear soft voices around her, the whistling of the wind and the soft snap of the fire. It seemed to drone on for hours. When she tried to open her eyes, her lids felt like they weighed as much as a small child. She could not seem to raise them. So she drifted off to sleep again only to awaken and feel moderately alert.

Struggling, she finally opened her eyes to a dim room and a roaring fire. Turning slightly, she noticed that someone was sitting next to the bed but she could not see who it was. Turning her head further, or movement of any kind, was simply out of the question. But she apparently moved enough so that it was noticed.

"Carington?" It was Kristina sitting next to her, her pale blue eyes wide. "Cari, are you awake?"

Carington took a deep breath, struggling to keep her eyes open. "I... I suppose ye could call it that," she murmured with thick lips. "What... what has...?"

"You have been unconscious for days," Kristina was almost sobbing. "We thought you were dead."

She did sob then and Carington blinked her eyes, struggling to focus on her young friend. "I'm not-a dead yet," she whispered. "My bairn...?"

Kristina slapped a hand over her mouth to stifle her weeping but she was not doing a very good job. "I am so sorry," she wept softly. "She was so beautiful but she was too small to survive. Father Massimo said Mass for her."

Carington closed her eyes and tears trickled down her temples. She was so weak that she could barely muster the strength to cry; the tears just fell of their own will. "My sweet bairn," she whispered. "Where is she buried?"

Kristina was a weeping mess. "Lady Anne insisted she be buried in the d'Umfraville crypt in town," she told her. "I remembered that you had told me once that your mother's name was Dera, so Lady Anne and I named her Dera Carington de Reyne. I hope that is all right."

Carington nodded, too overcome to reply. Kristina held her hand and wept with her. It was a painful moment for them both.

"Creed," Carington finally murmured. "Is he all right?"

Kristina sniffled and wiped her eyes. "Father Massimo says he is safe with your father."

"Thank God," Carington whispered. Then her eyes opened and

she weakly turned her head in Kristina's direction. "Is Father Massimo still here?"

Kristina shook her head. "He went back to tell Creed of... of...."

She could not finish as sobs overtook her again. Carington sighed weakly. "I wish he wouldna," she muttered. "It will only make him miserable that he is not here. There is nothing he could have done but he willna understand that."

Kristina did not know what to say. She held Carington's hand tightly. "There is so much more to tell you," she said. "The king's men have been here since the night you delivered Dera. They have not left."

Carington did not remember much of the past few weeks but she did remember the king's men. They had arrived when she was in labor and one of them, a knight named de La Londe, had been bold enough to try and question her. She had screamed at him. After that, she remembered little other than delivering a blue infant that she never had a chance to hold. But she knew, without anyone telling her at the time, that the baby was dead. Her conversation with Kristina only confirmed it. They had taken the infant away too quickly as the physic and Lady Anne struggled to keep her from bleeding to death. Her life was draining away and along with it, her consciousness.

After that, she remembered nothing until this moment. She felt strangely numb and exceedingly weak. She squeezed Kristina's hand faintly.

"I am thirsty," she whispered.

Kristina jumped out of her chair, wiping the remaining tears on her cheeks. She opened the chamber door into the main room beyond. "Lady Carington is awake," she announced. "She is thirsty!"

Kristina said it as if it was the most amazing event in the world. Suddenly, bodies filled the small bedchamber and Lady Anne came into view. Her handsome face was weary but she smiled sweetly at Carington, running a gentle hand over her forehead.

"Greetings, my lady," she said softly. "Welcome back."

Carington was very comforted by the woman's presence. The physic from Newcastle was standing beside her, his expression critical. He was a little man with a balding head.

"How do you feel, my lady?" he asked.

Carington sighed faintly. "Weak," she said honestly. "But I think I am hungry."

Lady Anne murmured a silent prayer of thanks and moved to get Carington some nourishment as the physic sat down beside the bed. He felt her pulse, put his hand on her head to determine her temperature, and a few other diagnostics. He pulled back the coverlet and gently pushed on her belly. As he did so, the milk from her swollen breasts stained her gown. Her body did not know there was no baby to feed. After several moments of analyzing his results, he covered her back up and fixed her in the eye.

"I was not sure you would awaken," he said frankly.

Carington's eyelids were growing heavy again, as if she had expended all of her energy from simply being awake. "We Scots are stronger than ye know," she told him, her emerald eyes fixing on him. "But my daughter… was there nothing to be done?"

He shook his head. "She could not breathe, my lady. There was nothing to be done for her. She was born too early."

The tears were returning but she fought them. "And me?" she whispered. "Will there be more bairns for my husband and I? He did so want a boy."

The physic patted her arm. "I do not see any reason why there cannot be more children. Your bleeding was caused when the sack that attaches the infant to the womb tore. I had to work to get it out of you before you bled to death."

She nodded, not particularly wanting to hear the details of the birth. The tears over her daughter's fate fell softly again. "Then I thank ye for yer skill," she whispered.

The physic watched her a moment, scratching his head wearily. He seemed lost in thought. Then he rose stiffly and quit the room just as Lady Anne entered with a bowl of beef broth. As Kristina stoked the blaze in the hearth to a ridiculous level, Lady

Anne fed Carington nearly the entire bowl. Feeling warm and nourished, Carington realized that she was feeling a little better, a little stronger. As Lady Anne handed the bowl over to Kristina, the physic suddenly returned with a bundle in his arms.

Carington and Lady Anne looked at him curiously as the physic unwrapped the snow-dusted swaddling.

"This child has no mother," he said, pulling away the blanket from the little face. "You are producing milk, my lady. It will do both you and the child well if you were to nurse her. I believe it will help heal your womb."

Carington was shocked as she recognized the blond-headed child of Lady Vivian. Her heart sank. "Good lord," she murmured. "Did Vivian not survive after all?"

Lady Anne, too, was momentarily shocked by the suggestion but quickly grew to support it. "She did not," she touched Carington's shoulder. "Stanton is beside himself with grief and the wetnurse has all she can handle with young Henry. Take the baby, Cari; take her and make her strong."

Carington was saddened by Vivian's death and by Stanton's ensuing grief. He had been quite proud of his wife and family. The thought of nursing Stanton's daughter did not distress her; in fact, it made her feel a little less devastated. Now, she had a purpose, small as that purpose was. After a moment's hesitation, she pulled back the coverlet and extended her arms.

"Give her to me," she whispered.

The physic laid the baby beside her and Carington found herself gazing into big blue eyes; they were Stanton's eyes. Her grief softened just a little more as she pulled back the neck of her shift, exposing a fully engorged left breast. As Lady Anne and the physic hovered over her to see if their little experiment would work, Carington offered her swollen nipple to the baby and was rewarded when the child quickly latched on to her. She latched on a little strongly, in fact, and Carington winced as the child suckled hungrily.

Lady Anne smiled gently at her, putting her soft hand against Carington's forehead in a motherly gesture. "Stanton will be so happy," she said softly. "He has worried greatly for his daughter since Vivian's passing."

Carington cradled the baby close, watching the little mouth work furiously. She touched the downy-blond head, imagining that it was her own daughter that she held. Somehow, it helped ease her heartache.

"What is her name?" she asked Lady Anne, still standing over her. "Vivian had not yet decided last I heard."

Lady Anne's gaze was soft on the blond haired infant. "As I recall, she liked Emma and Stanton wanted Mary," she said. "I do not know what they decided."

Carington looked back at the baby, now gazing up at her with her bottomless blue eyes. She stroked the blond head. "I like Emma," she said, lifting a dark eyebrow at Lady Anne. "Tell Stanton that Vivian and I have named his daughter. If he has issue with that, then he can discuss it with me. But warn him that he'll not like my response."

Lady Anne laughed softly, watching the infant tug at Carington's breast. "I doubt he will, my lady," she said. "In fact, I am sure he will unquestionably agree with you."

With a faint smile, Carington continued to nurse Emma until she fell asleep against her breast. When Lady Anne checked on the pair later that day, she found both Carington and the baby snuggled close in slumber.

The childless mother and the motherless child had found each other.

CHAPTER SIXTEEN

Five days after Carington's return from the dead, the skies cleared and all of the Northumberland was a brilliant winter wonderland. As far as the eye could see, a vibrant white blanket covered the landscape and the sky above was a magnificent shade of blue. It was cold and crisp and delightful.

Little Henry de Witt ran around the outer bailey and threw snow balls at his father and at Kristina, who had been hit a couple of times in the head. Henry had surprisingly good aim. But Kristina laughed it off, playing with the child who had so recently lost his mother. Stanton was still struggling with his grief but he was making a good effort at tending his son.

Inside the de Reyne cottage, Burle and his wife, a grossly rotund woman with a round head and frizzy red hair, helped Carington with baby Emma. Lady Anne had duties with her own boys who had been sorely neglected while women gave birth and babies died within the walls of Prudhoe. So Burle and Lady Frieda, having three grown daughters, lent a hand with Lady Carington who was only just now able to get out of bed. Frieda would fuss at her but Burle would encourage her. Then they would start bickering and Carington would find herself breaking up the fight. Like protective parents, they wanted to take care of her and she found it touching.

Business went on as usual now that things were settling somewhat. John's men were still at Prudhoe, still housed in a corner of the outer bailey away from the rest of the life at the fortress. The knight in command, Denys de La Londe, stayed well clear of anyone at Prudhoe except for Burle and Lord Richard. He did not deal with the rabble. And his impatience in Creed de Reyne's return was increasing.

In Creed's absence, Burle had been placed in charge. Since they only had two seasoned knights and one new knight for the whole of Prudhoe's five hundred man army, Burle had knighted Creed's squire, James, and now the tall blond lad had sentry duty along with his counterpart, Steven. They made a young and vigilant pair upon the battlements.

It was close to the nooning meal when there was a soft knock at Carington's door. Burle had long since left her to go see how his two newest knights were progressing so it was just Carington and Lady Frieda in the warm little cottage. As Carington sat near the hearth and fed Emma, Frieda went to the door and irritably opened it; she had expected to see her husband. But a strange knight was standing there, his blue eyes piercing.

"I have been informed that Lady de Reyne is in better health," he said. "I have come to speak with her."

With Emma suckling hungrily at her breast, Carington could see de La Londe standing in her doorway. He, too, had caught a glimpse of her so there was no use in denying that she was well enough for visitors. With her luscious dark hair freshly washed and pulled away from her face and clad in the yellow lamb's wool surcoat, she looked pale but healthy enough. Frieda was about to throw the knight out on his ear but Carington stopped her.

"Let him in, Frieda," she instructed evenly, grasping the end of the infant's blanket and discreetly covering her bosom. "I will speak with him."

De La Londe was a big man. He entered the cottage, his blue eyes inspecting every shadow, every stone. Such were the senses of a trained knight and Carington remembered that her husband did exactly the same thing when entering new surroundings. Their movements bordered on suspicion as if waiting for a sword to come flying out at them. Carington ignored the wary stance and indicated the stool across from her for the knight to sit.

"How can I help ye, Sir Knight?" she asked politely.

De La Londe gazed down at her; he had no intention of sitting and he had no intention of engaging in idle chatter. He moved straight to the point. "We must discuss your husband, my lady."

"What of him?"

"You are well aware that he is supposed to return to Prudhoe," de La Londe lifted an eyebrow. "I sent the priest who has been protecting him with a message."

Carington remained cool even though she did not like what the man seemed to be hinting at. "You did? I was not aware."

"I know. You have been ill since my arrival."

There was a strange rebuke in that statement but she ignored it. "What message did ye send?"

De La Londe did not mince words and he had no sympathy for the fact that the lady had delivered a dead infant three weeks earlier; he was only interested in finding de Reyne. The longer he was forced to wait, the more impatient he was becoming.

"Your husband is a fugitive, my lady," he replied. "My message to him is simple; if he does not return to Prudhoe immediately, I will take you to London to stand trial in his stead."

Carington's heart began to pound and her pleasant mood evaporated. "How dare ye enter my home and threaten me," she hissed. "Get out before I kick ye out."

De La Londe was not moved in the least. "My lady, it is very simple," he was matter-of-fact. "Your husband committed a crime. He must stand trial for that crime. Since he chose to flee like a coward, I plan to put you on trial in his stead. If he does not want this to happen, then he must return to Prudhoe and surrender."

Carington just stared at him. Then, she silently stood with the baby still attached to her breast and disappeared into the bedchamber. De La Londe watched her go, listening to her rustling about in the chamber as she cooed gently to the infant. Impatiently, he shifted on his legs, eyeing the round woman with the frizzy red hair who was gazing at him harshly. His gaze moved around the room, growing more irritated with each passing moment, when the door to the chamber suddenly flew open and a fire poker came flying at his head.

He saw it in his peripheral vision but was not fast enough to duck it entirely; Lady de Reyne caught a portion of his helm and sent him reeling into the wall. Before he had a chance to gain his balance, she swung it again and clobbered him on the shoulder.

"Get out!" she screamed, wielding the poker in front of her. "Get out before I beat ye within an inch of yer life. How dare ye come into my home and slander my husband. I'll kill ye the next time ye say such things about him!"

De La Londe leapt out of her way before she could swing the thing again. He glared at her viciously, his ears ringing from the blow to his head.

"That," he snarled, "was unwise. I do not care who your husband is; attack me again and I will snap your neck."

Carington was not entirely sure that he would not do as he threatened but she raised the poker again. "Get out," she growled. "I'll not tell ye again."

De La Londe backed up to the door, opening the panel although his eyes never left the lady. After a moment, he simply nodded his head.

"I will go," he muttered. "But rest assured, I will return. And when I do, it will be with shackles."

Carington did not reply; she kept her eyes riveted to him and the poker raised. When he shut the door behind him, Frieda rushed forward and threw the bolt. The women faced each other with shock and fear.

"Dear God," Carington breathed as she lowered the iron poker. "I thought he was going to strike back at me. Thank God he dinna."

Frieda rushed to her and put her fat arms around her. "You were so brave, my lady," she said gently. "He will think twice before threatening you again."

Carington let the woman hug her for a moment before gently pulling free and leaning the poker back against the wall.

"It isna me I'm worried about," she said, suddenly weary; her strength still had not fully returned. "I worry for Creed. If I know the man, and I believe I do, he is on his way back to Prudhoe. He willna let these men take me to London to stand trial against his charges."

"What will you do?" Frieda wanted to know.

Carington simply shook her head. "I must speak to Laird

Richard," she replied. "He will know what's to be done. You'll stay with the babe, won't ye?"

Freida nodded fearfully, going to the door as Carington peered from the windows to see if de La Londe was still around. Not seeing his big blond form, she nodded to Frieda, who opened the door.

"Lock this door when I've gone," she told the woman. "If I see Burle, I'll send him to ye. He will protect ye and the babe from that awful knight."

Carington bolted out of the door and into the bright, cold day. She heard Frieda throw the lock behind her as she made her way out into the slushy bailey. She was on edge as she scanned the bailey for signs of de La Londe but she saw none. She could, however, see his encampment on the western side of the inner bailey. She picked up the pace towards the keep.

The great keep was cold and dark as she entered. A servant was coming down the stairs as she closed the door behind her and she sent the man back up to Lord Richard's chamber. As she waited, she kept wandering back to the door and peering out into the bailey, waiting for de La Londe to come charging in after her. She had remembered the man from when she had been in labor, how he had forcefully entered the room in spite of the protests of Lady Anne. She would not put it past him to do something bold and underhanded, like drag her off in chains. She would have to be on her guard.

Richard joined her a few minutes later. He tried not to be too obvious about staring at her in the yellow wool dress; she had lost all of her pre-pregnancy weight but her engorged breasts gave her an hourglass figure the likes of which he had never seen. If she had looked good before, she looked even better now. It was difficult not to look at the woman and stare like a fool.

"You are looking well this day, Lady de Reyne," he said truthfully.

"Thank ye, m'lord," she replied.

"How is baby Emma?"

"She is growing quickly," Carington told him, but her smile

quickly faded. "I am afraid I have come to ye with a problem, m'lord. Creed always trusted ye with such matters and so will I. May we speak?"

His brow furrowed with concern. "Of course. What is the problem?"

Carington sighed faintly. "That knight – de La Londe – came to see me earlier. He told me that he sent a message to Creed with Massimo telling Creed that if he dinna return to Prudhoe, I would be taken back to London to stand trial in his stead."

Richard nodded his head faintly, lifting a pensive eyebrow. "I know," he said. "Massimo told me as much before he left for Scotland. I was hoping to spare you that little bit of information for a while, anyway. You have had a rough time of it."

She lifted her shoulders in resignation. "Although it is kind of ye to want to protect me, I fear that the knight intends to follow through on his threat. What shall I do?"

Richard rubbed his chin in thought. Putting his hand on Carington's elbow, he gently steered her into the small solar near the entry. The truth was that he had been contemplating this very thing for weeks. Now, he would have to make a decision. As bad as it would have been for de La Londe to capture Creed, it would be worse should he capture Carington.

"I have been attempting to figure out that problem myself," he admitted. "It is only a matter of time before de La Londe reaches his limit of patience. While you were ill, it was not an issue, but now that you are recovered, there is no longer any excuse to prevent him from taking you."

"I understand. Have ye figured anything out?"

He looked at her with a serious eye. "Aye," he said quietly. "Remove you from Prudhoe and send you back to Wether Fair."

She liked that idea. "We would have to be very careful," she told him. "We wouldna want de La Londe following me. The path would take him straight to Creed."

"Which is why leaving by darkness is our best option."

"Who will take me?"

"Stanton. Burle should stay here in case de La Londe and his men decide to cause trouble."

"When?"

Richard wriggled his eyebrows. "I suspect there is no time to delay. Do you feel strong enough to travel tonight?"

She nodded firmly. "I'll be ready, my lord."

"Good." He turned her towards the entry. "In the meanwhile, bolt your door and try to stay away from de La Londe. I will do what I can to keep him away from you."

She nodded, feeling confident now that a decision had been made. Moreover, she was excited at the prospect of seeing Creed again. With a smile at Lord Richard, she quit the keep with a sense of purpose. She would have to pack her necessities and then....

She suddenly came to a halt at the bottom of the steps. What was she to do about Emma? True, the child was Stanton's, but Carington had effectively been her mother for the past several days and they had bonded tremendously. Carington was torn between knowing she should leave the infant with her father yet wanting very strongly to take the baby with her to Scotland. Emma had helped heal so much in her that she could not bear the thought of leaving the baby behind. She had to find Stanton and talk to the man; perhaps he would let her take the baby. At least, temporarily.

Carington crossed through the inner bailey, into the outer ward where most of the activity was happening on this cold, bright day. Shading her eyes from the intense sunlight, her gaze moved over the battlements in search of Stanton. She saw Steven, who now seemed to be a permanent fixture on the walls, and young James who, because he was so tall, looked older and more formidable than his years. She waved to James when he looked down at her and he lifted a gloved hand in response. Still, she did not see Stanton. Lowering her hand, she was preparing to head for Stanton's cottage when someone suddenly grabbed her from behind.

Carington shrieked as her arms were wrenched behind her brutally and someone began to bind them. She looked up, shocked, to see de La Londe's face in profile as he concentrated on wrapping leather around her wrists. At that moment, all rational thought ceased to exist; she turned into a screaming, kicking banshee that brought the entire castle running to her aid.

De La Londe had her strongly in his grip. He had most of his soldiers with him, men loyal to the king who began unsheathing their swords as Prudhoe soldiers and knights began running at them from all directions. Steven practically jumped from the wall walk and James came flying down the ladder from the parapet so fast that he nearly lost his balance when he hit the dirt below. Soldiers were swarming from their posts and the outer ward was soon in chaos. The screaming, the fighting, had stirred up a hornet's nest.

De La Londe could see what was happening; he had expected it. He also knew that he had the advantage as he withdrew a small dirk, pulled Lady de Reyne against him, and put the razor-sharp blade to her neck.

"Come any closer and she dies," he bellowed.

The madness rushing at him came to an unsteady halt. Men were breathing heavily, looking at each other with uncertainty, wondering what they should do. Young Steven held de La Londe's attention while James circled around behind to try and catch the king's knight off guard, but the man was too seasoned. He knew what they were doing and he retreated into the huddle of his soldiers for protection.

"James!" came a holler. "Steven, back away before he gores her!"

Burle had bellowed the command as he came upon the group, his blue eyes serious. Stanton was right next to him, who had less control over his expression and looked mad enough to kill. But Burle was collected, and without his sword, as he faced de La Londe.

"What is the meaning of this?" Burle asked, although he already knew the answer. "How dare you betray the hospitality of Prudhoe by assaulting one of our women."

De La Londe was in no mood for games. He did not remove the

dirk as he faced Burle.

"This lady's husband is a fugitive from the king's justice," he said. "Since her husband is too cowardly to face justice, I am returning her to London to face justice in his stead."

In de La Londe's arms, Carington suddenly came alive. "I told ye not to call him a coward, ye stupid Sassenach," she snarled. "If I get my hands free, ye'll find yerself missing teeth."

De La Londe squeezed her, hard, to still her. Carington grunted with pain, grinding to a halt purely out of necessity. He had squeezed the breath from her. Then she tried to kick him in the groin and he shifted his grip, grabbing her silky black hair close against her scalp where it was most painful. She gasped with pain as he yanked her head back brutally. When she attempted to stir again, all he had to do was pull and she immediately ceased. He had her effectively trapped.

"That will be enough of that," de La Londe growled at her before turning to Burle again. "I will repeat my plans; I am taking the lady back with me to London. If you stand in my way, I will kill her."

Burle was stone-faced. "If you kill her, you will never make it out of Prudhoe alive."

There was something in Burle's gaze that made de La Londe dare to glance around him; there was an implied threat in the knight's voice that went beyond the normal rhetoric. He caught a glimpse of archers on the parapets, their arrows aimed at him. One word from Burle and they would unleash a rain of death. But de La Londe remained cool; he knew he held the larger advantage and he intended to use it.

"Open the gates," he ordered quietly. "We are leaving."

Burle continued to meet his gaze. He was preparing to reply when Richard came rushing in from the inner bailey, his dark eyes wide with surprise and anger. He pushed through the cluster of knights and soldiers, putting himself in between Burle and de La Londe. He held up his hands in a quelling gesture.

"Gentlemen, I beg for calm," he said quickly, looking at Carington in de La Londe's cruel grasp. "Knight, what are you doing with the lady?"

De La Londe lifted an eyebrow. "I am taking her to London to stand trial for her husband's crimes. This is the king's command."

Richard's dark eyes morphed into cool, simmering intensity as he put his hands down, slowly. "This lady only gave birth less than a month ago and nearly died in the process. She is still recovering. You cannot risk her over hundreds of miles of open road."

"I care not for her health, my lord."

"You are a knight. It is within your code to protect the weak."

"It is within my code to obey the king above all things."

Richard cocked his head in disbelief. "Do you want a prisoner so badly that you would portray the actions of a dishonorable knight by savaging a lady? If taking a prisoner is so important, then go find her husband. He is your true target. Capturing a small, unhealthy woman is cowardly."

Something menacing flickered in de La Londe's expression but was quickly gone.

"Unlike you, my lord, I follow the king's orders," he rumbled. "I do not hide fugitives from the king's justice."

Richard lifted an eyebrow. "If I were you, I would watch my tongue. I would be well within my rights to have you punished for slander."

De La Londe knew his limits and backed down; he would not tangle with an earl. "You would indeed, my lord, but I plan to leave Prudhoe at this moment. My punishment will have to wait."

It looked like there was no way out for Carington and she was verging on panic. But the sentries on the walls suddenly began shouting, distracting those in the bailey from the increasingly volatile situation. The soldiers near the gatehouse were apparently very excited about something. Burle did not move, nor did Lord Richard, so Stanton and the two young knights raced up to the battlements to see what the commotion was about. All movement in the bailey seemed to cease for a moment as everyone's attention was diverted to the parapets.

Stanton did not move for quite some time; it was apparent

that he was studying whatever had the sentries so excited. Then he began waving his arms at the soldiers at the main gate, who bolted into action and began churning open the great oak panels. The portcullis began wheeling up. When all was in motion, Stanton slid down the ladder to the bailey below, jogging back towards Burle and the others with his mail jingling a crazy tune. He was winded by the time he reached them.

"What is happening?" Lord Richard demanded.

Stanton's blue eyes looked from his liege, to Burle, and finally to Carington. He was staring at her when he spoke.

"Creed is coming."

Richard and Burle passed shocked glances. "Are you sure?" Richard asked.

"Sure enough, my lord. I can recognize the man's armor from a mile away," Stanton looked at his liege. "It looks as if he has brought an army of Scots with him, but more than that, I saw Hexham banners as well."

Richard's eyebrows flew up. "Kerr and Hexham united?"

Stanton couldn't help the smile of satisfaction that flickered across his lips. "United behind Creed."

As Richard and the others pondered the amazing scenario, Carington suddenly went mad. She began to fight crazily, jabbing de La Londe's dagger into her neck enough to cause a small blemish that streamed a tiny river of blood. It was a sheer miracle that she had not impaled herself as she struggled.

"Nay!" she screamed. "Tell him to go! Tell him to turn back! I will go to London in his stead; I am not afraid!"

De La Londe still had her by the hair so there was not much opportunity for her to fight him, but she was making a valiant attempt. He was forced to drop the dirk and put a big arm around her to keep her from flying out of control.

"Still yourself, woman," he growled.

But Carington ignored him. "Burle!" she was focused on the big Prudhoe knight. "Tell him to turn around! Tell him...!"

De La Londe managed to slap a hand over her mouth. In Carington's weakened state, it did not take long for her to wind herself. She simply did not have the strength she once did. Tears began to replace the energy so recently expended and she wept softly against de La Londe's hand. She tried to speak, several times, but her words were muffled against his glove. More than that, de La Londe's attention was now diverted to the open gates of Prudhoe; everyone's was.

An odd scene was unfolding before their eyes. Beyond the yawning gates, they could see a vast assortment of men in various stages of battle dress. Hexham colors flew overhead. But the strangest thing of all was that there were indeed a good many Scots intertwined with the English, their dark tartans seen against the white landscape.

As the army came to a halt, a group of mounted men continued down the road towards the main gate; in fact, an entire army that began to spill into the outer bailey and de La Londe instinctively took several steps back, away from the trickle of men in armor.

There was a particular knight in the front of the mass that continued to head in his direction even as the others stopped just inside the gate. De La Londe recognized the size of the knight, knowing Creed de Reyne on sight; the man was a giant whose legendary size only seemed to grow with time. Creed was coming at him like something horrifying and powerful, eventually dismounting his war horse and continuing on foot.

De La Londe continued to watch, feeling his heart beat with a rise of excitement; his prisoner had arrived and with that realization was also a hint of trepidation. As Creed raised his visor, de La Londe suddenly reclaimed the dirk he had once held at Carington's neck.

"Come no further, de Reyne," he pointed the tip at her white flesh. "Remove your weapons this instant. You are under arrest."

Creed's dusky blue gaze was fixed on a knight he had once considered a friend. Oddly enough, he did not stop. He kept walking. He walked right up to de La Londe and, as fast as lightning, yanked the dirk away from Carington's neck. Soon, she was trapped between them as Creed simultaneously pulled her from the man's grip and lashed out a big fist, making contact with de La Londe's jaw and sending him stumbling back.

"Had you not been holding my wife, I would have killed you where you stood," Creed rumbled. "The mere act of touching her warrants your death. You would do well to treat her like the Virgin Mary; untouchable by mortals and due your worshipful respect. Is this in any way unclear, Denys?"

De La Londe glared at him. "You are lucky I did not kill her. I could have easily slit her throat as you sought to engage in husbandly heroics. Be thankful I showed mercy."

Carington was sobbing softly at the sight of her husband but dare not attempt to speak to him. She did not want to distract him. Still, his presence beside her and the power of his hand on her arm was enough to drive her to tears. She could not adequately describe the intensity, the joy, of that moment. Creed shifted his grip on her as he pulled her gently behind him.

"I understand it was your intention to return her to London to face the charges levied against me," he said. "For that extremely cowardly and despicable act, you have incurred my wrath. It was for that reason alone that you find me returned to Prudhoe."

De La Londe knew he was in a bad way; he could see all of the men that Creed had brought with him and he knew he was easily outnumbered. He and his fifty men had no hope of taking Creed with this mob supporting him. And with that knowledge, anger began to bloom.

"Your threats do not frighten me," he replied. "Neither does the army you have raised to protect you. If they fear the king's retribution, then they will stand down and you will go peacefully. Otherwise, I will leave this place and return with an army such as you have never seen. Prudhoe will be laid to waste and you with it."

By this time, Galen Burleson had silently made his way to Creed, gently taking Carington from his grasp. Without even looking to see who had taken her, for Creed knew that it was one of his trusted men, he let her go and marched to de La Londe, his dusky blue eyes intense with fury.

"What has happened to you?" he hissed. "You were once

someone I considered a friend. You were part of the escort that brought Isabella back to England and were privy to everything that happened during that time. Why would you come to Prudhoe and threaten my wife against charges you personally know are false?"

De La Londe seemed to lose some of his confidence; he looked strangely at Creed, his jaw working as his emotions got the better of him.

"Someone must stand trial for the queen's indiscretions," he said frankly. "You are the most logical choice since she has named you as the man who fathered her child."

"But you know that is false."

"I know that you must stand to trial."

Creed's brow furrowed slightly, attempting to figure out the true motives behind his former friend's actions. "What have I ever done to you to make you turn on me like this?"

De La Londe's composure was slipping by the second. His breathing began to come in harsh, deep draws and he took a step back from Creed, his hands working and his jaw flexing dangerously.

"I am following the king's orders," he said, an odd strain to his voice.

Creed moved upon him, drawing closer. He would not let the man back out of this. "Answer my question. Why would you turn on me like this?"

De La Londe unsheathed his sword, drawing a gasp from Carington several feet away. In fact, Galen also unsheathed his sword, followed by dozens of others as they saw Burleson move; he was the only one close enough to actually see what was happening. The deathly sound of metal grating against leather in a sing-song ring filled the cold air of the ward.

Creed threw up a clenched fist, silently ordering his men to stand down. He could hear their weapons being drawn and did not want his men to move; at least, not yet. He wanted an answer to his question which, so far, de La Londe seemed unwilling to provide. His dusky blue eyes pummeled the man with their intensity.

"Answer me, Denys," he rumbled. "Why are you so determined to see me punished for a crime you know I did not commit?"

De La Londe's eyes narrowed dangerously even though it was apparent that his control had fractured. He was trying to take a stand and was not doing a very good job.

"Because someone has to take the fall," he finally replied. "It must be you."

"Why?"

The sword in his hand twitched. "Because the king is going mad thrashing the men who accompanied Isabella from France," he finally snapped; it sounded as if he had sharply exhaled the entire sentence. "You have no idea what it has been like, Creed. He has taken our lands and tortured our families. He took my own wife as prisoner and will hold her until I return you to London. Is that explanation enough for you?"

Creed just stared at him; suddenly, a great deal made sense. He understood why it had appeared the man had betrayed him. More than that, he was not shocked by the king's actions. He was, however, appalled.

"My God," he breathed. "Is this true?"

De La Londe nodded wearily, as if all of his strength had suddenly left him. "It is," he replied quietly. "There were six of us who went on that mission; you, me, de Wolfe, de Russe, St. John and Wellesbourne. All of us, to some degree, have been punished by the king for his wife's pregnancy. Wellesbourne even had his lands confiscated. But we would not condemn you; none of us would. The more the king threatened, the more we stood united."

"But you have come to arrest me," Creed pointed out softly.

De La Londe's pain was evident. "I stood with the rest until the king abducted my wife. Then I had no choice."

Creed continued to stare at the man, horrified. He suddenly looked to Galen, standing several feet away and still clutching Carington.

"Bring the priest to me immediately."

The knight let go of Carington and went off in search of

Massimo. As he did so, Creed's gaze suddenly fell on his wife and for the first time since his arrival to Prudhoe, he allowed himself to focus on her. He had been afraid to before; afraid that he would lose control and turn into a raving lunatic. But now, with the situation somewhat in his control, he allowed himself to drink in the sight of her. It was more, and better, than he could have ever hoped for. And with that realization, the dam he was struggling to hold back suddenly burst.

She was dressed in the delicious yellow lamb's wool, looking more beautiful than he had remembered. His heart began to do strange things against his ribs and a lump formed in his throat. He lost his composure altogether and went to her, capturing her roughly against him and listening to her soft sobs in his ear. It sounded like heaven.

There were tears in his eyes as he whispered against her ear. "Massimo told me that you... the birth...."

Carington held him tightly around the neck, a death grip she never intended to release. "I am fine, English," she wept softly. "Now that ye are with me, I am fine."

The tears in his eyes spilled over onto her hair. "Are you sure? Massimo said...."

She could feel the wetness from his tears and hastened to reassure him. "I am sure," she pulled back to kiss the small amount of flesh that was exposed by his lifted faceplate. "'Tis true that I was sick for a time, but I feel better every day."

He just looked at her, tears on his face and his lower lip quivering. She shushed him softly, wiping the moisture off his face with a free hand. She knew there was a dual reason for his tears; one reason he could hardly bring himself to voice and another one he'd not yet managed to express. There was still the unspoken matter of the baby. She would not let him torture himself so over it.

"There will be more bairns for us," she murmured, strongly endeavoring to compose herself since he was showing such unbridled emotion. "The physic said so. What happened... 'twas just a tragedy, English. 'Twas nobody's fault and there was nothing ye could have done had ye been here. Ye mustn't blame yerself."

He nodded as if he agreed with her but she knew, deep down, that he did not. He would shoulder the undeserved guilt. "I am sorry," he murmured. "Sorry I was not there for you during that time. I am sorry I was unable to comfort you."

She shushed him again, gently, kissing him and tasting his tears on her lips. "Her name was Dera de Reyne and Lady Anne buried her in the cathedral in Prudhoe," she told him. "Someday... someday we will go and visit her."

He nodded, his tears welling again but he fought them. He held her close once more, simply glad that she was alive. Truthfully, he had no idea what he would find when he had arrived at Prudhoe. To see his wife wrestling in the bailey with de La Londe had not been among the possibilities in his mind.

"I am simply grateful to God that you are healing," he said softly. "Your health is the most important thing in the world to me."

She patted him on the armored shoulder. "I told ye; I am fine," she repeated bravely, pulling back from him enough to look in his face. "But what about de La Londe? What are ye going to do?"

He took a long, deep breath, his gaze scanning the bailey for Massimo. The priest was not hard to spot as he emerged from behind some horses and began heading towards him. Galen was a few feet behind him, following.

Beside her husband, Carington was not watching the priest or Galen; she was looking at all of the men Creed had brought with him. It was an awesome sight. She leaned into her husband, pressing herself tight against him as if fearful of the sheer numbers. Rows upon rows of men in tartans and armor. Until this moment, she'd hardly given notice.

"All of these men, English," she murmured in wonder. "Where did they come from?"

He gave her a gentle squeeze. "The English are from Hexham," he told her. "The rest... well, you will have to ask your father where they came from. He is the one who raised them."

She smiled faintly. "I recognize the Scots," she said. "I see Maxwell and Graham tartan. But where is my Da?"

"He is outside the walls, somewhere." He focused on the priest as the man drew close and his gentle mood vanished as he addressed him. "Why did you not tell me that the king had punished the knights who had accompanied me to France? De La Londe just told me that the king has wreaked havoc with them in his anger over Isabella's pregnancy."

Massimo held his ground. "Because I was attempting to protect you," he said. "Had I told you the truth, you would have ridden to London and gotten yourself killed."

Creed's brow furrowed angrily. "So you withheld the truth? By what right do you make such a decision for me?"

"Because you would have condemned yourself."

"I will not let my friends take the king's wrath in my stead."

Massimo gazed at him a moment before shaking his head. "So now you know. What do you intend to do about it?"

Creed threw out his hands in frustration. "I cannot allow Denys' wife to be used as a threat."

"I repeat my question; what do you intend to do?"

"Ride to London and settle this once and for all."

At his side, Carington came alive. "No, English," she tugged on him in a panic. "Ye cannot go. The king will kill ye!"

Massimo, too, put a hand on Creed's arm, his pale face intent. "She is correct; the king only wants to make an example out of you. The man is vile, petulant and evil. You cannot become a martyr. You cannot let him win."

There was something in the way that the priest said the last sentence that made Creed look strangely at him. There was a good amount of power behind the emphasis on the word. There was almost anger behind it.

"Win?" he repeated. "This is not a game to be won or lost. What I do, I do to save my friends who have been protecting me for well over a year. It should have never gone this far and I blame myself and my distorted sense of self-preservation. Everyone was trying to hide me or help me flee, but I should have stood my ground and faced the charge like a man. Perhaps I was indeed a coward to run."

At his side, Carington was weeping softly again. Galen, Burle, Stanton, Richard and Denys had all heard the exchange. They began to move closer, no longer able to remain bystanders to what Creed's apparent intentions were. The man that they had been harboring and protecting for months was now on the verge of disrupting all they had tried to do for him.

"The priest is right, Creed," Denys insisted weakly. "The king will only make an example out of you."

Creed swung on him. "You came all the way to Prudhoe and threatened my wife because you wanted to take me back as your prisoner," he said pointedly. "And now you change your mind when I am set to comply? This makes no sense."

Denys was unsure how to reply. He lifted his shoulders wearily. "As I said, I felt I had little choice," he said quietly. "But perhaps… perhaps I am hoping you will come up with an alternate solution. Truth be told, I do not want to arrest you. But I do not want to see my wife held captive, either. If there was only an option to allow both of us what we wish I would gladly take it. I have prayed to God since this madness began for the wisdom to end it but I cannot think of anything; the only option, in fact, seems to be to give the king what he wants. He will accept nothing less."

Creed stared at him, hearing Carington weeping softly and taking a moment to touch her cheek gently to quiet her. He looked around to the faces surrounding him, men that were ready and willing to die or kill on his behalf. Men who had always protected him. He had to end this; he knew that. It all started with him and it would end with him. As he wracked his brain for an answer, an idea slowly began to occur.

"The king wants me dead or alive," he muttered thoughtfully.

De La Londe, Richard and Galen were the closest to him. The earl nodded firmly. "If you go to him alive, he will kill you in the end," he said quietly, eyeing Carington as he did so. "You know this."

Creed nodded, thinking of his brother and what Ryton would say to all of this. The man always had an answer. But Ryton was dead at the hands of Jory and there was no answer to be found….

Or was there?

Creed looked at the earl. "If the king is going to kill me regardless, then perhaps… perhaps he would be satisfied if I was killed in the attempt to capture me. Perhaps he would be satisfied to be presented with my body."

Richard's brow furrowed. "Your body?" he repeated. "What are you talking about?"

Creed's mind was working furiously as he looked at Denys. "If you were to bring a body back and tell the king that it was me, do you think he would be satisfied?"

De La Londe scratched his head. "He knows you on sight. He will want to see the body and he will know right away if it is not you."

Creed searched for a solution to that issue. "But what if the body was damaged somehow? Perhaps the face was obliterated. It could easily happen in a sword fight, for example, if I were to resist you."

"Or it could have happened in the battle at Hexham." They all turned to look at Galen as the man stepped forward. He was following Creed's train of thought and took it a step further. "We lost many men in that battle, including your brother."

Creed's eyes narrowed as he tried to follow Galen's line of thought. "What are you saying?"

Galen cleared his throat softly, his gaze moving between Creed and the earl. "We have many bodies from that battle," he said quietly. "Suppose we produce one and send it on to London with de La Londe. It would be decayed beyond recognition and we would tell the king that it was you."

Richard was the first to respond to the idea. "It could work," he replied hopefully. "Yet we would have to find a man of Creed's size and hair color. Do we know of any?"

Everyone was busy scratching their head in thought or mulling over a potential subject when Creed's quiet voice suddenly filled the air.

"Jory," he muttered.

The earl looked at him as if he could not believe his ears. "D'Eneas?"

Creed sighed faintly and looked at his wife, who was very much interested in the conversation now that it meant her husband was not going to turn himself over to the king. He smiled weakly at her and looked back at the earl.

"Aye; Jory," he nodded, thinking of the decaying corpse now buried in Prudhoe's cathedral because Baron Hawthorn, upon learning the circumstances of his son's death, did not want the body returned to him. "Although I am twice his size, when a man's body has decomposed over the months, it is difficult to know just how big, or small, he truly was. But our hair is the same color. If I was killed at Hexham those months ago, then it is possible that Jory's body could pass for me."

Richard was interested and doubtful at the same time. "But his face… the king would recognize the features as not yours."

Creed's dusky blue eyes fixed on him. "I will take care of that," he murmured vaguely. "For Ryton's death, for all of the hurt and anguish he put me through, let him now save me. I will help him right the wrongs he cast against my brother and me."

Richard sighed heavily and shook his head. "He would not like that in the least."

De La Londe interrupted. "But what of the men I brought with me?" he wanted to know. "They have seen you, Creed. They will know that you were not killed at Hexham months ago."

Creed's gaze moved to the north end of the outer ward where several of the king's troops were gathered. They were seasoned men, sworn to the king. He thought a moment before turning back to Denys.

"Unsheathe your sword and be prepared for a mock battle of epic proportions," he muttered. "By the time you and I are finished, out of their line of sight of course, they will know that you killed me in your attempt to capture me. The brutally destroyed corpse you present to the king will confirm it."

De La Londe lifted his eyebrows. "It will be a stretch. The corpse we will present to the king will be months old as opposed to weeks old."

"I know. But we will do our best to be convincing in every aspect."

"It may not work."

"It will if you are convincing. How badly do you want your wife back?"

He had a point. As Denys digested the plan and worked it through in his own mind, Massimo, having remained largely silent through the conversation, interrupted.

"Am I to understand you will send a corpse back to the king and tell him that it is Sir Creed?" he demanded.

The men in nodded to varying degrees. Massimo lifted his eyebrows at the scheming group. "And you are going to disfigure the face of the corpse so the king will not be able to recognize that it is, in fact, not Sir Creed?" he wanted to make sure he understood.

Again, everyone nodded; especially Richard. Massimo frowned fiercely. "I cannot condone the desecration of a body no matter what the reason."

Before Creed could answer, Carington let go of her husband and moved to the priest. All attention was on her as she put her soft hands on his arm, her emerald eyes glittering. Now, she was composed and prepared to help her husband any way she could. They had a plan; they needed everyone's cooperation to make it work. Massimo would have to be convinced.

"Let me tell ye what kind of man Jory d'Eneas was and then if ye still wish to protest, I'll not fight ye," she glanced over her shoulder at her husband. "Finish yer plans, English. I will have a little talk with the priest on how Jory is doing posthumous penance for the sins he has committed against ye in life. I believe he will see our point of view."

Creed smiled as he watched her walk away with Massimo, her delicious figure as it swayed beneath the yellow gown. He had never loved her more than he did at that moment, his heart swelling with emotions and gratitude that he could never find the proper words to express.

Not surprisingly, Massimo was eventually agreeable to the plans for Jory's rotting flesh. Exhumed and sent to London with de La Londe, King John was not entirely convinced that it was Creed but rethought his position when the fifty men at arms that had witnessed most of the battle between de La Londe and de Reyne confirmed the story. No one had seen the death blow, that was true, but they had seen most of the battle. And it had been a brutal one.

Therefore, Jory d'Eneas accomplished something in death that he would have never given consent to in life. He saved the man who killed him.

He saved Creed.

EPILOGUE

1213 A.D.
Throston Castle, Northumbria

Carington's foot was tapping with impatience; the wedding was two days away and they had to leave now or they would never make it in time. It was November in Northumberland and the weather could be fickle, and Creed was eager to leave while the weather was moderately calm. So she stood at the base of the stairs in the great keep of Throston Castle, ready to explode with annoyance. Arms crossed, she spoke with more patience than she felt.

"Ladies?" she called up the steps. "Yer father is waiting and he'll not wait much longer. If yer not down here this instant, I'll send him up to retrieve ye."

There was a good deal of hissing and conversation going on upstairs; Carington could hear it. She could hear the sounds of running feet. But, so far, she had yet to see any one of her six young daughters who were, even now, sorely testing their father's patience. Creed was a saint of tolerance when it came to the girls, but they were already an hour late in departing for Prudhoe. His patience was not infinite.

Not that he would be cruel with the girls when angered; he was, in fact, quite the opposite. He was, as Sian Kerr so kindly put it, a rug beneath his daughters' feet. The tears would come when Carington, far less patient than her husband, would explode and the girls would sob as if she had broken their hearts. Then they would turn to their father to pick up the pieces, which he would calmly and sweetly do. Carington reflected on the innumerable times such explosions had occurred over the past twelve years. And with the girls growing older, the incidents were only gaining in frequency.

Carington sighed again, resisting the urge to run upstairs and begin swatting behinds.

"Emma?" she called to her eldest. "Get the girls moving. I want everyone downstairs this instant."

She could hear Emma's voice above the rest, sternly telling her sisters to do as their mother instructed. She could identify the voices who were opposing Emma's instruction; strong-willed Cora and Gaira, at nine and seven years respectively, would not be pushed around. Annabella, their elder sister at eleven years of age, was calm like her father and tended to stay clear of controversy. Then she heard Moira, the five year old who knew everything, and Rossalyn who, at three years, apparently knew more than all of her sisters combined. Four out of the six were bred in the fiery image of their mother; Creed still laughed over that while Carington was close to pulling her hair out as the girls grew and their strong personalities developed.

"Cora?" Carington yelled up the stairs. "Gaira? Stop arguing with Emma and get down here. If I have to come up there, I'll take a stick to ye!"

Annabella suddenly appeared, carrying her satchel with her. She was a lovely girl with her father's dark hair and dusky blue eyes. She had his temperament, too. She smiled at her mother as the only obedient child in the lot. Carington touched her daughter's cheek affectionately and indicated the open entry.

"Go to yer father," she instructed. "Yer brothers and the nurses are already in the carriage."

"Can I hold Ramsey, Mama?" Annabella wanted to know. "Emma always gets to hold him and I want to hold him for a while. Please?"

Ramsey Ryton de Reyne was three months old, a fair haired son that was beginning to look a good deal like his long-dead name sake. Carington nodded shortly, trying to hasten her daughter out the door.

"Aye, of course," she said hurriedly. "Now scoot."

Annabella disappeared out the entry as Carington turned back towards the stairs; one daughter down and five to go. She could hear her youngest daughter's saucy voice, a child who she had personally dressed an hour ago. She had been ready to go then and Carington was at a loss to understand the delay. She hollered up the stairs again.

"Rossalyn de Reyne!" she snapped. "Ye come down here this instant. If I have to go up and get ye, ye'll be sorry!"

Little Rossalyn appeared on the stairs as if by magic. The spitting image of her dark haired, green-eyed mother, she looked like a little porcelain doll. Her father was especially attached to her. . Rossalyn took the stairs timidly and Carington reached up to lift her off the last several steps. She gently set the child down.

"What are yer sisters doing up there?" she asked.

Rossalyn was as sassy as a jaybird. She lifted her shoulders disinterestedly. "I do not know," she fidgeted. "Mama, can I have some cake?"

"Not-a now," Carington took the child's hand and forced her to stand next to her. "Stand here with me and be a good lass."

As Carington and her squirming daughter waited for the next wave of girls to descend the stairs, a scream suddenly caught their attention. Carington looked to the keep entry in time to see her eighteen month old son Cormac burst through the door with his father hot on his heels. Creed grabbed the boy before he could run any further, swinging him up in the air and listening to him squeal. As he kissed the boy's red cheeks and the baby shoved at him, trying to break free, Creed's gaze fell on his wife and youngest daughter.

"He got away from me," he explained as Cormac tried to twist his way out of his father's iron grip. "Where are the rest of the girls? Annabella is the only one in the carriage."

Carington nodded with limited patience. "I have been attempting to get them downstairs." She raised her voice so that those upstairs would hear her. "I am about to go up there and blister backsides."

Creed knew she meant it. He handed Cormac over to his mother. "Let me see if I can impress upon them the importance of getting themselves down to the carriage before their mother lets loose."

Carington repressed a grin as Creed took the steps. "Dunna coddle them, Creed," she said sternly. "They'll only argue with ye."

Creed waved a patient hand at her as he maneuvered his enormous shoulders through the narrow stairwell. The first face he came into contact with was Emma; gorgeous, blond and blue eyed Emma was the image of her father, Stanton. But those years ago when Carrington had tended the newborn had seen the two irrevocably bonded. Stanton allowed Carington to take his infant daughter and raise her as her own, something Creed was not displeased with. She was such a sweet, delightful girl that Creed could not have loved her more had she been his own flesh. He smiled at her as she went to him for an affectionate hug.

"Where are your sisters, Em?" he kissed her on the top of the head. "Your mother is about to have fits."

As if on cue, Cora, Gaira and Moira emerged from their large, shared chamber with their arms full of bags and blankets. They began thrusting the items at their father, who held out his enormous arms to accommodate the clutter. They piled it on.

"Dada, I want to wear Cora's green traveling cloak but she will not let me," Gaira complained. "Tell her that she must let me use it, please?"

Creed shook his head. "If she does not want you to wear it then that is her choice," he said evenly. "You have many other cloaks to choose from."

Gaira's lip stuck out in a pout, much as her mother's did in times of displeasure. She did, in fact, look a good deal like her fine-featured mother and Creed kissed the little girl on the forehead. "Your blue cloak is lovely, honey. Please wear that one; it would make me happy."

Gaira brightened, though only slightly. "Very well," she said, turning for the chamber. She happened to pass Cora on the way in and she stuck her tongue out at her. "Selfish."

Cora stuck her tongue out in return but did not pause on her way out of the chamber. She went straight to her father. "Dada, how long are we staying at Prudhoe?"

"For a few days," he replied. "Until Gilbert's wedding is complete. Are you ready to leave? We must hurry."

Cora was another fair-haired child in a family that was dominated by black hair. But she had brown eyes when no one else in the family did and was already quite the doe-eyed beauty. Fussing with the traveling cloak that her sister had so wanted to wear, she indicated to her father to help her secure it. He obeyed and fastened the ties.

"Will there be dancing at the wedding feast?" Cora turned to him, adjusting her collar.

Creed nodded. "I would expect so."

Cora cocked her head thoughtfully. "And plenty of young men?"

This time, Creed's composure took a hit. He puffed out his cheeks. "Good lord, lass; you are only nine years old. Why are you asking about young men?"

Cora lifted her slender shoulders, thrusting her pert little nose up in the air. "Because Marion de Witt is already betrothed and she is only a year older than I am. I do not want to be an old maid, Dada."

Creed just looked at her and shook his head. "Marion de Witt is betrothed to Rory Burleson from Hexham because they are close neighbors. And I promise that you will not be an old maid."

Gaira came back out of the chamber she shared with her five other sisters, sneering as she fussed with the blue cloak on her shoulders. "And Romney Burleson has his sights set on Emma," she taunted her sister. "She has the breasts of a woman and you are as flat as a board."

Cora turned red-faced. "I have so got breasts!" she thrust out her flat chest. "See? They are growing larger every day."

Creed put his hands over his ears. "Stop!" he roared, scaring the girls into silence. When he saw their wide-eyed expressions, he quickly regrouped. "Downstairs, ladies," he said calmly. "Now, if you please."

"Dada, do you think I am as flat as a board?" Cora asked.

Creed whistled loudly, pretending not to hear her. Receiving no answer from her father, Cora resumed sticking her tongue out at her sister but dutifully descended the stairs. Emma was right behind the battling pair while Moira, the five year old, was still fussing inside the large chamber. Creed stood in the door of the big, cluttered bower, watching his black-haired, blue-eyed daughter dig under her bed.

"Moira, my love, we must go," he hissed gently. "What are you doing?"

Moira's head came up. "My poppet, Dada. I cannot find her!"

Creed set down the bags and cloaks in his arms and found himself on the floor, in full armor, searching under the bed for a doll.

"If you cleaned some of the clutter out from under here, you might be able to find her more easily," he told her.

"Please, Dada!"

Creed grunted as he was forced to stand up and move the bed aside in order to retrieve the doll. But Moira's happy face soothed any irritation. He cupped her little head in his massive hands and kissed her cheek.

"Happy?" he asked.

She nodded. "Thank you, Dada," she said sincerely.

With his child in tow, Creed picked up the bags and cloaks once more and descended the stairs only to find the entry hall at the bottom empty. Holding Moira's hand, he quit the keep and descended the exterior stairs into the bailey. There was an entire entourage of de Reyne soldiers waiting to escort the baron and his family to the nuptials of Sir Gilbert d'Umfraville. Oddly enough, the spoiled young lad had grown into a rather calm and handsome young man, so the nuptials were something of a joyous occasion.

A soldier came running to him as he neared the entourage, taking the baggage from his arms and going to load it on one of the pack wagons. Creed approached the carriage that held his five daughters, two sons and two nurses and lifted Moira up into the cab. Making sure everyone was properly settled, he looked at Carington as she stood next to the carriage. Their eyes met and he smiled.

"Ready?" he blew out his cheeks in a heavy sigh.

She nodded wearily. "Finally."

"Do you want to ride with me for a little way?"

She looked into the cab, already seeing that Cora and Gaira were not getting along. They tended to be the most aggressive pair and she shook her head sadly.

"I'd better not," she said. "I canna leave the wolf pack alone for too long. They might eat each other."

"Can I at least take Rossalyn? She loves to ride with me."

Carington shook her head. "She stays with her sisters. I dunna like her on that snappish charger and ye know it. 'Tis no place for a young lady."

His looked disappointed, yet resigned, as he pulled her into his arms. His dusky blue eyes were soft on her. At thirty-one years of age, she had hardly a line on her face. She was still as beautiful as she had been when he had first met her at nineteen and there were no words strong enough to describe his adoration for her. He worshipped her.

"I have said it before and I will say it again; the girls act just like you," he murmured, bending down to kiss her tenderly. "You only have yourself to blame for their wild streak."

She wrapped her arms around his neck, her body filled with the fluid warmth she associated with her husband. Something about the man filled her, comforted her, like nothing else. He was her rock.

"Then it is my duty to ride in the cab and keep the beasts at bay," she murmured. "I'll not be far away if ye need me."

His lips were on her ear. "I always need you."

She smiled, feeling him kiss her ear, her cheek. "Which is why we've had seven children in twelve years."

He pulled back, grinning, and released her. "Complaining?"

She shook her head slowly, her emerald eyes filled with reverence. "Never."

He began to close up his helm in preparation for mounting his warhorse. Carington watched him proudly, gradually distracted by the squabbling in the cab. Forced to look away from her beloved husband, she glared at her tussling daughters.

"Cora," she snapped. "I am going to sit in that cab between ye and Gaira for the entire ride to Prudhoe and so help me, if either one of ye utter a harsh word, I'll tan yer hides."

Cora and Gaira immediately shut their mouths, their eyes wide at both their mother and father. That lasted about two seconds until Moira decided she was chilly and yanked the traveling blanket off of Gaira. That started the avalanche all over again and Creed stuck his head into the cab.

"Ladies, please," he said softly, reaching out a massive mitt to still the tussling hands. "If you behave yourselves, I promise that when we arrive at Prudhoe, I will take you into town and buy you all something very pretty."

The girls squealed with excitement. "Me, too, Dada?" Annabella wanted to know. Being the only obedient girl in the bunch, she didn't want to be left out of the bribe.

He reached out and touched her dark head. "Of course, honey. All of you." He looked back at the three squabblers. "Agreed?"

"Agreed, Dada," they said in unison.

Creed stood back from the cab and winked at his wife. He was not sure if he believed the girls but he had to try; he hated to see their mother punish them and he knew from experience that she would. Carington just pursed her lips at him in disapproval.

"Ye spoil them, Creed," she admonished softly.

He took her elbow and leaned down to kiss her cheek. "I treat them like I treat you."

Carington had no snappy reply to that. She allowed her husband to help her into the cab, receiving a tender kiss from him as he departed. The last she saw of her husband was as he made his way back towards the head of the escort.

Creed was smiling as he made his way to his warhorse. Life was good and there was no reason not to smile. Furthermore, he was thinking of Ryton this day, so many years after the man's death at Hexham. Every time he returned to Prudhoe, he thought of his brother. He wished the man could see him now.

A conversation lingered in his mind, one he had reviewed many times over the years as one daughter after another was born. He could just see Ryton's reaction to six daughters; the mere thought always made him laugh. He knew what Ryton would have said.

Creed, you're a saint.

He was not a saint. But he had certainly found heaven.

Bonus Chapters of the exciting Medieval Romance **LORD OF THE SHADOWS** to follow.

1215 A.D.: The reign of King John means dark days for all of England. Not one man, woman or child lived without fear.

Magnifying this fear is the man they call The Lord of the Shadows - a terrifying figure who sits at the right hand of the King, manipulating the royal moves like a puppet master. The Lord of the Shadows has been known to tear men apart with his bare hands and can, with a snap of his fingers, alter the future of anyone he chooses. The nobility is terrified of him, and for good reason. That is - the nobility that know of his existence.

Lady Sheridan St. James has been drawn into the political arena by her father - having no sons, he bequeaths his power and knowledge to his eldest daughter, a stunningly beautiful and bright creature. Upon his death, Sheridan finds herself at the head of the mighty House of St. James, a major leader in the rebellion against the crown.

During her first visit to London she becomes acquainted with a massive knight who has, in kindness, saved her sister's life. She has no idea Sir Sean de Lara is the man known as The Lord of the Shadows, but even when she is told of his horrible deeds she still cannot not believe it. Sheridan and Sean draw close despite the influence of the horrendous affairs of state sweeping London. All she knows is that he is handsome and kind, and although Sean is well aware of the lady's status, it makes no difference that she is, in perception, his enemy. To Sean, Sheridan is quickly becoming his reason for living - but out of necessity his responsibilities to the king become stronger than his love for Sheridan and he is forced to perform his duties or risk death to them both.

Still, Sean swears to her that his days as the Shadow Lord are numbered even as rival factions cruelly separated them. It soon becomes a test of Sean and Sheridan's love to find each other again in a world which is determined to keep them apart.

".... I should have known from the beginning not to concern myself. We have so many choices in life, in every situation. One choice can mean the difference between life and death. This choice, for me, would come to mean both...."
The Chronicles of Sir Sean de Lara
1206 - 1215 A.D.

CHAPTER ONE

Tower of London
January, Year of our Lord 1215

He shouldn't have bothered. He knew from the moment he observed the situation that he should have walked the other way and pretended not to notice. He was hidden by the fortified entrance of the White Tower from the group that had gathered near the newly constructed buildings on the eastern wall. It would have been so easy for him to slip away. But for some idiotic reason, he remained.

A drama was unfolding in the morning hours of the ninth day of January of the New Year. A young woman with bright red hair was hanging from a second story window of the structure as someone desperately attempted to pull her inside. Through all the screaming and drama, he could see that the red-haired girl was determined to leap to a nasty death below. He left the safety of the shadows, morbidly intrigued by the life and death struggle. Like the allure of a good beheading, it was pure entertainment.

The closer he moved, the more the players came into focus. It was frenzied and dangerous. The redhead was half out of the window, set upon a narrow protuberance of the stone that comprised the exterior of the building. She was howling, struggling to break free of the hands that held her. He couldn't hear what she was saying but, being female, he surmised that it probably wasn't terribly important. Better to let her jump and be done with it.

His attention then moved to the woman attempting to prevent the suicide; he couldn't make out the features at this distance, but he could certainly distinguish the blond hair that shimmered against the afternoon sky as gold would shimmer against the sun. He found himself more intrigued by the beauty of the hair than by the chaos unfolding around it.

He moved closer still, the hair luring him. As he arrived on scene, the few people that were standing about noticed his presence and quickly moved away from him. The movement was innate, like oil parting from water. No one with a sane thought in their head would dare stand within proximity of Sean de Lara. Like cockroaches, they scattered.

He didn't notice when the group shifted away from him. That was a normal happening and not worthy of his regard. Furthermore, he was looking overhead; the redhead was most of the way out of the window by now, the woman with the blond hair pleading urgently for her to come inside. Surely things were not as bad as they seemed, she said. But the redheaded woman was lamenting loudly. She was apparently unworthy, unloved, and wholly unsuited to remain in the land of the living. The blond assured her that none of this was true. She loved her dearly. *Please come inside, Alys!*

He maneuvered himself towards the window. He didn't know why, but he could see what was coming. The fall wouldn't kill her, but it could seriously injure her. He didn't know why he should bother with this idiocy. Perhaps to make up for all of the evil he had done in his life, there would be one good thing he could list as a contribution to Mankind. He saved a silly girl from breaking her neck. He could imagine St. Peter laughing him all the way back to the depths of Hell for that natty little side note to an otherwise problematical life.

He was almost directly beneath the window now. The redhead slithered out onto the narrowed shelf but the stone was slippery and she was unable to gain a foothold. Just as he reached the base of the window, her grip slipped and she plunged straight down.

She was still screaming when he caught her. She wasn't heavy in the least and he had stopped her fall with ease. But her flailing hands had clipped his nose and he could feel a trickle of blood. The girl stopped screaming, her mouth still open, when she realized that she was not a messy, broken blotch on the ground. Her startled blue eyes looked at her rescuer with such surprise that, for a moment, he actually thought he might crack a smile. He'd not done that in years. In his profession, there was nothing to smile over. He was sure he'd lost the ability long ago.

She must have stopped breathing at some point, because she suddenly took a huge gasp of air with her wide-open mouth. It was like looking at a fish. Without a word, Sean set the woman to her feet. She was shaken and her legs did not seem to work correctly. He steadied her when she couldn't seem to stand. Her mouth finally closed and she looked at him with a sickeningly yearning expression.

"My lord," she gasped. "I… I do not know what to say. Thank God you were here to save me, else… else I do not know what would have become of me."

He couldn't help responding. Stupidity always provoked his irritation. "You would have seriously injured yourself just as you were attempting to do. God had nothing to do with my appearance."

She clutched him for support. "But… my lord, I am sure that God sent you to save me. I am positive of this!"

"He did nothing of the kind, my lady."

"I am in your debt, forever and ever."

"Unwarranted, my lady."

"But I am your *slave*."

He was thinking that he should perhaps disengage her hands and leave quickly. He did not like the way she was looking at him.

"I assure you that is not necessary," he removed one of her hands and was in the process of removing the other. "I would suggest you stay away from windows until the urge to climb out of them leaves you."

The young woman would not let go. She continued to clutch at him, re-grasping him every time he peeled her fingers away. For ever digit he removed, two would take its place. He swore she had nine hands.

"Please, my lord," she gasped softly. "I must know the name of the man who has saved my life."

"Suffice it to say that I am a knight who has done his duty. No more thanks or obligation is necessary."

The redhead was still pawing him when he caught a glimpse out of the corner of his eye. The blond hair he had seen two stories above his head was suddenly in his midst and for a moment, it was as if time itself stood still. Startled, he found himself staring into the magnificent face of the woman with the hair of gold. Nothing about her was foul or defective. She was, in a word, perfect. For a moment, he thought he might actually be gazing upon an angel. He could think of no other explanation.

But the exquisite woman wasn't focused on him. She was out of breath, evidence that she had run the entire way from the apartments above. From her expression, it was clear she had not known what to expect. Seeing the other woman alive, when she had presumed otherwise, was nearly too much to bear.

She grasped the hands of the hysterical redhead. "Alys," she breathed. "Are you hurt?"

Alys shook her head. "Nay," she suddenly seemed weak and faint, dramatically so. "This brave knight saved my life. He is my redeemer, I tell you. He snatched me from the very jaws of death."

The blond woman turned her attention to Sean and his heart began to thump loudly against his ribs. She was an incredibly lovely creature with luminous blue eyes and long, dusky lashes. Her skin was creamy, her nose pert. He tried to get past his fascination with her beauty, struggling to focus on her softly uttered words.

"My lord," she said. "My sister and I cannot adequately express our thanks. We are forever in your debt."

So they were sisters. *Strange,* he thought. When the redhead had expressed her indebtedness, it held no attraction to him. But with this sister....

"Obligation is not necessary, my lady," he said quietly.

She smiled the most beautiful smile he had ever seen. "You are too kind," she said in a sweet, lilting voice. "Consider the House of St. James your loyal servants, my lord. No favor you would ask of us is too great."

Something in Sean's expression grew dim. It was like a shadow falling over the sun, imperceptible to all but the experienced eye. But whatever warmth had been brewing was instantly quelled.

"St. James?"

"Aye, my lord."

"And your names?"

"I am the Lady Sheridan St. James and this is my sister, the Lady Alys."

His response was to gaze at the pair a moment longer before silently, yet politely, excusing himself. It was nothing more than a slight bow and he was off across the compound, an enormous man with arms the size of tree limbs. He walked with the stealth of a cat, disappearing into the shadows from whence he came. As quickly as he had appeared, he was gone.

The girls watched him go, puzzled by his swift retreat. Alys was positively crestfallen.

"You frightened him away," she said accusingly. "He said that no obligation was necessary. Why did you press him?"

Sheridan's lovely face darkened as she looked at her sister. "You silly cow," she snatched the girl by the wrist. "You frightened him with your insane behavior. What on earth possessed you to climb out of the window? Had he not caught you, you more than likely would have fallen on his head."

"That's not true!"

"He had no choice but to catch you."

Alys' pale face flushed. "How *dare* you. God sent him to save me!"

"Blasphemer," Sheridan hissed. "Be silent and come back inside with me. We will speak no more of this day or of your behavior. Mother would have your head if she knew what you have done."

Alys rose to the fight, but her face suddenly crumpled. She became overdramatic again.

"But he left me," she moaned. "He left in the night. His steward said so. What choice did I have but to end my disgrace?"

Sheridan tried to retain her dignity in the face of the crowd that still lingered. They pointed and whispered, but no one approached. She put her arm around her sister, hustling her back towards the entrance to the apartments.

"I do not know why he left, Alys," she said quietly. "Perhaps we shall never know. But that is no reason to kill yourself."

"But… but he said he loved me."

"Perhaps he was mistaken."

"How can you mistake love? And… and I believed him. I allowed him to…"

"Hush. We will speak no more of this, Alys. Not another word, do you hear?"

"But I am so humiliated," Alys wept softly.

Sheridan did not want to speak of her sister's plight. This wasn't the first time she had fallen for a man of unscrupulous character that had taken advantage of her. She was always falling in love with one man or another, pliable to their whims and lust. And this wasn't the first time she had threatened to end her suffering.

"You must be strong," Sheridan did not know what more to say. They had been through this too many times in the last few years of Alys' young life. "You must be strong and wait for the proper man to come to you."

Alys' expression brightened with unnatural rapidity. "Perhaps God sent the man who saved me to replace him. Perhaps it was fate, Dani. God sent my savior to save my life and mend my broken heart. Do you believe in love at first sight?"

"I do not."

Alys' tears faded as they entered the dark, cool corridors near the Flint Tower. "My savior must have felt something for me. Why else would he risk his life to save me?"

Sheridan could only roll her eyes in disbelief.

***

Nestled deep in a long stretch of ancient stone and mortar, the solar of the king was a dark place at any given time. In the day, it was gloomy, but in the night, it was positively sinister. Phantoms lingered in the shadows and the heavy smell of alcohol reeked throughout the room. The king liked his drink and had a tendency to pass out with tankards in his hand, which then spilled upon the floor and seeped into the expensive carpets.

Tonight was no exception to the usual dreariness and stench. The dinner hour was swiftly approaching and the hall of St. George was filled with servants, vassals, and the finest food that England could provide her people. But the king's solar was reserved for Henry II's youngest son and the most prominent members of the king's circle to attend him in conference.

It was a somber group that gathered this eve around their king, John Softsword. William Fitz Osbern of Monmouth lingered by the hearth, while the volatile pair of Humphrey de Bohun of Caldicot and Walter Clifford of Clun huddled a few feet away. Lesser lords with minor titles and lands completed the evening's royal guest list; Bernard de Newmarch, Richard Fitz Pons, and Payn St. Maur. These men, and their immediate retainers which could number four or five additional men each, filled the solar to near capacity.

It made John feel secure to have these men around him. He was tortured by inner demons, hounded by a lifetime of failure and insecurities brought on by an insecure upbringing. He was essentially weak minded and needed those of strong mind and opinions hovering close. Physically, he was a man of small stature, bad hygiene, and one heavily lidded left eye that gave him a rather dull appearance.

"Henry St. James, 3rd Earl of Bath and Glastonbury, died last year," Monmouth continued the conversation they had been involved in since entering the private solar. "I was aware that the Bishop of Bath was in London on the widowed countess' behalf, but not the daughters."

"He fought with my father," the king said, his usual cup of wine in hand. He was getting drunker by the minute. "He did, in fact, fight always on the side of my father. He has ever been against me."

"There are many in London at this time that raise opposition to you, sire," Monmouth replied. "We have kept watch of them, have no fear. Ask your Shadow; he will tell all."

Attention turned to the darkened recesses of the room near the servant's entrance. Back there, in the depths, lingered the king's bodyguards. These two men were sworn to protect the king, sworn to do his will and fulfill every perverted and outrageous whim. To speak of them struck fear in the hearts of even the bravest of men. Gerard d'Athée and Sean de Lara were strong-arm men without an ounce of compassion if it ran contrary to their sworn duty.

"De Lara," the king spoke to one of the two lingering in the blackness. "This news of the St. James' women has come from you. Tell us all you know so that we may assess the threat."

Sean came into the light. His deep blue eyes were fixed on the king, unwavering, cold and calculating. He was an enormous man, even larger than d'Athée and twice the size of any other in the room. He had been rumored to kill men with his bare hands, appendages as large as trenchers, and there wasn't one in the room who did not disbelieve that. He had been with John for several years, far more feared than his bear-like counterpart Gerard, because there was one great difference between them: Sean had intelligence. A dangerous man with a brain was a dreadful prospect. And he had the ear of the king.

"My lords," Sean spoke with a voice that seemed to rise up from his feet to exit his mouth. "I can tell you that we have seen a collection of opposition barons gather in London in the past few weeks, much more than we have ever seen before. The House of St. James is merely one of many."

"Who else is here that we may not know about?" Fitz Pons demanded. He jabbed a finger in Sean's direction. "We know you have spies that report to you, de Lara."

"I have spies," Monmouth muttered, out of turn.

"We *all* have spies," Clifford interjected impatiently. "But our spies are spread out over our lands as well as in London. They run thin at times." He glanced at Sean, his old eyes sharp and wise. "De Lara knows all, sees all. He knew that the House of St. James was at the Tower and told us so, last week. Today he has met the daughters, which is of no consequence to us. I care not for the women, but I do care for Jocelin. That is where the true power lies."

The mood of the chamber was growing uncomfortable. Jocelin, Bishop of Bath, was an influential man with a tremendous voice within the church. The House of St. James was allied with the man and, consequently, most of the West Country. With all of England in civil war and conflict, alliances and enemies were of supreme importance at this time.

"The Earl of Lincoln arrived yesterday," Sean continued. "Worcester, Coventry and Rochester have been here for weeks. I am also told that Salisbury, de Warenne and Arundel are on the road and due to arrive within days. De Braose rides with Salisbury."

One could have heard a pin drop. It was more than they had imagined. The mood turned from uncomfortable to ominous as the shock of the information sank deep.

"De Braose is the most powerful lord on the marches. As we speak, he is waging war against the Welsh," the king's voice was tinged with bitterness. "Why does he come to London?"

"Reginald is on the marches, sire," de Lara replied. "His son Guy rides with Salisbury."

"God's Bones," Fitz Pons hissed through clenched teeth. "Two of the three most powerful marcher lords ride to London, not to mention Arundel. What does this all mean? Why are they all converging on London?"

"They ride against the king, of course," de Lara said steadily. He paused, eyeing the crowd, wondering if they were ready for the rest of his report. "There is more, my lords."

John glanced up from his nearly empty chalice. "What more?"

"I am also told that Fitz Gerold, Fitz Herbert, Fitz Hugh and de Neville are expected from the north, though I cannot be sure. The information is unclear and several weeks old. And then there is the matter of de Burgh..."

"Hugh de Burgh," John slammed his chalice to a table, missed it, and it clattered to the floor. "I will punish that man, I swear on my father's grave. He defies me, my old tutor. I will strip him of everything my father ever granted him and call it swift justice."

John's rage was up. If it became worse, he would throw himself down on the rushes in fits. It was important that he remain in control, important for his cause that he put on a strong appearance. No doubt nearly every man de Lara named would be in attendance at the feast tonight and they must see nothing other than a collected monarch. Sean glanced at Gerard, the great hairy beast of a man, and with a silent gesture sent him in search of the physic. He was well aware of the signs of impending convulsions.

The nobles sensed this as well. De Lara took a step towards the group and immediately the men moved to vacate the chamber. There was a feast awaiting and much plotting to attend to. They would leave de Lara to calm the king.

When the room was empty and John sat twitching in his chair, Sean took a moment to study the man. He was attempting to assess just how close he was to seizures.

"Sire," he said quietly. "You needn't worry over those who would oppose you. Your loyalists are just as strong. This is an old story and an old issue. We have dealt with worse. The monarchy will prevail, I assure you. It always has."

"But the church stands against me," John was salivating as he spoke. "Worcester, Coventry and Bath are in London, no doubt to assist the barons in plotting my downfall."

"They are men of the church, sire. Perhaps they are merely in London on papal business."

John grunted. "The church has ever been against me. And that nasty little business a few years ago…"

"Your excommunication was short-lived, sire."

"But I had to prostitute myself and my country in order to please that bastard, our gracious, sympathetic and illustrious pope," John's rage was gaining again. "He damn near emptied our coffers with his demand for tribute. But it was of no avail. The man is *still* against me."

"Even if that is the case, sire, you count the bishops of York, Northumberland and Chester among your allies. They understand your vision for England and for her holdings."

"Pah. They understand nothing but tribute and penance. I must pay for the sins of my father and those before him. That is the foundation of their hatred, you know. The sins of my entire family. 'Tis not just my political stance that has provoked the abhorrence of the church."

He was speaking with the petulance of a child, exaggerated, with dribble flying from his lips. Sean knew that paroxysms were imminent. His next words were specifically designed.

"As you say, sire."

"Of course I say. The church is full of idiots and mercenaries."

"The church favors those who pay well for its loyalty, sire. And I have heard that Northumberland has been well-courted by William Marshall as of late."

John's eyes widened. "My brother's chancellor? He lures my greatest supporter?"

"Money is sometimes greater than faith, my lord. Or the love of a king."

John's rage exploded and he was twitching on the rushes by the time the royal physic arrived.

"... Lo, there did I see my destiny when I gazed across the room on that fateful night...."
The Chronicles of Sir Sean de Lara
1206 - 1215 A.D.

CHAPTER TWO

"Did you ever imagine what Adonis must look like?"

Alys was lying horizontal on the great bed that she shared with her sister. She was half-dressed for the evening meal, most of her time having been spent in the land of silly daydreams. Sheridan had been attempting to hurry her up for the better part of two hours. But Alys moved, as always, on her own time.

"No," Sheridan was gazing into a polished bronze mirror that was strategically affixed to the chamber wall. "I have not imagined that. And you should not waste your time. You must finish dressing or I swear that I will leave without you. The bishop will be here at any moment."

Alys turned to watch her sister as she pulled a bonecomb through her silky dark-blond tresses. Sheridan's hair was thick and straight, while Alys had more natural curl than she could handle. Still, Sheridan was able to roll her hair with strips of cloth at night, resulting in cascades of curls for the following day. In a world where beauty was judged on natural attributes, Sheridan often felt inadequate as far as her hair was concerned. But she did possess the loveliness of face and figure so as not to feel completely unattractive.

Alys never thought her sister was unattractive. In fact, she was proud and jealous of her beauty at the same time. She finally decided to push herself off the bed and go in search of her hose, which could take some time to locate. She was a messy girl and her clothes were generally strewn all over the room.

"Surely my savior has the face meant for Adonis, do not you think?" Alys bent over when she came across her shoe. "Did you not notice how handsome he was?"

Sheridan was in the process of pulling the front section of her hair back and securing it with an enormous comb in the shape of a butterfly. "I noticed how big he was, to be certain. The man was three times your size."

"But he was beautiful," Alys sighed.

Sheridan had not given him a second thought, but she did seem to recall unnaturally clear blue eyes and a square, firm jaw. Upon deeper reflection, she supposed he had been rather handsome in a rugged sort of way.

"I presume so. I did not give much notice."

Alys found her hose. "Do you suppose he will be at the feast tonight?"

"If he is one of John's vassals, I am sure he will be."

That prompted Alys to move faster. She yanked on her hose, affixed the garters, and put on her shoes. Then she snatched the comb that Sheridan had been using and began furiously brushing her hair.

Sheridan frowned at her sister's pushy demeanor. Fortunately, she had finished securing her own hair and moved aside so that Alys could have full control of the mirror. . She went to the wardrobe to collect her slippers.

"Good Lord," she grunted as she bent over for the shoes. "She cinched my corset far too tightly."

"Who?"

"The maid."

"Oh." Alys had brushed her hair so roughly that it was turning into a giant frizzy ball of red hair. She smoothed her hands over it furiously. "Look, now. What do I do?"

Sheridan went to her rescue. They had been through this routine before, too many times. She put beeswax and a slight amount of oil on her hands and smoothed them over her sister's hair, again and again. Most of the strands tamed, but some clung to her as if alive. It was like trying to tame a wild beast.

"If he is there tonight, do not make a fool of yourself," she muttered as she smoothed Alys' hair. "You already thanked him. There is no need to throw yourself at his feet."

Alys was appalled. "I would do no such thing."

Sheridan worked the oil into the ends of the hair until it was absorbed. "I know you far too well, baby sister. What have I told you before? You must be cool and pleasant. 'Twill make you more appealing than if you lay at his feet like a door mat."

Alys made a face, rolling her eyes. Then she yelped as her sister pulled a single, painful strand. "I am sure he will want to dine with me if he is there, do not you think?"

It was Sheridan's turn to make a face. Alys never listened to reason, from anyone. Finished with the hair-salvage, she fastened a delicate black hairnet over Alys' head to compliment the red dress with black accents that she was wearing. When all was said and done, Alys' wild mane was nicely contained.

"There," Sheridan said. "Now you look presentable. Have the maid beat the wrinkles from the dress before we leave."

The little maid they had brought with them from their home at Lansdown Castle was in the larger antechamber airing out the heavy cloaks her mistresses would wear. The woman came when Alys beckoned, bearing the large paddle made from water reeds normally used to beat bed linens and rugs. The red haired sister put her arms up and the servant girl went to work, smacking out the wrinkles from the linen that had formed when Alys had lain all over the bed during her daydreams.

With Alys finished, Sheridan returned to her final touches so that she would be presentable before the finest courtiers in England. It was, in truth, intimidating. She gazed at herself in the mirror, assessing her reflection; she wore a gown of iridescent green, like the color of the sea on a warm summer day. The sleeves were long with trailing cuffs, the neckline daringly low, and the bodice tapered at the waist to emphasize her slender torso. A lovely necklace of rough-cut emeralds finished the look.

As she inspected her face, she noticed that her lips were chapped again. She had to constantly rub a solution of beeswax and salve on them to keep them from cracking and bleeding. On special occasions, she added a touch of ocher to the mix and turned her lips a delightful shade of red. It was perhaps a bit much, and a little daring, but she liked the result when she was brave enough to do it. Tonight, she decided, was just such a night.

She wasn't aware that Alys was also watching her as she went through her closing preparations. Alys' blue eyes grazed her sister, from head to toe, wishing yet again that she had been blessed with even half the beauty her sister had. Though their facial features were similar, Sheridan's were refined and delicate and Alys' tended to be broader. Sheridan had lovely white teeth, with slightly protruding canines, that added charm and character to her beautiful smile. Alys had slightly protruding front teeth that made her look like a rabbit. Sheridan also had a slender neck and shapely shoulders, whereas Alys' neck was a bit thick. In fact, her entire body was a bit thick; not fat, but full. Sheridan had a trim waist made even more slender with the corset, which only made her breasts appear rounder and firmer.

Alys often wished she had been born in Sheridan's figure. Perhaps it would have made a difference with the men she had fallen in love with. Perhaps they would have stayed. But she wasn't bitter, strangely enough. It was simply something she lived with.

A knock on the door sent their hearts racing with excitement. The little maid flew into the antechamber and opened the door for Jocelin, Bishop of Bath and Glastonbury. A rotund man who had been close friends with their father, Jocelin had taken it upon himself to assume the paternal role for the girls when their father passed away suddenly the year before. Lillian, their mother, had not fared well with the death of her husband and the family had been in emotional need. Jocelin had stepped in, not only for the family's requirements, but also as a promise to Henry St. James.

The men had been united in their alliance against the oppressive monarchy that had driven a bitter wedge through the heart of the country. Henry's death was unfortunate, as there was still much to accomplish in that arena and Jocelin knew they were well on their way. Tonight, the first festival feast of the year would be an excellent opportunity to assess the growing opposition and reaffirm alliances. The king, allies and enemies alike would be in attendance and Jocelin was eager to gauge the playing field.

Unfortunately, the notion was on Sheridan's mind as well. He knew the moment he looked into her angelic face that she was thinking the same thing he was. Henry St. James had no sons, and Sheridan had been inevitably directed into the role. She was the eldest child, intelligent and wise, and like her father in every way. She would have made a fine son and heir, and Henry had raised her as if she had been male. Truth be known, part of the reason Jocelin had assumed Henry's mantel to keep Sheridan out of trouble. As Lady Bath's daughter, she wielded the power of an important earldom and in these days of political upheaval, wise council was needed more than ever.

"Greetings, ladies," Jocelin said in his great booming voice. "How lovely you look this eve."

Alys grinned and spun about to display herself. Sheridan shrugged off the comment and accepted her cloak from the maid.

"I am told de Warenne is on his way to London," she said. "He was an old friend of my father's. When he arrives, I should like to see him."

Jocelin helped her with the heavy, fur-trimmed garment. "We will both see him upon his arrival. Tonight, I have arranged for us to be seated with the Bishop of Coventry. William is a very old friend and a strong supporter of our cause." When Sheridan turned to face him, adjusting the neck of the cloak, he lowered his voice so Alys would not hear. "We will speak to him about arranging a meeting with the other allies."

"How soon can this be done?"

"I do not know. There are many we must arrange this with, and it must be done in all secrecy. Should the king discover our plans...."

"He'll arrest us all and execute us for treason."

Jocelin bobbed his head with resignation. "It is possible. I also understand that William Marshall will be at the feast tonight, another mark in our favor."

"William Marshall?" There was excitement in her tone. "Do you think we could arrange to sit with his party? No offense meant to the Bishop of Coventry, but William Marshall is legendary. The man has served three kings and I, for one, would be eager to bask in his presence."

Jocelin patted her shoulder patiently. "In time, little one. You do not invite yourself to the Marshall's table. You wait to be summoned."

"But..."

"Tut," he held up a finger, cutting her off. Now was not the time to continue this discussion. To change the subject, he lifted his voice to Alys. "Are you ready, my dear? There is much food and festivity awaiting us. We must hurry before it is all over with."

Alys bolted from the door with Jocelin and Sheridan close behind. A small contingent of the Bishop's men and of St. James men await in the hall, commanded by a knight who had been Henry's captain for many years. Neely de Moreville was a powerful man with an unspectacular face, but of calm and good character. He bowed to the ladies, paying particular attention to Sheridan.

"If my lady is ready," he extended an elbow.

Sheridan took his offered arm and followed him down the corridor. Jocelin and Alys were immediately behind them, followed by four St. James guards and four Ecclesiastical guards.

The Tower of London was a labyrinth of dark corridors, a grand hall and cramped rooms. It had recently seen some expansion; a new moat had been added, filled by water from the Thames, and several buildings and apartments were added on the south side of the White Tower. The largest addition, however, was the Bell Tower that loomed high above the fortress.

The group left the east apartments and crossed the bailey towards the White Tower. The feast would be in the keep's great hall. Sheridan's gaze moved over the new, enlarged surroundings.

"I have never seen such a large structure," she said. "Surely this is the strongest and most impregnable fortress in the world."

Neely took any opportunity to speak with Sheridan. Being his liege's daughter, he had watched her grow from a sweet child into a dazzling young woman. But he knew his place, well aware of their difference in station.

"It has quite a history, my lady," he said. "Especially over the past few years with the contention of power between King John and his brother, Richard."

"I heard tale that John laid siege to the tower several years ago while Richard was in the Holy Land."

Neely nodded. "Richard's chancellor, William Longchamp, initiated a massive expansion project, the results of which you see now. John took advantage of his brother's absence and attacked the new defenses. Longchamp was forced to surrender not because the fortifications failed, but because the Tower ran out of supplies."

Sheridan thought on that a moment. "'Twould seem that John will stop at nothing to gain what he wants."

"Keep that in mind, my lady."

Having served the House of St. James as long as he had, Neely had been trusted with their innermost secrets. He was well aware of Henry and Sheridan's position on John. He was, in fact, extraordinarily uncomfortable that she was here at the core of King John's wickedness. It had been, in his opinion, foolish of her to come, but this journey had been planned for a long time and nothing would stop Sheridan from accompanying Jocelin in her father's stead.

Neely knew more than he let on about the king, as did Jocelin. They both knew the man had no morality. He had been known to seduce the wives of his advisors while the men were powerless to stop him. For those who tried to resist him, he had them thrown in the vault and took the women anyway. Sometimes the men were left in the Tower to rot. One did not refuse the king and live to tell the tale.

Which was why they were particularly fearful for Sheridan. She was a magnificent creature and it would only be a matter of time before John saw her. When that time came and the royal summons arrived, Neely was still uncertain to what he should do. Jocelin wanted to whisk her to a convent if and when the occasion came. Not even the king, with as much trouble as he had historically experienced with the church, would violate the sanctity of a convent. But the problem was that once she was committed, she would have to remain. For a beautiful young woman and the heiress to a massive earldom, that was not an attractive option. Therefore, being in London, at this moment in time, was risky in more ways than one.

Sheridan knew none of this, of course. They had decided not to tell her for fear of upsetting her. Though she was a stable and wise girl, still, they were attempting to protect her. No use in worrying over something that they could not control. But they could be on their guard.

The entrance to the White Tower loomed ahead. The keep was constructed of pale stone that gave it a ghostly glow in the moonlight. It was so tall that it appeared to touch the night sky. The St. James party mounted the steps and entered the small foyer immediately inside the structure. There were two stewards there to greet them, ushering them further down the corridor and into the great hall beyond.

Lansdown Castle was a grand enough place with a large hall. But even the homey fires of Lansdown's hospitality could not compare to what they soon witnessed. It was as if they had entered an entirely new world; never had Sheridan seen so many tapers, slender beams with gracefully lit tips. They gave the hall an unearthly glow. The room was also very warm, not only from the amount of people in it, but because there was an enormous fire in the two massive hearths that bordered the east and west walls of the room.

More servants greeted them, dressed in finery affordable only in the house of the king. There were several long tables, all decorated with phials of wine and seasonal fruit. Nobles, such as they do, sat on benches, tables, and all around the room. They were everywhere, the men who harbored such power in England. On Neely's arm, Sheridan watched it all quite closely. It was an intimidating sight.

Power and wealth reeked from every facet of the massive, fragrant hall. While Neely deposited Sheridan at the table and faded into the shadows, as other knights did as their masters took seat, Jocelin sat between Sheridan and Alys. Their soldier escort fell back against the wall directly behind them. The party was barely settled as Alys snatched her goblet and held it aloft for wine.

A servant was at her side almost immediately, filling the goblet. Alys downed her allotment and demanded more. Sheridan settled herself on the bench, smoothing her gown and kicking off the dried rushes that had adhered themselves to her slippers. All around the room gathered groups of men and women, the gaiety of laughter filling the warm, stale air. In the gallery above, a group of minstrels played a haunting tune. Sheridan twisted her head around, watching the group overhead for a moment, before returning her attention to the brilliant room.

"Do you see anyone that you recognize?" she whispered to Jocelin.

Jocelin's sharp eyes scanned the hall. It was like being in a roomful of predators; each man had the look of both killer and prey. There was an odd air about the place, of both suspicion and friendship. His gaze came to rest on a group several yards to their left and he visibly perked. "See there," he said quietly. "The Bishop of Rochester and his party. And I also see with him the barons Fitz Gerold and Fitz Herbert, men from the Welsh marches."

"Do you see de Warenne?"

"Nay."

"Coventry or Rochester?"

"Not yet."

Sheridan tried not to be too obvious about staring. "If you

point out these men to me so that I may recognize them," she whispered, "perhaps I will be able to set up the meeting we've all longed for. No one will suspect a lady in these circumstances of subversion."

Jocelin cocked an eyebrow. "'Tis only subversion if what we are attempting to accomplish is thwarted. If successful, we shall be loyalists."

"There is no one that disputes our rightness," her voice grew stronger. "No one on earth that would dare to..."

Jocelin cut her off. "Look," he almost gestured but caught himself in time. "There is the Earl of Arundel. I haven't seen the man in years."

Sheridan caught sight of a short, red-haired man as he disappeared into a well-dressed crowd. Before she could comment, Jocelin crowed again.

"And look there," he bordered on excitement. "William Marshall in the flesh."

Sheridan found herself gazing at a man that was relatively close. He was tall and lanky, with thinning gray hair. When he turned in her direction, she was struck by the sharpness of his gaze. His eyes fell upon Jocelin and he walked straight for him. Jocelin rose to his feet and extended a hand.

"My lord," Jocelin said. "It's been a long time."

William Marshall brushed his lips against Jocelin's papal ring. His dark eyes twinkled. "Too long," he said. "I am surprised you have managed to stay out of trouble since the last I saw you."

Jocelin grinned. "Who has been spreading such lies? Trouble is my bed fellow. We're good friends and keep each other company."

William laughed softly. Then his gaze fell on Sheridan and he bowed gallantly. "My lady."

Jocelin took the opportunity to introduce her. "My lord William Marshall, may I present the Lady Sheridan St. James, eldest daughter and heiress of the late Henry St. James, 3rd Earl of Bath and Glastonbury."

The Marshall appraised her courteously. But Sheridan felt as if

God himself was scrutinizing her. She curtsied before the man and he took her hand chivalrously.

"My lady," he greeted. "I knew your father. He was a righteous and cunning man."

She smiled, mortified that her lips were twitching with nerves. "Thank you, my lord. May I say that it is indeed an honor to finally meet you."

"And you."

"May I introduce my sister, the Lady Alys."

William turned to the redhead. "My lady."

He took her hand in a gentlemanly fashion and touched his lips to her fingers. But that was the end of it. With a lingering glance at Sheridan, the Marshall turned to Jocelin and the two of them lowered their voice in private conversation. Sheridan looked over at her sister, now on her third goblet of wine. Alys was gazing adoringly at the Marshall.

Sheridan went pale.

"Oh, no...."

***

The feast commenced when the king entered the hall. It was with great pomp and ceremony, as befitting the monarch. Barons called to him, women waved at him. John, a short man with a droopy eye and noticeably bad hygiene, gestured benevolently to the group in the hall. It was reminiscent of the Pope making his rounds among his admiring subject, with all the flair of a holy parade. Some of the older men who had served his father were less friendly towards him, yet there was respect as due the king.

It took several minutes for the king to make his way to the dais where the royal table was lodged. Festooned with a variety of fine goblets and a huge centerpiece of marzipan sculpted into naked cherubs, John took his leisure time in reaching his seat. He was more intent to linger over the adoration of his subjects.

Jocelin watched him with disgust.

"He is not his father's son," he grumbled. "Henry was ruthless and deceitful, but at least he could call himself a man. His son lacks even that privilege."

Sheridan leaned in to him. "I hear they call him John Softsword because of the loss of all of his holdings in France."

"'Twas ten years ago that he acquired that name," Jocelin said. "That name and a few others."

Sheridan suppressed a grin. "I was not allowed to hear those other names, Your Grace."

"If I know Henry's mouth, then I doubt that is true."

Her smile broke through and she lowered her head so that the others would not suspect her joviality was at the expense of the king. She collected her goblet and took a long sip of the tart wine. . Glancing up just as the king took his seat, she noticed several soldiers and retainers to the rear of the royal dais. Though most were finely dressed nobles, some wore weapons and armor. One man in particular looked familiar; he was so enormous that he was twice the size of nearly every man in the room. About the time she began to realize where she had seen him, Alys grabbed her arm.

"Look, there," she hissed. "The knight behind the king, dressed in full armor. Do you see him?"

Sheridan's initial shock sharply cooled. "I do."

Alys' fingers dug into her flesh. "My savior! He is behind the king!"

Jocelin couldn't help but hear the commotion between the girls. Alys had jostled him about in her excitement. "Here, here, what's this? Who are you two talking about?"

The girls leaned close on either side of him, their focus on the royal party. "The massive knight that stands to the king's right hand," Alys was pointing and Jocelin took her hand and put it in her lap. "Do you see him?"

Jocelin found the source of their curiosity. His eyes narrowed. "Aye," he said slowly. "I see him."

"Who is he?" Alys demanded.

Jocelin watched the large man for a moment before answering. "Why do you wish to know?"

"Because he saved my life today," Alys said, oblivious to the tone of Jocelin's voice. "I… I had an accident."

Jocelin looked at her then, sharply. "An accident?"

Alys didn't want to explain herself. "Aye, I… I fell. He saved me. Who is he?"

By this time, Jocelin's behavior had Sheridan's attention. She wondered why he suddenly looked so tense. She tugged on his sleeve gently.

"Do you know him?"

The bishop shook his head. "I do not know him, but I know of him." He lifted his cup, regarding the ruby liquid inside. "If you must know, the barons call him the Lord of the Shadows."

The disclosure caused both girls to look back to the royal platform. "Lord of the Shadows," Alys repeated dreamily. "That's marvelous."

Jocelin gulped from his chalice. "Nay, young Alys, that is *not* marvelous. The man is a demon."

She was indignant. "What do you mean?"

"What I mean is that he is the Devil's disciple. He is the king's protector and used by the king for the most evil of purposes. There is no man in this kingdom that does not fear him. His presence, his very name, is synonymous with pain and death. If you see the man, run for your life."

The girls looked at the dais with a bit more recognition and dread. "What do you mean when you say that the king uses him for evil purposes?" Sheridan almost didn't want to know.

Jocelin debated whether or not to tell her; de Lara would be the one to come for her should she catch the king's eye. "Evil, Dani," he said quietly. "The king sends de Lara to commandeer women for his conquests."

Sheridan tried not to appear too horrified, but Alys was unimpressed. "But what's his name?" she insisted.

"Sean de Lara."

"Sean," Alys whispered, feeling it roll across her tongue. "Sir Sean de Lara. What a beautiful name."

Jocelin turned on her. "Listen to me now, Alys. I know your

penchant for the opposite sex. I know of your naïve views and your trusting ways. Though I do not know the circumstances of de Lara's involvement in your accident, I will tell you this; stay clear of him. Remove him from your thoughts. He is no prince to sweep you away nor a man to be trifled with. I promise you that the only reason John still sits upon that throne is because of de Lara. No one is brave enough to attempt his removal, and the man is deadly in more ways than one. Not only is he physical power, but he has intelligence. His tactical knowledge is without compare. No army will go up against John during these times because of de Lara's very presence. You will, therefore, heed my words; forget him. Harbor no false notions of his good character."

Alys' eyes were wide with disappointment. Her gaze moved from the bishop to the dais and back again. "Are you sure? He didn't seem that way to me."

Jocelin patted her hand. "I am sure, little Alys."

She didn't look convinced, but to her credit, said nothing more. During Jocelin and Alys' conversation, Sheridan's gaze never left de Lara's distant face; she had remembered the man from their afternoon encounter. He was three times her size, that was true, but he wasn't misshapen or ugly as a giant would be. He had crystal blue eyes, the clearest she had ever seen, and a square jaw that projected power and astuteness. His features had been even and extraordinarily attractive. In fact, the man positively reeked of masculinity. He was striking.

Nor had he been impolite or unkind to them. He had, after all, saved Alys' life. At no time did she receive the impression of death or hazard from him. He seemed polite and chivalrous. Puzzled, yet resigned to Jocelin's words, she returned to her goblet and put the notion of the mysterious Sean de Lara out of her mind.

The meal was lavish and plentiful. Huge slabs of pork and mutton were on display, served by the fancily-dressed servants. William, Bishop of Coventry, eventually showed himself; a slight man that reeked of alcohol, he seated himself and several retainers across the table from Jocelin and the St. James women.

He greeted Jocelin amiably, introduced himself to the ladies, and spoke well of Henry St. James. He seemed congenial enough. But he finished the otherwise normal conversation by running an inviting foot against Sheridan's leg.

Strange that his gesture did not shock her. She had heard tale of men of the church seducing women and had seen a few questionable actions in her lifetime, enough to know that these men were not entirely celibate. It was well known that they could be quite corrupt. She casually shifted so that her leg was not within reach of his dirty toes, but it seemed the bishop had long legs and managed to stroke her ankle once again with his cold digits. When she cast him a baleful glance, he ran his tongue over his lips and grinned.

Disgusted, she rose from the table with the whispered excuse to Jocelin that she was in need of the privy. She couldn't even look at the Bishop of Coventry, infuriated that his leering attention had forced her from the table. He had managed to unnerve her enough so that she needed to collect herself. That was not a usual occurrence with her; Sheridan was normally steady in a world filled with flighty women. But the events of the day and the excitement of the evening had shaken her otherwise steady constitution. She needed a breath of air. When Neely tried to follow her, she called him off.

She walked from the warm, fragrant hall and out into the corridor. It was several degrees cooler in the long hall. There were an abundance of guards and servants about, each one of them asking to assist her. Sheridan shook the first two off but allowed the third, a young lad dressed in red bloomers, to show her to the door. He took her to a small exit seldom used that led out into the yard just south of the Tower. Long, stone steps led down to the dirt below.

The moonlight illuminated her way, a bright silver disc against the night sky. As she reached the bottom of the stairs, she glanced up to admire the evening. It was a lovely night and she inhaled deeply of the winter fragrance. From the cloying warmth of the hall to the airy chill of the evening, it was refreshing. She thought over the bishop's actions for a moment longer before putting it out of her mind. The man was a supporter of their cause and she could not let anything interfere, not his apparent lust or her distain. If it happened again, she would be forced to speak to him in no uncertain terms. She hoped it would be enough.

It was actually quite cold for January and Sheridan was without her cloak. But she enjoyed the cold, unlike most. She found it invigorating. She moved away from the steps, strolling into the yard and gazing at the Wakefield Tower several hundred yards to her right. It was a massive cylinder framed against the black sky. Now and again she could see the guards upon the wall walk, going about their rounds. It was a busy place, this living, breathing heart of England. Another few steps had her at a large oak tree that stood solitary and alone in the vastness of the empty yard. Glancing into the thick branches above, she heard a voice behind her.

"My lady is without a cloak," the tone was so low that it was a growl. "'Tis cold this eve to be taking a stroll without cover."

Startled, she whirled around. De Lara was standing a few feet away. She had never even heard him approach. All of the things that Jocelin had told her about the man suddenly came crashing down and it was an effort to keep steady.

"I… I enjoy the cold, my lord," she hoped her voice didn't sound as startled as she felt. "This is nothing but a balmy eve."

Sean stood his ground, his clear blue eyes focused on her face. Never did they wander in an evil or suggestive manner. Nevertheless, Sheridan was on pins and needles as they confronted one another.

"Bravely spoken," he said. "Where is your cloak?"

"Inside."

"Then I shall go and retrieve it for you."

"That is not necessary, my lord," she said quickly; *too* quickly. "I shall return to the hall. You needn't trouble yourself."

The glimmer in his eyes changed, though his expression remained unreadable. "No trouble at all, Lady Sheridan. 'Twould be my pleasure."

Sheridan could see that he would not be deterred. Remembering Jocelin's words, panic began to snatch at her. "No need, I assure you. I shall return to the hall this instant."

She was half way to the steps by the time he replied. "Why would you want to return to that den of depravity and gluttony? You are in much better company out here with the moon and stars."

She paused although she knew, even as she did it, that she should probably continue running and never look back. "It is a lovely evening, of course."

He began walking towards her, slowly. "Then why do you run like a frightened rabbit? This is not the woman I met this afternoon. She was far more controlled and coherent."

The panic that pulled at her suddenly gripped her full force. She threw out a hand as if to stop his forward progression. "Come no closer. If you try to take me to the king, I'll scream as you have never heard screams before. I'll fight as you have never seen a woman fight. I'll... I'll kill you if you try, do you hear me?"

It all came out as a rapid stream of high-pitched threats. Sean stopped in his tracks and his eyes widened. After a moment, he broke out in laughter. In all his years, he'd never seen or heard anything so hilarious. For a man who had not openly laughed in ages, it was a liberating experience.

"So that is why you run?" he said, sobering. "My lady, I assure you that I have no intention of taking you to the king."

Sheridan's heart was thumping in her chest. She could hardly catch her breath out of sheer fright. But above her racing emotions, she realized one thing; de Lara had an amazing smile. His straight, white teeth were bright against the moonlight and dimples that carved deep channels into both cheeks. Had she not been so terrified, she would have been completely entranced.

"What...?" she swallowed, torn between wanting to trust him and the inherent instinct to run. "You mean you have not come here to abduct me for the king's... the king's...?"

He shook his head. "Nay." His voice was a rumble. "I saw you leave alone. I came to make sure that you did not come to harm."

There was something in his manner that put her at ease. It was probably foolish, but she felt it nonetheless. "But I am not your concern, my lord. Why would you do this?"

"Because a woman wandering alone is not safe," he said. "However, after your threats of great bodily harm, I would hazard to say that you are no ordinary female."

"I am not."

"You can more than likely take care of yourself."

"I have been known to win a fight in my time."

"Is that so?" He appeared genuinely interested. "Against what mighty warrior, may I ask?"

She pursed her lips reluctantly. "Only my sister. But she packs a wallop."

"Of course, I have no doubt," he said sincerely. "She seems the fighting type."

"She is."

The conversation died for the moment, but it wasn't an uncomfortable pause. Sean stood several feet away, watching the reflection of the moon off the lady's fine features. As he had noted in his initial impression of her, there was nothing imperfect about the woman. He shouldn't have followed her outside, he knew that; but he had seen her from the moment he'd entered the great feasting hall and, try as he might, he couldn't seem to ignore her. When she left, he had followed. He didn't know why. He didn't even know what he was going to say to her should he have the chance. But here he was and the conversation had come easily.

"Are you really going back inside?" he asked.

She shrugged. "I probably should. My family will wonder what has become of me."

"I would be deeply honored if you would walk with me for a few moments."

If you see the man, run. She couldn't shake Jocelin's words. But the knight standing before her didn't seem the death and destruction type, at least not at the moment. His manner was quite gentle. It emboldened her. Never one to shy away from the truth, she looked him squarely in the eye.

"For what purpose?"

He was silent for a moment. Then, a well-shaped eyebrow slowly lifted. "Because it is a lovely evening and I should enjoy the company of a lovely lady."

She considered his kind request. "Won't the king be looking for you? I am told that you are his protector."

He could see where this was leading and he wasn't surprised. For the first time in his long, illustrious and hazardous career, he felt a twinge of shame. For once, he wished he could keep his chosen profession out of this. He'd never wished that before and it was a strange awareness.

"Our king is amply protected," he said simply.

He extended an enormous mailed elbow. She gazed at it a moment, her deliberation evident. Then, she looked at him. "May I ask a question?"

"If that is your pleasure, my lady."

"Very well. If I was your daughter and a man of your reputation asked permission to take me on an unchaperoned walk through the Tower grounds, what would you, as my father, say?"

A twinkle came to his eye. "What do you know of my reputation?"

"Probably more than I should."

He didn't lower his elbow. "Walk with me and we shall discuss it."

"We shall discuss it now or I will go back inside."

The twinkle in his eye grew and he lowered his arm. "As you wish, my lady. What would you like to know?"

She felt comfortable enough to ask him. Besides, she was still close enough to the Tower to make a run for it should she anger him. "Are you really as malicious as I have been told?"

His expression didn't waver. "I would not know. What have you been told?"

She didn't want to offend him. But she wasn't sure if she trusted him, either. Surely Jocelin would not lie to her. Brow furrowed in thought, she began to walk. Sean took pace beside her.

"We must be honest, my lord," she said after a moment. "It would appear that you and I are on opposite sides."

"'Twould seem that way."

"Then I am your enemy."

"In theory."

"I had not heard of you before this day. What I was told was quite unflattering."

"To you or to me?"

She looked at him. "To you, of course. I was told that you are not only the king's protector, but that you assist him in his… his dastardly and distasteful deeds. Everyone is afraid of you. Is this true?"

He drew in a long, deep breath. Thoughtfully, he gazed up at the sky. "It is far more complicated than that. Politics always are."

"But you are kind to me. I do not fear you even though I am told that I should. Why are you kind to me?"

"Because you were kind to me."

She stopped walking, lifting her hands in a confused gesture. "How would you know that? I only met you this afternoon. I said but a few sentences to you."

He looked down at her, so diminutive and sweet against his massive size. "It wasn't what you said, but how you said it. Your manner was kind."

There was something in his expression, barely perceptible, that brought her an odd sense of pity. "You are unused to people being kind to you."

His reply was to lift an eyebrow. When he put his elbow out, this time, she took it. They resumed their walk.

"I suppose there are those that would call me foolish for even speaking to you," she said.

He was enjoying the feel of her on his arm. It had been ages since he'd last experienced such satisfaction. "Absolutely."

"And if my family were to see me at this moment, I would be in for a row."

He glanced at her. "They will not beat you, will they?"

She met his gaze. "That is a strange question coming from a man..."

"Of my reputation."

She smiled sheepishly. "I should have worded that more carefully."

He just smiled at her and they resumed their walking in silence. Sheridan was beginning to grow cold in spite of her assertion that she was immune to such a thing.

"You did not answer my question," she said.

"What question was that, my lady?"

"If a man of your reputation were to take your daughter on an unescorted walk, what would you do?"

"Kill him."

He wasn't joking. She knew from the tone of his voice that he had never been more serious. It wasn't a boast, but a fact. In that statement, she could see that everything Jocelin had told her about him was true. He was a man of deeds bred of evil. Still, she did not sense that Sean was an evil man. In their first meeting and now their second, she had never received such an impression.

But the mood threatened to grow odd and strained. She did not want that. Instead, she chose to make light of his comment.

"Do you plan to kill yourself, then?"

He gave her a crooked smile. "Nay, my lady. I intend to behave as a chivalrous knight should."

She stopped walking again and looked at him with the utmost seriousness. "Sir Sean, you have been nothing but chivalrous since our first meeting this afternoon. And for saving my sister, I will always show you kindness no matter... well, no matter what our politics."

Sean was genuinely touched. His life was full of subversion and deadly threats and he truly couldn't remember, in recent times, when he'd had a moment that had been even remotely pleasant. There was no comfort in his life. As wrong as it was, he was finding comfort with an enemy.

"I thank you," he said quietly.

The moment was sweetly awkward. At a loss for words, Sheridan resumed their walk yet again. She could have walked all night on his arm, letting the conversation flow as easily as honeyed wine.

A cold breeze suddenly blew off the river and enveloped them both, swirling with frenzied intensity. When it died as abruptly as it came, Sheridan shivered. Sean noticed immediately.

"My lady is chilled," he said with concern. "I shall return you to the hall."

"I am not cold, truly," she insisted. "I would rather walk."

He looked at her. "Your lips are gray."

She lifted an eyebrow. "We're standing in moonlight. Everything is gray."

The normally unreadable expression turned suspicious. "Even as you speak, your lips quiver. That is not my imagination."

He was right, but she made a face that suggested it was a reluctant surrender. Feeling somewhat pleased with his victory, he turned her around in time to see a figure emerging from the shadows of the White Tower. He caught the glint of a blade and knew before the shape came fully into view that it was an assassin sent to kill him. In his world, it could be nothing else.

Normally, he took a sadistic pride in proving his worth as an adversary. He was the living example that no man could kill the Lord of the Shadows. But this time it was different; he had Sheridan on his arm and his heart lurched with fear for her safety. . Sheridan saw the approaching blade and let out a strangled cry a half-second before Sean shoved her out of harm's way.

The assassin wielded the light-weight blade with practiced agility. It sang an eerie cry of death as it sailed through the air, three successive thrusts at Sean's head. Weaponless, de Lara stood his ground as the weapon hurled in his direction. With a defensive move that had him spinning rapidly to his left flank, he ended up behind his attacker. Reaching down, he grabbed the hilt of the sword and used the palm of his right hand to strike a brutal blow to the back of the man's neck. The force of the jolt was hard enough to snap his spine. The man fell to the ground, dead, with his blade in Sean's left hand.

Sean stood there, gazing impassively at the corpse. This was not an unusual occurrence and he had faced better. Sheridan, however, stood several feet away, her mouth gaping in shock. It took Sean a moment to remember that she was still there.

"Are you all right?" he tossed the blade down and went to her. "I did not mean to be rough with you, but I did not want you in the line of fire. I pray that I did not hurt you."

She just stood there. "My lady?" he prodded gently.

She blinked. Then her knees buckled and she threw out her hands as if to grab hold of something to steady herself. Sean was the nearest object and he took hold of her so that she wouldn't fall.

"I think I need to sit down," she whispered tightly.

He looked around but there were no benches within walking distance. He put one arm around her slender torso and took firm grasp of her right arm, holding her fast.

"You'll be all right, my lady," he said with quiet assurance. "I'll not let you fall."

They took a few slow steps in silence. He could feel Sheridan quivering like a leaf and guilt swept him. He held her tighter.

"That man," she gasped. "He was... he tried to *kill* you."

"Aye," he said steadily.

"But why?"

He lifted an eyebrow. "If you know anything of my reputation as you have said, then you can answer that question."

She took a deep breath, struggling to regain her composure. "I know, but that was so... so bold, so brutal."

"I know."

She looked up at him; he had not even worked up a good sweat. He looked completely unruffled, the same as he had appeared the moment they realized the man was upon them. It infuriated her. "And you are so calm?"

He shrugged. "Panic is deadly. One must think clearly in order to survive."

She stared at him a moment longer before shaking her head. "Then surely I would have died because I cannot imagine being calm in the face of a deadly attack."

"It is an acquired calm, I assure you."

Her eyebrows flew up. "Are you saying this sort of thing has happened before?"

He didn't answer. He continued to walk with her, holding her against him so that she would not collapse. Even when he thought she might be stronger, he continued to hold her simply because he liked it. As they neared the narrow steps that led back up into the Tower, a herd of men came flying through the doorway and down the narrow stairs. Even in the moonlight, Sean recognized the St. James colors.

Neely came rushing at them with his sword leveled. Shaken but not senseless, Sheridan could see what was about to happen and threw up her hands.

"Neely, no," she cried. "Put the weapon down."

He came to a halt several feet away. His dark eyes were twitching with alarm and anger. "Let her go," he shouted at Sean.

Sean was completely calm, completely impassive. "The lady has had a fright." His voice was as cold as ice. "If I release her, she may fall."

Sheridan could see that there was no easy way out of this for any of them unless she took action. She patted Sean gently on the arm that held her. "It's all right," she told him. "I am well now. You may release me as he has asked."

He did as she bade, but his eyes never left Neely. It was like a marauder tracking its quarry. Sheridan sensed the deadly tension as she went over to Neely.

"Put the sword down," she ordered quietly. "Sir Sean has committed no wrong. He has saved me from an assassin."

She pointed to the body several feet away in the shadow of the White Tower. Neely could see it faintly in the dark and he looked at her, puzzled as well as frightened.

"We heard the scream," he looked her up and down. "Are you

well?"

"Indeed," she didn't like his hovering manner. "As I said, Sir Sean saved my life. He should be commended."

Neely looked at Sean. The last thing he would do was praise the man. After a long pause filled with hostility, he spoke tersely. "We are grateful."

Sean didn't reply. Though he was watching Neely, his peripheral senses were reaching out to every man around him. There were at least eight. With a lingering glance at Sheridan, he took several backwards steps, fading back into the shadows where the assassin lay. Sheridan held his gaze until he disappeared into the blackness.

When he was sure de Lara had left, Neely turned his full attention on her. "What happened?" he demanded softly. "How did you end up out here? You said that you were..."

She put up an impatient hand. "I know what I said," she snapped, heading back towards the narrow stone steps. "I needed a breath of air. I was attacked and Sir Sean saved my life. Leave it at that, Neely. No more questions."

He shut his mouth, but he wasn't happy in the least. They both knew this would get back to Jocelin and there would be hell to pay.

"...Not to act on my thoughts would have been the wiser. My error was in the act of doing...."
The Chronicles of Sir Sean de Lara
1206 - 1215 A.D.

CHAPTER THREE

"Did she say anything of value, then?"

"Nothing that I would consider, my lord."

"But you conversed for some time."

"It was light conversation, I assure you. Politics barely entered into it."

These meetings were always clandestine; dark alleys, dark rooms, stables, anywhere they would not be easily recognized. Such had been the way for years, since Sean's induction into the service of the king.

The meetings were no more than once every three months or so. To attempt a more frequent encounter would be to invite suspicion. As it was, Sean had to make sure his schedule and activities were nothing out of the ordinary. It was the middle of the night, after the king had retired for the evening, and Sean was in the stable bent over the hoof of his immense charger. The other half of the conversation came from the loft above, well hidden in the mounds of freshly dried grass. They never spoke face to face.

"I am truly not sure how much she knows," the voice said. "Her father died last year and left her with a great earldom. From what I understand, she has assumed his mantel in every way. What Jocelin knows, she knows. If there is imminent rebellion in the wind, she will know it."

Sean used an iron pick to clean dirt out of the horse's hoof. "If there is imminent rebellion in the wind, then you would know it, too."

The voice grunted. "Not necessarily. Some of the barons believe I am too far removed from their cause and that my head is swept up in the storm of politics. Some believe my time came and went with Richard. In any case, I wield power, aye, but only within my own troops and close vassals. I do not have the pulse of the common man."

"And you believe that she may?"

"'Tis possible. She is rooted to the rebellion on a much more grounded level."

"Then what would you have me do, my lord?"

"You have made contact. Perhaps you should maintain it, simply to see if she will provide you with anything useful."

Sean had planned on doing that regardless. "She has a security force. It will not be a simple thing to communicate with her."

"You are the Lord of the Shadows. Stealth is your gift."

Sean was silent a moment as he dropped one hoof in favor of the other. Although there were stable boys to do this work, none of them would go near his charger for fear of being trampled. Bred in Galicia by a man whose family had been breeding big-boned war horses for a hundred years, the animal's military reputation was beyond compare. Sean was the only one who could get near the beast.

"What else do you know of her?" he asked casually.

The voice hissed, the gesture of an individual with strong opinions. "That she will make some man a very wealthy husband. She is quite lovely as well, but I am sure that escaped your notice."

Sean knew it was a jab but he chose to ignore it. "Does she have suitors?"

"Nay. Jocelin has told me that she has refused every man her father attempted to contract with. Now it is the bishop's duty to find her a husband, which will be no easy task. The man actually listens to her opinion. He is a fool."

Sean didn't reply. The voice continued. "Has the king seen her?"

"Not yet."

"It is only a matter of time. He will demand her, you know."

Sean's movements slowed. "That is possible."

"You will have to bring her to him as you have the others."

Sean remained silent. The voice spoke more loudly. "Sean? Did you hear me?"

"I heard you."

"Why do you not respond?"

"Because I have nothing to say on the matter."

The tone of the voice turned to one of disbelief. "You cannot actually be thinking of refusing him?"

"As I said, I have nothing to say on the matter."

"I have listened to you speak of the St. James woman for the past half hour. I know you, Sean. I have known you for thirteen years. If I did not know better, I would say that you have an interest in her."

"Think what you will."

The voice fell still for a moment. "No matter what you feel, you cannot refuse him. You have not refused him for nine years."

Sean let the hoof fall. He leaned up against the horse, his gaze moving out into the darkness of the stables. His manner, normally steady, suddenly turned bitter.

"Aye," he muttered. "For nine years I have catered to his every repulsive whim. For nine years, I have kidnapped men's wives and delivered them to the king like a gift on Christmas morning. For nine years, I have cleaned up his leavings, disposing of the women who have died as a result of his lust and delivering those who managed to survive back to their homes." He tossed the iron hook against the wall, so hard that it lodged in the wood. "No matter how much I have convinced myself that the king's behavior was of no consequence, deep inside, I knew that it was. For the women that died as a result of his lust, I made sure they had a Christian burial. For the women who survived, I made sure they were cleaned and fed and delivered to those who would care for them. For every evil I helped create, I also tried to right it. No one knows that I orchestrated anything other than the evil, of course, other than God. The king's sins are my sins in the eyes of men."

The voice in the loft was silent. Long moments ticked by before it spoke again. "Though I have always suspected your feelings on the matter, this is the first I have heard you speak openly of them."

"I am getting foolish in my old age."

The voice snorted softly. "Take care, then. You are as we had always hoped for you; the most feared man in the kingdom. Your reputation is without equal. You are finally where you can accomplish the most good. Be strong, de Lara. The day will come when you will be rewarded for your loyalty."

Sean broke from his cynical, thoughtful stance and moved around the horse. He picked up a currycomb and ran it across the silver hide. "I hope that day will come soon. I grow weary of being seated by the Devil's right hand."

"As would any rational man, but you are by far the strongest of us all." The straw in the loft shifted, raining down on the horse's back. "Keep your focus, Sean. You are where you are most valuable now. The barons are clearly amassing and I sense that John's days are numbered. But you are critical to this success. Is that clear?"

"It is, my lord."

"If anything crucial happens, you know how to contact me. Otherwise, I will contact you again in a month or two. We shall meet again."

Sean didn't answer. The straw stopped falling on the horse's back and he knew his contact had slipped from the loft, out into the dead of night. He normally left these meetings feeling a new sense of purpose. Tonight, he left feeling disheartened.

When he finally slept in the last hour before dawn, his dreams were of luminous blue eyes.

***

"What did I tell you about him?" Jocelin exploded. "Did you not hear a word I said? The man is dangerous!"

Neely had waited eight whole hours before confessing the evening's events to the bishop. Sheridan had been rudely awakened by Jocelin's shouting shortly after dawn. Now, in the antechamber of their apartments, she found herself on the defensive. Completely missing the point of Jocelin's rage, as usual, Alys sulked in the corner because her sister had gotten to speak to the mysterious Sean de Lara and she had not.

"I have told you twice what happened," Sheridan said evenly. "And I know what you told me about de Lara. But he was a complete gentleman, I assure you."

"He is a wolf in sheep's clothing," he fumed. "What possessed you to go outside the Tower in the first place? You are mad, girl, mad."

She lifted an eyebrow at him. "If you are going to insult me, then this conversation is over. I should like to wash and dress for the day."

"You are not dressing just yet," he jabbed a finger at her. "You will provide me with satisfactory answers."

She sighed with exasperation. "What would you have me say? That I was tired of being preyed upon by your friend, the Bishop of Coventry? That I was, in fact, disgusted by the man rubbing his feet on my leg, so much so that I was compelled to get a breath of fresh air or vomit?"

Jocelin looked at her with shock and she nodded her head, firmly. "Aye, he did that, the old fool," she insisted. "So I had to take a walk to clear my thoughts. As I was walking, a man tried to attack me. Had it not been for de Lara, I would not be here at this moment. Now, may I please dress?"

Some of the wind went out of Jocelin's sails. "Oh, Dani," he whispered. "Why didn't you say something to me? Why not tell me about William where I could have confronted him?"

She waved him off. "I would have told you, eventually. I simply did not want to embarrass your friend in front of you."

Jocelin sat his bulk down in the fine sling-back chair adjacent to the hearth. . There was peace now where there had been fury seconds before. "It is not a matter of embarrassment," he muttered. "I cannot believe that he would betray me so."

He seemed genuinely distressed. Sheridan went to him, leaning over to kiss his bald head. "He did not betray you. He rubbed his toes on my ankle. Perhaps it was an accident and he really meant to rub the table leg. In any case, you needn't feel bad. It's over and done with."

Jocelin grunted. "Over and done with, aye. But at what cost? Putting you at the mercy of de Lara."

She pursed her lips with frustration. "How many times do I have to tell you that he was a perfect gentleman?"

He didn't have an answer. He was much more concerned with entertaining the horrible scenarios. Leaving Alys half-asleep and still pouting on the chair opposite the silently brooding Jocelin, she retreated into the bedroom.

Her maid had a porcelain bowl of warm water waiting for her. Rose petals floated on the surface. Removing her night shift, she washed her face and used a soft linen rag to run warm water over her body. She always felt better when she washed in the morning. The maid briskly dried her and rubbed rose-scented oil on her skin to soften it. Just as her lips were constantly dry, her skin was also. The oil helped.

Her favorite dress was a soft blue linen sheath with long sleeves and a simple belt that draped around her hips. With it, she wore the silver and sapphire cross that her father had given her. The maid brushed her silken hair and wove it into one long braid, draping it over a shoulder. Sheridan finished her toilette by rubbing beeswax on her lips from her ever-present pot of the stuff.

The window of her chamber was open and she could hear the birds beyond. . She went to the opening, leaning out over the yard below and remembering the previous day when Alys had nearly plunged to her death from the same window. Thoughts of the event brought thoughts of Sean de Lara.

She leaned against the windowsill, gazing into the gentle blue sky and wondering if de Lara would ever speak to her again. The way Neely had chased him away last night, she wondered if she had made an enemy. She'd never seen Neely so edgy, which only lent credence to Jocelin's tales of de Lara's dark reputation. Her father's captain had known of the man; that much was apparent. She would have wagered that every male of political awareness knew of the man. Still, she continued to doubt what everyone seemed to know.

"If you are thinking of jumping, I wouldn't."

The voice came from below. Startled, she looked down to see Sean leaning against the wall directly below her. It was the first time she had seen him without his armor; he wore a bleached linen tunic, heavy leather breeches and massive boots. Without his helm, he had light brown hair, close cropped and riddled with flecks of gold.

The full lips set within his square jaw were twitching with a smile and the clear blue eyes were glimmering, as if he knew something she did not. It was an amused expression. He was, in fact, excruciatingly handsome now that she had a chance to see him in broad daylight. He looked nothing like the horrible Shadow Lord she had been warned about. She realized that she was glad to see him.

"What are you doing down there?" she asked.

"Waiting for a St. James sister to fall into my arms," he replied with a twinkle in his eye.

"Ah, I see," she smiled down at him. "Which one?"

He pushed himself off the wall, turning around so that he could see her lovely features better. "Must you really ask that question?" He held out his arms. "It is your turn."

She laughed. "No, thank you, my lord. I have no desire to see if your strength will hold out a second time."

He smiled broadly at her, resting his fists on his hips. "Then allow me to say good morn to you, my lady," he bowed gallantly. "I do hope you slept well after your harrowing experience last night."

"I did, thank you for asking," she said. "And you?"

"I never sleep."

"That's terrible. How do you survive?"

"By my wits alone."

"That must be terribly difficult."

He lifted an eyebrow. "Are you suggesting my wits aren't up to the task?"

She laughed, a dazzling display of lovely teeth and tinkling gales. Before she could reply, the door to her bedchamber opened.

"Dani?" It was Alys. "Who are you talking to?"

Sheridan quickly stood up, wondering why she suddenly felt so horribly guilty. "I...," she faced her sister. "A... person was passing by as I was looking out of the window and I simply said good morn."

Alys was at the window and pushed her head through. Sheridan was positive she would see Sean and the entire morning would be filled with lectures and angry exchanges. Sheridan turned back to the window, her eyes falling upon the last place she had seen Sean and fully prepared to make excuses to her sister.

But a strange thing occurred; Sean had disappeared and there was nothing below but dirt and stones. Curious, not to mention disappointed, Sheridan scanned the area but saw nothing. It was, yet again, as if he had simply disappeared. Alys, bored with the featureless view, went over to the bed and threw herself onto the mattress.

"I am so miserable, Dani," she threw her arm over her forehead. "The only man I was every truly attracted to has apparently decided he is interested in you."

It occurred to Sheridan that her patience for Alys' self pity was very thin. An unselfish sister would have been happy that she had found some interest in male companionship. But Alys could see nothing but her own disappointment.

"If you are speaking of de Lara, then I would suggest you find another subject," she said. "Jocelin warned us about him. My encounter with him last night had, shall we say, brutal moments. You'd best forget about him." Alys peered at her.

"What about you? Will you forget about him?"

Something in Sheridan changed at that moment. She had never lied to her sister in her life. But she decided in that flash of time to keep her feelings about de Lara to herself. Alys would only create misery if she knew that her sister actually had some curiosity towards the man. And it wasn't the fact that it was de Lara; Alys created misery if her sister showed interest in any man. If Alys could not be the center of male attention, she had always been determined to ruin her sister's chances.

But Sheridan said nothing of what she was thinking. She promised herself at that moment that she would keep her feelings to herself. It would be safer for all of them if she did. Moreover, if her bizarre interest in de Lara was something to last for only a day or two, she did not want to be embarrassed. Alys created quite enough embarrassment to go around with her own dalliances.

"He is forgotten," she said simply. "Now, what will we do today, darling? What is your preference?"

Alys shrugged. "I do not feel like doing anything. I do not want to see anyone or be seen. Perhaps we will stay to the apartments and contemplate our pitiful existence."

Sheridan didn't feel like staying to the apartments. She felt like walking out on the grounds on the off-chance that de Lara might find her again.

"As you say," she said as lightly as she could, heading for the massive wardrobe against the wall. "I plan on going to the chapel this day and having the priest say mass for father."

They all knew how Alys hated attending mass. Too often, she fell asleep in the middle of it and snored like an old dog. "You go ahead," the redhead snorted. "I will wait for your return."

Sheridan dug through the wardrobe, coming across the delicate black mass shawl that had belonged to her grandmother. She really had not planned on paying for mass today, but it was as good an excuse as any. Her stomach twitched with an odd, giddy excitement and she knew in the same breath that she was being foolish. De Lara was more than likely long gone, maybe forever. But she didn't care. The urge to see him again, to speak with him, was strangely overwhelming.

She blew into the antechamber where Jocelin was still glowering. She was mildly startled to see another body present; she'd never even heard him enter.

"My lord Marshall," she dipped into a polite curtsy. "I did not know you were here, my lord."

William Marshall sat opposite Jocelin, his gray eyes piercing as they gazed at her. "I have only just arrived, my lady," he stood up. "My old friend and I barely had time to speak last night. I went to his chamber and they told me he had come here. I apologize if I have intruded."

"You have not," Sheridan assured him, thinking he looked different from when she had met him last night. He looked as if he'd slept in a field; there was hay in his hair and on his tunic. He looked exhausted. But those thoughts were cast aside as she realized that she was very glad to have Jocelin occupied, as he would not insist on accompanying her.

"If you will excuse me, I plan to have mass said for father this morning," she said. "I am on my way to the chapel."

"What of Alys?" Jocelin asked.

"She prefers to say here." Sheridan tossed the shawl over her shoulders and went to the door. "I shall take an escort, have no fear."

She was halfway through the door as Jocelin called to her. "Neely is in the hall."

Sheridan acknowledged him with a wave. She didn't want Neely escorting her, of all people, especially if they ran into de Lara. In the dim, cool hall near the Flint Tower, she caught sight of the knight several feet away in a small alcove. His dark eyes fixed curiously on her.

"My lady is leaving?" he asked.

She couldn't decide if she was still angry with him for spilling the evening's events to Jocelin. Neely had only done what he felt he should do, and that was to protect the St. James family even when they could not, or would not, protect themselves. For as many years as she had known him, he was more like family to her, and family always forgave family. But she still did not want him escorting her.

"I am going to church," she said. "Give me a guard and I'll be on my way."

"I will take you myself."

"Nay, you will stay here," she lifted an eyebrow. "Alys is in one of her moods and I need you here should she decide to jump from the window again. I will depend upon you, Neely."

He knew what had happened yesterday but, to his credit, had not said anything to Jocelin. Whatever Alys St. James did anymore didn't surprise him.

"Is it bad?" he asked.

"Bad enough," Sheridan replied. "Please do me this favor. I do not want Jocelin catching wind of her antics."

Neely nodded in resignation. He and Sheridan had spent a good deal of time over the past few years concealing Alys' peculiar behavior. He motioned to two of the guards standing against the wall. "Lady Sheridan wishes to go to church," he said. "See that she is amply protected."

It was more escort than she wanted, but she didn't argue. Leaving the cold halls of the apartment tower, she descended the steps into the cool, bright January sunshine. The Tower grounds were fairly alive with activity, mostly soldiers as they went about their business. There were, in fact, many different Houses on the grounds, probably more than the Tower had seen in quite some time. .

People tended to keep to themselves, however. There weren't great social gatherings due to the tense political climate between the king and most of his barons. It was a heady world of intrigue and enemy, of suspicion and loyalty, and no one could be certain that their ally of the moment would be their ally tomorrow. Lives often depended upon silence. Therefore, nearly everyone Sheridan passed barely acknowledged her.

The Chapel of St. Peter was on the opposite side of the compound against the west wall. She walked past the White

Tower on her way to the chapel, gazing up at the massive structure and remembering the previous evening with clarity. . The yard in which she had met Sean was on the opposite side of the building and she was unable to catch a glimpse of it. Instead, she walked through the dry, cold grounds, thinking the whole place to feel rather desolate.

When she reached the chapel, she left the guards outside. The chapel itself was a long, slender chamber with a soaring ceiling and massive support columns. Long, needle-thin lancet windows lined the walls, running nearly floor to ceiling. There were no pews or benches, only a bare floor of hard-packed dirt. At the back of the chapel, near the door, stood the prayer candles, lit by those who paid a pence for a priestly prayer.

It was an empty chamber for the most part. Sheridan put the shawl over her head and began to walk towards the front of the hall, keeping an eye out for a priest or acolyte. As she drew near the altar, she caught sight of two priests in the shadows, conversing with each other. Taking a quick knee in a show of respect for the altar before her, she folded her hands in prayer.

It wasn't long before she heard footfalls approach. Opening her eyes, she gazed into the face of a young man who could not have been much older than she. His hair was cut in the traditional priestly fashion, the crown of his head shaved bare in piety. He wore rough, if not slightly dirty, brown robes with a large wooden crucifix hanging around his neck. His blue eyes were kindly.

"I am Father Simon," he said softly. "May I be of assistance to my lady?"

She stood up. "I would like a mass said for my father."

"Of course. A shilling it will cost."

She fumbled around in the small purse she had attached to her wrist. All the while, she wondered if it had been foolish for her to think de Lara even went near the chapel. This whole thing had been a ruse. Perhaps it had been a wasted one, and now it would cost her a shilling. Well, perhaps not a wasted trip, but she had truly hoped to catch sight of him again. The Lord of the Shadows more than likely did not suffer the illumination of God's house. She was beginning to feel foolish.

She handed over the money. Father Simon smiled. "Mass will be said at Vespers. Your father's name?"

"Henry St. James."

"Of course. Good day to you, my lady."

As he turned and walked away, Sheridan noticed straw on his robes, embedded near his shoulders, as if he had been laying in the stuff. It stuck her odd that William Marshall had been covered in the same substance. With a shrug, she gave it no further thought. Perhaps all men at the Tower suffered the affliction of mysterious straw.

Sheridan returned to her apartments near the tall, dark Flint Tower without catching another glimpse of Sean de Lara that day.

Read the rest of **LORD OF THE SHADOWS** in Kindle format or in paperback at Amazon.com or Barnes and Noble.

ABOUT THE AUTHOR

Kathryn Le Veque has been a prolific writer of Medieval Romance Novels for twenty years.

Visit Kathryn's website at www.kathrynleveque.com for more information including ordering more novels. Kathryn lives in La Verne, California.

Order at www.kathrynleveque.com

CPSIA information can be obtained
at www.ICGtesting.com
Printed in the USA
LVHW080952151021
700543LV00022B/403